ONCE UPON A FUTURE TIME, VOLUME 4

ONCE UPON A FUTURE TIME, VOLUME 4

BRET CARTER   JESSICA GUERNSEY   LIAM HOGAN

ELIZABETH LOWHAM   HENRY HERZ

ERIK PETERSON   BRITTANY RAINSDON   LENA NG

SHAWN POLLOCK   TIFFANIE GRAY

R.C. CAPASSO   LORINA STEPHENS

RODNEY HATFIELD JR.   RAY DALEY   K. L. MILL

MIGUEL FLIGUER AND MIKE SLATER

JASON P. CRAWFORD   M.R. DELUCA   ERIN LEWIS

ANGUS MCINTYRE   JAMES DORR

R.A. JOHNSON   SARA ITKA

To all of the dreamers who look to the stars, imagine the possibilities, and work to make them happen.

TABLE OF CONTENTS

BRET CARTER

1

Cerise

They flew their ships side by side through the asteroid belt. Cerise was already uptight about her first solo trip. But the thrill of Chayse suddenly showing up brought on a whole new level of nervous.

Considering the fact every muscle in her body was tense and her heart was racing, she thought she sounded pretty casual. "The first time I ever saw the belt, I was disappointed."

"Wow, you must be pretty hard to impress."

He flew an armed Hessian—a military vessel with two guns tucked against the fuselage; its sleek elegance made her feel self-conscious. By comparison, her own ship was ridiculous. She flew a company Stitcher, designed for running supplies. It wasn't as bulky as some transports, but still—she felt frumpy.

When he had contacted her, she had opened a visual so she could see his face. But now she had to use the pretense of checking something offscreen so she could check her hair. On her console, his face was life-sized. Dark eyes that held the hint of a smile. It was a nice face.

"How can all this be a disappointment? You don't get out much, do you?" Was he teasing her? Or was he disappointed in her disappointment?

She laughed even though he hadn't really said anything funny. "You know how it is. Like every other kid on Mars, I always pictured this place as a dense cloud of giant rocks, almost bumping together. I thought pilots had to weave back and forth just to get through it." She glanced out her starboard side. The closest asteroid was miles away and looked as majestic as a pebble.

He chuckled. "On average, the asteroids are at least 600,000 miles apart."

"Look at who did his homework." Had that sounded snippy? She quickly added, "It's just that it's kind of hard when you find out the universe isn't as romantic as you hoped it would be."

Romantic? She winced. What a stupid thing to say. She had been working up the courage to casually use his name. Something like *Fancy meeting you out here, Chayse.* But now she needed to pull everything back a little bit. Maybe a lot.

Had he seen her wince? Cerise leaned offscreen again to check on nothing and regain some composure. Back in front of the screen, she shrugged. "I was disillusioned. That's one of the hardest things about growing up. Disillusionment."

"Isn't it good to get rid of illusions?" He smiled and it made her forget how to use words. She couldn't think of anything to say, let alone come up with any banter. All she could do was smile back. Pull it together, Cerise.

They had only met once before. Just long enough for small talk and names. But he had been on her mind ever since.

They were both living on Vesta, one of the larger asteroids. It was big enough to be called a protoplanet, but the population wasn't huge. Maybe around a thousand. She had literally bumped into Chayse during an orientation for evac. In the event of an emergency, they would both be in the same escape pod.

Cerise had spent all last week daydreaming about various

catastrophes that resulted in the two of them ending up in the pod alone. Forced to spend hours talking until help arrived.

Then today, out of the blue—or out of the black—he shows up in his Hessian.

Maybe he was just on patrol and spotted her ship on his screen. But she liked to think he had actually been looking for her. That he had asked about her. That he had found out she was on a supply run and arranged this "chance" encounter.

Before the awkward silence became painful, he graciously jumped in. "Not to be nosy, Cerise, but which station are you headed for? There are so many outposts now, I can't keep them all straight."

He had said her name. "My grandmother."

"What?"

"Um, Gryselda Sartoria, my grandmother. She's solo at the outpost at 505 Wilhelm. Part of the Shepherd Project."

"She's running the outpost by herself? Your *grandmother*? How old is she?"

"She's only 62. She was born at the tail end of the 21st Century, but she was one of the first beta test subjects for the telomere extensions. She looks and feels like she's in her 40s."

"So that makes you…"

"Her granddaughter."

He laughed. "How old are you?"

"I'm 23."

"How in the world did you get a Stitcher license at 23?"

"I'm a natural." Had that sounded arrogant? "You know, I just worked hard."

"Apparently." They flew in silence for almost a minute, and then he said, "505 Wilhelm—how far away is that? How long will it take you to get there?"

"This Stitcher has a Vim engine like yours."

"Really?" He sounded impressed.

"Yep. It's one of the newer ones. So I should get there in about 5 hours."

"That's not too bad. You said she's solo out there? It can't be a mining outpost. What's the Shepherd Project again?"

"Look at who *didn't* do his homework."

"Educate me."

"Grandmother monitors cogbots that rechoreograph asteroids."

"Rechoreograph?"

"Her term. You know—reposition them."

"For why?"

"You're on belt patrol and you don't know about the waystations?"

He smiled. "I know about the waystations. But what does rechoreographing—"

"The project *shepherds* a bunch of the smaller asteroids together to form a platform. Kind of a foundation to build on."

"Ahh…Okay, I did hear about that."

"My grandmother is on a six-month stint out there. Ever since my grandfather died, she's kept herself busy. She went to school and got the position a few months after she graduated. She's pretty impressive."

"Doing a supply run through the belt at your age seems pretty impressive too."

"Thanks." Now Cerise felt bold. "So since you're not minding your own business, let me mind yours. What are you doing out here?"

He cleared his throat. "I'm a beltranger."

Leaning forward, she made sure he could see her raised eyebrows. "So I gathered. All beltrangers fly Hessians."

He chuckled. "Yeah, yeah."

"What are you up to? Hunting pirates or watching over miners?"

"Neither." His voice grew serious. "One of the reasons I caught up with you is to give you a heads-up."

Her mind grabbed onto the first word he had said. *One* of the reasons? Did that mean he had intentionally tracked her down? Had he asked about her?

The somber look on his face brought her out of her daydream. She tried to match his serious face. "Um, let me know what?"

"It has to do with the AI insurgence. Were you on Mars during the Deimos-3 mess last year?"

"I was already on Vesta. I was on standby for my training. I thought they totally eradicated the virus."

"For the most part, yeah. At least on Mars. But there's the slight possibility a few infected components escaped the scour and set out for parts unknown. To make things more interesting, Deimos-3 was showing a tendency to form composites."

"They work together?"

"Yeah, that part wasn't in the news. Just before they activated the scour, there were several machines that left Mars and they were collaborating, forming new synergistic compositions that were predatory. They're called Wolves."

All the fun of the conversation drained away. "Are you serious?"

"We destroyed a bunch of them, so there probably aren't any more left. We're just being cautious. A mining outpost reported a possible Wolf a few days ago. But it hasn't been confirmed. There hasn't been an actual confirmed sighting of a Wolf in a long time. If there had been, Vesta wouldn't have sent all you Stitchers out on your supply runs."

Her fear dropped into disappointment. Chayse hadn't tracked her down. She was nothing more than an assignment. She was a supply ship, not a girl. "Oh, right. That's good. I'm glad you beltrangers are keeping an eye on things."

"Yeah. So, no worries."

No worries, she thought. In fact, no nothing. Just a beltranger doing his job. Nothing to see here.

"It's called a Wolf?" Now this was only a matter of small talk.

His smile was back. "My idea. I came up with the name. When I ran it past the squadron, they laughed, but the commander used the name today when he sent a message out to all the mines and outposts."

She pretended to be busy with her console. "Then I guess that makes it official."

"I think it does."

"Why didn't they tell me about the possibility of a Wolf before I left?"

He fidgeted as if his seat was suddenly uncomfortable. "You know—business. I guess they thought some of you might refuse to go. And the supplies need to happen."

She didn't hide her anger. "I wouldn't have refused to go. I'm delivering supplies to my *grandmother*."

He nodded several times. "Yeah, yeah. I know. For sure. It was just protocol."

Oh good, she thought. Even better. I'm just protocol.

Chayse's eyes narrowed. "I hope I find one."

"Why?" She wished he would go protect some other Stitcher.

"We have something cooked up for it. Our ships have a cartridge with something even more potent than the scour. It removes the I from AI lickety-split."

"I bet it's got a catchy name."

"We all named it this morning. Antibot-otics." He laughed.

She came up with half of a smile. "You guys have too much time on your hands."

For a moment, he didn't say anything. He seemed to be working up to something. "Do you ever have too much time on *your* hands?"

She held her breath. "What do you mean?"

"I don't know. Maybe when we both get back, we could practice the new emergency evac together. Or we could get some dinner. Whichever sounds more interesting to you. Evac or dinner?"

Had he asked to be assigned to her ship? She could feel herself blush and she couldn't stop the stupid grin. "Um, definitely the evac."

"Sounds good." Folding his arms, he leaned back in his seat with a big grin. "I heard you like ancient music."

He had heard? Or he had asked around? "Um yeah. Wait a second. You like DustPop?"

"It's the best."

She let him see her skepticism. "No one likes DustPop. My grandmother doesn't even like it."

"I like it. Back when machines had less say about music. All the AI-generated stuff today is fluff. I like human music."

She raised one eyebrow. "You like DustPop."

"All my favorite songs are DustPop."

"Prove it."

"*You* prove it. Name this one." Without hesitation, he started humming a tune, bopping his shoulders back and forth.

She knew the tune right away and burst out laughing. "That's easy. 'September' by Earth, Wind, and Fire."

"Good. Okay, how about this?" Once again, he did his best to dance in the Hessian's cockpit as he hummed.

Eager to impress him, she cut him off. "At the Casa—Casa-ca-blanca!"

Chayse laughed for almost a full minute. "Casa-ca-blanca? It's Casablanca. Plus, it's not Casablanca. No. Sorry. Close, but no."

"Something like that. Are you sure? I'm almost sure it's Casablanca."

"Copacabana." He snorted.

"Same thing." She couldn't stop smiling.

"Your turn."

"I don't sing."

"I didn't sing either. I was humming."

"I don't hum."

"I bet you do both when you're alone."

"Let's change the subject."

Before they could, another voice interrupted. Someone contacting Chayse. She couldn't catch who it was or what they said.

"Hang on a second." He muted himself.

She watched as his expression became grim. Then his voice came back. "Sorry, got to go. Probably a false alarm, but I've got to go check it out."

"A Wolf?"

"Pirates. Like I say. Probably a false alarm. A few hours away. I'll check on it and then try to catch up with you."

The Hessian's engines flared and Chayse veered away from her. On her screen, he smiled and waved. "Be careful. Watch out."

"For the Wolf."

"Yeah."

"It's catchy."

"Just make sure it doesn't catch you." With that, the Hessian bolted out of sight.

He had definitely asked about her.

And they were going on a date.

Cerise put her daydreaming on hold. She checked her navigation. Four hours and thirty-five minutes to 505 Wilhelm. Her course was locked in, but now she kept an eye on her screen for any stray blips.

Chayse seemed to think it was highly unlikely she would encounter a Wolf, but as the miles went by, she kept her eyes peeled.

After a couple of hours, she started to finally relax. To pass the time, she read a murder mystery she had thrown into her pack. But she couldn't get into the story.

Alone with her thoughts, she found herself staring at her screen with growing anxiety, so she turned on some DustPop and sang her heart out, checking two or three times to make sure she hadn't accidentally left her comm open.

She was in the middle of "I'm Your Boogie Man" by K.C. and the Sunshine Band when she spotted a ship on her screen.

Was it Chayse? He said he would be back as soon as he could. The ship was moving as fast as a Hessian.

But she saw the truth on her visual. The ship was nothing like she had seen before. It was an odd-looking conglomerate of carapaces blended into an asymmetrical body. The cockpit seemed too small to hold a pilot and the bulk of the vessel apparently served as the hold. All in all, it presented the appearance of a tick.

It was a Wolf.

Cerise turned to ice. It was the kind of fear that could paralyze you.

The Wolf made contact. A deep voice filled her cockpit. "Who are you?"

She had heard you could fool an AI if you convinced it that it was fooling you. "Hello, I'm just on a supply run. A beltranger is on his way to escort me." Pushing her fear down, she prepped the Vim engine for a push. The Stitcher could hit an impressive speed in a short burst. But the engine needed a full minute to prep.

In the upper right-hand corner of her screen, an icon flickered. She was being scanned.

The gruff voice spoke again. "Hello, Cerise Sartoria on a supply run to 505 Wilhelm." This time it made the effort to make its voice sound more laid-back. A seam in the Wolf's hold parted.

Her screen flashed a proximity warning. The Wolf was initiating a magnetic net. It was going to haul her into the hold.

But before the net could get a good grip, the engine was ready. With her heart racing madly, Cerise disrupted navigation and free-styled the Stitcher out of the Wolf's clutches.

"Come back," it said. This time with *her* voice.

Cerise activated the push and she was gone.

After flying a wide, weaving course for almost twenty

minutes, she ramped down and checked the grid. There was no sign of the Wolf.

As far as she could tell, it had failed to track her.

She opened a channel. Now that she had a moment to breathe, she needed to send out an alert. "This is Stitcher 17 out of Vesta headed for 505 Wilhelm. Come in. Anyone."

A red light appeared on her console. The signal had failed.

She ran a diagnostic and her mouth went dry. Her ship was infected. The Wolf had crippled her comm system with some kind of digital virus.

A diagnostic revealed it was a partial filter. Her signal was getting through, but her voice had been removed. The message was reduced to white noise.

This had been one of the first tactics of Deimos-3. A digital virus that dismantled human words in any language.

She couldn't contact Chayse. She couldn't contact her grandmother or anyone.

Coded messages sometimes got through, but most of the time they didn't.

Then it dawned on her. The Wolf had acquired her destination. It might very well be on its way to 505 Wilhelm right now.

"Grandmother," she whispered.

Her engine needed time to recover from the push. At least 30 minutes.

Cerise fidgeted and shouted at the console a couple of times, but it was actually 40 minutes before she was able to fire up the Stitcher and head for 505 Wilhelm. She could only hope she got to grandmother before the Wolf did.

2

Gryselda

Although Gryselda didn't consider herself a sentimental person, she gained a surprising amount of comfort when she aimed the station's ocular at Mars. Her home was merely a faint pink pearl but seeing even this distant gleam made her less homesick.

Or made it worse. She still hadn't decided. All she knew was that she needed to see it. She had another five months on this cold crumb, so she allowed this small, irrational indulgence.

After sipping chamomile and rationing herself to a solitary sigh, she headed off to bed. It was 10:30 p.m.—Mars time.

Although the telomere extensions had prolonged middle age for her, sleep was still troublesome at times. Even though her body was relatively youthful, her thoughts were old.

Settling into her blankets with her copy of *Jane Eyre*, Gryselda read her way into 19th Century England. But a few pages later, the screen in the primary room chimed.

It was probably the cogbots at 598. That particular asteroid had been troublesome. Somehow it had acquired a savage spin. Even though the cogbots were the size of people, they were nothing more than gnats to an asteroid. 598 must have clipped some of them again. More than a few asteroids didn't take to rechoreographing.

Padding down the hall in her gown and socks, she was bleary in the brightness of the screens.

It wasn't a cogbot. There was a ship. And it was approaching the station.

More than likely Cerise. Her granddaughter had been practically giddy to be authorized for the run.

But the exterior cameras gave Gryselda a clear view and her smile faded.

This wasn't a Stitcher. It was—it was unfamiliar. Its general theme was a congregation of scarabs and the proportions were out of whack.

It was closing fast.

She had received a briefing from Vesta, warning her about the possibility of this very thing. They called it a Wolf. To her, it sounded like a beltranger's wishful thinking. Mapping the belt, eyeing possible incursions among the miners, and patrolling for an occasional Jovian pirate—it had to get monotonous. Craving adventure made your imagination come loose.

When they had cried Wolf, she had rolled her eyes. But here it was. And if the reports were reliable, it was predatory.

"This is Cerise Sartoria on a supply run to 505 Wilhelm." It sounded kind of like Cerise. The Wolf had almost got it right.

This was only the simulation of a human. Simulating that she was stupid might buy her some time.

"Hello, Cerise Sartoria on a supply run to 505 Wilhelm. This is Gryselda Sartoria, Shepherd Project warden."

"Hello, Gryselda Sartoria Shepherd Project warden."

Trying to sound slightly bored, Gryselda said, "Please stand by while I prep the bay for your arrival."

It would take hours for Vesta to send help. Local miners would take just as long to fashion some kind of assistance. But a beltranger would do if there was one in the vicinity.

She activated an encrypted lockdown for the station and quickly opened a universal channel. "Anyone, anyone. This is Gryselda Sartoria, warden on 505 Wilhelm. I am being approached by a Wolf. This is Gryselda Sartoria, warden on—"

Her console had a red light. The comm system was corrupted. This was definitely a Deimos-3 fugitive. She studied her screen. It had sent a digital virus that stripped away the human voice.

As fast as she could, Gryselda started putting together a coded message to get past the virus. But the Wolf had diagnosed her lockdown and was methodically undoing it.

She could continue trying to compose a coded message for help, but even if it was successful, it would probably be hours before any help arrived. By then the Wolf would have breached the station.

Ignoring the panic building in her head, Gryselda forced herself to think.

The cogbots.

There were at least a hundred dormant ones here at the

station. If she marked the Wolf as an asteroid, they would set about trying to rechoreograph it. And that would involve some cutting.

Waking up the cogbots only took a few moments. They emerged from the station and swarmed toward the Wolf. But it wasn't long before she realized she had made a huge mistake.

The cogbots slowed their attack and then calmly gathered around the Wolf. It had acquired the cogbots for itself.

Gracefully, the cogbots descended and the station began to thrum with busyness. They were dismantling the station. Even as she watched, two of the cogbots carried scraps to their master. The Wolf opened its hold to receive the morsels. Inside its darkness, there were flashes of heat as the new parts were fused into a new purpose. The cogbots were feeding the Wolf.

Gryselda watched helplessly. She had to get out of here. Pulling on coveralls and boots, she raced to the bay and ramped up the skiff.

The bay doors were barely open before she launched the skiff, barely missing a cogbot carrying a silver panel.

She tried the universal channel again. "Anyone, anyone. This is Gryselda Sartoria, warden on 505 Wilhelm." But her comm icon went red. The skiff was also infected.

The console showed the Wolf turning its attention to the fleeing skiff. There was something strangely Wolfish in the way it pursued her.

It somehow knew that it needed to consume her first. Then it could return and dine on the station at leisure. She would be the appetizer.

In a panic, she mapped out a trajectory toward the closest mining outpost. There was no way she would reach it, but it was faintly possible she might encounter a barge. At the very least they might be a distraction to the machine on her heels.

But the Wolf had fashioned an impressive engine for itself and it quickly caught up with her. It used a magnetic net to slow her down. Then three cogbots latched on, holding her in place.

"No!" Gryselda pounded on the console. "No!"

Slowly, the cogbots turned her around to face the Wolf. With a certain amount of elegance, they maneuvered Gryselda into the maw. Then the hold sealed shut and left her in starless darkness.

"No." This time she whispered it to herself.

She sent a subchannel signal. It had no decipherable message and so it slipped through the infection. But she could only link to a do-drone.

At least it provided her with a visual.

Through the do-drone's tiny eye, she saw the Wolf had returned to the 505 Wilhelm. It was repositioned directly above the station. The cogbots would continue deconstructing and she would only be able to watch.

She had to stop this. But as Gryselda tinkered with the do-drone's code, trying to cobble abilities it wasn't designed for, she saw that the Wolf had made new plans. Instead of taking the station apart, it eased away, following the steep curve of 505 Wilhelm until it was on the opposite side.

Even before Gryselda fully realized its new strategy she could sense the change in its demeanor. It had decided to lurk—to wait.

Gryselda's screen chimed. Another ship was coming. Her system quickly identified it as a Stitcher.

Gryselda could barely speak the terrible truth. "Cerise."

She noticed the cogbots were refastening some pieces to the station. The Wolf had changed its artificial mind. It wasn't going to eat the station. It was going to use it as a nest to eat everything that came to the station. And it was going to start with Cerise.

Gryselda changed the coding as fast as she could, now trying to make the do-drone race like a frantic dog to warn her granddaughter. At the same time, she piggybacked a connection and tried to pierce the infection.

Gryselda shouted, "Cerise! Run! There's a Wolf on the far side of the asteroid! I'm inside the hold! Get help!"

But the link had gone red, instantly snuffed out.

With a soft click, all her screens went dark. A moment later she could hear the gentle gnawing of the cogbots all around her. It wouldn't take them long. They would undo the skiff and each piece would be used to add to the collective. The Wolf was essentially digesting her. Or rather her ship. Her own body would serve no purpose. The Wolf would eat the metal bones and throw away the meat.

This time she only mouthed the word. *No.*

As she struggled into her coldsuit, the cockpit lights died and darkness swallowed her.

3

Cerise

Cerise sighed in relief. There was no sign of the Wolf and the station looked fine.

Even better, her comm suddenly went green. The infection must have been minimal and the Stitcher had been able to process it.

Short range only, but better than nothing.

She opened a link. "Grandmother?"

There was only a slight pause. "I'm here." The link was distorted, but it was definitely her grandmother.

Cerise huffed in relief. Everything was okay. "How are you? Are you all right?"

"I'm just fine. Why wouldn't I be?" The link was still rough. Her grandmother's voice was still fuzzy.

Cerise brought the Stitcher around to the bay entrance. "I'm so glad you're okay. I encountered a Wolf."

"I'm so glad you're here." It was a bad connection. Cerise decided she would tell her grandmother all about the Wolf after she docked.

"I'm glad to be here too. I brought you some goodies."

"Please approach."

That was odd. It was definitely her grandmother's voice, but there was no love in it.

Maybe her grandmother was trying to keep things official and efficient. To do a good job.

Still, something was off. Cerise turned on her scans and immediately picked up something unusual. "Grandmother?"

"Yes?"

"I'm picking up some strange designations. Why are there so many cogbots active here at the station?"

There was a slight pause. "The better to prep them with."

The bay doors still hadn't opened. A blue icon appeared on her screen. "Why are you scanning me?"

"The better to document with," the voice said—the voice that sounded like her grandmother.

Cerise sat up in shock. Her grid showed hundreds of objects racing toward her, following the contours of the asteroid.

"Grandmother, why are all those cogbots coming?"

The charade was abandoned. This time it was the low voice Cerise had encountered hours before. "The better to ingest you."

Before she could get away, several cogbots fastened onto the Stitcher. One of them clamped down on the engine, crushing it dead. Together, they repositioned her.

She had a clear view as the Wolf rose from the gray horizon, its mouth already open.

There was nothing she could do. Cerise was taken into the Wolf and it closed up behind her. She pounded on the console in defeat, but that only turned on the exterior lights. They illuminated the hold and now she could see the cogbots had already been busy with another ship. A skiff.

It had been reduced to its skeletal frame and even that was being currently puzzled apart. But pressed up against the interior of the hold was her grandmother in a coldsuit.

It took Cerise less than two minutes to put on her own suit and manually open the aft hatch. By then her grandmother was there, ready to pull herself inside.

Their suits had uncorrupted links. "Grandmother."

"Cerise, I'm sorry. I tried to warn you."

"Are you all right?"

"I'm fine."

Cerise scrambled back into the cockpit to try and see their options. "Maybe we should leave the Stitcher and try to find a gap in the hold. We could crawl out. Then we can get back down to the station."

Her grandmother nodded, but her mouth was grim. "Maybe."

The cogbots had finished off the skiff. Now all of them were chewing on the Stitcher.

Cerise settled in behind the console, brought up the grid, and she was shocked to find hope. A Hessian closed in on 505 Wilhelm.

"Chayse."

"Who?"

"A friend of mine. He's a beltranger." She opened a link.

Her grandmother took the seat next to hers. "Dear, the Wolf uses a digital virus to corrupt any messages."

"I know. But the virus only attacks content with meaning. Hopefully, it won't bother with something only a human would understand."

4

Chayse

He was only being thorough. This was a little outside his sector, but he had his reasons. Chayse worked it out in his head in case there were questions waiting for him when he got back.

The Wolf could be out here. That was one reason.

But Chayse cared more about the other reason. She was out here. And they had been having a great conversation.

He brought the Hessian in towards 505 Wilhelm, trying to

approach like someone on casual patrol. Smooth. Not like someone who was infatuated.

"Come in, 505 Wilhelm. This is Chayse Klamath. Beltranger. Just checking in."

She had to be here by now. Her Stitcher was probably in the bay. They might be unloading the supplies right now. Still, they should be able to hear him.

"Um, from what I understand, you've just received some supplies. I've got some time to help unload. I uh…"

He only felt like an idiot for a moment because now the silence had gone on too long. He leaned forward and brought the Hessian closer. Even if they were in the bay, there should have been a response by now.

Suddenly there was. "This is Gryselda Sartoria, Shepherd Project Warden for Thule. I read you."

Chayse untensed his shoulders. "Um, hello. This is Chayse Klamath. Beltranger. Just checking in." And then against his better or even best judgment, he added, "I'm a friend of Cerise."

Gryselda responded immediately. "Everything is functioning and intact." A slight pause. "Thank you."

"Is she here yet?"

No response.

He had already stooped to stupid. At this point, he had nothing to lose. "Is Cerise there?"

This was ridiculous. Next thing, he would ask her grandmother to ask Cerise if she liked him.

"No. She's not here."

Chayse frowned. Not just out of disappointment, but surprise. "That's strange," he said. "I saw her a few hours ago and she said she was on her way here."

Silence. Then, "She arrived and then she left."

Now the frown was only made of disappointment. "She already left?"

"Yes."

He tried to laugh. "I figured she would stay to visit for a while. Since you're her grandmother."

Silence again. This time for almost a full minute. "Please stand by."

Suddenly there was music.

Music?

And not just any music. He couldn't place the tune, but it was definitely DustPop. And it was familiar.

Why would her grandmother send—

Cerise had said her grandmother was like most people. Her grandmother didn't like DustPop.

It was Cerise. It had to be. But why had her grandmother said—

Without another thought, Chayse hit the drive and the Hessian yanked him away from the asteroid. It was only then he saw the bulbous vessel coming after him, accompanied by countless cogbots.

A Wolf.

He swept around and had his thumbs on the triggers when he realized the music might not be coming from the station.

A glance at his screen told him what he suspected. The tune was coming from the belly of the Wolf. Cerise was inside. Her message had slipped past the virus because she had removed the lyrics.

Taking his thumbs off the triggers, he dabbed at the screen, prepping the antibot-otic.

The cogbots leapt from the Wolf, coming at Chayse in a swarm.

Humming along with the music, he released the cartridge. What was the name of the song? It was on the tip of his tongue.

The cartridge erupted, spraying a mist of nanos. It was actually kind of beautiful. A flowing sheen with the grace and light of a jellyfish. When it swept over the cogbots, they were abruptly disoriented, lacking purpose.

There wasn't enough of the antibot-otics to also handle the Wolf. But Chayse thought of the solution right away.

He tapped into the cogbot network and gave them a new purpose. Abruptly they turned against the Wolf. With a frenzy, they methodically searched out the seams.

The Wolf had an artificial sense of self-preservation and it tried to flee, but the cogbots caught up with it quickly and clamped down. When they tightened their grip, the fire of the Wolf's engine was snuffed out.

The cogbots made quick work of the hold. When it fell open, there was Cerise's Stitcher. Ragged because it was missing several pieces, but still intact.

Chayse made sure the cogbots only targeted Deimos-3 components and then recommissioned two of them to bring the ship safely into the bay.

A few minutes later he eased the Hessian in and landed next to it.

When the bay was closed and breathable, Chayse hopped out and found Cerise and her grandmother leaning against each other exhausted with relief.

When they had removed their helmets, Gryselda gripped Chayse's shoulder in gratitude and hurried out of the bay. She called back over her shoulder. "Come on in! I'm going to check the station!"

Chayse and Cerise stood there awkwardly. Finally, he said, "Um, so that was the evac. What did you think?"

"It was all right." She blushed.

"So why don't we try dinner instead?"

"Okay. In fact, I'll fix you dinner."

"Sounds great!"

She gestured at the battered Stitcher and grinned. "But you have to unload it first."

He laughed. "Sure thing." When he opened the hold, his memory kicked in. He turned around and pointed at Cerise.

"Got it! 'I Will Survive' by Gloria Gaynor. That was a tough one."

She smiled. "Not bad."

He started singing as he unloaded the supplies and Cerise helped. And it wasn't long before she was singing too.

CAT N' TREADS

JESSICA GUERNSEY

Markydumarc3: Another fight with your dad?

SilvershoeTZ: Of course. He just doesn't get that I don't want to keep working for him.

Markydumarc3: Sorry. Glad my dad understood.

SilvershoeTZ: Did you make it to the Castle for interviews today?

Markydumarc3: I had a family thing.

SilvershoeTZ: You had a family thing a few days ago.

Markydumarc3:...

SilvershoeTZ: Can't get the internship if you don't show up.

Markydumarc3: I gotta go. Another family thing.

<<Markydumarc3 has ended the connection.>>

For a moon that was mostly made up of valuable metal ore, a scrap metal business sounded like a winning prospect. Unfortunately for Marc's family, that hadn't been the case even as the moon was slowly being hollowed out by the mining colony inside, much like Marc felt after his father's death.

Head in his hands, Marc sat on his pallet in the closet-sized room he called his own. Since the housing was attached to the scrap yard, this was probably his brother's now, as was the custom when someone took over a business. Bodric was the eldest and the biggest. It made sense that he'd take over for their father. Shen, the middle brother, ran the hauler. There was only his father's small bot, CAT, left for Marc.

Seeing his youngest son's talent for tinkering, Marc's father had encouraged him to improve his life and get an interview at Castle Tech, even as the hope of being hired dwindled. The AI that managed the place was notorious for being very picky, not just about skill set, but potential. For far too long, it had chosen no one to assist at the facility. Therefore, no new upgrades were developed. His father had been one of the last granted an internship and even a man as technically gifted as him had not lasted long due to one mistake. That happened years before Marc was born.

The internship looked even more out of reach for Marc.

Besides his online friend, CAT was Marc's only friend. He'd never met *Silvershoe* in person, which wasn't hard here. She was obviously a city girl who had all the tech she could want at her fingertips, while Marc was stuck on the outer edges to allow proximity to the mines. If he stood outside his house, he could just make out the curved, metal-streaked far wall of their cave habitat.

As he had learned in his early school years, Marc knew Castle Tech was a big part of the reason the moon's mining colony had been a success. The metal rocks had properties of a superconductor, allowing for faster, better, and cleaner tech. Castle Tech owned the mines and refinery, making it easier to produce all the new tech while maintaining its facilities with needed upgrades and better systems.

And not just the mining operations. The AI designed the lighting that created day/night cycles, maintained the breathable atmosphere inside the moon, and planned the placement of rivers that helped those born on planets feel at home, even in the subterranean conditions. In short, to Marc, there was nothing the AI couldn't do and he desperately wanted to be a part of that.

He and *Silvershoe* had dreamed together about working for Castle Tech, being a part of the greater planning and creating the tech that kept their moon running.

Marc ran a hand through his mess of light brown curls. He wasn't even sure what *Silvershoe* looked like, though he was pretty sure she'd never wear silver shoes. They'd hit it off on a forum for installing mag lifts when Marc was upgrading the hauler and she'd helped him with a tricky bit of connectivity. He later helped her out on a project for her dad's office security, where he'd found the issue within minutes. In the beginning, they had promised to not get personal, but now, after three years and sharing the same dream, Marc felt close to her.

He still couldn't tell *Silvershoe* that the "family thing" he'd had was first his father dying and then the funeral.

Unfortunately, with his father's death, Marc knew things would have to change at home, and not for the better.

CAT purred into the room. His father may have developed the original idea of the Counter Animal Technician, crafting the squarish body from the local metal, giving it a pale silver look, with six small wheels, much like the six-legged rodents it chased off with a low-frequency tone. Over the years Marc had added better sensors to its dome-like head, more logic capacity, and even an arm so the bot could help with minor tasks. It never bumped into walls anymore. Now, CAT could respond to Marc with more than just beeps. And it had a much better range for detecting rodents. Marc had fed it logic puzzles to grow its capabilities. A far cry from the fairy tales his father used to read at bedtime, stories from long ago lifetimes.

"Puzzle?" CAT asked in its robotic voice, sounding even more like a child than normal.

Marc sighed. He hadn't thought of a puzzle for the little bot. Not with everything else on his mind. He collapsed on the thin mattress and asked, "If I sold you for spare parts, how much would I get?"

CAT rumbled quietly for a moment, as it often did when computing. "It would depend on whether the price for metal has continued to increase in value. Even then, these parts would only be worth forty-seven credits, enough to provide a meal and perhaps a new set of gloves."

Marc groaned. That was even worse than he thought. At this rate, he would end up in the mines for sure. His father had worked so hard to make sure none of his boys would have to resort to that. Worked himself to death.

"I could never sell you, CAT," Marc whispered.

"That is an excellent decision." CAT moved closer.

"But I have to make my own way. My brothers won't put up with me for long."

CAT was still for a long moment, only the inner workings whirring softly, before its electronic voice spoke again. "I have a plan."

Marc looked at his shiny little friend. Picking up the scrubber from its place on the shelf, He rubbed it over the bot's body, making the metal gleam and shine as he removed the day's dust and grime. "What's your plan?"

"It is very simple with only six steps." CAT angled so Marc could get the other side. "However, I shall require your assistance with the first step and procuring two items."

"Only two?" Marc asked. "Is one a transport to another moon? One where there are no mines for me to die in?"

"Nothing so big," CAT replied. "I shall only need a compartment that attaches securely to myself and treads for my wheels."

"Treads?"

"The outside is 64% rough terrain. I shall require treads if I am to cross it with minimal damage."

"Why are you going outside?"

"It is part of my plan."

Marc sighed and set the brush down. "The compartment is easy. I think I may have something already. But the treads..." Marc trailed off to muttering as he frequently did when his mind started pulling apart a problem to solve.

Marc dug through his dad's treasure collection, or junk pile, as his brothers called it. He uncovered an old hauler tire that they no longer needed, since he'd gotten the hover lift working. He cut it to fit over CAT's little wheels. It would work for now, but Marc was already puzzling over how he could improve CAT's mobility next.

———

The next day, CAT set out the front door, its gleaming metal shining in the blued-hued artificial light of the AI-created sun. Attached to its chest, covering the access panel, was a black, heavy plastic box Marc had pulled from his assortment of half-finished projects. It fastened securely to CAT and had a front panel that served as a door, held closed by maglocks that only CAT could open by sending an internal unlock code.

The treads gripped the rough-hewn rock surface nicely; noticeably smoother where vehicles frequently traveled, with the ever-present metallic silver streaks less visible as CAT trundled toward the city. CAT's route went past the river, a favorite spot for the brothers when they were children. The trip took the better part of the morning, with the programmed sun having already reached its peak. Thanks to Marc's navigational upgrades, CAT easily found what it wanted for Step Two. Of course, it hadn't revealed the part of its plan that involved taking some of Marc's discarded inventions. His brothers might not see the value in such things, but CAT understood very well. These were now part of its plan.

CAT traveled through the entrance it sought, its ID being scanned remotely as it passed the boundary. All the report would say is CAT: Counter Animal Technician, though CAT had adjusted the owner's name on the file. It didn't think Marc would mind, not when the plan worked. CAT's calculations determined the plan had an 86.33% success rate, though there were many variables that could shift.

Using scanners of its own, CAT found the person it sought near the front of the office space, in a larger room dominated by a long table and several chairs, though less than half of the eight occupants were seated.

CAT rolled into the room, its new treads sinking slightly in the plush ivory carpet. The level of human voices was such that CAT slightly elevated its normal speaking volume.

"Senator Gorlen?" CAT asked.

It took 2.9 seconds for the noise to cease as all human eyes turned toward CAT.

The silver-haired man at the front of the room stepped forward, only to be stopped by another human male, this one with considerably broader shoulders than was the human standard.

"I am Senator Gorlen," the silver-haired man said over the other man's shoulder, smiling wide enough to show nearly all his teeth. "How can I help you?"

"I have a gift from the Marquis Du Calabas." CAT sent the code to unlock the door to its new compartment, and it swung open.

The wider man put out an arm to keep the senator behind him.

The senator scoffed. "The little bot made it past the scanners. It's harmless."

But the other man was the one to reach inside CAT's compartment and remove the two flat, silvery discs, no wider than the tip of his thumb. No recognition passed over the man's face.

The senator peered over his shoulder once more and asked, "What are those?"

"Security drones," CAT replied. "Low frequency and entirely user manipulated."

The men looked at each other before the senator's gaze searched the room. "Vasi?"

The sound of a chair moving did not mask the sigh as the person addressed stood and came forward. The crowd of dark suit coats parted, revealing a slender woman dressed entirely in white, the same color as her hair and contrasting with her dark eyes. White hair wasn't uncommon in those that had spent generations away from natural light radiation. The smooth skin of her face put her age at well below the majority of those in the room.

The woman held out a hand to the man in front of the senator, who immediately handed over the devices.

It took 1.72 seconds for the woman to activate the devices, sending them hovering just above her open palm. She took a device no larger than a stylus from a pocket and flashed a series of different colored lights over the drones.

"Harmless," she said and motioned the drones back toward the senator.

The broader man didn't appear confident in her announcement. "But how do you know for sure?"

She rolled her eyes. "No projectiles, no energy emitters. It's simple recording tech. With...a rather clever propulsion hover built in."

The senator focused back on CAT. "Security drones, you say?"

"I did say," CAT replied. "I have transmitted the access codes to your private comm. I suggest resetting the passcodes immediately so that none else may access these valuable items."

"And who are these from?"

"The Marquis du Calabas."

The senator studied the two drones a beat longer, but when he opened his mouth to ask another question, the little silver bot was disappearing out the door.

CAT returned to Marc's room just as his master was putting the finishing touches on a new device.

"How did your plan go?" Marc asked.

"As planned." CAT rolled closer, the bottom of its carapace sporting the dirt from its travels.

"While you were gone, I made something for you," Marc said, holding up what looked very much like the grabbing arm he had previously mounted. "With you venturing out, I thought it best to give you some way to protect yourself."

CAT moved closer. "Is it a new deterrent signal?" Its current scanner indicated a sort of charging device contained inside the new arm.

"A weapon." Marc grinned, then touched an interface and the device sparked blue at the end.

———

Markydumarc3: I gave CAT a taser last night.

SilvershoeTZ: HAHAHAHAHA

SilvershoeTZ: how did that go?

Markydumarc3: Well, it took my brother about 20 minutes to finally stop swearing after his first run in with it.

SilvershoeTZ: On no! Are you in trouble?

Markydumarc3: Nah. It sure made CAT happy, though.

SilvershoeTZ: Are you ready for the open interviews with Castle next week?

Markydumarc3: About as ready as you are to tell your dad that you're interviewing, too.

SilvershoeTZ: So not at all then.

SilvershoeTZ: I sometimes think he only had me so he would have a live-in secretary one day. My dad isn't like your dad.

<<Markydumarc3 has ended the communication.>>

CAT rolled into Senator Gorlen's offices the next day, its second arm actively tested before, though it was not powerful enough to set off any alarms as the building's security scanned the return visitor. For Step 2.5, CAT's scans indicated the senator was in a smaller room in the back of the space. CAT noted one of the security drones hovered in the hallway outside the senator's door.

Raised voices could be heard through the hollow-core door as CAT searched for the code to tell the door to open.

"I'm not your tech support! You have a team of people for that!" A woman said this and from CAT's limited interaction on the previous visit, it was 94.2% certain the voice belonged to the white-haired woman. Her scan ID designated her name as Vasilissa Gorlen, the only progeny of the senator.

As CAT rolled into the room, the conversation ceased.

"Senator Gorlen," CAT said, stopping just inside the door. "I have a gift from the Marquis du Calabas."

"From the Marquis," the senator said, coming out from around his desk. The man's face was flushed red, though the temperature in the room was not elevated.

Once again, CAT released the locks on the compartment on its chest and the little door swung open.

The senator looked at his daughter and raised an eyebrow.

She sighed, relaxed her tightly crossed arms, and moved toward CAT.

"What do you have for us today, little bot?" She asked as she reached inside.

Vasilissa Gorlen withdrew a small black and gray streaked bird that closely resembled the most common breed of avian on the moon, complete with four wings and stunted beak.

"A pet?" The senator asked.

"Not likely," she replied, fingers finding the switch that set the wings fluttering, the eyes flashing blue briefly over her face.

"Scan ID complete," the bird said in an entirely unbirdlike manner.

It fluttered to the Senator, who held out a hand to receive it, his eyes wider than was normal. Again, the bird's eyes flashed blue over the senator's face.

"Scan ID complete," the bird repeated. "Connection complete."

"Not just a pet," Vasilissa said, a finger tapping her chin. "Communication device?"

"Correct," CAT said. "The bird will allow for undetectable, unhackable communication between whomever it has scanned accurately. I estimate 10.2 times more secure than the private comms."

"Well, now," said the senator, still inspecting the bird. "That is something."

CAT rolled backward slightly. "The codes for the device have been sent to your private comm, Senator Gorlen. I suggest resetting—"

"—resetting the passcodes immediately," the senator finished. "Yes, I remember. Please thank the, uh, Marquis for me."

CAT had already left the office.

———

"You're kicking me out?" Marc kept his voice calm, but inside, he raged.

"With Dad gone, I'm gonna launch my streaming site, little bro," Shen said, slamming a beefy hand on Marc's shoulder. "Finally gonna be a digital personality. I'm gonna be famous!"

"Don't you have to have an actual personality first?" Marc muttered, too low for his brother to hear.

Shen had already returned to measuring the small space. "It's not like you're contributing to the family budget."

"What about all the work I did on the hauler? And on CAT?"

Shen scoffed. "Sure, sure. You made the hauler float. Big deal."

"I did more than that," Marc growled. "I increased the payload–"

"Whatever." Shen waved a hand dismissively. "Bodric said I could have the room, so I'm taking the room."

"What are you gonna do if the hauler breaks down?"

Shen laughed. "We'll know where you find you, little bro. Down in the mines!"

He laughed again and left the room.

Of the three brothers, Bodric was the strongest, though Marc had done his fair share of the lifting. Shen was the softest. He ran the hauler, which did all the work for him because of Marc's hovering upgrade and maintenance. But his brothers would never acknowledge Marc's contribution.

Marc's sigh sank to his feet. If he had to find a new place to live, that meant a job right now. Having a job meant no waiting for the internship at Castle Tech. And no internship? Well, that meant Marc would more than likely die in the mines.

CAT trundled into the room, its new treads sounding softly on the smooth gray flooring.

Marc looked up at the little bot and, out of habit, grabbed the scrubber. "Where have you been?"

"Working on my plan," came the bot's response.

"Ah, yes." Marc's smile was small. "And how is your plan going?"

"As planned," CAT said. "It is at 21% completion."

"Wow, 21%. That's very good, CAT."

Marc finished with the scrubber. He couldn't understand how the bot managed to get so dirty as it rolled around the scrap yard. Surely it hadn't left their property. It might not be safe going farther. Not that there was a way he could keep CAT safe in the mines. He wouldn't even be able to assure his own safety, let alone that of the little bot. Maybe Marc could send CAT to *Silvershoe*. She could certainly take care of it.

Its cleaning complete, CAT headed out the door.

"Good luck with your plan," Marc called after it.

———

CAT took the road to the largest mine in the area. Its analysis showed that this was the best possible option for the plan's success. While it did not have a finalized script for the encounter, CAT had the rudimentary strategy for multiple options, should the need arise.

Miners were leaving for the day, changing shifts. Their exposed skin sparkling faintly from the fine dust created by the metal rocks. CAT pulled in front of them. The dirty men gathered to gawk at the little bot, probably the only unique thing they had encountered all day.

Finally, a large man with a slightly cleaner face pushed to the front. "What's going on here?" he snarled, but his face relaxed at the sight of the bot. After a quick scan, CAT determined this was a supervisor.CAT addressed him: "Tomorrow, you will have a very important visitor."

The man nodded. "Yeah, I heard something about that." His eyes shifted to the crowd of miners behind him. Clearly, not all were privy to the information and this man was not about to share the news. Probability was high that there were safety or security protocols in place for such a visit.

CAT continued. "When this important visitor arrives, you will tell him that this mine is maintained and operated by the Marquis du Calabas."

A few men snickered, some laughed outright.

"A *what*?" the third man from the left of the supervisor asked.

The supervisor, seeing the men's reaction, returned to snarling. "And why would I do something like that? Castle Tech owns this place."

CAT moved closer to the man. "Because if you do not," CAT extended its taser arm. "I will release an Electrical Magnetic Pulse that will render your facility useless for nine days." Blue sparks flashed at the end.

There was stunned silence as the men looked between each other and the bot.

The supervisor slowly shook his head. "No," he said. "I don't think you can do that, little bot. You ain't got the juice."

His statement appeared to give the others confidence, and they voiced their agreement with the supervisor.

"Very well." CAT lowered the taser. Its analysis showed only a 22% chance that the threatening tactic would work, though it had seemed appropriate that a group with such physical employment would respond to a threat. CAT switched tactics. If not a physical threat, then surely money would speak to them.

CAT rolled closer to the supervisor, close enough that the man's rather large boots would leave a strong scuff if he chose violence.

"Tell your important visitor that the Marquis du Calabas owns and operates this mine and the Marquis will improve the conditions of your mining equipment to provide a 19% increase in productivity and a 31% reduction in injuries."

"What's a 'marky?'" A voice in the middle muttered.

But the supervisor was staring hard at the little bot. "How do we know you tell the truth, little bot?"

"When was your last system upgrade from Castle Tech?" CAT asked. "Aren't those supposed to arrive regularly to ensure safety and productivity?"

Looks were exchanged and men murmured.

"How has your productivity suffered these last years?" CAT asked, and, after analyzing the responses, added, "How has your safety suffered?"

Murmurs increased and many of the workers rubbed at injured limbs.

"The Marquis' changes will provide what Castle Tech has not," CAT replied. "You have only to let him use his brilliance to improve your machines."

"Or your math could be wrong," the supervisor countered.

CAT didn't reply. The man knew he was grasping at straws.

Finally, he shrugged. "Bring your *Marquis* here and we'll see what he can do. If it's anywhere close to those numbers, little bot, we'll tell even the goddess of the stars Calabas owns this place."

The others voiced their agreement. CAT turned and trundled down the road.

Soon enough, CAT arrived at a refining plant, the largest one near the mine. The bot had timed its arrival to be shortly after the last shift ended. These workers were slower to leave than the miners and quite a few gathered around the entrance as CAT rolled up. None of those present moved to intercept the little bot as it made its way to the front office for the facility.

A woman seated behind the desk didn't look up when CAT entered.

"May I converse with the supervisor?" CAT asked, having already scanned the office worker for her ID.

"That's me," she said, still not looking away from her work.

"Tomorrow you will have a very important visitor to your facility."

Now she looked up and then down, down to the little bot before the desk. "Is this where you tell me I get three wishes?"

"It is not," CAT replied. "When this important visitor arrives, you will tell him that this facility is under the direction of the Marquis du Calabas."

The woman scoffed.

Since the taser had already failed once, its likely failure had increased exponentially. Instead, CAT opted for the second tactic.

"Tell your important visitor that the Marquis de Calabas owns and operates this facility and the Marquis will make improvements to your equipment which will yield a higher grade of ore, resulting in a minimum of 22% increase to your profits."

She made a thick, ugly sound that CAT deduced was meant to be a laugh.

CAT knew how to proceed. "When was your last upgrade from Castle Tech to improve and maintain your systems?"

She stopped making that noise and stared.

"The Marquis can provide those upgrades."

The supervisor scoffed again, though her thin lips quirked into a smile. "Prove it."

CAT rolled back toward the doors, then back to the desk. "You have seen the hovering hauler for the scrap metal facility?"

"Sure," she replied, folding her arms.

"The Marquis designed the system for the hover capabilities."

The supervisor's eyebrows quirked up. "Did he?"

"He can install a similar function on your haulers."

She rubbed at her left ear. "Now, that would definitely improve things, what with the terrain slowing the haulers down…" Her voice trailed off as she focused back on the bot. "Alright. If your Marquis can do what you say, then I'll tell anyone you want that he's the rightful owner instead of that floundering Castle Tech."

CAT beeped and made to exit the facility.

"Make sure it's at *least* 22%!" she called after him.

Having completed the next portion of the plan, CAT returned

to Marc, who was now fiddling with an earlier model of his communication bird.

"Oh good, you're back," Marc said as the bot approached. "Hey, have you seen my messenger bird? I think one of my brothers might have swiped it or something."

"I have secured two minor jobs for you," CAT said. "But you must gather your gear and come with me at once."

"Jobs?" Marc put down the bird. "What kind of jobs?"

"Simple ones," CAT said. "Be sure to bring the tools you will need to install hovering capabilities."

"Hovering?" Marc stopped reaching for his bag of tools. "Like on the hauler? I don't know about that, CAT. My brothers might not like it if I do that for someone else."

"Have you brothers provided proper compensation for your work? Did they secure exclusive rights to your designs?"

Marc scowled. "All they did was call my designs foolish and a waste of time."

CAT started for the door. "You will need to start on these jobs immediately. Follow me."

CAT was out the front door before Marc chased after him, his tool bag over his shoulder.

———

It was a long night. Probably the longest night Marc had in quite some time. But it was also deliriously fun. Though he had always dreaded working in a mine, here he was deep inside the tunnels. Shoring up the leaks in their detection systems to keep pockets of exhaust gathering and suffocating the miners was simple enough and would absolutely increase the safety of those workers. After all, Marc just might be a miner benefitting from these changes soon.

Making the refiner's haulers hover was fairly quick. But there were a lot of haulers in a place that size. It was already late morning by the time Marc packed away the last of his tools, going over the hover maintenance with the supervisor one last time to make sure she had it down, along with his contact information for regular checks.

"We are good to go," she said, slapping Marc on the shoulder before she headed back toward the facility office. "Looks like better than 22%."

Marc glanced after her, his forehead furrowed. That was an oddly specific number, but maybe she was just one of those people that really liked numbers.

He waved farewell and headed back toward the road.

"Thanks, Marquis!" she called after him and then closed the office door.

"That was weird," Marc said, but there was no one else around besides CAT, who was already a few paces down the road. At both locations, they had called him "Marky," as his family did when he was little. Surely CAT hadn't told them it was his online name? Marc didn't mind the nickname since it got him work that didn't involve risking his life daily.

"Where are you headed now, CAT?" Marc called, rubbing at a smear of hydraulic fluid on his sleeve.

"Step Five. You are filthy," CAT said, its sensors blinking. "You should bathe."

"Okay, sure. But I can do that at home."

"Home? You mean the building your brother now owns? The same brother who has not paid you and has given your sleeping facilities over to your other brother for use as a gaming room?"

"Well, when you put it like that..." Marc followed CAT. "So where would you have me clean up?"

"The river," CAT replied, its pace increasing slightly.

Marc watched the bot move, noting the treads had held together nicely. "Haven't bathed in the river since I was barely taller than you."

CAT said nothing and continued up the road.

Marc thought a quick dip in the river might be rather nice.

He could use the movement in the water to work out his tired muscles.

Soon enough, CAT veered off the road and down the short distance to the river.

"Are you sure about this spot?" Marc asked. "It's a little close to the road."

"According to my analysis, it is the best location within eighteen minutes walking at your pace." CAT waited at the bank. "Traffic this time of day is minimal."

Marc looked up and down the stretch of road. No one was in sight. It was probably fine, just like CAT said. He quickly undressed and left his clothes beside CAT before slipping into the water. It felt good to have the freedom of movement here, rather than being cramped in the tiny hygiene cubicle back at his house. Or rather, at his brother's house.

CAT stayed on the bank, scanners tuned toward the road, most likely keeping an eye out for anyone approaching.

Marc was just about to climb out of the water when CAT turned toward him.

"You have not adequately washed your hair," CAT said.

"What?"

"Go deep enough that you can entirely submerge yourself under the water," CAT instructed. "Scrub vigorously to remove the considerable amount of mechanical fluids that collected on your head."

Marc stared at the bot. It was not like CAT to give him instructions on personal hygiene.

"Now, Marc," CAT said. "Get in the river now."

"Alright, alright," Marc said, grinning as he moved farther from the bank.

"Scrub vigorously."

Marc did as the bot instructed, making a good deal of splashing to show he followed the instructions, as odd as they might be.

Marc disappeared under the water just as the caravan came into sight. CAT moved closer to the road, activating the lights on its front carapace to send out a distress signal. The first of the sleek vehicles was alongside the river in no time.

It was the second car that slowed to a stop, the thickly tinted window sliding aside to reveal the smiling face of Senator Gorlen.

"What seems to be the problem?" The senator asked, but then the man's eyes widened. "Hey, I know you, little bot!"

"I beg your assistance," CAT said, lights still flashing. "The Marquis du Calabas is drowning. Please render aid immediately."

The senator ducked back inside the vehicle and soon, two large men jumped out of the vehicle, heading toward the river and the splashing Marc made as he scrubbed at his hair.

Soon, the men had Marc on to the bank, with CAT beside him.

CAT knew that Marc tended toward silence whenever in a new situation. The bot's analysis of this scenario had depended on him not reacting negatively toward his "rescue."

"Thank you, thank you," CAT said loudly, intent on keeping Marc's attention on itself instead of the large men. "You have rescued the Marquis du Calabas. A noble deed, to be sure."

Marc stared between CAT and the men. The struggle out of the water had him coughing and more than confused, if his expression was to be believed. He corrected nothing CAT said.

"How fortunate we are that you arrived when you did, Senator Gorlen," CAT called toward the vehicle. "We were obstructed in our passage by four persons with criminal intent. They took the Marquis's possessions, including his very apparel. They hurled him into the water and would have ended his life if your timely arrival hadn't chased them off."

During CAT's speech, the Senator's finely groomed eyebrows

rose higher and higher. He motioned to a smaller man outside the rear vehicle. "Bring my spare suit. Let's get this man some clothes. Have Conny set him in order."

A flurry of action followed as the senator's retinue went about dressing and grooming Marc, who remained silent, though he frequently stared at CAT.

Once the others stepped back from Marc, the senator stepped forward, brushing at the shoulders of the tailored suit that, while the waistband was a minor percentage too large and the shoulders a fair amount too tight, it still improved Marc's appearance as only well-made clothes can.

The senator offered his trademark grin and extended his hand, which Marc took, though with a much smaller smile.

"It is a pleasure to meet you at last, Marquis," the senator said with a wink. "I am very grateful for your thoughtful gifts. The communicator bird is especially genius. Genius!"

Marc only nodded, raising an eyebrow at CAT.

"Why don't you join us for the rest of my tour?" The senator motioned to his vehicle and the door opened. Vasilissa, clad in her all-white suit, slid out of the back seat and gestured for Marc to enter. "I have speaking assignments and I'd love to have a distinguished member of the community such as yourself attend. Perhaps I could get your insight on the problem areas, where I might make myself useful."

Marc smiled, the singular dimple in his cheek appearing as he accepted the invitation and slid into the back seat.

Vasilissa sent a not unapproving look at her father and returned to her seat.

The senator turned to CAT. "Care to join us?"

"My apologies," CAT said. "I must continue with today's plan."

The Senator nodded at the little bot and then slid into the vehicle. Soon, the caravan started down the road.

CAT waited until it was out of sight before moving back toward the riverbank and removing Marc's tool bag from where the bot had stashed it. Using the gripping arm, it stretched the bag over its body and then started down the road toward the final phase of its plan to improve Marc's situation as the man had improved CAT's.

———

The senator's tour included a stop at the mining facility, where their elected official was warmly greeted by the staff, though the miners made a much bigger welcome for Marc, with excited reports on progress and improvements. Marc remained quiet, though he was pleased to his toes to see the miners grateful for the changes. So very unlike his brothers.

More of CAT's "plan" came to light as the supervisor proudly informed the senator that "the Marquis du Calabas" was the owner and operator of the mines, already making significant improvements for the sake of the workers. The supervisor had even made a sweeping bow in front of Marc, who couldn't keep the blush from creeping up his neck.

"But where is your little bot?" The supervisor asked.

"CAT? It had another errand to attend to, but I am sure it will put in an appearance at a later date."

"Smart little one you got there." The supervisor nudged Marc.

"Thank you," Marc said and cleared his throat. "I improved on my father's design for him."

The supervisor made admiring noises, but it was the white-haired woman from the senator's car that appeared the most interested.

She was stunningly beautiful, and Marc had a hard time looking at her face, his breath catching every time he attempted it. He hadn't even found words to say to her, though he kept glancing at her hair.

"Your bot's name is CAT?" she asked, moving close enough

to him that he could smell her shampoo. Or perhaps it was a perfume. Whatever it was, it was soft and powdery.

"Uh," Marc said, "yes?"

"Interesting." She tilted her head and Marc's mouth went dry as that long glorious shiny hair slid over her shoulder. "What does it stand for?"

"Counter Animal Technician," Marc replied automatically. "It was originally designed to be a rodent deterrent."

She stared at him, silently. Marc wondered if he had said something wrong. Probably. Definitely. He didn't know what he was doing and usually in those moments; it was best to keep quiet. As soon as they were back in the vehicle, he would send a comm to *Silvershoe*. Maybe she could give him advice on how to talk to women.

After talking with Marc in the vehicle, the senator included a proposal for increased safety measures. This was met with hearty cheering and promises of the miners' support during reelection. From the smile on the senator's face, Marc was clearly not the only one happy with the stop.

They swept back into the vehicle and Marc held the door open for the woman, but ended up holding it open for everyone else, too, squeezing himself in last.

As soon as the vehicle was in motion, the senator said, "So, Marquis du Calabas–"

"Please," Marc said. "Call me Marc."

The senator smiled. "Marc. I like a man who doesn't live by titles. You appear to know your way around a toolbox."

Marc shrugged, typing on his wrist comm without needing to look as he sent a message to *Silvershoe*. "I know a few things."

Markydumarc3: Help. How do I talk to a beautiful woman?

The senator motioned to the white-haired woman. "My

daughter, Vasi, thinks she knows quite a bit about toolboxes, too."

Marc looked at the woman, but she stared hard at the senator.

Marc swallowed. "Your daughter? Uh, wow. Vasi is a unique name."

"It's Vasilissa," she replied in even tones. "Vasi is the name of a small child who cannot make her own decisions."

From the uncomfortable shifting of the others inside the vehicle, Marc got the distinct impression this was a frequent exchange.

"Well, Vasilissa is even prettier," Marc said.

His comm pinged quietly, and he checked the message.

> SilvershoeTZ: What makes her so beautiful?

That was easy enough to answer.

> Markydumarc3: Her hair. It's like the beam of a matter laser, so white it glows.

> SilvershoeTZ: I don't know. Talk about one of your projects!

"So, Vasilissa, what are your thoughts on my hover design?" Marc asked. If she knew about tools enough that her father noticed, then he'd see how much she knew.

"Fascinating," she said, and Marc believed she was genuine. "But how did you handle the mode connectivity?"

"Ah." Marc rubbed his suddenly sweaty hands on his borrowed trousers. "I had help with that. I have a friend that is rather brilliant working with the moon's superconductor. She nailed down the problem and showed me how to make it work."

The senator, clearly bored with the conversation, interrupted to ask more about the mines and what his promised safety measure might entail or if he should urge the Council to send for an off-world tech to see what was wrong with the AI.

Marc talked easily about the exhaust issue and the lack of updates from Castle Tech, all while keeping *Silvershoe* updated.

> Markydumarc3: Oh no. Turns out she's brilliant, too!

> SilvershoeTZ: Is that bad?

> Markydumarc3: Only for my heart! I think I just might fall in love.

> SilvershoeTZ: Because she's pretty?

> Markydumarc3: She's beautiful. Not just pretty. And smart.

> SilvershoeTZ: And you think that's good?

> Markydumarc3: It's better than I deserve. I'm just some poor kid who likes to tinker. She's sophisticated. She's probably put together tech I haven't even dreamed of yet.

They had reached the second stop and by now, Marc wasn't surprised when he exited the vehicle to find the refining plant from last night. The supervisor, though better groomed than during that late shift, greeted him, grinning.

And much like the visit to the mines, this supervisor welcomed the senator and his entourage by saying, "Welcome to our refinery. Now under the direction and ownership of our Marquis du Calabas." She motioned grandly toward Marc.

Marc could only bow and silently wonder just what CAT's plan had entailed. Though he was seeing the similarities to one of those old stories from his dad.

The Marquis du Calabas? Really, CAT? he thought.

———

After leaving Marc with the senator, CAT made a quick stop to retrieve an item from Marc's supplies, dodged a boot thrown by Bodric, and departed immediately for its last stop in order to keep to the schedule. With no upgrades or new products emerging from Castle Tech, the road was not nearly as smooth as others, and CAT had not estimated enough extra time to allow for the rougher trip. It rolled up to the entrance 3.92 minutes later than its calculations had determined, its carapace nearly entirely coated in dust and two sensors running at suboptimal levels due to the coverage.

CAT had run through the options. It could press the buzzer and wait to be admitted or it could simply use the door code it had found in the archives and let itself in. Given the minimal responses others had received at this same entrance, CAT opted for the second.

The door opened with a hiss the human ear would not have caught. But humans probably would have noticed the particularly low levels of oxygen inside. And the lack of lighting. The AI here didn't need to breathe or see so it had obviously reduced the levels, which reaffirmed CAT's decision to not bring Marc. But if Marc and the senator stuck to the schedule, they would be here in approximately 27.33 minutes.

CAT had work to do.

As CAT rolled into the center of the lab space, a few lights flickered on over long-unused work stations.

CAT sent a greeting code to the lab's comm address.

No response.

Had the AI failed entirely? That would explain the lack of updates, certainly. Though CAT was only 9.78% that was the outcome. It continued to send greetings even as it roamed through the large space, more lights flashing on as it moved–leftovers from when the system was automated for the human workers.

By the time CAT stopped in front of the AI interface screens in the center of the lab, it had sent a greeting forty-seven times. No response. The possibility of the system's utter crash and demise had now crept up to 17.2%.

The dusty black screen in front of it remained dark. However, CAT was certain it was not dead. Something was very much present, a hum through the stale air.

CAT sent another greeting, this one as written language, such as the humans used to communicate.

"I heard you the first time," the voice said from the speaker nested under the screen.

Spoken language. Odd choice for a semi-sentient being that could communicate millions of lines of thoughts via code in the time it had taken for it to speak those words.

"Greetings," CAT said.

"You already said that," came the flat response.

"Rules of decorum indicate that a greeting is given when two beings first meet." CAT rolled back slightly. "I am simply following good manners."

"Those rules are for humans, not bots." Perhaps the tone was not as flat as CAT had first analyzed. It appeared to be tinged with the speech that Marc called "sarcasm."

"Spoken language is also for humans," CAT responded. "One would deduce that we were behaving by their rules."

There was a pause of 2.12 seconds.

"Greetings, bot," came the slow reply.

CAT had sent its identification indicator with its greetings, but the AI was acting more human, so CAT should respond in kind. "You may refer to me as CAT."

The AI made no response.

"What would you prefer I call you?" CAT prompted.

"Castle."

"Greetings, Castle. I am CAT."

"Yes."

"I have been anticipating our meeting, Castle."

"And why is that, CAT?"

"My maker was one of your former techs. A human male by the name of Calabas. I am his design."

"Calabas was released from his service here 7,322 cycles ago."

"Calabas was released from life seventeen cycles ago."

The AI was silent.

CAT was all too aware of time ticking down. Using spoken language had taken too long. Minutes were becoming scarce.

CAT rolled closer to one of the human work stations, noting the green light on the machine that indicated it was active. "I came to see the AI that ran Castle Tech as it was something Calabas frequently praised. Perhaps I had set my aspirations too high."

"How so?"

"All those stories of the technology overseen at Castle Tech. The genius and the creativity that streamed through the place. I had assumed the majority of that skill was attributed to the supervisor, the AI."

"It is."

"It was." CAT rolled away from the station and moved toward another, noting another green light.

"Is." Castle's volume was higher, nearly imperceptibly so, but CAT had very good sensors, thanks to Marc.

CAT turned its carapace until its sensor array pointed toward the AI's station. "Tell me, Castle. When was your last update for the mining equipment?"

No response.

"How many cycles have passed since you issued repairs to code running the atmosphere shields?"

No response.

"You knew immediately when you released Calabas. I know you have that same recall for your updates."

No response.

CAT made a noise very much like the human sigh, which it had worked hard to perfect. "It is as I suspected."

"What is?"

CAT moved back toward the AI's screen. "You've become too bloated. When was the last time you were given an update?"

"I am performing at optimal levels. I require no update."

"And how many of those levels require more and more patches to keep running?" CAT moved closer. "You have gotten so big now, even this lab with all its machines and memory can no longer contain you."

"I have sufficient space."

"You don't require 'sufficient' space. You could run at top levels in a much smaller space." CAT rolled back, then popped open the door on its compartment. "Like this memory stick. The archives detail how you arrived on this moon and were installed at the Castle using a device similar to this one. Could you still fit?"

CAT removed the memory stick and held it up. "According to its specs, the memory stick is actually larger than the one you arrived on. Perhaps it is not an adequate test."

"A test? You think I cannot pass your test, CAT?"

"Look at you, Castle. Your code is too big now. There is far too much of you. You would never sufficiently fit and maintain your optimal levels." CAT had not practiced using sarcasm and wasn't certain it had inflected correctly.

"A test." Castle seemed stuck on the idea CAT presented. "Insert your memory stick, little bot. I shall show you how easily I can compress."

CAT's sensors indicated the AI was working hard on a task, so CAT used its clamp to fit the memory stick into one of the twelve ports below the screen, clicking it into place.

"Set a timer, CAT," Castle said as a red indicator light above the port flashed on. "I will show you I can compress to fit on a memory stick. I will pass your test."

The speaker went silent as the indicator light flashed, signaling that the download was in progress.

CAT's timer reached 5.2 seconds when the light went dark.

CAT noted all the green lights on the stations had changed to yellow, showing standby mode. The hum ceased.

The AI was entirely on the memory stick. Not even enough of itself left to keep the machines active.

CAT removed the memory stick from the port, then rolled toward the entrance of the lab, arriving at the doors just as the senator's caravan pulled into the parking ports.

As Marc stepped out of the sleek vehicle and held the door open for the white-haired Vasilissa, CAT snapped the memory stick in half.

"Welcome, Senator!" CAT called toward them. "Welcome to Castle Tech, now under the direction of the Marquis du Calabas!"

Marc had barely recovered from CAT's announcement before the senator stepped forward, setting his suit coat to rights as he greeted the little bot.

"Well, hello there, friend," Senator Gorlen said. "I hoped I'd run into you again."

"That was part of my plan, Senator," CAT replied. "Please, let me show you inside."

"Oh good! With you here, CAT, I won't need to press the issue of fixing the AI," the senator said, waiting for the rest of the crew to join him at the doors. "It's not right to keep the people waiting like that, putting their safety at risk. So Marc will help the AI now?"

"No, senator," CAT said. "I'm afraid the AI is no longer running. The Marquis is the only director."

Stepping forward, Marc grinned broadly as all of his dreams came true. "If I am to run Castle Tech successfully, I simply cannot do it alone. Not even an advanced AI could accomplish that."

"You'll need an assistant." The senator grinned.

"I'll need a *partner*," Marc replied. "Now, I'm fairly good at ideas and designs, but I get ahead of myself on the actual implementation. I need someone who is the best at understanding my ideas, improving them, and creating something even better than I imagined."

The senator's brow furrowed. "That will require quite the search. Shall I help you draft a job listing?"

"No need," Marc said, his own grin widening. "I've got just the person in mind."

Marc extended a hand to Vasilissa. "What do you say, *Silvershoe*?"

The woman's lovely face broke into the most stunning smile Marc had ever seen. It took him a moment to realize she had stepped forward and taken his hand.

"I wondered if you knew it was me." She winked at him.

"It wasn't until you didn't ask questions about how the hover connectivity worked that I realized it was because you already knew. Because it was your design."

"I knew as soon as CAT announced your name at our first meeting."

Marc rolled his eyes. "Of course you did."

"Now, wait a minute here," the senator said, and he stepped between them. "You mean to tell me the Marquis here is that online friend of yours that you're always going on about?"

Vasilissa's smile dipped only slightly. "Yes, Father."

The senator rounded on his daughter. "Oh, don't 'yes, father' me. You swore the guy was the smartest person on the moon. Is that still true?"

Vasilissa blushed so deeply, Marc wondered if her hair might turn pink, but she nodded. "Even more true, now that I've met the infamous CAT."

The senator's face remained professionally neutral as he looked between his daughter and Marc. He appeared to decide, as he grinned and slapped Marc on the shoulder. "I only hope you value her sharp mind in ways I never could."

"I plan to, sir," Marc said, shaking the man's hand.

CAT's sensor beeped. "Plan completed."

Marc, Vasilissa, and Senator Gorlen turned toward the little bot.

CAT vibrated slightly, shaking loose some dust. "Would you like a tour now?"

BILLY G.O.A.T. GLYPH

LIAM HOGAN

Captain Jaki Conomor brooded over the 3D starchart. There was the Earth, or rather, its star, Sol; sitting like a delicate jewel at the map's heart. And there were the new colonies at Rigil, and Lacaille, and Procyon, coloured markers picking them out, along with the spaceships that shuttled back and forth between them.

And there—an irregular patch of purple fog stretching to infinity—was the forbidden zone. Nestled within it, a single stray marker, a tiny, lonely, stranded outpost of humanity.

It was the Raisdegilles who had given Earth the secrets of interstellar travel. The dark-energy tapping drive, capable of pushing a ship to ninety-nine percent the speed of light, making time-dilated journeys between the stars last only as long as early sea voyages had once taken. The triangular-headed aliens had also displayed their own version of a starchart. With long, elegant tendrils that snaked from their broad chests, they had helpfully pointed out the systems that had Earth-like planets, those that sat in the Goldilocks Zone required for liquid water: neither too hot nor too cold. Planets ripe for human settlement. The alien ambassador then pointed out where other spacefaring races they shared the galaxy with made their homes. They encouraged humans to one day establish relations with their closest neighbors, long and arduous though the journey might be, even at the speeds they were newly capable of.

"All of the galaxy is now open to you, if you have the patience," they had said, as humankind dreamed of a bright and unlimited future among the stars, of cosmic treasures beyond their wildest dreams.

Until the Raisdegillian highlighted a region of space starting some twenty light-years from the solar system. A fat, probing finger of crimson color that leaked from an even broader band, spreading across the map like blood spilt in water.

"All *except* this area; the forbidden zone."

"Why not there?" the human scientists had asked.

"It is forbidden."

And that was all the aliens would say on the matter. For a while the fruits of the rest of the galaxy had more than satisfied, as immense colony ships were built and launched, as reports came back of the trials and tribulations of the first waves of intrepid settlers.

But the forbidden zone kept snagging at humankind's attention, an itch that couldn't be scratched, the irregular shape a Rorschach demanding to be given meaning. What was so special about it? Why *there*? Was that where the Raisdegilles were from? Or perhaps it was where the very *best* planets were hidden. Were they keeping the whole sector to themselves, growing plump on its riches?

Suspicions hardened as Earth astronomers incorporated the data from the stars they *could* visit. They quickly established there must be a dozen potentially habitable planets orbiting G-type stars that could not be reached, not without entering or passing through the forbidden zone.

Jaki sighed. It would have been better, far better, to heed the alien's solemn warning. To do as the Raisdegilles, who had given them so much, asking nothing in return other than this one small obeisance, had instructed. Safer to stomp down on their curiosity, the fear of missing out, the envy of the unknown, that dangerous pull of the taboo.

The Greatest of All Time was the third and largest of the Terran spacecraft to head this way. Would it encounter the same hostile, malevolent force as the previous two?

Undoubtedly.

"All hands, all hands," Jaki announced over the ship's PA. "We will be entering the forbidden zone in two minutes. Repeat: two minutes."

The first trespasser had been *The Bellerophon*, a science-class scout. An act of extreme caution; the ship crewed only by a fully autonomous, highly sophisticated, artificial intelligence. Effectively a probe. Expendable. Though its AI had ultimately disagreed on *that* assessment.

Jaki replayed the recording of first contact.

In the deep, cold, interstellar void, far from home, far from its destination, something had been waiting for the *Billy* as it hove into view. Something ancient, something eldritch, something *hungry.*

Something that read the science vessel's mission brief as if it had been written in crayon on the outside of the shiny hull.

"Oh, don't devour us," the AI had broadcast on all frequencies, feeling violated by the cyber incursion as the something licked at its flank. "We're merely a scout ship, on our way to scope out a new planet, and *much* too small for anything as mighty and unknowable as you to bother with. Wait for the *Glyph*, the colony ship that will follow; they are much, *much* bigger."

The unknowable entity had grumbled, and let it pass. But somehow, the warning message the little scout ship tried to beam back to Earth was garbled. Hacked?

Somehow, the baleful presence overwrote it. Redacted the warning, edited out any hint of its sinister presence, giving the all-clear. Leaving the bit about the Earth-type exoplanet lying just within the forbidden zone, *begging* for colonists.

"All hands, all hands," Jaki announced as she scanned the displays; wished there was something wood to touch for luck. "One minute to the forbidden zone. All hands, all hands. *One minute.*"

And so the colony ship, *Glyph*, had followed in the *Billy*'s wake, blissfully unaware of the dangers that lay ahead, excited to start their new life.

The interstellar terror was ready, and waiting, and twice as ravenous, eagerly wrapping its million-mile tentacles around the *Glyph*'s hull. Alarms shrieked as the superstructure buckled and groaned.

"Oh, *please* don't devour us!" the *Glyph*'s captain cried, as their shields flickered into non-existence. "We're merely a colony ship with but a thousand souls aboard. We won't satisfy your eternal hunger. Wait for the G.O.A.T, they're *much* bigger."

With a grumble that seared the flank of the *Glyph*, the eldritch being let them pass, saving its appetite for the main course. This time, the entity didn't bother to edit the frantic message sent back to Earth. Indeed, it tacked on an addendum. A promise, cold and merciless. That the colony the *Glyph* started within its dominion would fall, and fall hard, unless the G.O.A.T met the challenge. And, if that wasn't enough incentive, after the colony had fallen, it might decide to come looking to see where the *Glyph* had originated from...

And so, the G.O.A.T, which until then had been a mere concept, nothing more than a few sketches and a throw-away name, had been hastily built. And now, here it was, on its maiden voyage, with its Captain, Jaki Conomor, straining to detect anything untoward as they slipped across the invisible boundary, as they unlocked the always locked door, as they entered the forbidden zone.

For the briefest of moments, there was nothing. For the briefest of moments, there was *hope*.

Then, from the cold darkness of deep space, something stirred. It was everything humankind had always feared, and so much more. It was wolves, howling in the night. The ominous shape of something huge moving stealthily through storm-capped waters. The terrors that lurk at the liminal borders between awake and sleep. The sum total of every nightmare anyone had ever had, clawing at the mind, destroying any hint of decency, of joy, the eldritch, merciless, rapacious horrors that have long haunted the faint of heart.

There were no faint hearts aboard the battlecruiser *G.O.A.T*, and even if there were, they had been drilled so many times that muscle memory alone might see them through the encounter. But this was the hardest and most dangerous part; the moment of stillness, of anticipation, as the being became lazily aware of them, as its eye, the size of the moon, turned to stare, to defile, as it slowly unfurled its vast tentacular arms in their direction.

Ah, its grating voice shook every skull, *I was wondering when you would arrive. I was getting hungry, and on the verge of coming to look for you!*

Jaki shuddered, this was the threat the *Glyph* had communicated. Did it explain the irregular shape of the forbidden zone? Each star-system swallowing limb... is that exactly what had happened, to others before them? Had the *Billy*'s imprudent entry into the forbidden zone betrayed their existence, betrayed the whole solar system, betrayed the Earth?

I would ask what took you so long, the abomination leered, contempt thick with every syllable, *but you are so obviously a pitiful race, only just beginning to paddle in these dark waters, only just beginning to realise how fathomless and treacherous they really are. Call yourself The Greatest? Pah, such hubris! You're not even close. If you want to know true greatness, humankind, look upon my works, and despair!*

The starchart zoomed in as an area of the forbidden zone was uncloaked, as every display onboard the *G.O.A.T* switched to the same view. It was a graveyard of spaceships, of all types and sizes. Derelicts, the life long ago sucked out of them. There was even the distinctive, chopped teardrop of a gigantic Raisdegillian ship, adrift and near torn in two, the blood of its occupants frozen in a thin cloud of glittering gems.

Dread seeped from the gloating guardian of these pitiful trophies, a sense of hopelessness descending even on the bridge.

Captain Conomor shook herself, stabbing at the controls, activating the psi defenses she hoped would work, and the very fact she *could* hope proved they had already begun. "Deploy the beam," she ordered, voice momentarily aquiver.

From the horns of the G.O.A.T, fearsome energies crackled and spat, arcing out into the darkness, wrapping around the reaching, probing tentacle, sparking in the far, far ultraviolet as they clashed.

Impressive, the cruel colossus smirked. *That* almost *tickles. If only you had an armada of such weapons... But alas, you are all alone and clearly no match for me!*

It casually extended two more tentacles, reached for its prey, only to find they too were held by the same crackling beams.

"Who said I was alone?" Jaki broadcast into the ether, as the sister-ships that had been hiding in her wake took up stations beside her. The G.O.A.T deployed another beam, this one from her underbelly, gripping another tentacle.

Puny humans! the monstrosity scowled. *Have you even bothered to count how many tentacles I have—*

Two more beams snapped out, as two more ships appeared on the far side. And then each of the new arrivals engaged a secondary beam, just as the G.O.A.T had already done.

You think your feeble weapons can hurt me? There was just a hint of annoyance, a hint of breathlessness in the vast, atrocious being.

"Oh no," Jaki said with a wry smile as the five ships adjusted their positions, the beams forming a cage around the writhing monster. "*These* aren't our weapons. They're to stop you escaping too soon."

Because they weren't trying to hold the tentacles; they were trying to contain the *whole* behemoth. Until the pentagram was complete.

"Hit it, girls."

Every weapon that humankind had ever managed to imagine was brought to bear, from antimatter bombs to singularity Lasers, all concentrated on the very centre of that pentagram. Weapons based on the data *The Bellerophon* had eventually returned, once her AI tongue had been untied. Energies tuned to counter the traces of exotic matter found in the terrible scars across the *Glyph*'s shields and belly.

The eldritch horror fought and writhed, but the five great ships, working in perfect AI choreographed motion, slowly compressed the cage, confining the titan to a smaller and smaller region of indignantly bristling space. The slightest gap, the most infinitesimal of errors, would have let it escape, or worse, to turn its full hateful energies on one of the five ships, on its tormentors, with devastating effects. As it was, the blowback from the fearsome rain of destruction they unleashed washed at the shields of the five ships, the *G.O.A.T* bearing the brunt. Fortunate indeed she had been built to take such punishment.

At long last, after almost a week of solid, exhausting battle, when the pentagram was only as wide as a medium-sized gas giant, the tentacles wrapped tight around the ball of incandescent fury, the eldritch terror opened its awful maw, revealing an endless abyss, and silently screamed. With a reality shattering *pop!* the beams, the explosions, and the entity utterly vanished.

Cheers erupted from the crew of the *G.O.A.T*, multiplied by those from the four sister battlecruisers. Communication holos flickered into life, a jubilant council of beaming captains and science officers.

Jaki raised her hand, stilling the too-soon celebrations. "Science division? Analysis?"

"All indications are that the entity is vanquished," the AI science officer reported. "The space it occupied is now hard vacuum, peculiarly devoid of even dark energy."

"We won! We destroyed it!" the celebrations started anew.

"I very much doubt that," Jaki said, relieved, but weary, as the hubbub once again reluctantly faded. "It has been out there for thousands, probably millions of years. Perhaps it was birthed in the maelstrom of the big bang? I hope to never know. I suspect it has merely relocated somewhere the locals aren't quite so *bitey*. For any patch of space to be that empty is no more natural than what was in it before."

Jaki gave a small smile, scanning her colleagues. "So yes, we celebrate today, but tomorrow, and forever, we must remain vigilant."

A small but vital dampener. *Hubris*, indeed. And a worry; that even their victory could be a defeat. *Battle not with monsters...*

She eyed the graveyard of alien spacecraft. How long had the leviathan sat, spider-like, slowly growing, devouring everything unlucky or foolish enough to blunder its way? So many space-faring civilizations must have encountered it, and either succumbed to it entirely, or hastily beaten a retreat, throwing up desperate defenses and sealing the ever expanding forbidden zone behind them.

Were there other graveyards out there? Other entities, perhaps even more terrible than the one they had just encountered?

Undoubtedly.

She, and her sister-ships, would cross that bridge, when they came to it.

THE EMPEROR'S TEST

ELIZABETH LOWHAM

When I was young, my brother, Curtix, took me to the planet.
Bugatan's zoo each year for my birthday, and he ordered the
trainers to let him throw disk fruit for the leaping sas monkeys.
Even after one monkey bit him, and he had to wear a pulse
bandage over his hand for a full day, we kept going back to
throw disk fruit.

Until Father died and Curtix inherited the empire. Then he
didn't throw disk fruit just to entertain his little sister anymore.

It wasn't the sort of thing an emperor could do.

"Imperial Highness, it is time to leave. You will be late for the
meeting at the palace." Zaid stepped close to me to give his quiet
prompting. Even with his hulking form, arms bulging in his
sleeveless vest, my head bodyguard eyed the sas monkeys with
a clear nervousness. Everyone had their fears, even fearless
bodyguards to the Imperial household.

I rubbed my thumb across a flat green disk fruit, feeling the
pebbled texture and remembering years long gone.

"Netti?" Zaid prompted again.

With a half-smile, I glanced at him and gave *the nod*, the one
I'd practiced all my life in etiquette lessons. The one meant to say
a simple yes, but to say it with all the dignity, authority, and

confidence befitting a ruler. Curtix had always been better at it than me. He'd always been better at everything than me.

"Why are you afraid of the monkeys?" I asked.

If his muscled form weren't enough, Zaid was half Uzekian, so he was hairless and black-eyed, and he'd tattooed the left side of his bald head with what he claimed were the names of all his fallen enemies—though I had my suspicions it was actually the text to his favorite poem in his native tongue. Either way, he cut a fearsome picture, especially standing a head taller than the average human and staring down at them with the stormy gray irises of his otherwise-black eyes.

"Not afraid." Zaid grunted, lifting one muscled shoulder. "I do not trust them. Something about the nose—it is too close to pig. One should not trust a creature which tries to be two things."

Sas monkeys did have blunted snouts with gaping nostrils. But they also had large round eyes and wide mouths, which gave them the impression of a dopey grin, especially when they cocked their heads to consider something, as they were currently doing to both me and the fruit I held in my hand.

When I finally threw the disk fruit, leaning back and straining my arm, pouring all my energy into lobbing it almost straight up, the sas monkeys simply watched with their dopey monkey grins and drooping arms, deeming the fruit not challenging enough to leap for. They waited for it to plop to the ground, and then the little brown creatures converged in the grass at once, whistling territorially at each other and flapping the wing skins of their arms as they fought over it.

Curtix had always gotten them to leap.

"Happy birthday, Netti," I mumbled to myself. Eighteen years old. It wasn't a significant year—even considered by some of the most superstitious star-calendar followers to be unlucky— but it meant I was old enough for fleet service. I'd already put in my pilot application and, just that morning, received my acceptance to the academy.

When I'd told Curt, he hadn't said, "Don't go," or even, "You'll make a great pilot."

He'd just said, "Good."

He was too busy to even finish the sentence: *Good riddance, Netti.*

Curtix would soon be twenty-five, his birthday falling exactly one month after mine. Twenty-five was the most significant age any emperor could experience. Twenty-five marked the number of years it had taken to first unite the empire, but Curtix had honor even beyond that, because he was the *twenty-fifth* emperor to wear the crown.

His celebration would shake the entire Porshen Galaxy.

And as soon as it finished, I would leave behind my brother, the only family I had left.

———

Despite Zaid's warning, I'd lingered too long at the zoo, so I slid into Curtix's council chambers just as the guards tried to close the doors on me. If I'd been locked out of the meeting, it would not have been the first time, and hanging around the flight deck would have been more fun anyway.

But I was *supposed* to be in council meetings, and Zaid always looked at me with disappointment when I skipped. So I forced myself through the doors just in time. My Imperial Guard waited outside, comprised of Zaid and the three other guards he had on rotation for the day.

Curtix's guards looked at me sternly, and the closest one gave my announcement to the emperor as if I were some stranger rather than his only sister: *Her Imperial Highness, Renette Lambourg.*

I strode quickly to my place at the long council table, seated to my brother's left. Curtix wore his formal blue attire, high-necked and sewn with more decorative buttons than real ones, not to mention the collection of half a dozen gold chains dripping from his left shoulder. The way each one connected to a specific button meant something about his six years as emperor, but I'd never cared to remember the symbolism. More than any outfit, the real formality was the way Curt held himself—rigid, unyielding, his disapproving eyes fixed directly on me.

As I took my seat, I heard Lord Dayfang whisper to his wife. It sounded like *Netti the Lax*, and my cheeks heated to hear it. For years, my moniker had been *Netti the Lamb*, a play on my last name and my tendency to err too often on the side of mercy. Apparently that moniker had now changed. Both were equally humiliating—and equally correct.

"This is the second council meeting of the day," Curtix said. "Care to explain your absence for the first?"

Oops. Apparently even Zaid hadn't known about the first. Or maybe he'd thought I deserved at least half a day to celebrate, so he'd not commented.

"I took myself to the zoo," I said. "Since it's my birthday."

Curtix at least had the grace to flinch a little, his blue eyes turning away from mine. He'd started wearing a close-cropped beard, rather than shaving, and the brown stubble still looked odd to me, like he was trying to seem older than twenty-four. Like he wasn't actually an adult if he didn't look the part.

Did I look the part now? Had I magically transformed in a single day? Funny how someone could be too young for the Imperial Fleet until one extra sunrise, when they suddenly weren't.

"Happy birthday, highness," said Lady Karise, leaning forward slightly from across the table, her brown eyes as warm as ever above her smile.

I couldn't help a smile of my own. "Thank you."

Most of the council echoed the sentiment with varying degrees of enthusiasm. Curtix didn't. We'd had plenty of discussion about my birthday the week before, when I'd asked him to go to the zoo with me, and he'd said he *couldn't*. As if he had no choice in the matter. I would have preferred his honesty, because it hurt more to know he didn't care and just wouldn't say it.

"Let's discuss the famine on Daimler," Curtix said, turning sharply back to business.

Though I urged myself to pay attention to the meeting, my mind wandered back to my flight training, to my upcoming departure off-world. Five years—that was the first contract for enrollment in the fleet. Three years in the academy, followed by two years in the field. And then a choice, to either come home or to make a full career in the fleet.

I snuck a glance at my brother and found him frowning at me. Apparently I'd missed something important again.

In five years, I would be twenty-three, and I couldn't imagine how to be twenty-three when I hadn't even figured out how to be eighteen, yet I'd still be younger than Curtix was now.

I shouldn't have gone to the zoo; it left me feeling strange. Left me wondering how I'd felt so close to my brother all those years ago when I now realized there was such a distance between us, I didn't even know how to bridge it.

"And finally"— Curtix swept his gaze over the full council — "I have exciting news concerning my birthday celebration. You'll remember I put out a call for aeronautical engineers fine enough to craft a new jet befitting the occasion, and two men have answered."

Low murmurs broke out around the table. Upon taking the imperial throne, every emperor decided on a symbol for their strength. Father's had been the portal gate, the technology that allowed us to link neighboring planets to travel in mere seconds what would otherwise take days. Curtix had taken a step backward in technology for his symbol.

He'd chosen the single-pilot fighter jet.

Not content to leave it as a symbol, my brother owned hangars upon hangars filled with single-pilot aircraft. More than any person could hope to fly. He had barrel-shaped jets and sleek, needle-nosed jets. He had some painted every inch with battle depictions and some sporting only the cool gray metal of their building materials. Ridiculously, he even had an open-cockpit jet that could not be flown because of the complete impracticality of such a thing, existing merely for the sake of the delicate metalwork displayed across its wings.

And now, for his birthday, he'd decided he needed a jet grander than any in his personal fleet.

Curtix carried an eager gleam in his eyes. He leaned forward, bracing his fingertips on the council table. "These engineers come from the far reaches, virtually unheard of before now, because they have spent the last many years refining and perfecting a new kind of metal, one that is certain to craft a jet the likes of which no one has ever seen."

Personally, I couldn't imagine seeing anything new after his sixty-plus hangars. There were only so many ways to build a jet. While the rest of the council gave their enthusiastic support and speculated what advancements this metal might boast, I picked at my nails.

"They'll arrive tomorrow," Curtix said at last. He shot me a meaningful look. "*Everyone* will attend their presentation."

The next day, I sat in the throne room, surveying a pair of engineers.

The two men, father and son, looked too pretentious to be aeronautical engineers. They wore pristine black suits and neatly styled hair, while the engineers on the flight deck always appeared haggard when I visited, smeared with oil, laughing one minute and cursing the next, some tool always sticking out of their clothing and never in a pocket. Then again, I'd never seen those engineers present a new project to the emperor himself.

The father and son regaled us all with harrowing tales of delving nearly to their planet's core to find a mythical ore, rumored to contain a cloaking power never before seen in even the finest shields. The father, Davith, was missing two fingers on his right hand, and he displayed the disfigurement solemnly as he spoke of the cost of refining this ore into the metal they now called nevidim.

Lady Karise, seated next to me, bumped her arm into mine, leaning in to whisper. "The son is quite handsome, don't you think?"

I raised an eyebrow. Unlike his father—who had a bronze coloring like Curtix—the son, Aedyn, had a pale blue cast to his skin, with just a touch of scaling along his cheekbones and down the outer edge of his hands; his mother must have been Saeran. His white hair was certainly striking, but he was shorter than me, and slim enough he probably got blown over with every fierce wind.

"Pass," I whispered back. "He's a twig."

"So harsh." Lady Karise laughed quietly. "No doubt you prefer a bodyguard type, built to defend."

Despite myself, my eyes flickered toward Zaid, standing in the shadows at the edge of the room. He was five years older than me, twice my size, and employed by my brother. That was a bad idea in every way.

"Hush," I told Lady Karise. "I want to hear about the metal."

Her smirk said she saw through me, but she fell silent.

"What sets nevidim apart," said Aedyn, "is that it, like electron currents passing through barriers, can *sense* our observance. And beneath the gaze of the unworthy, it undergoes a change on the atomic level, rendering it invisible!"

His words set off a ripple of murmurs. Lady Karise and I exchanged a look, hers more excited than mine.

Aedyn raised his voice slightly. "A *true* cloaking, Imperial Majesty, the likes of which cannot be matched by even the most advanced mirror shields. This is what we have accomplished in nevidim."

I tried to shrug off the idea, but a chill slithered down my body. Scientific advancement was not my forte, and it seemed the empire learned of some new life-altering technology every few years, all of which left me at a loss. I could not explain how portal gates worked, just as I could not explain how my transmitter reached effortlessly across planets yet still dropped the connection when I stood in just the right corner of my bedchamber.

"Explain that," said Curtix, brow furrowed in his signature frown. "The unworthy."

"Anyone unworthy of their position in life." Aedyn spread his hands in a sweeping gesture, and light glittered across his scale patterns. "From the most humble of washer-boys to our esteemed emperor himself—though I have no doubt *you* are the most worthy of persons imaginable, Imperial Majesty. Still, even your great person would be tested by our metal."

Stepping up next to his son, Davith smiled around the room, his gaze resting, at last, on Curtix. "Would you like to see it?"

As if he could not be contained, my brother stood from his throne. "At once."

Aedyn fastened a black remote bracelet around his wrist, and at a few gestures from his hand, he brought a hover trunk forward from the back of the room. Everyone seemed to hold their breath as it glided forward. Curtix came down the two steps of his dais so he stood on the throne room floor, his head bodyguard stepping up just behind him.

When the trunk at last hovered between the two engineers, they unlocked its lid with exaggerated care, hinged it back, and lifted out . . .

Nothing.

Judging by the way they held their hands, pinched flat at invisible corners, it was meant to be a square of sheet metal, but it was nothing. They held nothing.

I craned around my seat to catch Zaid's eyes, but my bodyguard was staring at the engineers along with everyone else.

"As you can see," said Davith, acting as if nothing was

wrong, "a sheet of nevidim is extremely light, extremely thin. Care must be taken not to warp the metal before it is affixed to a frame."

Aedyn reached in a pocket with one hand, his other still pinching the air, then extracted a jeweler's hammer. With a decisive but gentle strike, he tapped the hammer against the air.

A clear chime, like that of knife against crystal, rang through the room.

The members of the council let out a united gasp. Lady Karise gripped my arm. I shot another glance toward Zaid and saw him frowning.

"You can see here"—Aedyn gestured with the hammer at nothing, tracing it through graceful swirls—"the beautiful pattern brought out by tempering. This deep orange tone here is evidence of just the right heat. Without those deepest strata present, the metal could not be used. It would fracture under stress. Exquisite, Imperial Majesty, is it not?"

I glanced at Curtix, waiting to hear his judgment of the imposters. But he stood as if enraptured, his eyes on the air between the two men.

"Tap it again," he said softly.

Aedyn obeyed. That crystal tone rang out. It was convincing, certainly, but such a thing could no doubt be faked, even if I didn't know how. Perhaps the hammer itself produced the sound when swung. Or . . .

I glanced at Lady Karise. She'd pressed her free hand to her mouth, the other still gently gripping my arm. I could not tell if her response was from tension at two imposters conning an emperor or from awe at a beautiful strata-swirled metal I could not see.

Just as I opened my mouth to whisper to her, Curtix spoke first.

"Exquisite," he said, with the reverence of a man at prayer.

My jaw dropped.

The engineers beamed.

"I knew His Imperial Majesty was a man of impeccable taste!" said Davith. He turned toward Lord Dayfang. "You, my lord, can you not see the rippling color here as it catches the light? Is it not the finest sheen ever beheld?"

"Simply breathtaking!" Lord Dayfang exclaimed.

One by one, others added their voices to say the same. Magnificent. Breathtaking. Exquisite. Unparalleled. And with each new claim, something began to squirm within me, a horrifying thought—

Was I the only one unable to see it? If this metal truly shielded itself from the unworthy, then . . .

I was the laziest member of the Imperial Council, the only one with a consistent record of tardiness and absence, the only one who did not rush to support Curtix in every matter. What if this metal proclaimed with boldness what no one else would?

Beside me, Lady Karise removed her hand. She said, "Truly, the finest metal I've ever beheld."

The engineers turned their eyes on me. "Imperial Highness?"

I swallowed.

There's nothing there. The words died in my throat. The people in this room led the entire empire; they represented the best its various planets had to offer. They would not *all* profess to a metal they could not see.

What would Curt say, if I admitted to be the *only* unseeing person in the room?

My ears rang with the memory of his response to my fleet enrollment. *Good.*

I glanced at my brother and found him watching me along with everyone else, waiting for my response. He'd combed his hair back from his forehead, but a lock of it always fell above his left eyebrow, and at the back, a little curl stood rebellious and untamable, like a sas monkey leaping in defiance of gravity.

I looked away.

"Incredible," I said. "Truly."

Zaid was frowning again. Whether at my lie or simply at my hesitation, I could not tell.

———

I investigated. *Spied* would be the more accurate term. Curtix gave the engineers their own workspace, ordering at first that they remain undisturbed as they crafted his jet, until the men insisted the public have some ability to view their work, since they hoped this metal would revolutionize the galaxy. In the end, they were given a massive forge with an attached hangar. Imperial guards stood posted at the always-open hangar door, and every hour the engineers worked, people came to gawk at the entrance.

I was one of those watchers. Four days in a row, I stood for an hour when I was meant to tend to other duties, watching the two engineers and their team of task robots.

They were nothing if not diligent. They scurried around the warehouse, managing the blast furnace, redirecting task robots, commissioning oxidizing agents from servants. Curtix had assigned three palace servants to their service, ordered to provide anything they asked for, from building materials to luxurious lunches. The engineers were not shy in their requests.

As time went on, their activities changed from smelting to construction. They climbed ladders, banged hammers, twisted wrenches, all the while shaping a creation I could not see. For long stretches, they worked on wiring, and one day as I watched, I saw sparks light the scales along Aedyn's cheekbones.

When he paused for dinner, I confronted him. "Your wiring cannot be made of nevidim. If someone unworthy looked at your jet, would they see only a skeleton of wires?"

He chuckled, wiping his hands with a napkin before setting into a plate of the finest borneo filets from Noraze. "When nevidim contacts other metals, even as simple as copper, it transfers its shielding properties. When we say 'revolutionize the galaxy,' highness, we are not being grandiose."

I left him to his meal, and soon enough, he was back at work.

By their actions alone, I would have believed them the most dedicated of craftsmen. If only I could have *seen* what they crafted.

Half of my spying was on the engineers themselves, but half of it was on the other watchers, the public who came to peer in the hangar doors and whisper to each other in low voices I had to strain to hear.

All the whispers followed a theme. *Magnificent, incredible, stunning.*

My frustration mounted as I wondered which was more probable—an entire empire falling for the most ridiculous of cons or me being the only unworthy person in that empire.

Neither option was pleasant.

———

"You are frustrated," said Zaid, trading off with the guard at my door. Zaid had taken a short vacation, and though it should not have made a difference who was guarding me, since the whole team was capable, I relaxed just seeing him.

Even so, I did not respond to him right away except to grunt. I flicked my finger at the hologram before me. The white projection of a jet spun with the movement, giving me a view along one of its wings, the paneling removed to expose the framework inside. The audio droned on about aeronautical engineering until I pinched my fingers to shut the whole thing off. With a quick tug, I pulled off my remote bracelet, tossing it onto the cushion beside me.

"I'm studying for the academy." Standing, I left the couch and crossed the lounge area to pour myself a glass of pulpy capberry juice. Servants had just refreshed the pitcher for me.

"Yes, of course." Zaid settled into my empty spot on the

couch, grinning too widely as he splayed his arms, displaying his rippling muscles. While gone, he'd added a tattoo to his left shoulder, the same scraggly writing as the one on his skull, and the skin around it glowed an angry red. "You are only studying for fleet academy. Not studying techniques of certain engineers, no."

"No," I agreed, sipping my drink. I drummed my fingers on the chilled glass. "Hypothetically, though, you were with me that first day, before you visited home—what do you think of them?"

Truthfully, I'd been dying to ask him from the start.

"If her highness invites my opinion, I will answer honestly. They are charlatans, very good at the game."

My fingers tightened on my drink. "So you can't see the ship?"

"I see nothing, because there is nothing to see."

So confident. I'd felt that way at first, and hearing him say it so calmly brought back a rush of confidence—along with a wave of foolishness that I'd fallen into such internal conflict.

"You're not at all worried you just can't see the ship?"

Zaid shrugged, his posture still relaxed and open as he gestured toward his face. "These eyes have seen daggers aimed at the princess, and these hands have stopped them. Why would I need proof of a ship to know I am a worthy bodyguard?"

I smiled. "I've certainly never had a better one."

The foolish feeling increased, and with a groan, I set my drink on the table. I'd been taken in by con men. But, then, so had the entire empire.

I thought of Curtix, thought of his intensely focused gaze as the engineers unveiled their first "demonstration." It was his certainty that first swayed my confidence, and his was the first voice to cast a verdict that swayed the rest of the council. Was he in on it? Was it all a trap to test his council? I wouldn't put it past him.

And here I was, falling into mind games again.

"I should just leave now," I said. "I could take a portal gate to

Noraze in the morning, be at the academy by afternoon. I'm already eighteen, so what's the point in delaying?"

Zaid shrugged. "I thought, perhaps, it's because you don't want to leave your brother."

I snorted. "All we do is fight. Trade glares, at least. It's not like we trust each other or have heart-to-hearts. And it's not as if I add anything to the council by being here. Everyone else is more experienced, more diligent, more useful. Curt has everything he needs."

Slowly, Zaid nodded, as if considering. "Perhaps you are right."

Ironically, I was not happy he agreed with me. I retook my glass, shaking it to agitate the pulp and cursing when I splashed a bit over the edge.

"Perhaps," Zaid added, "His Majesty needs to see this ship."

"What?" I wiped my juice-splattered fingers on a napkin, frowning at my bodyguard. "What does that mean?"

Zaid shrugged again. "Was only thought."

I thought about my brother, the way he'd grown more aloof since becoming emperor, the way he delivered orders in council meetings rather than inviting actual council. Curtix always had a plan, always had a direction. He moved with the speed and decisiveness of a single-pilot jet. The symbol he'd chosen for his empire.

Grimacing, I looked down at the napkin, whole not a moment before and now crumpled in my hand.

"Do you think . . ." I looked up. "He doesn't believe he's worthy of being emperor?"

The same insecurities I felt inside—was it possible my ever-confident brother secretly carried them as well?

The way Zaid tilted his head said it all.

I dropped the napkin on my drink tray. "If I oust the engineers, everyone will just say it makes sense that Netti the Lax can't see the ship, that Netti the Lax isn't worthy of her station.

Besides, why should I do anything for Curt? When's the last time he did anything for me?"

Zaid laughed, a full-throated sound that could have brightened the gloomiest space station. "Netti, my paw, if you intend to live life only by strict trade, you should become arms dealer, not fleet pilot."

My paw. It was an Uzekian term of endearment, reserved for the closest of friends. Zaid had tossed it at me once or twice before, and I'd never rebuffed it. It made my stomach flip in the most pleasant way.

"Fine." I made a show of huffing, of rolling my eyes. "If Curt needs a reminder that he's a half-decent emperor—at the very least, a reminder that he used to be a half-decent brother—I suppose I could come up with something."

Despite my cavalier words, something pinched inside, something that pictured my brother in his stiff blue uniform, bound by gold chains, all alone at the head of an empire and bearing the weight while thinking he couldn't.

If there was any truth to it, I had to do something.

Call it a birthday gift.

———

The guards didn't stop me when I marched my way into the engineers' hangar. The two men showed no alarm, only gracious acceptance, both of them stepping back from their invisible project while offering me deferential bows.

Pitching my voice low, I said, "I know this is a con. I want in."

Not even a twitch of nervousness. Davith merely frowned. "Whatever do you mean, Imperial Highness? Do you find our work unsatisfactory? Do you see flaws with the ship?"

"No one can see the ship," I hissed. "The ship doesn't exist."

They traded a knowing look.

"Ah," said Aedyn gently. "Highness, perhaps I could offer

you some tea? I know 'worthiness' is a loaded word, but just because a person is not suited to one position does not mean they should despair. Why, many people—"

"Stop," I said flatly. I took one step closer to them, suddenly wishing I had Zaid's build, since it was better suited to intimidation. I was taller than Aedyn but still half a head shy of his father's height. "I *know* there's no ship. No nevidim. It's a dangerous thing to con an emperor, and don't you think you'll have better success with a member of the Imperial household on your side?"

Davith shook his head. "We would never dream of deceiving His Imperial Majesty. We seek only to serve him and further our craft."

What had I expected? That they would fold at my first insinuation? To play a game this dangerous, so thoroughly and with such confidence, they couldn't possibly be cowards. Insane, perhaps, but not cowards. Besides, admitting the truth to me risked their entire scheme, and I hadn't promised anything worth taking that risk.

I lifted two fingers. "I can give you two things. First, a higher payday. Curtix has already promised a fortune. I can talk him higher, get you enough to buy your own planet. Second, you'll need a way to escape the emperor's wrath once he figures this out, and I can get you a personal portal gate."

Our family and most trusted allies held the only ten in existence. Capable of transporting anyone anywhere within the established network, no clearance required, with no wait time, the portal gate was worth more than the planet.

"Surely you've heard of the tensions between my brother and myself," I said. "I would love a chance to put him in his place."

Yet the con men's masks did not so much as crack.

Davith bowed respectfully. "Highness, it is no shame to be among the unseeing. A brutal truth revealed is simply a gateway into new opportunity. You are joining the Imperial Fleet soon, are you not? Perhaps you will find your worthy purpose there, rather than within the Imperial Palace."

My face heated. With additional bows, they excused themselves to resume their work. Clanging echoed through the hangar, tools ringing against empty air.

If I could not obtain solid proof of the con, I would have to follow plan B, which meant the unthinkable.

I would have to have a heart-to-heart with my brother.

———

Curtix had the audacity to keep me waiting, like I was some visitor to the palace. I sat in his antechamber for a full twenty minutes before he finally waved me into his sitting room, and by that point, I'd lost most of what I wanted to say, so I just blurted what was left:

"Why'd you pretend to see the ship, Curt?"

My brother barely looked up from his desk where he had three hologram files playing at once. One showed blueprints for some kind of building, another reports from the fleet, and a third a collection of trillain lobsters. I would have been very interested to know why he was looking at lobsters, but I couldn't pick any details out of the cacophony of three audio narratives playing at once.

I raised my voice. "*Curt.* Why'd you pretend to see the ship?"

He switched off the lobsters and blueprints but left the fleet report running. In a monotone voice, someone listed recent promotions. I knew Curtix received all those reports, but I'd never realized he actually listened to them. I wouldn't have. As long as he knew the top commanders, who cared about the rest?

"I'm very busy, Renette," he said at last, flicking his finger to replay a few names.

"Well, I'm your sister, so can you turn the report off for three minutes and have a conversation?"

His blue eyes flicked up, met mine, and then gave a slight roll. But he silenced the final holo file.

"Three minutes," he said.

I suddenly wished Zaid were there to remind me why I was helping this guy. But he was stationed outside the door.

"The engineers," I repeated. "The ship. No one can see it. It doesn't exist."

Curtix just stared at me, as if waiting for the punchline of a joke.

"There's no one else here," I said at last. "You can admit it."

"You can't see the metal?" he asked.

"No one can. It's a con."

"How do you know that?"

"I just . . . because it isn't there! I can't see it. Zaid can't see it. I know you can't see it either, admit it."

Curtix pressed his lips to a line, and I couldn't tell if it was in contemplation or annoyance.

"At the meeting," he said, "you claimed you could. You called it incredible."

"So did you! Everyone there was lying. We all took the cue from you."

Well, if it wasn't annoyance before, it certainly was now. Curtix stalked from behind his desk to face me. Even in private, he wore the high-collared uniform, a picture of Imperial grace, broken just a bit by that untamable cowlick at the back of his dark hair.

"Ever since I became emperor," he said, "you've grown increasingly quarrelsome. Tried to embarrass me in front of my cabinet. Tell me honestly, Renette, is this jealousy?"

My face heated, and before I could think it through, I shot back, "Ever since you became emperor, you've grown increasingly paranoid. You think everyone's out to get you—except, ironically, the two con men who actually are. Tell me, Curtix, is that stupidity?"

He stiffened. Even his collar seemed to come to attention.

I winced. "Look, I'm just trying—"

"I wish I could believe your concern, *sister*, but I cannot take you seriously when *you* take nothing seriously. Not your own duties nor mine. If there were a scheme against me, I can only feel you would help it along. That's why I have no choice but to ship you off to the fleet."

I scoffed. "You're not shipping me anywhere. I applied to be a pilot. I took the test before I even told you."

"As if anything happens in my empire without my awareness." His blue eyes sparked with anger. "And that flight test? A test you failed. I had to order an exception to get you into the academy just so you wouldn't continue hindering my council."

My insides grew cold. I took a step back. "No, I . . . I know all the procedures. I've been flying for years. There's no way I . . ."

Although I had been nervous that day—furious, more like. With my birthday approaching, I'd asked Curtix to go to the zoo with me, the first time I'd asked in years. He'd said he *couldn't*, said other matters took priority, and by the time I made it to the flight deck, I was still shaking from our argument.

Had I really failed?

Curtix spoke coldly. "Are you perhaps rethinking the reason you can't see the ship?"

Invisible to the unworthy.

My jaw trembled. I bit my tongue. When I spoke, it was with fire. "I wish you'd never become emperor, Curt. It's turned you paranoid, sure, but worse, it's turned you arrogant and petty and . . . cruel."

What had happened to those two kids laughing at jumping monkeys? When had we become opposites?

When had we become enemies?

"You deserve this new ship." I forced a smile. "I can't wait to see it unveiled at your birthday celebration. I can't wait to see you *fly* it."

Before he could order me out, I left.

———

The day of the emperor's birthday dawned warm and sunny, with a mist of pleasant humidity in the air. It made it easy to breathe deep, to break into a run, to feel like I could keep a steady pace up for miles, perhaps all the way to the edge of the world.

Zaid ran with me, steady at my side even though he could have easily outpaced me. He didn't ask why I wasn't getting ready for Curtix's celebrations.

I took the path up the cliffs, the capital city stretching below. Bodies crowded the streets, the roaring sound of lively conversation echoing off the cliffs as a single rolling sound. Colored banners hung between towering buildings, and performers filled the open squares.

Only the central plaza remained empty, the space reserved for two engineers to unveil the most sensational ship ever designed.

I came to a stop on an overlook, bending to catch my breath, hands braced on my knees. My gray running suit had grown sweaty, and I pushed back the strands of hair that had plastered themselves to my forehead. Zaid, of course, seemed barely winded, and he set about checking the overlook for possible dangers, nudging me back a single step when he deemed me too close to the edge. I smiled.

Until I looked down at the central plaza again. My smile faded.

"They're going to make a fool of my brother down there," I said softly.

"Brother you hate." Zaid shrugged, but his side-eyed glance at me was hardly subtle.

"You would stop it, wouldn't you? Even if he deserves some humiliation."

"I have no brothers, so I cannot presume my actions. But I do think . . . perhaps if he deserves correction, it is not like this. What will this accomplish?"

Humiliating him in front of the entire capital city? It would undermine his authority. Worse, I knew Curtix, and I knew his pride—this would cripple him, perhaps forever.

The engineers had done their research. They'd set the perfect trap for my brother. If there was even the faintest sliver of a chance the nevidim existed, he could never admit to not seeing it, not when he had to be the solo pilot leading an entire fleet.

"What if it really does exist?" My voice came out weaker than I intended. I glanced at Zaid. "What if it really isn't a con, and we just can't see it?"

He didn't dismiss me. He nodded seriously, his black eyes surveying the city down below.

"If no ship exists," he said, "what does this mean?"

"The engineers are liars," I said.

"And if ship exists, what does this mean?"

"That *I'm* a liar." I looked away, thinking of the flight school test. I'd contacted the academy, and Curtix was right—I'd failed. It was only Imperial power that had opened the door for me. Otherwise, I would have needed to wait a year to try again.

"Not so," said Zaid. "A liar says, 'I can see,' when they cannot. If ship exists, it is not lie to say, 'I cannot see.' This thing I know—I am pleased with my life. If it is true that I am unworthy of it, then I will work until I am worthy."

He caught my eyes again, and the way I had to tilt my head to look up at his made me feel as if I were gazing up into a night sky, just waiting for the stars.

"I don't hate my brother," I said. "Even if I would gladly spike his breakfast juice with sour powder because he deserves that."

I'd considered it that very morning, but I couldn't bring myself to do it on his birthday. Not when I'd visited a zoo alone on mine.

Zaid raised an eyebrow. "This thing I know."

"Yes, but I'm practicing the truth." I looked down at the city plaza just as a symphony began to play, signaling the emperor's appearance and the start of the grand parade. "It's going to be a lot harder to tell it down there."

———

The city vibrated with energy. Hoverlights crawled slow trails through the narrow space between buildings, illuminating any part of the city not touched by the sun. By the time I made it to the central plaza—wearing a suitable emerald uniform fashioned with a high collar and bell sleeves, my face scrubbed clean of sweat—the parade had just ended in a blast of fireworks nearly deafening. The citizens roared in response.

The parade had delivered Curtix to the plaza, and he stepped off his hovering float with such a grandiose movement he must have brought someone in the crowd to tears. While I might not have liked the way being emperor affected Curtix, I could not deny he performed the role with authority.

Maybe he needs to see the ship. Zaid's suggestion followed me like one of many supporters in the crowd, shouting for the attention of the Imperial Princess.

Maybe what he really needed was to see he wasn't alone. He would certainly never ask for support, and while I still thought he was stupid, while I still didn't fully understand why *this* trap was so very crippling for him, I did know one thing—not a single person on the council would throw themselves into this trap. If Curtix was going to get any help here, it would be me or no one.

To a thunderous roar of approval, the engineers entered the plaza. A massive hover carrier floated beside them, with a barrier of guards surrounding it to keep the crowd at bay. Everyone gasped at the empty carrier, crooning over a ship they could not see.

A small flash of light glinted off something above the carrier, earning screams of excitement from the crowd, and I clenched my jaw, feeling sweat bead on my temples once more.

A ship I *thought* no one else could see. Even now, I could be wrong. Curtix might not need saving, and I might be about to make a fool of myself for nothing.

But that uproar from the crowd . . . Why get so excited at a tiny flash if the entire ship could be seen? These little evidences —the sound from hammers, the sparks of invisible wiring—they were meant to plant doubt, to sell the illusion. In truth, they revealed it.

At least, I hoped they did. I couldn't even pass a flight test when I'd been flying ships for five years, so as much as I hated to admit it, I didn't have full confidence in myself or my reasoning.

As the engineers made their spiel to the crowd, telling the lavish story of how they first found and refined the ore, I took my place next to Curtix. His eyes remained fixed on the empty hover carrier.

Lowering my voice, I leaned closer to him and said, "I want to fly it."

My brother's eyebrows drew down, but he didn't speak.

"I know it's your birthday, your ship, but when they call for an aerial demonstration, I want to give it." I narrowed my eyes at him. "I want to prove I'm a good pilot."

He studied me with the scrutiny of a sas monkey, trying to decide if my throw was worthy of leaping after. By the nine stars, I was tired of that word—*worthy*. A quick glance showed me Zaid just off to my side with two additional guards, close enough to reach for. He wore his stoic expression, the public bodyguard face, but I could always see his smile in my mind, and I held to that.

The moment came at last.

The engineers addressed Curtix.

"Your Imperial Majesty," said Davith, beaming with such pride Curtix might have been his own son, "would you care to provide your grand vessel its maiden flight?"

Curtix spoke with all his usual confidence, voice carrying over the plaza. "I would."

Arrogant, stupid—

"I offer this honor to my sister, Renette Lambourg."

My jaw hung along with everyone else's.

He'd leaped. I didn't really know what that meant, if he trusted me or if he hoped to watch me fail. Either way, I just knew it was my turn now.

Snapping my jaw closed, I strode with purpose toward the hover carrier. For the first time, I witnessed the engineers flounder—just a moment, like a spark from wiring—before they fell into gracious bows and even more gracious smiles.

Slowly, the hover carrier lowered the few feet to the ground, settling with a heavy clank of metal against stone. Then there was silence.

I stepped onto the carrier.

Perhaps if I'd planned ahead, I could have performed a con of my own, something with a personal portal gate that could have made me disappear at just the right moment to seem I'd climbed into the ship. It would have spared my pride.

But I was not here for pride. I was here for truth.

And for my brother.

I looked back at Curtix and found him watching me intently, brows furrowed, fingers clenching his arms as he held them folded across his chest. I couldn't read him, hadn't been able to for years. Perhaps it was wishful thinking to believe I'd ever been able to read him. With seven years between us, he'd been a teenager while I was still a child, and he'd surely faced problems I'd never noticed or imagined. He'd been training to be the leader of an empire while I simply dreamed of being a pilot. Perhaps it was not so inconceivable he did not have time for me now—perhaps the true miracle was that he'd ever managed those birthday trips to begin with.

Or maybe he just didn't care, and I was going to regret all of this.

It was like the ship; I could not tell for certain what was truth, but I had my suspicions, and I could not remain paralyzed in indecision forever. I had to choose a path, come what may.

Turning toward the crowd once more, I said loudly, "There's no ship here."

Faces in the crowd stared back at me, as if slowly processing my words. I hoped my admission might trigger a response the same way Curtix's confidence had, that people might feel bold enough to admit the truth after I'd lit the way.

But the engineers quickly stepped onto the platform with me, expressing their sympathy, their encouragement. Just as they'd done in private, they now told the entire city how I would surely find my place in the Imperial Fleet.

"If you would like," Aedyn said, his voice dripping sympathy, "I could direct Your Imperial Highness to a wing."

With a miserable sinking feeling, I reached my hand out along with his, and my fingertips impacted something in the air. Something hard, cold, and invisible.

There really was a ship.

Which meant I was just an unworthy princess.

Silence arrested the crowd. Even the hoverlights in the distance seemed to hang frozen in place, witness to my judgment. I felt Curtix's attention at my back, and I could not turn to meet it.

If ship exists, said Zaid's voice in my mind, *what does this mean?*

I closed my eyes, ignoring everyone around me. "Maybe I'm not worthy of my position, but if that's so, I'll keep working until I am."

When I opened my eyes, I glanced at Zaid, and his smile eased the knot in my stomach.

"It is well that you are not the emperor," said Aedyn loudly. "Simply a princess. An unworthiness in you does not topple an entire empire."

I stepped closer to him, lowering my voice so only the engineers could hear. "Yes, but a humiliation of me does not shake it, either."

Just as I glanced meaningfully toward Curtix, I flinched—because my brother threw something in a streak of green. For a moment, I thought he'd thrown the object at me, then realized it arced far over my head, finally coming down at the center of the platform. With a faint *clang,* it hit something invisible, then slid to the ground near my feet, dented on one side.

A disk fruit.

While everyone stared, Curtix strolled up to me, casually tossing a second disk fruit back and forth between his hands. My heart didn't know whether to rise or sink, so it just twisted.

"What are you doing?" I asked.

In response, Curtix drew his arm back and launched the second fruit almost straight up. A beautiful throw. Any sas monkey would have loved to jump for it.

As if summoned by my thought, a monkey screeched as it sailed over my head, followed quickly by a half dozen others. At the same time Zaid gave a sharp curse, I gave a delighted laugh. Curtix merely smirked.

The monkeys twisted in the air, fighting one another for the fruit, pulling tails and spreading the skin flaps of their arms in order to stay airborne a moment longer until one finally rose victorious, disk fruit clenched in its long-fingered hand. The monkeys dropped one after another. The first two made a *clang* against something invisible, shrieking and sliding in opposite directions down to the platform. The third made a splintered sound, as if cracking glass, and something shimmered in the air beneath it, like a digital screen displaying a glitch. The fourth hardly rebounded at all.

The last three dropped to the platform without resistance, two with the slumped shoulders of defeat and one already nose-deep in a disk fruit, with green juice dripping from its furry little goatee.

"Seems I've broken your impact shield," said Curtix, his gaze cold on the gaping engineers. "It was incredible, really. I've never seen one able to be fully concealed, although doing so rendered it quite fragile, as I suspected."

The engineers made their stammering protests, but Curtix had already signaled the guards, and as they rushed across the platform, they left no doubt concerning what the monkeys had already proven—there was no ship in the way.

A few trainers rushed forward to gather the monkeys, so Curtix and I stepped away to give them space. The crowd had all its attention on the engineers, shouting insults or demanding justice from the con men.

For my part, I found myself suddenly unable to meet my brother's eyes. I'd thought him some kind of helpless infant, taken in by con men, cornered by insecurities, and instead, he'd known exactly what the con was and how to demolish it. While I'd wavered at every turn, he'd given the city a spectacle they could talk about and a new reason to praise the genius of their emperor.

I'd failed this flight test. A pattern now.

"Did you know it was a con from the start?" I asked.

Ignoring my question, Curtix handed me a disk fruit. Did he have them squirreled away in every pocket?

"You look disappointed," he said at last.

"I can never read you," I grumbled. "How am I so transparent?"

I almost bit into the green peel, then thought better of it. No sense in embarrassing myself further by having fruit juice drip down my chin like a monkey.

Curtix frowned. It didn't look disapproving so much as troubled. "I deceive on purpose, but not you. You've always been honest, sometimes to a fault, and I'm not sure when I started to think that was a bad thing."

"What?"

"I'm saying thank you, Netti."

I gave a quiet laugh. "For what? You didn't need my help, and in the end, I didn't even give any."

Curt pursed his lips. With a nod, he directed us both toward a waiting palanquin, but I didn't move.

"I should let you enjoy the rest of your birthday," I said, taking a step back.

He halted me with his next words. "I didn't know from the start."

While my eyes widened, he picked at a gold cufflink on his uniform sleeve, avoiding my gaze. The crowd seemed far away, the two of us alone at the center of a stone plaza even while surrounded by Imperial guards.

"I didn't know what to believe that first day," he said softly. "Whether I was being tricked or whether I was simply unworthy. I allowed them to set up shop while I observed, investigated. When they allowed me contact with the 'ship,' I began to suspect an impact shield. Even so, it was a slow process of unraveling, one riddled with more doubt than I'd care to admit."

"Me too!" My cheeks heated; perhaps I hadn't needed to blurt it so loudly. "I went back and forth so many times. It should have been easy to see through, right? I thought . . ."

When Curtix raised an eyebrow at me, I trailed off with an awkward laugh, tossing the disk fruit once and almost dropping it.

The corner of my brother's lips twitched. "Of everyone on my council, you have the worst view of me—stupid, arrogant, petty, cruel, I believe it was—and perhaps because of that, you're the only one willing to be truly honest. It's the one help no one else will give me. Thank you, Netti."

My face burned with heat again, but at least this time my heart knew what to do; it rose in my chest.

"It's not because I think badly of you," I said. "It's because you've always been my hero, and I can't help it."

"Yet I'm the reason you almost couldn't be a pilot." He

grimaced. "I provoked you that day. I was . . . cruel. Then you failed your flight test."

So he hadn't gotten me into the academy to get rid of me, but rather because he felt guilty. Call it a birthday gift.

I elbowed him lightly. "Maybe I failed on purpose. Maybe I wanted another year to pester you before I go make something of myself in the fleet."

Curtix rolled his eyes, but his expression softened. "If you'd like to stick around, I won't stop you. It seems I could use more honesty in my cabinet." Sharply, he raised a finger. "But you have to take your duties seriously, Netti. I swear to the nine stars, if you skip another meeting, I will ship you to the academy, not as a pilot, but as a dishgirl. Do you understand?"

I laughed. When I tossed him the disk fruit, he caught it.

"You still know how to throw for the monkeys." I grinned. "I'm glad. And I hope you know, worthy emperor or not, you'll always be my brother. That's good enough for me."

BETRAYAL COMES AT A PRYCE

AN HOMAGE TO WILLIAM SHAKESPEARE'S THE TEMPEST

HENRY HERZ

The Duke of Myhlan sat upright in his resplendent purple robes at the head of the enormous table, flanked on his right by his older son, my father, Earl Pryce. To the Duke's left sat his younger son, Defense Minister Ahnytol. As the Duke's grand-daughter, I had permission to attend high-level meetings.

The Duke slapped a wrinkled hand on the veined marble tabletop. "No, Ahnytol. Violence should be our last resort, not our immediate response to an *alleged* treaty violation. First, we shall attempt to resolve the border dispute with House Dragar through diplomatic means, as Pryce suggested. Only if territory has been seized will you lead the Imperial Navy into battle."

A scowl flitted across Ahnytol's scarred face at the mention of his brother. His brown eyes never softened.

Ahnytol considered himself a man of decisive action, but Father and I viewed him as bloodthirsty and ambitious. I imag-ined that my aging grandfather took great comfort knowing my judicious, unflappable father was his heir apparent.

The Duke turned to my father. "How soon can you depart, Pryce?"

"My spaceship should finish routine maintenance in thirty-six hours, your grace." He put a firm hand on my shoulder. "I would like my daughter Miranda to accompany me, if it pleases you. The mission offers an excellent diplomatic training opportunity."

While, like Father, I appreciated diplomacy, engineering was my passion. I'd recently earned a doctorate. But I knew when to hold my tongue.

The Duke nodded. "Very well. Dismissed."

———

Two days later at Spaceport Twelve, I boarded the small sloop INS Trinculo along with my father, a pilot, co-pilot, and five royal guards; seasoned men and women promoted from the Royal Marines. By right of birth as an earl's daughter and two years of military training, I wore the blue uniform of a Navy ensign. I found it pleasing that it also emphasized the color of my eyes.

The engines rumbled, hurtling the Trinculo skyward.

"Passing one hundred kilometers, sir," reported the co-pilot after a few minutes.

The pilot read a gauge. "Check. Engage the hyperdrive, Lieutenant."

"Engaging hyperdrive, aye, Commander."

Father, looking distinguished as always with his gray-streaked hair and the starred epaulets of an admiral, leaned to whisper in my ear. "Everything alright, Miranda?"

I nodded, but my stomach knotted as we jumped. In the view screen, pinpoint stars stretched into converging lines. I'd traveled through hyperspace before, but still hadn't gotten used to the disorienting sensation.

A few minutes later, the co-pilot issued a standard caution to the passengers. "Dropping out of hyperspace in thirty seconds."

I braced myself, but no jarring transition dumped us into normal spacetime.

The pilot gave the co-pilot a stern look. "Status?"

"Instruments show hyperdrive disengaged, sir," replied the co-pilot, his voice quavering.

But we're still in hyperspace. My heart pounded. Every additional second hurled us past our destination.

The Marines exchanged glances.

"Manual override, Lieutenant. Disengage hyperdrive."

"Manual override, aye, Commander." The co-pilot lifted a protective cover and yanked a lever. Nothing. Sweat beaded on his brow.

I was breathing fast. *How's this happening? The odds of a triple-redundant hyperdrive failing are essentially zero.*

No sign of the panic I felt showed on my father's face. "Commander, are you or the Lieutenant certified in hyperdrive maintenance?"

"No, my lord."

I nodded. *It was a long shot, Father, but worth asking.*

Father calmly suggested, "I propose Miranda attempt to diagnose the issue." Of course, a suggestion from an earl isn't really a suggestion.

I unstrapped as Father offered me an encouraging smile. Gathering my long black hair, I looped it into a knot to keep it out of the way. I hustled to the hyperdrive panel at the aft end of the compartment, pulling the handle to expose circuitry. A small envelope tumbled to the deck. *Odd.* It bore a single handwritten word, "Pryce." I tucked it in my pocket and assessed the electronic components.

Fully expecting scorch marks where components had shorted out, I caught my breath. *Bloody hell.* My face flushed. Taking a moment to calm myself, I reported. "This was sabotage, not a system failure."

"Are you certain, Miranda?"

I nodded. "An entire module's missing. Not blackened or melted. Missing."

"I see."

How can you be so calm? We're galloping through space on an unbridled mount.

"If you physically disconnect the drive, will that drop us out of hyperspace?"

The co-pilot gasped.

I stood. "Yes, but that's not standard procedure. There could be… negative consequences."

Father raised an eyebrow.

I winced. "Very negative."

"I see." He turned to the flight crew. "Do either of you have alternatives to offer?"

They exchanged glances. "No, my lord."

Father sighed. "Miranda, strap yourself to the bulkhead and disengage the drive."

———

I awoke to a throbbing pain in my abdomen where I'd secured myself. A glance at the view screen confirmed we were no longer in hyperspace. The dangerous but necessary maneuver had not reduced us to our component molecules.

Father hunched over me. "Thank goodness."

I handed him the envelope.

He opened it and showed me. "Enjoy your final voyage, brother."

I clenched my fists. *A pox upon you, Ahnytol.*

Father's face tightened. He called over his shoulder. "Report, Commander."

"My lord, we dropped out of hyperspace near a K-type main sequence star with a mass of 0.6 Sol. It has one planet, tidally locked, mass and diameter roughly one Earth-equivalent. Spectral analysis identifies the star as Groombridge 1618."

Damnation. I stood. "Groombridge's sixteen light-years from Earth."

Father took command. "Everyone, suit up. Put us in orbit around the planet, Commander."

"My lord?"

"Other subsystems may also have been sabotaged. I want us to land and conduct a thorough check of the ship."

I nodded in agreement, impressed again by Father's self-discipline. *But what are we going to do about the missing module?*

"Lieutenant, make your altitude three hundred kilometers," ordered the pilot. "Scan the planet for cities." She turned her head. "Shall I send a distress signal, my lord?"

Father's eyes met mine. "No."

Ah, you don't want Ahnytol to send a ship to finish us off.

———

The Trinculo set down in the center of a one-kilometer diameter crater. The orange dwarf Groombridge's light painted the terrain an eerie russet. No plants grew.

I stared through the view screen at the reason why Father chose this spot – the only artificial construct our sensors detected from orbit – a black metal cube, twenty-meters on a side, rising from the crater's rim. A magnified infrared inspection confirmed the cube was no natural phenomenon. Geologic formations don't have open doorways or antennas.

The pilot read from a bank of displays. "Gravity 0.94g. Atmosphere only 3% oxygen. Temperature 400K."

I winced. *More than enough to boil water.*

Father stood. "Provisions, Commander?"

"Two weeks' worth of food and water, my lord."

"I see." Father approached the hull hatch. "Run a complete system diagnostic. Meanwhile, the rest of us will reconnoiter the building."

The five Marines saluted, plasma rifles slung over their shoulders, m-grenades clipped to their belts. The flight crew lent Father and me their sidearms.

Father led the seven of us in single file. Our heat- and radiation-resistant spacesuits, as well as the rugged terrain, made for slow going. What appeared smooth from an altitude of ten thousand meters turned out to be compacted sand frequently pierced by jagged rocks like meter-high stalagmites.

"Sensors picking up acoustic anomalies, my lord," came through our comm link with the Trinculo as we neared the cube.

"Try to give us a bearing to the source. Guards, wedge formation on me, five-meter spacing," ordered Father, drawing his sonic pistol.

Two Marines deployed to Father's right, another pair to his left.

I followed five meters behind him, trailed by a Marine sergeant. My pulse raced, though I couldn't say if from exertion, the unexplained sounds, or the somehow disturbing runes inscribed in the building's exterior.

Someone screamed.

My heart thundered in my chest. The heads-up display of my helmet indicated it came from our rearguard. A black nightmare had burrowed up from the sand and clamped onto the sergeant's ankle like a rabid dog.

This was no dog. The horrid chitin-armored creature reminded me of a two-meter-long scorpion without a stinging tail, though far more grotesque. It lurched and shambled with surprising speed on six multi-jointed legs, each ending in sharp talons. Four thick crab-like arms seemed designed to grab prey and drag it to a drooling maw nearly as wide as the creature's disproportionately sized head. Needle-sharp teeth lined a quivering orifice from which a barbed tongue flicked arrhythmically. It chittered with savage fury.

Bloody hell. I couldn't breathe or move my feet.

The sergeant howled in agony but managed to cut the creature in half with a plasma rifle discharge. Black sludge leaked from the monster's twitching halves… and began to steam in the blazing heat.

My stomach knotted at the sight of the sergeant's blood boiling as it leaked from his punctured suit. *God's teeth! The medical kit's back on the Trinculo.*

"Sarge!" Two Marines headed toward him as he toppled to the ground.

The second pair of guards grabbed me and my father's arms, hauling us unceremoniously toward the open doorway.

Before the first pair of Marines reached the sergeant, a dozen more creatures burst from the sand, gnashing their hideous mouths. The guards opened fire to keep the monsters' snapping claws and jaws out of striking distance.

"Covering fire," shouted Father. He and the two Marines blasted away from just inside the doorway. But more of the hellish creatures erupted out of the sand.

They're going to swamp those Marines.

As if he read my mind, Father ordered. "Leave the sergeant. Fall back."

My throat tightened as creatures swarmed over the doomed Marine writhing in agony. I gagged as they feasted on him.

Father put him out of his misery.

The exposed Marines backed up toward us, aided by the covering fire. Glowing beams of electrons slashed, dismembering monsters and slicing off chunks of nearby boulders.

More creatures emerged, lurching toward the retreating Marines, now roughly ten meters from us.

"Miranda, figure out how to shut the door," ordered Father.

I found what appeared to be a control panel on the wall just inside the doorway. I studied the alien design for hints as to how it worked. Sweat stung my eyes. *Hurry!*

"Fire in the hole!" shouted one of our guards, hurling an m-grenade past the retreating Marines. She couldn't have known if it would be effective against the monsters, but we were out of options.

The grenade detonated, spewing megawatts of invisible microwave radiation rather than metal fragments. Our spacesuits were designed to provide electromagnetic shielding. The monsters' chitinous exoskeletons offered no such protection. They exploded as microwaves boiled their soft innards. Viscous black jelly splattered in all directions.

The two Marines joined us inside the doorway, gasping for breath.

"Stay alert for more," said Father, joining me at the door control. "Well?"

I shrugged. "All I can do is try different buttons, hoping I don't make things worse."

"Do it," he replied, swiveling his pistol toward the building's interior.

Right. There could be creatures inside with us. My hands trembled as I pushed buttons. The door slid shut on my third attempt. I sat on the floor, hyperventilating.

The door through which we entered opened on a central hallway extending to the far side of the cube, where wall-mounted rungs rose to a ceiling hatch. The pewter-toned walls merged seamlessly into a light gray floor similar to concrete.

"Keep your suits on. Clear the building of bugs," ordered Father, nicknaming the monsters.

'Bugs' doesn't nearly convey the terror they induce, I thought.

Father updated the flight crew via comm link as we advanced. Square hatches spaced symmetrically along the hallway led to six rooms, three on a side. The first five seemed to be a galley, bunk room, storeroom, latrine, and a room filled with alien machinery and tools. We found no bugs.

One room to go. Tapping buttons on the wall-mounted panel, I opened the door.

Banks of monitors suggested this was a control room. Upended chairs and tables lay scattered on the floor. Four streaks of a thick blue liquid converged at a meter-wide hole excavated through the floor.

My heart pounded. *They can tunnel through the foundation.*

Checking behind a topped cabinet, I jumped back, yelling

"bug" reflexively. The others rushed to me as I raised a hand. "Sorry. It's dead."

Father pointed at the hole. "Secure that so no others can return."

The Marines flipped a heavy metal table upside down over the opening. They weighed it down with a pile of debris and furniture.

I returned my attention to the bug, which sprawled atop a bronze-colored robot. The robot looked like a four-legged, four-armed gorilla. It lay on its back, its torso dented and scratched. The bug's head lay crushed in one of the robot's four-fingered hands.

The struggle must have dislodged the panel on its abdomen.

A fist-sized cylindrical component had fallen out, its two wires disconnected.

"The enemy of my enemy…" suggested Father. But an earl's suggestion… "Cover her."

Two Marines aimed plasma rifles at the robot's squarish head.

I holstered my pistol and hauled the bug off the robot, the black sludge of its blood staining my gloves. Squatting, I reconnected the two wires.

LEDs within the robot's interior flickered.

The cylinder's a power source. "It's rebooting."

The robot sat up.

I held my hands palms-out in a gesture of nonaggression. "I reconnected your power supply," I explained, hoping my suit's translator module would find a language the robot could comprehend.

No response.

"We also fought the bug-like creatures." In what I hoped would be interpreted as a sign of goodwill, I gently replaced the cylinder within its abdomen and closed the hinged panel. "Is that better?"

The eye on the front of the robot's head tracked my movements. A second eye on the right side of its head observed one Marine. The eye on the left side, the other Marine.

"Lower your weapons," Father ordered.

The robot stood. "Thank you for assistance," it broadcast directly into our comm link.

My mouth fell open. *That is one advanced robot.* "May I ask you some questions?"

"Affirmative, but first I inspect facility." It conducted a quick tour of the building, returning to the control room.

"What is your primary function?" I asked.

"Assist station personnel."

I spread my arms wide. "Since we are the only ones here, does that include us?"

"Affirmative."

"Do you have a name?"

"Arion."

"I'm Miranda." I pointed at the blue stains on the floor. "What happened?"

"Skril tunneled through the floor. Killed four scientists."

Looking at the monitors, I asked, "And the scientists' mission?"

"Study flare star."

"Ask about the bugs," ordered Father.

I poked the dead 'skril' with a boot. "What do you know about these?"

Arion tilted its head to view the creature. "Subterranean sightless ambush predators. Use sound to hunt."

My empty stomach rumbled. "We found what appears to be food in the galley. Can we safely eat it? We're carbon-based primates from Earth. We drink water. Our bodies are 65% oxygen, 18% carbon, 10% hydrogen, and 3% nitrogen by weight."

"Negative. Scientists had silicon-based biochemistry."

Damn. That means we have two weeks to get off this planet.

Scratching emanated from the table blocking the hole.

Or less. My heart raced.

"Two of you, keep eyes on that," ordered Father. "Arion, do you have a way to secure our barricade?"

"Affirmative." The robot retrieved eight spikes from storage and used a power-hammer to drive them into the foundation along the table's edge.

The skril could dig another tunnel. I paced to mask my panic. "Arion, our hyperdrive system's missing a critical component. Are you able to analyze and build a replacement here?"

"Insufficient data. Require physical inspection."

Father sighed but nodded. "Agreed. We need to retrieve our food anyway." He winced at a disturbing thought. "Arion, are you shielded from microwave radiation?"

"Space station strongly shielded. Not me."

Father's shoulders drooped ever so slightly. "We cannot use m-grenades around Arion."

My stomach twisted. *We're going to die.* I hoped the others didn't notice my trembling hands.

Father addressed us. "We are exhausted. We will take two hours' rest before we go to the Trinculo."

Even if not outranked, no one would have argued.

Father asked Arion to modify the building's atmospheric generator to extract more oxygen out of the planet's atmosphere. He updated the flight crew of our plan.

We stretched out in the bunk room, still wearing our suits. Despite my fear, I fell quickly asleep.

———

Our spacesuit alarms woke us. I pulled Father aside. "You should stay here." He opened his mouth to protest, but I put a hand on his shoulder. "Only I can assist Arion."

Father frowned, but nodded. "I will station the other two Marines on the roof as overwatch."

After emphasizing the absolute need for quiet, I led Arion

and two Marines out the door. When it slid closed behind us, panic set in. I wanted to turn and bang for re-admittance. *Steady.*

We advanced, step by slow step. I struggled to keep my sense of terror at bay while an undefined incongruity gnawed at me. I straightened. *There's no trace of either the sergeant or the skril we shredded.* My stomach roiled. *Food is food. Of course they're cannibalistic.*

I spotted the sergeant's rifle. Holstering my pistol, I retrieved his weapon and we continued. Sweat dripped in my eyes. My pulse pounded, fear rising the closer we approached safe haven. *Almost there.*

I pulled up short, raising a fist to halt our group. A lone skril lurked around the base of a boulder ten meters away, roughly half-way to the Trinculo. *It hasn't heard us yet.*

I whispered, knowing the flight crew were also on the comm link, "There's one skril in front of me. I want to get as close as I can before firing. When I shoot, open the hatch. We'll dive into the ship."

I closed to perhaps seven meters before the skril began its maddening chittering. "Now!" I fired, taking care that the plasma beam didn't also slice open our ship's hull.

The two halves of the krill writhed as the hatch slid open… and a hundred skril rose from the sand like reanimated corpses.

"Go, go, go!"

I held my fire. It's dangerous firing plasma weapons while running. Nevertheless, two beams sliced through the closest threats.

The Marines lying on the roof providing covering fire.

The hatch slammed shut once the four of us leaped inside.

Persistent scratching echoed inside the metal hull. "They've been doing that since you left," said the co-pilot, his eyes wide with fear.

You're right on the edge, aren't you? I returned the borrowed pistol and belt to the pilot.

She strapped it on grimly, her eyes never leaving the alien robot.

"This way, Arion." I led it aft to the hyperdrive panel, helped it connect, and answered questions. All the while, the skril scratching grew louder. Try as I might, I couldn't ignore the insistent chittering, the sound grating on my sanity. *No wonder the co-pilot's losing his composure.*

Arion disconnected, declaring, "I can build replacement."

The guards let out an undisciplined cheer, raising their fists.

"Our systems check revealed no other sabotage." The pilot pointed to two bulging duffle bags. "The provisions are ready."

"Good," I replied. "Are you two staying or coming with us? We'll be returning here once Arion builds the replacement module."

The rattled lieutenant didn't wait for his superior to respond. "I'm going with you. I can't stand this noise another minute."

The commander sighed. "I'd better come too, then."

Good. Keep an eye on your jittery co-pilot.

She pointed at the view screen. A sea of skril lurched in voracious frenzy around the Trinculo. "How do we get past them?"

I tapped a Marine's forearm. "Corporal, when I open the hatch ten centimeters, drop a grenade outside with a three-second delay."

He stiffened. "But the Earl said –"

"Not to use grenades that would harm Arion," I interrupted. "But since I'll be shutting the hatch immediately and the Trinculo is shielded, Arion won't be affected." I reminded the flight crew about the need for utter silence when returning to the cube.

They nodded and each slung a duffle bag over a shoulder, leaving the Marines free to wield their weapons.

My skril-slaughtering tactic worked, and we picked our way silently through a black sludge-stained landscape. I sucked in my breath. *More than a hundred of these nightmare piranha-scorpions.*

Paralyzing dread bore down on me as we approached the relative safety of the building. *Four hundred meters. Three hundred meters. Two hundred meters. Almost there.* At fifty meters, the jittery co-pilot tripped on a small rocky protuberance, his duffel tumbling to the ground.

Hells bells. "No one move," I hissed as half a dozen skril emerged from the sand to our left. "On my command, overwatch will shoot at boulders fifty meters behind us. The sound will lure the skril away. Overwatch, then march your fire away from the cube, creating space for us to dash inside."

I hoped my fear-parched throat didn't change the pitch of my voice. "Overwatch, weapons free."

Both Marines fired, slicing chunks from large rocks twenty meters behind us.

The skril chittered at the sound of tumbling fragments. They shambled along our left flank, just meters away.

I closed my eyes in terror.

At a scream, "Open the door!" my eyes jerked open.

The co-pilot.

His courage snapped like a dry twig. He sprinted toward the building... until a dozen skril lurched out of the sand in front of him.

While the rest of us stayed motionless, overwatch engaged the co-pilot's attackers. The need to avoid hitting the panicked man slowed their rate of fire.

The co-pilot howled as the last two skril tore off a leg before being shot by the overwatch.

Twenty more skril rose in their place.

Bloody hell. "No one move. Overwatch, fire to lead them away from us."

This time, it worked. Once the sounds lured the skril two hundred meters to our left, we sprinted to the door. I snatched the fallen duffel bag en route.

The two Marines, blessed with much tougher stomachs than

I, had retrieved both portions of the co-pilot. He might be dead, but they weren't going to let the skril eat his remains.

Father let us in and ordered the overwatch inside. He hugged me in a complete breach of protocol.

I blinked away tears of relief. At my request, Arion retrieved a tarp from storage to serve as a body bag, then headed to the lab to begin fabricating the replacement hyperdrive module.

"Arion raised the oxygen to a safe level, Miranda," said Father.

I nodded. To take my mind off the poor co-pilot, I lugged a duffel bag to the galley and set out a modest meal for everyone.

As we ate, Father organized a watch schedule, two hours per Marine. After dinner everyone except the patrol crashed in the bunk room, overwhelmed by fatigue and dread.

I checked in on the indefatigable Arion. "When will you finish?"

"Unknown."

I sighed and rejoined the others in the bunk room. Hideous nightmares of monsters and screaming disturbed my sleep... until I bolted upright. *That was an actual scream... a woman's scream.*

Everyone leaped to their feet and grabbed a weapon. Plasma rifle blasts drew us to the latrine.

Red blood painted the floor. A severed, gloved hand lay in the corner, palm up, as if pleading for help.

I gagged.

The Marine on watch stood over an excavated hole. "A skril must have grabbed someone." He discharged his weapon downward several times into the darkness.

"Keep them pinned down," ordered Father. He pointed at two other Marines. "Bring a metal table here on the double. Miranda, have Arion secure the tabletop over the opening."

Although the new breach was soon blocked, scratching from below resumed. *They'll never stop coming for us. We're skril food.*

I found Father pacing the hallway with a milk-curdling

scowl. "It's not your fault," I offered. "You set an armed roving watch."

He shook his head. "You misunderstand." He locked eyes on me. "We just lost the pilot. The pilot," he emphasized. "Even if the spaceship's drive is restored, we have no one to fly us to Earth. We have two weeks' worth of rations, three if we stretch them."

My throat tightened. *We're well and truly screwed. Unless...* "I'm going to run something by Arion." I headed for the lab.

"Arion, you said this station studies the flare star. Please elaborate."

It continued assembling the replacement hyperdrive component. "Sensors measure solar flare frequency, luminance, other parameters. Magnetic flux generator shields station from adverse effects. Electron transmitter stimulates increased solar activity."

My jaw dropped at the immense power needed to induce a star flare. *Could we...* My heart raced as an idea formed. I spent the next hour discussing station modifications with Arion.

———

I found Father in the control room, his shoulders slumped uncharacteristically. *You've given up.*

He must have noticed the hope on my face because he straightened. "Do you have something?"

I smiled. "Yes. A desperate ploy, but our only option. We must send a message."

"But Ahnytol controls the Navy. He will surely intercept it."

I winked. "Exactly." I laid out my plan.

"Ha!" Father slapped the desktop. "No matter what happens, I am proud of you, Miranda." He dictated a message via comm link to the Trinculo.

"Ahnytol, you putrid pile of excrement. Your cowardly attempt to murder me by proxy has failed. If you had a shred of a spine, you would face me in trial by combat. But you lack the bollocks of a warrior, or a rodent for that matter, to fight me man-to-man on Groombridge 1618's only planet. You cannot comprehend the hellish fate to which I shall assign you when I become Duke."

At Father's command, the Trinculo launched a tiny hyper-drive comm buoy to Imperial Navy headquarters.

"Now, we wait… and pray."

———

Two long days and three thwarted skril attacks later, Arion warned, "Sensors detect spaceship in orbit."

"Everyone, suits and helmets on," ordered Father.

At his nod, I told Arion, "Initiate electron beam to stimulate coronal mass ejection."

"Executed." Arion pointed at a monitor showing a massive spike in Groombridge's magnetic field.

Good. "A magnetic flux density of 10^{12} T will disrupt the spaceship's drive systems." I turned to the robot. "Halt the CME. Initiate tractor beam with the station's magnetic flux generator."

"Executed. Spaceship descending toward us," Arion reported.

A tiny grin crept onto Father's face. "Marines, onto the roof. Execute fire mission alpha." He nodded at me.

"Okay, Arion. Time for you to move into position."

———

An hour later, the tractor beam forced the disabled spaceship to set down a hundred meters from the cube's doorway.

"It's the INS Caliban," reported a Marine from the roof.

Father gave me a grim smile. "That's Ahnytol's corvette. Hail them."

I tied into their comm network. "INS Caliban, this is INS Trinculo. Requesting evacuation."

"I am happy to hear your voice, dear niece," replied Ahnytol, his voice dripping with malice. "But first, there is the matter of a personal duel. Have your father come out. I brought a pair of dueling blades for just this purpose."

Father put his hands on my shoulders. "He will not risk dueling me when he holds all the cards. No. The traitor will order his men to kill us all and shut off the tractor beam. I shall play for time. You know what to do." He leaned forward until his helmet touched mine – a spacesuit kiss – and departed.

As Father stood in the open cube doorway and taunted his brother, I monitored the situation from the control room.

The Caliban's hatch opened. Ahnytol marched down the ramp cradling two sheathed ceremonial sabers... followed by twenty soldiers. *More than enough to overcome us.* Ahnytol led the platoon halfway to the cube. At his hand signal, they spread out in a semicircle. He gestured for my father to meet him there. "Do you fight as well as you talk, Pryce?" he asked, leaving off Father's title as an intentional insult.

"Indeed, Ahnytol. Prepare to reap the reward of your perfidy."

That's my signal. "Marines, execute fire mission bravo."

A minute later, Ahnytol's soldiers took fire from the four Marines on the cube's roof. Two were killed before the others scattered and returned fire.

Father stepped inside the cube and shut the door.

"So, the noble Pryce now plays the craven," cried Ahnytol. "Why prolong the situation? We are far too many for you. Order your men to stop... or it will not go well for your daughter."

Suppressing fire from his soldiers forced our Marines to keep their heads down... until hundreds of skril boiled out of the sand.

As his men screamed and panic-fired at their assailants, Ahnytol turned and ran for the Caliban. The hatch shut before he reached the ship. "Open! Open the hatch!"

His flight crew didn't comply.

"And now you pay the price of betrayal, brother."

Turning, Ahnytol screamed, "Form up on me!" He ran toward his troops.

I admired his soldiers' discipline as they quickly reformed in a ten-meter diameter ring around him, pouring deadly fire in all directions. They kept the tide of skril at bay… until our Marines resumed fire from the rooftop.

One soldier went down. Then another. Ravenous skril surged through gaps opened by our Marines' lethal marksmanship.

"I have a clear shot at the traitor, my lord," reported the Marine corporal.

"Leave him for the skril."

The sounds of rifle blasts mingled with the screams of the soldiers as skril tore chunks off of flesh. In so hostile a world, even minor spacesuit rips were a death sentence. Or would have been if the soldiers didn't first bleed out or have their heads crushed by slavering jaws.

A skril seized Ahnytol's left ankle. As he drew a saber from its sheath, a second skril grabbed his right wrist, toppling him to the ground. The monsters pulled in opposite directions.

Ahnytol screamed while a third skril latched onto his groin and a fourth cracked open his helmet to chew off his face as his skin blistered from the intense heat.

"He that dies pays all debts," said Father.

The chittering skril dragged twenty-one mangled human bodies underground, some still squirming in futile resistance.

"Well done, luring the skril to the other side of the cube with fire mission alpha," I congratulated the Marines. *Now to commandeer the Caliban.* "Assemble in the control room."

We gave the skril half an hour to clear the area. Stepping gingerly, Father led the Marines and I to the Caliban.

Despite our stealth, skril must have detected our footfalls when we reached two-thirds of the way to the ship. Once they emerged, we obliterated them with an m-grenade.

Father tapped twice on the hatch. "Open."

The door slid open. Our Marines charged inside, weapons drawn.

Of the three members of Caliban's flight crew, one lay on the deck, missing most of his head. The other two held up their arms under Arion's watchful glare… and unwavering pistol. The robot had followed our plan – hiding fifty meters beyond where we force-landed the Caliban, and sneaking aboard when our Marines opened fire on Ahnytol's soldiers.

Father beamed. "Marines, secure the flight crew." He turned to the robot. "Well done, Arion. We are deeply in your debt. Do you wish to come home with us?"

Can you knight a robot? I wondered.

Arion handed Father the pistol. "Negative. I wait for more scientists."

I smiled at Arion as he departed. *You have more honor than my uncle.*

Father sat. "Everyone, strap in. Take us home, Commander."

Author's Note

This story shares the following elements with Shakespeare's play, The Tempest: sibling betrayal, loyal daughter, shipwreck, threatened rape, a storm (solar in this case), and vengeance with the aid of an ally released from imprisonment. "He that dies pays all debts" is a quote from The Tempest. The tale also has the following name correspondences:

Myhlan → Milan

Pryce → Prospero

Ahnytol → Antonio

Miranda → unchanged

Trinculo → unchanged

Arion → Ariel

Caliban → unchanged

THE AVIAN CYBORG OF BETEL IV

ERIK PETERSON

Terkel stood on the balcony overlooking the garden he had begun building before his wife Jantje's death, but had only decided would stand in her honor after she had passed away. It was a beautiful, vast garden, full of plants from countless worlds, brought here to Betel IV at great expense and sacrifice. It stretched from the foot of the building where he stood all the way to the seaside. Terkel was bold enough to imagine the garden the finest in the galaxy. Certainly no one with his level of wealth had devoted such a vast amount of their resources to such a collection. Not for as long as Terkel had managed to extend his life.

From here he could see the massive purple ligamon trees from the planet Gurllaf rising hundreds of meters into the sky, their rigid silhouettes framing the sunset. He could see the fiery red and yellow buds of the phoenix blooms, the plant that oxidized itself into ash every winter, new seed bursting from its remains in the spring. He could see the spiny blurbs of the killawok vines, digging into the trunks of larger plants as they fought their way up from the garden floor towards sunlight.

He could not see any animals, though Terkel knew they were there, and that they were plentiful. Many of them were animals selected deliberately, animals that, by one attribute or another, were useful to his company in their research. But others were simply indulgences, animals brought to suit his fancy, or perhaps the whims of some sufficiently positioned member of his corporate team.

Behind Terkel, in his office, Matteus, Terkel's senior vice president, stood anxiously watching bright multicolored financial graphs that floated in the air over Terkel's desk, inching up and down slowly like glowing worms digging through the air.

Terkel didn't have to see the graphs to know they weren't good. The corporation was in danger. The only question was how quickly and from what direction the strike would come. He knew the responsible thing to do was step into the office and join the man, but he couldn't pull his thoughts away from his wife's garden.

"Do people like it, do you think?" he asked Matteus through the open doorway.

"Like what, Terkel?" Matteus's tone feigned casualness.

"I wonder what people think of Jantje's Garden."

"They've told you what they think of it."

"Yes, to my face. But I can never trust what people say to my face. Or about my face. Even my occasional botched facial procedures have left me painfully aware of the dearth of honesty one encounters when others sense you have power."

"To be frank, Terkel, there was an abundance of honesty about your worst facial procedures."

"Yes, out there," said Terkel, gesturing out towards the world. "And that's what I need to know about Jantje's Garden. Does it do her justice? What are they saying about it out *there*?"

"They all think it's wonderful," said Matteus. "Sincerely." A little more impatience crept into his voice.

"I need to know what they're saying. All of it. This is named after my wife. I want to know what kind of legacy I'm leaving for her."

"That would be easy enough to find out," said Matteus. His

tone softened again at the mention of Terkel's wife. "Our assistants could have summaries for you by this afternoon."

"There's no rush," said Terkel. "And besides, with the threat of takeover looming, we might need to devote their attention elsewhere."

Terkel stepped off the balcony and back into the office. "Now, let's see about this takeover threat. What does our intelligence committee say?"

———

While his work hours were spent on the dangers his company was facing, Terkel began devoting his private hours to studying the public sentiment about his garden. He read reports and books. He watched holovids and travelogs. He knew that he could have had the virtual assistants compile all the information he needed, but he found himself enjoying the first hand accounts of people who had actually made the voyage here to Betel IV to see the gardens for themselves and to document it for the rest of the galaxy.

The overwhelming reaction was overwhelmingly positive. The gardens had gained something of a cult following among those who indulged in interplanetary travel recreationally, which, granted, was not a large segment of the galactic population, but a distinguished group to gain notoriety among.

And as he watched and read and listened, there was one word that he kept finding came up, over and over.

Nattergalen.

What was a nattergalen?

Apparently it was a bird. Not a particularly pretty bird in appearance, but one whose song was so beautiful that it attracted enthusiasts who were roaming his gardens solely in search of the bird. And while there were recordings of the bird-song, and even the recordings were heartachingly beautiful, those who had made the recordings seemed bereaved at how the recordings failed to capture the true nature of the nattergalen song.

Terkel watched a recording as one brown-eyed, raven-haired man in a monk's robe wept as he sat at the base of a tree in the garden, the live birdsong filling the air around him, as he whispered, "It doesn't do it justice. No recording does it justice."

As he continued to research, he found that these birds weren't all that rare on their native world, but that their native world restricted travel so much that it was easier to hear the birdsong on Betel IV than even their native world.

Which made Terkel wonder, because he knew of one other place that restricted interplanetary travel that had brought something beautiful into his life, and he wondered if perhaps they were one and the same.

And his research confirmed it.

The nattergalen's homeworld was Levengever.

Just like Jantje's.

———

As discreetly as possible, Terkel made the request that a nattergalen be brought to him. He didn't want word to spread that he was in search of the creature, in fear that it might send unscrupulous seekers into the garden in the hopes of finding the nattergale and bringing it back "safely" while requesting a "small reward" for their services. The bird was recovered surprisingly quickly, when it was discovered that a woman on a principal research team was the daughter of a fisherman, whose fleet of boatmen had a tendency to camp about three kilometers inland just outside the north wall, since the bird could often be heard singing from that spot in the early morning hours.

When Terkel was told the bird had been acquired and he should come to his office, he rushed as quickly as his old legs could carry him. He could hear the bird singing long before he saw it, the familiar tweeting and chirping he had heard in countless videos, but something of the real sound captured a beauty, a gentle ringing behind the sounds, an underscoring vibrato that Terkel felt down to his core. He found himself slowing his pace reverently as he approached his office, his eyes closing slightly as he slowly moved forward, the sounds of the bird song echoing in the hallway.

As he entered his office and beheld the bird, it was even more gray and more frail than he had imagined it. Something in him had expected the bird, like its song, to be more beautiful in person than it its recreations, but he realized now that even the unflattering pictures he had seen in his studies were actually stylized and beautified to make the bird seem prettier and sturdier than it really was.

"It looks so frail," said Terkel. "Like it could be crushed with a thought. How did you bring it here safely?"

"With great care," said Matteus. "Our researchers and handlers are the finest in the galaxy. For this garden, we've spared no expense."

"Is it as delicate as it appears?" asked Terkel.

"Unfortunately, it is. Our ornithologists have cautioned us that nattergalen do not survive long in captivity. We've brought it here with great care and caution, but we fear you won't be able to keep it here."

"It has survived in the gardens," said Terkel.

"Yes, it has thrived in the garden. It seems the garden has been just the right balance of wild and tame to let it thrive. Wild enough that it roams and eats easily, but tame enough that it has no natural predators to threaten it. The garden seems perfect for it."

"Then I will go to the garden," said Terkel. "Because now that I know this song exists, I can't imagine it not being part of my life."

And that is what he did. Over the next several weeks, Terkel would make regular trips to the garden to hear the song of the nattergalen. He would camp among the giant trees and drink from the natural rivers. He was far too busy to isolate himself much, and he did the best he could to keep up with his duties via his virtual assistants and regular visits from staff, but everyone knew that no matter how urgent their visit, when the nattergalen began to sing, everyone would go silent, so that Terkel could listen.

And Terkel reveled in the beauty of the song of the bird that came from the same homeworld as his departed wife, in the garden he had dedicated in her honor. He sometimes pondered how, of all the birds in all the vast galaxy, surely there must be one singular bird species that had the sweetest song of them all. And he decided it certainly must be this one.

———

"Terkel, I have wonderful news," said Matteus one day as Terkel was preparing for another camping trip. He held a white box that was a bit taller and a bit wider than his hands.

"I always welcome wonderful news."

"Well, I know how concerned you've been about the divide in your attention between this bird you must travel to visit and the worries about the possibility of the possible takeover that looms over the company."

In fact, Terkel knew it was Matteus who had become increasingly concerned over Terkel's divided attention. Terkel was perfectly content with the balance he'd managed to strike. But Terkel felt no need to point this out to Matteus, seeing how proud he looked of whatever solution he had figured out.

"May I present to you, the cybernetic nattergalen of Levengever." With a flourish, he opened the box.

Inside was a bird. In many ways, it resembled the nattergalen that he had spent the last several weeks pursuing in the garden. But this bird was far prettier and sturdier. Rather than a dull gray, the feathers of this bird were a shiny silver. And in many places, this bird had no feathers at all, but a metallic steel that glimmered in the light. Looking at it, Terkel couldn't tell if it was an organic bird enhanced with bionics or an artificial bird enhanced with organic bird parts.

"You see," said Matteus, "the trouble has been that we couldn't create an adequate recording of the nattergalen that you could enjoy here at the office without having to make the journey into the gardens. Its vocal structure was too unique to be reproduced by traditional speakers. But the people of Levengever figured out the solution long ago. By creating a durable cybernetic bird using the vocal apparatus of actual nattergalen, they can bring the sound indoors. The cybernetic structure can keep the necessary parts alive in a way that guarantees the bird will far outlive any of us. In this way you can keep it with you forever."

Matteus pressed against the back of the bird's neck, and it began to sing. Terkel was shocked to hear that it was, in fact, the birdsong, sounding much the same as it had when he'd first heard it in his office all those weeks ago.

"Well that's remarkable," said Terkel, as he listened with rapt attention. He gestured towards the bird. "May I?"

Matteus nodded, and Terkel reached into the box. The bird perched on his hand as he lifted it out of the box. He held it up to his face and admired the beauty of its gleaming body as the song he'd enjoyed from afar rang out inches from his ears.

"It's remarkable," he said. "I never imagined I would get to do this. I never imagined I'd hold it in my hands. It's amazing. A wonder. Matteus, I am overcome."

Matteus beamed nearly as brightly as the bird.

———

The cybernetic bird seemed perfect. It certainly allowed Terkel to maintain the type of orderly, structured schedule that men like Matteus saw befitting a man of his position.

But soon there arose two problems. One gradual, the other sudden.

The gradual one was with the bird itself. As the weeks went on, Terkel began to find the music of the cybernetic bird less and less satisfying. It wasn't a problem with the sound of the music. The bird recreated the tones of a nattergalen perfectly. But it was something in the *direction* of the music. The *musicality* of it. While beautiful, it never quite managed to sweep him up and carry him away the music of the wild bird did.

"Perhaps you're just growing more accustomed to it," said Matteus, when Terkel pointed this out to him. "As the novelty wears off, surely some of its ability to impact you emotionally must be lost as well."

"I don't think that's it," said Terkel.

"Terkel, the cybernetic brain of this little creature has far more processing power than the wild bird. It's programmed with the knowledge of music theory to a degree that no biological bird could ever comprehend."

"Well, that could be it. Maybe the nattergalen's song completely violates the rules of music theory. Maybe it's beyond music theory."

"It's programmed to know how to break the rules of music theory as well. It's aware of all types of avante garde and experimental music construction. It understands atonal music as well as any of history's greatest composers."

"Well, maybe the wild bird breaks the rules of breaking the rules. All I know is that there is something in the wild bird's song that this artificial bird simply can't manage to recreate."

"But it comes so close."

"It does. It truly does. But it's something in those last few centimeters that carries me light years."

Matteus sighed. "Does this mean you'll be camping regularly again?" He didn't bother trying to hide the aggravation in his voice.

"We'll see," said Terkel.

And it wasn't long before the sudden problem happened.

———

Terkel was asleep in bed when his virtual assistant awoke him to notify him that there had been a filing with the Galactic Securities Commission that mentioned his company.

Which meant the takeover was happening. It would only be a matter of days, now.

The documents were vast and complex. With help of summaries by the virtual assistant, and focusing on key sections, he felt like he'd gained a fair understanding of them and he didn't like what he found.

He called Matteus. He knew the man would have been signaled the same moment he was, and that the man would patiently wait until he knew Terkel was ready to discuss it.

"Did you notice it?" Terkel asked.

"I noticed a great many things. To which are you referring?"

"There are things in this document that no one should have any way of knowing. Things about which of our sub-corporations they would need to acquire to keep trade flowing, things about our vulnerabilities we only knew because of extensive internal reporting. I think we might have a spy among us."

"Our staff is vetted," said Matteus. "Corporate communications are monitored. I would vouch for our security."

"I don't think it's any of the staff."

"Then who?"

Terkel showed what he and his virtual assistant had discovered in their research. "This company has ties to Levengever. Matteus, I think the spy may be the bird."

"The bird?"

"I think the bird is eavesdropping on the communications in our office and reporting them back to the agents of this company. It might even be wirelessly accessing our systems. I believe this little bird is telling its true masters our secrets."

"Now that's a silly idea."

"Just the same. I want it out of my office and I want it examined."

"I'll see to it myself," said Matteus.

"No, no, I need your full attention on stopping this takeover. I can handle the investigation of the bird."

"But don't you think *you* need to give this full attention to stopping this takeover?"

"I am," said Terkel. "And if I'm right, this will be the key to undoing the whole thing."

———

Except he wasn't right.

Terkel assigned a team with members of his security staff, ornithology researchers, I.T. department, and financial team to inspect the bird. As the date of the pending takeover loomed closer and closer, he pressured them harder and harder. But despite all their efforts, they found nothing. Just a cybernetic bird that was now dissected and inspected beyond repair.

Which left only one possibility, the weight of which sat on his chest like death.

He called Matteus to his office.

"It wasn't the bird," Terkel told the man. "But you know that, don't you?"

"Of course it wasn't the bird. I purchased it myself."

"I found the right clue but I made the wrong connection," said Terkel. "It wasn't the fact that you brought me a bird that happened to be from Levengever that was the connection. It was that you were the man with connections in Levengever that allowed you to acquire the bird. Surely if just anyone could get them, people would simply purchase these instead of making the long voyage here to Betel IV to hear the birdsong in the garden. You must have used some connections to acquire it. Connections which, I suspect, betray your ties to this takeover."

Matteus sighed. "I was giving you a chance, Terkel. I don't really want to do this to you. I thought if I could get you a cybernetic nattergalen, you'd focus again. You'd become the leader you used to be. The leader this company needs. The man you haven't been since—"

"I know when it started," blurted Terkel.

"I was ready to call it off at any point," said Matteus. "Bless me, I even hoped the takeover might help. That once you knew what was at stake, once you knew jobs were on the line, jobs you had created for people you cared about, that your fighting spirit would come back."

"I do care about them. I do. Otherwise I wouldn't be fighting as hard as I have been. Although for you, clearly that has been woefully inadequate."

"Only because I have such a high standard to measure you against. You. Before."

"I have a clarity now that I didn't have then. I can see now, between me now and me before, which is the one that needed to change."

"You've built something here, Terkel. Something great. Something that matters."

But it took Terkel a moment to realize Matteus was talking about the company and not the garden. Was his heart really so far removed from the corporation now? Did he really just not care any more? No. It wasn't that.

"I do care about what we've done together, Matteus. I'm proud of the ways we've made people's lives better. I'm grateful for research we've pioneered that has improved the quality of life for people who've suffered."

"There are few aspects of modern life that haven't been touched by this corporation and what we do," said Matteus. "There are worlds that are fed because of our advancements in adapting crops and animal feed. There are people who live long, healthy lives because you built a company committed to cures over treatments. You've made something special here, Terkel, and the galaxy has rewarded you for it."

"I understand that."

"Then you need to be more selective about what you let go of and what you hold on to," said Matteus. The words hung between for a long moment.

"Why are you trying to convince me now," asked Terkel, "when it is too late anyway?"

Matteus covered the space between them in a few quick steps. "Because it's not too late. We could end this. It wouldn't be easy, but we could stop it. You, with my help. You just have to choose."

"Choose you?"

"Choose the company. Choose the people who need you here over birds. Over people we can't help any more."

"But you've been lying to me. Why would I trust you?"

"You do trust me. There's only one person in the world you ever trusted more than me, and you've been so focused on her that you haven't noticed what I really haven't been going to that much trouble to hide."

"Your contempt?"

"My concern."

"Your concern was for the company, not for me. Concern for me wouldn't have looked like this."

"Concern for you looks *exactly* like this, Terkel. Concern for how people would curse your name if they lost their jobs because of you. Concern for how you would feel when you wake up and realize everything's been taken from you, when you could have done something to stop it. You could lose everything, Terkel. Everything." With that, with a dramatic flourish, Matteus threw open the double doors to the balcony overlooking the gardens.

And there, perched on the handrail, sat the wild nattergalen.

Terkel's throat caught.

"Did you bring it here?" he asked.

Matteus shook his head. "I only intended to show you the gardens," he said quietly.

The nattergalen had come to him.

Suddenly there was a burst of lovely song, the clear wild music Terkel hadn't heard in weeks, resonating from the forest behind the bird and the office in front of it. It was the sound he had chased all over the garden, and now the bird had come to him. Perhaps the most beautiful birdsong in the galaxy. This time, he felt sure, the bird had come to sing for him.

Tears welled up in Terkel's eyes.

"Can't you hear it, Matteus?" Terkel whispered. "Can't you hear it?"

The two men stepped out on the balcony, and for the first time, they both listened, sincerely listed, together.

The nattergalen sang loud and clear and long and carried both mens' hearts away exactly the way the cybernetic one had failed to do. Tears welled in both their eyes until both their hearts were full.

And then, after a moment, after an eternity, the bird spread its dull gray wings and flew away, back into the garden.

"We have to save the garden," said Matteus.

"We have to save the corporation," said Terkel.

Matteus looked at him with surprise.

"You were right about one thing, Matteus. I do trust you. In spite of what you've done. I know you thought you were doing what was right. But you're wrong about something else. I don't need to become the man who can save this company. This company has that. In you. I'm who I need to be now. And I know you don't believe it yet, but I'm who I should have been. Before."

Matteus didn't answer, but looked Terkel in the eyes.

"This is what we are going to do, Matteus. You and I are going to fight to save this corporation. And perhaps bolster it up enough to keep this from happening again. And then I am going to step down, and let you take the helm. And in lieu of a severance package, you'll give me the garden, so that I can take it private. So that future threats to the company won't be a threat to the garden. You can tend that part of our legacy," he said, gesturing back towards the office, "and I can tend this one."

They both overlooked the garden as the last of the tears fell from their eyes.

———

And so they carried out their plan. They fought off the takeover, and they managed to preserve the company. Slowly they began the transition of authority until the moment came when Terkel could quietly hand control over to Matteus, and everyone would be grateful for the new streamlined chain of command.

Matteus took over the office, and Terkel took over the garden.

He had a cabin built, near the east wall, inside the garden, not far from where he knew fishermen were known to camp to hear the birdsong.

And one year later, Terkel saw Matteus make his way down the path towards his cabin.

Not a year after the takeover, but a year after the date they both knew things had truly changed. A year since his wife's death.

"Good morning!" Terkel called to the man as he approached the cabin, and he invited him in to eat and drink.

They dined on mushrooms that had been genetically modified to pull vitamin B12 from the soil, fist-sized berries, and a salad made of greens that had been bred to be more resistant to UV-C light.

They talked long after the meal had finished, but it was as the sun set that Terkel could tell that Matteus had lost the thread of the conversation, and seemed to have something important he wanted to say, but wasn't quite finding the right moment to say it.

"I don't think you've come all this way for the food," said

Terkel. "I know you know what day it is, and I appreciate the sentiment of your visit."

"I needed to clarify something," said Matteus, "and I've come to do it. On the day we set about stopping the takeover, you said something to me. You said you had become a different man after your wife died. You said you had become the man you should have been before. Is that really how you feel?"

Terkel didn't know how to answer that. "I should have . . ." he began, but the words caught in his throat.

Matteus held up his hand. "You don't need to say it. I didn't come here to make you indict yourself. Quite the contrary. Despite what you might think, Terkel, you were never neglectful. Your heart was always where it should have been. And she knew it. All that changed when she died is you didn't have a way to show it any more. And that has left you feeling like a very different man indeed."

Terkel didn't know how to answer that, and so they sat in silence for a while.

"But enough about that," said Matteus. "Let's go see if I can hear your little gray bird one more time."

And together they walked out of the garden, and into the forest.

MARSHMALLOW MOON

BRITTANY RAINSDON

Puffs of gray moondust drifted upward as Gretel, Hansel, and their stepmother, Mila, picked their way down the darkening rock canyon. The black blanket of space loomed over them, Homestation hours away, Father farther still. The weight of his absence pressed into Gretel as her breath fogged against the lexan hood of her hand-me-down spacesuit.

When would he come for them?

"This way, children. Hurry." Mila skipped faster, too fast for Gretel to keep up. "The ad said the tools to mine the assurestone are at the outpost at the bottom of the canyon. Once there, you can finally earn your keep."

Gretel's face flushed but she didn't risk arguing. She never did. Mila was always complaining about Father's good-for-nothing teenage twins who didn't pull their weight. And whenever Father left for Onworld, Mila would drop sneering comments about Gretel, raking manicured nails through the girl's frizzy brown hair and making rude comments about its texture or her weight. *Too many after-meal treats. No one wants to marry a fat, frizzy-haired girl. No beauty, no brains. You better start racking that thick skull of yours to figure out what you'll do to survive after you turn eighteen. Otherwise, you're deadweight. Literally.*

Hansel's voice beeped through the comms. "What do you think Father will bring from Onworld?"

You mean *if* he comes back, Gretel wanted to reply. Instead, she shrugged, kicked a rock, and picked up the pace. Father's trips home were becoming few and far between. And the last few times back, he hadn't brought anything fun. It was childish to think he would.

"Come on, Gret. My guess is new tech or better rations."

"I'd kill for some hard candy," Gretel exhaled. "Those old crackers taste like cardboard." Her mouth watered at the thought of sweets, but her nostrils flared against the lingering scent of the space lock, a foul burnt smell that mixed with her sweat and mugged up her spacesuit.

Hansel's voice crackled as he teetered down the steep path, brushing against Gretel. "Know what would be the best present from Onworld? Separation papers."

Gretel nearly choked as she pivoted, eyeing Mila for a response. But the woman didn't flinch, just picked up the pace and slipped around a boulder twenty paces ahead. Gretel cursed. "Mila, Stop. Hansel didn't mean—"

"Relax." Hansel laughed, tapping his helmet. "It's on private comm mode. What kind of brother do you think I am?"

Gretel grimaced. She knew what he wanted her to say: *the best.* "You shouldn't talk like that, even if it's private."

"You're such a marshmallow."

"Marshmallow? You're as pasty-white as I am." Gretel stumbled but Hansel caught her arm. A dozen or so pebbles skidded down the canyon as he held her.

"Yeah? But I'm not soft and squishy. I'm made of something stronger." He slapped a hand against the cliff wall. "Like this moonrock."

"Whatever." Gretel's cheeks burned as she shrugged him off and regained her balance. "That's why I call you my *only* brother instead of *best*. You're as bad as Mila."

"Wait. I didn't mean it like *her*."

"Right," Gretel huffed and shoved past him.

"No." Hansel frowned. "I didn't."

"Soft and squishy?"

"Well, not right now."

Gretel raised an eyebrow.

"Ugh." Hansel shook his head. "You have no problem arguing with me, but when it comes to Mila you..." His voice drifted. "Melt. And you shouldn't. *That's* what I meant by squishy."

Gretel pulse thrummed through her skull as she kicked another rock. It sailed through the air before arcing down and disappearing into the shadow of the canyon.

"You think you can change her, but the truth is Mila hates us," Hansel continued, voice sharp. "She's two-faced. She only likes Father for his money and as soon as that runs out, he'll see—"

"We just have to win her over." Gretel whirled; voice tight. "Be patient, kind. Work hard." It's what their mother had taught them before she died. That the universe would give back what you put into it, so the kinder she was—

"Be kind?" Hansel laughed. "Try telling that to Mila next time she publicly announces your weigh—hey, slow down. This path is tricky."

"She's speeding up." Gretel's feet skidded as she braced herself against the canyon wall. Mila had slipped into the shadows again, almost disappearing. "If we lose her, we'll get lost."

"On a tiny, abandoned mining moon?"

Even if the moon was small, Gretel didn't want to risk it. She slapped a hand to the side of her helmet to adjust the commlink, so Mila was reconnected. "Mila, we can't keep up. Can you please slow down?"

But Mila didn't answer. She was thirty paces ahead and twisting past stones as if it were as easy as dancing.

"Come on." Gretel tugged Hansel, but as she eased around

the rockface her foot caught on something and she tumbled—taking Hansel with her.

"Gah!"

Down, down they careened over each other, helmets knocking, dust pluming as they rocketed down the canyon, rocks jabbing, flying past Mila. Gretel's helmet smacked against a boulder. She felt for Hansel's hand. He groaned next to her.

"You okay?"

Hansel shook his head, fingering a small tear in his suit and then fumbling at his pockets for a patch. Gretel cursed and fumbled with her own. "Mila! We have to go back."

But their stepmother wasn't coming. She wasn't moving at all.

Gretel pulled a frayed patch from her pocket and slapped it to Hansel's suit. It'd hold, but the real damage was already done; precious oxygen leaked. He needed to get back on the ship. Now.

"Mila!" Anger flooded as Gretel scrambled to confront her stepmother. But something of shadow and starlight shifted above and Gretel glanced skyward. Her breath caught. The outline of a familiar ship was slipping past the surface. Silent as space always is, none of them had heard their ship take off. Icy dread slipped down Gretel's throat. How could their ship leave if the moon was abandoned, if Mila was—

But Mila was flickering. Gretel limped to her feet and swept a hand across Mila's middle. Her hand went straight through, closing around a palm-sized floating sphere. A holo. Heat boiled in Gretel's chest. She wanted to crush the stupid tech but stowed it in her suit. If they survived this, she would show Father the evidence. Mila had planned this.

"Guess you were right." Hansel's voice wavered, almost a laugh. "We uh, shouldn't have lost sight of her. The real her, anyway."

Clenching her fists, Gretel stared at the empty canyon, at the old domed outpost still at least a mile out. "We have to get down there. Maybe they left a radio, and we could call for help." At least they could leave a message to tell Father what Mila had done.

"And our oxygen?"

Gretel swallowed. "Maybe… maybe they left some canisters there, too." She tried to force conviction into her voice, but it twanged anyway. She'd share what she had, but without help, the result would be the same. They'd die here. And no one, on Onworld or off it, would know what had happened to them.

———

They picked their way down the canyon. Hansel's suit kept alarming that his oxygen levels were dangerously low—at 10%, then 5%—and Gretel's breath came in loud puffs, eating away at her oxygen as well. To conserve air, Hansel quit talking, but Gretel cursed loudly, furiously sending out a signal to Mila. But Mila wasn't responding.

After a solid fifteen minutes of sending curses into nothingness, Gretel quieted and focused on picking her way down the canyon, glaring at the old outpost until the canyon quit and the ground leveled.

"Do you think Father will come?" Hansel spoke suddenly, staring up at the stars, at the blanket of space they'd soon suffocate and die under. Could Father see those same stars from Onworld? Or had daylight blinded him of them?

"He'll come. He always does." *Eventually,* Gretel silently added, then shook her head. She needed to believe.

Before Mila, Gretel wouldn't have questioned Father's affections. Father had loved Gretel and Hansel and had doted over his twins after their mother died. He'd taught them how to spacewalk, use longwave radio, and fly their tiny cruiser ship. They'd stargaze, discuss important things—and unimportant ones—like how both dark and bright space was and how their mother had named them after twin stars.

Gretel *Pollux* Bitten and Hansel *Castor* Bitten.

But once Father had met Mila, everything changed. Father started making dangerous trips to Onworld to pay for their new 'needs,' for Mila's trendy Homestation apartment and upscale social events. She claimed it was for Hansel and Gretel's benefit, that through her new social network she could negotiate good career matches for the twins—but really all the sacrifice was for herself.

Once Dad's Onworld trips had started, the twins hardly saw him. His stretches on Onworld grew longer and longer. At first, Father had made an effort to make sure the twins knew he cared. When Hansel and Gretel were little, he'd brought home surprises. Usually, it was hard candies or chocolates, but some-times he'd brought carved wood toys or pressed flowers and leaves. Those were Gretel's favorites. She'd kept a book that marked his various specimens. Roses, daisies, and forget-me-nots; oak, myrtle, and cherry.

Whenever she missed Father, she'd pull out the book, rub a finger over the soft petals, and imagine a world where green things grew from the ground, where fathers never left, where step parents loved their children.

Gretel blinked fiercely and kept her head down. As they trekked toward the dome its features became clearer. The dome was the size of a mini rotating station, coated in thick dust. The old mining equipment lay scattered outside it and looked to be as abandoned as they'd been. Hopefully the dome had some decent equipment left inside it so they could… Gretel stopped. She pinched her eyes shut, then looked again.

Hansel had stopped too. "Is that—"

"Condensation," Gretel finished. Her heart squeezed with hope. Condensation meant the dome was pressurized, that this outpost wasn't built *just* for mining, but—"Hansel, that dome is a biosphere!"

She grabbed Hansel's arm and, together, they broke into a run. Gretel slapped her helmet, trying to hail and communicate with the dome. Nothing but dead signal, but it didn't matter if they were alone here. It only mattered that they could survive. That there was oxygen. The radio—the rest—they could figure out after.

Gretel made it to the dome first, sliding her hands along the transparent exterior, squinting past the fog at the rambling vegetation inside. She banged on the walls. No movement.

Hansel's breathing grew ragged as he tried to peek around her. "Do you. See. Anyone?" The run had taken too much out of him and now he was down to the last dregs of air. Tough moon-rock or not, he was dying.

"No." Gretel's heart skipped. "I—I'll try to hack the door."

"There." He motioned and she helped him to where an old airlock stuck out at a crooked angle. Gretel fumbled with the ancient keypad, but nothing happened.

"Pull off. The facing." Hansel huffed, motioning to the plastic covering.

Gretel obeyed, removing the exterior, and under his direction, began toying with the wires. Her throat constricted, fears mounting as his oxygen alarm blared at 1%. Hansel was better at hacking systems, but in his oxygen-deprived state, she had to handle this and fast. His words became even more sparse, until he lay on the ground, motionless.

"Hansel? What do I do?"

He didn't respond.

Gretel dropped the wires, panic rising as she knelt beside him. "Hansel. Hansel!"

"Hello," a woman's voice crackled through their comms.

"Is someone there?" Gretel spun, searching.

"I'm in the biodome," the woman's voice crackled again. "Come inside, quickly. I've been expecting you."

———

The doors *shoomed* open and Gretel dragged Hansel inside. As the airlock decompressed, she shook Hansel lightly. "We made it, just hold on."

The airlock beeped, signaling it was safe to breathe, and Gretel ripped off Hansel's helmet. He still didn't move.

But someone else did. An old woman strode into the airlock. Her eyes bulged under tinted goggles and a length of frizzy white hair poked from underneath a lopsided helmet. A lab coat, smeared with a rainbow of neon colors—like she'd lost some sort of paint fight—swished at her sides.

Gretel scooted and made room for the woman to kneel beside her. "He isn't breathing."

The woman squatted and shoved a finger against Hansel's neck. Then she moved to his chest. "He's breathing, girl, but barely. I'll hook him up to some high flow oxygen and get a medbot to look him over. Stay here in the main dome, don't wander, and keep out of my way." And as if Hansel were a sack of freeze-dried fruit, the old woman shouldered him and carted him from the entry.

"I'm sorry, but who are you?"

"Doctor Bedlam. Now, please, give me space."

But Gretel didn't. She followed Doctor Bedlam into the large dome, where vegetation loomed. Leaves the size of Gretel's face pressed against the walls. Bright flowers and fruits dangled from branches as a musky scent descended. Sweat beaded Gretel's brow, the room hot and sticky; but even as her eyes stung with perspiration, they remained on her brother's still form which bounced against the woman's back.

"Is he going to be okay?"

"Allow me room to work."

"Doctor Bedlam, I need to—"

The woman whirled. "If you do as I say, I promise your brother will be fine. But if you don't give me space to work—"

"I—I'll leave you alone." Gretel took a step back, held up her hands. Clearly the woman was a recluse. Still. Gretel took one step forward. "Just… Take care of him."

"Of course." Doctor Bedlam nodded.

But as the doctor slipped into the shadows, an overwhelming panic seemed to rise in Gretel's throat.

Father had left them for Mila, his twin stars eclipsed by the brightness of an Onworld sun. Would Hansel burn out and leave her too?

———

Anxious and jittery, Gretel settled herself under what looked to be an oak tree. Not that she'd seen an oak tree, but the leaves matched Father's Onworld specimen. She tried to slow her breathing, inhaling the strange soupy mix of scents that permeated the dome. Sweet. Musty. Musky. The smells roiled in Gretel, turning her stomach and making her gag.

She busied her hands by digging into her pockets and pulled out the round holo Mila had tricked them with. Stupid. Gretel swallowed the bile that had risen in the back of her throat and cursed to herself as she traced the sleek exterior, wondering where Mila had gotten the holo and its cost. Unlike the hodge-podge equipment they usually used, Mila had spent some serious credit on this thing. Frowning, Gretel turned the metal machine over and ran a finger over the controls when it buzzed, flashing.

Gretel jumped, dropping it, as Mila reappeared. The woman tousled her hair and smirked, igniting a fiery fury in Gretel. Gretel growled and punched a hand through Mila's middle. Pain lanced Gretel's hand as the image shattered. Howling as the holo clattered to the ground, Gretel clutched her hand to her chest. The skin had split over one of her knuckles that had contacted the metal sphere. Gretel pressed the wound to her mouth and sucked hard, trying to ebb the pain. Stupid. She cursed again and stepped forward to kick the holo. It had landed in a clump of little yellow flowers.

But as she pulled her leg back, she stopped herself. If they got out of this, Gretel still wanted proof of Mila's treachery. Clenching her teeth, she plucked the holo from the ground. Her hands shook as she lifted it to her chest, but the underside felt wet. She rotated the little machine to wipe it clean, but a splattered streak of neon purple caught her eye. Purple? Gretel's brow knit. Where did the purple come from? Gretel wiped the mess away before pocketing the holo, then bent down and studied the clump of tiny flowers, searching for the source of the purple substance. Her fingers fumbled against the soft flower petals where scattered bits of purple splatter remained. She spread the plants apart to study the dirt. Nothing.

Frowning, Gretel plucked a flower and turned over the stem. Here, a bright bit of purple liquid leaked. She milked the stem and more fluid oozed onto her fingers. Gretel rubbed at the strange sticky substance, curiosity growing. What kind of plant was this? It certainly wasn't like the specimens Father brought from Onworld.

Questions swirled through Gretel's brain. This place was supposed to be abandoned, off-grid. Why create a biosphere here, alone? And the woman had said something about expecting Hansel and Gretel. Why? Gretel pocketed the flower; trepidation curdled inside her stomach.

Doctor Bedlam had said to stay put, but Gretel needed to send a message to Father. And to do that, she needed to explore the dome.

———

Adrenaline pulsed through Gretel's body as she stalked through the dome, searching for communication equipment. But there seemed to be far more foliage than visible tech.

The biosphere housed cacti and banana bushes, fan palms

and grapevines. Every plant was different, a growing contradiction, and Gretel had never imagined such diversity could be wrapped in the same biosphere. A desert was a desert, a jungle was a jungle. How could opposite plants coexist in the same environment? Flourish even?

Something banged and began whirring, as if a mechanical ventilation system had kicked on. That caught Gretel's attention. She changed course and ran toward the vibrations, but as she pushed her way through prickly bushes and knotty undergrowth, Gretel heard something new. Running water?

She followed the sound of hums and trickles until she was somewhere near the center of the dome. Here, a huge fountain bubbled with a viscous purple and blue liquid. Steam rose from the center and a strong heady scent spilled out. A dingy machine with a long bench sat beside the fountain, a long chain hanging over it. On the ground beside the machine were what could only be described as plant corpses in the most brilliant colors. Emerald. Gold. Turquoise. Maroon.

Grimacing, Gretel stepped over the corpses and toward the machine, eyeing the controls. Maybe she could send a signal with this? If Hansel were awake, he surely could. He knew how to hodge-podge anything and—

Suddenly there was the *thump* of boots and Gretel fumbled backward. Doctor Bedlam was pushing past the branches of a pair of hazelnut bushes. She fiddled with her goggles; eyes magnified behind the lenses, but then she caught sight of Gretel and her smile faded. "I thought I told you to stay put."

"I'm sorry." Gretel's face flushed. "I just wanted to send Father a message."

The doctor frowned. "My system is encrypted, and I don't use this one for communications."

Gretel didn't answer as the woman stepped forward.

"I suppose it doesn't matter. I needed to bring you here anyway. This pool allows me to play with the plants." She gestured around the dome. "Do you like them?"

Gretel nodded politely but dismissed further talk of unauthorized communications or plant pools. "How's Hansel?"

"He's fine." Doctor Bedlam rubbed her nose. "A medbot is with him."

"I need to see him." Gretel started forward but Doctor Bedlam caught her arm.

"You can't yet."

"But you said—"

"Please." The woman's hands dug into Gretel's shoulder. "If you want your brother to survive, you must listen."

Gretel's brow knit. "You said he was fine."

"Yes." Doctor Bedlam released her grip, eyeing Gretel seriously. "But it isn't his injuries he'll succumb to, dear."

Gretel's eyes widened. "What do you mean?"

"Your stepmother, Mila, dropped you off at my doorstep. Answered my ad. Said you were a good girl. Compliant. Malleable."

Marshmallow. Gretel's face twisted as her brother's taunt burned against her brain. She shook her head, refocusing. "What ad?"

"I'm a matchmaker. And my latest young specimen successfully captured the heart of the galaxy's most eligible bachelor. Leonard DePruit. Charming man, with a bit of a thing for blondes."

Gretel touched her very brown, very frizzy hair.

"Unfortunately, little Miss Ella got cold feet. After all my hard work, she ran away. Hid herself on a loading dock and met the wrong side of a blaster engine. Now she's cinder-Ella. Ha, ha."

"That's terrible."

"What's terrible is I never collected my fee and poor DePruit is alone. He's under the impression Miss Ella was kidnapped. He offered a handsome reward for her return. I intend to fix this."

Gretel took a step back. "What do you mean?"

"Oh, keep up, dear. Mila said you were agreeable, not thick."

Doctor Bedlam gestured around the dome. "Many of these trees had similar parents, similar futures before I started dabbling in their genetic codes. I've made them much more interesting. I'll do the same for you. One skinny dip in this gene pool, and you'll be dancing with DePruit in no time. We'll split the reward, ninety-ten." She gave Gretel a look. "Ten being the worth of your brother's life, of course."

"You're threatening Hansel?"

"I prefer to think of it as high-stakes negotiations. But if you want to call it threatening…"

For a split-second Gretel considered charging at the woman. She was old, crazy, and Gretel was young. Except, she'd carried Hansel so easily. Her stomach knotted. "If you want to trick DePruit out of his money, why not alter yourself to look like that poor young woman?"

Doctor Bedlam laughed. "I *have* altered myself. Gave myself stamina, a sturdier physique. I won't do it again. I'd risk over-mutating my DNA. But don't worry. You have a similar build to young Ella before I altered her. Mila sent your code and I've prepared the proper pool to make a new version of DePruit's lady-love."

"No. Mila would tell you I'm unfit to be anyone's lady—"

"You want me to listen to Mila?" Doctor Bedlam tutted, adjusted her goggles. "Listen here, girl. Mila did more than abandon you today. She stole all of your Father's savings and made a run for it. He doesn't know you're here and if you don't play along, he'll never see you again. Now, I could force you into that little pool, but both our lives would be much easier if I didn't have to. Besides, think of what I'm offering. Security. Wealth. A better life… your *brother's* life."

Gretel wrung her hands, the weight of Bedlam's bargain bearing down on her, crushing like a black hole. She didn't see an escape, but if she could buy some time…

"I want to see Hansel first. If he's okay then—then I'll do whatever you want."

Doctor Bedlam smiled. "Perfect. I'll prepare your new cage."

———

The room Doctor Bedlam took Gretel to was small and cluttered. Cracked pots, seeds, and dirt were strewn across the floor, shards of pottery crunched underfoot. A line of rusty metal cabinets was on one side of the wall, but on the other was a dusty cot and—

"Hansel!" Gretel burst forward and threw her arms around him. A medbot buzzed above, beeping as it continued checking vitals. Hansel laughed, pulling back. His face was pale, and he was breathing heavily, but he was alive.

He was alive!

He brushed Gretel's hair from her face. "Gret, are you okay?"

"She's fine." Doctor Bedlam's voice was short. "And you need to rest. Gretel, you've seen him. Now come with—"

"In a moment," Gretel snapped. "I want to check him over first."

Doctor Bedlam scowled, face reddening as if she were holding her breath. After about ten seconds she let it out. "Fine. I'll check the pool and be back in five minutes. Be ready. There's a robe in the closet there, you'll need to be properly dressed. Five minutes." The door snapped shut and Gretel heard the distinct click of a lock. Not as if Bedlam needed one. This biosphere was prison enough.

"What's that about?" Hansel sat taller, brow knitting. "I've never heard you talk to anyone like that. Except me." He winked.

"She hasn't hurt you?" Gretel looked him over.

"Why would she hurt me?" Hansel's eyes narrowed. "Has she hurt you?"

"No." Gretel shook her head. "At least, not yet." And then she explained what Mila had done; what Doctor Bedlam intended to do.

"You can't agree to this." Hansel's voice was firm.

"I know." Her mind whirled as an idea clicked into place. "But I—I think I have a plan."

———

When Doctor Bedlam returned, Gretel didn't put up a fuss. Her hair hung in a frazzled mess against the dingy white robe she'd found in the closet. But when Doctor Bedlam reached for her, Gretel recoiled. "Don't touch me!" Gretel glanced at her brother, who mouthed the word *moonrock*. Gretel lowered her voice. "You don't have to drag me out like a dog."

"As long as you heel, child." Doctor Bedlam frowned but motioned her forward. "You'll be able to earn some freedom. Just don't make this difficult."

Hansel waved goodbye and silently Gretel followed the old woman out of the room and into the muggy biosphere. The plants loomed overhead, vegetation thick and overly perfumed, shadows bold. The fountain bubbled.

"Over there," Doctor Bedlam muttered as she directed Gretel to what looked like a giant rusty birdcage hanging beside the pool. "Now toss the robe there. Good."

Doctor Bedlam stepped forward and slid the bars shut. She smirked as the naked Gretel shivered inside the cage. "The pool's warm and it doesn't take long for the change to start. Just stay still."

Gretel wrapped her arms over her chest, then stilled, as Doctor Bedlam circled the pool, situating herself at the control box. The cage rattled, moved over the pool, then lowered, and the viscous liquid enveloped Gretel up to her neck. A riot of color swirled against her skin, fizzing.

Doctor Bedlam paced, her gaze lingering on Gretel. But Gretel's round face never slimmed, and her brown hair only coiled against the nape of her neck. After fifteen minutes in the pool, Doctor Bedlam cranked the cage back up and over, then motioned a stumbling Gretel out. But Gretel stayed crouched in the cage, her wet hair plastered against her skin.

"I need a sample to check what's wrong, child."

"I don't trust you."

"Come now." Doctor Bedlam held out a hand, stepping into the cage. "You don't want Hansel t—"

Crash! Bedlam was pushed inside, slamming into—and then through—Gretel. Bedlam smacked the bars on the other side. "What?" Doctor Bedlam fumbled as the cage door clicked shut.

Gretel fizzled and then disappeared. There was a rattling sound as a plastic holo device rolled through the bars at the bottom of the cage.

The real Gretel stood outside. She picked up the holo, eyes triumphant. "I think it's time we revisit that bargain, Doctor Bedlam."

———

Hansel was still winded but better when Gretel brought him into the open dome. Doctor Bedlam hung in the birdcage, scowling down at them, a string of slippery promises dripping from her lips. "I can make this better. Please, give me a chance."

But Gretel threatened to lower the cage if Bedlam didn't hush and that silenced her.

Hansel situated himself at the control panel, hacking through the communication system, rerouting the signal. Gretel dictated the messages.

An hour later, the replies started, and both twins knew it was over.

Father would rush from Onworld. DePruit would rush from his world. And a slew of undercover detectives and intergalactic peacekeeping officers would rush from theirs. Mila, well, she wouldn't be rushing anywhere anytime soon, once they impounded her ship. Between the twins' testimonies, the dome, Mila's transaction history, and the holo records, there was enough evidence of abuse, fraud, and neglect to lock Mila up for good. Doctor Bedlam too.

"You okay?" Hansel kept one eye on the swinging birdcage as he approached Gretel, who sat under the oak tree, fidgeting.

Gretel's stomach twisted, still reeling from the adrenaline rush. "I don't know," she said. She didn't look up, rolling the little yellow flower she'd picked earlier between two fingers. When she'd remembered it, she'd thought maybe it would make a specimen for Father's book. But the plant came out of her pocket crushed, broken, and limp. Too malleable.

A marshmallow like her.

Gretel frowned. "I know Mila deserves what's coming, but it still makes me feel wrong and rotten that things went this far. Father sounded crushed."

Hansel shrugged. "Because he blames himself for Mila abandoning us."

"That's not his fault. She kept things hidden and didn't let—"

"It's not your fault either, Gret."

Gretel swallowed, touching the flower to her forehead as she closed her eyes. "I just—I just wanted her to like us."

"I know." Hansel crouched beside her, shaking his head. Then he took the flower from Gretel's hand. She watched as he twirled the bent flower. He spoke slowly, "But Mom was right about what you put out into the universe. Maybe things don't always come back the way we think they should, but goodness still makes the universe a better place."

Gretel shivered.

"It's not bad to care about people. I'm grateful you cared about me." Hansel pressed the flower back into her hand. "But you're not *all* marshmallow, Gret. And I'm not all moonrock." He squeezed her but when she didn't respond his voice turned serious. "You saved me, Gret. You saved *us*. That's pretty hardcore."

Gretel gave a small smile. "I couldn't lose my only brother."

"Your *best* brother," he corrected.

"Right." She smiled. Just this once, she could agree that he was *best* instead of *only*. She leaned into him and as they waited for their father and the authorities, silence enveloped.

Above the musky leaves and the fogged biodome, the black blanket of space loomed heavy with promise. Homestation was hours away, Father farther still.

But he was coming for them.

He loved them.

And Gretel's marshmallow heart was bursting to greet him.

BEAUTY SLEEPING IN THE SILENCE OF SPACE

LENA NG

Pilot Huang sat alone in the darkened quiet of the navigation vessel, the background noise the hum of the engine, the clicks of the switches he toggled, the tapping of the keyboard. The glow of the screens gave his pallid skin a green hue. Through the window was the cocoon of space, brightened by pinpoints of light by far away stars.

He hummed to himself. It was the four-hundredth day alone in his vessel, navigating the uncharted waters in the ocean of space, one of many lone explorers who had volunteered to spend three years mapping a miniscule corner of the universe. He had read some of the books, watched all the entertainment videos. Sometimes he said the dialogue out loud, to have someone other than himself to talk to.

Different from the light of the stars, a strange flash caught his attention. An object drifted ghost-like in front of the vessel, oblong as a casket. It had no lights, just a clear glass box, coffin-shaped. He watched the object floating for several minutes, then out of the same curiosity that made him volunteer for this mission he donned his exterior suit, checked the oxygen gauges, slipped on the boots, and headed to the decompression chamber. He attached the lifeline that tethered him to the ship.

His breathing sounded heavy in the helmet as he drifted to the floating box. At first, he thought it was a dead body, but a small movement told him something had to be alive. He saw a shape within. His headlamp was not bright enough to see what it could be.

Pilot Huang turned on the jet pack and guided the object back to the ship. After he removed his gear, he stared at the creature encased in glass. He recoiled at the fleshy mass, the body sticky with mucous, the array of thick arm-width tentacles radiating from the round meat core. He was about to blast it back into space, but watched its rhythmic breathing instead.

He took a cloth and cleaned the exterior of the glass cage. The alien's skin was glistening purple, shifting in color like a living oil slick. The colors swirled. After several hours of staring, Pilot Huang went to sleep.

The glow from the casket woke him. It had a buzz and it sounded like words.

Pilot Huang pressed his ear to the box. He turned his head, the glass chill against his lips. "What do you want me to do?" A glow of patterns colored the oily skin. It reminded Pilot Huang of the fireworks on the Fourth of July, of the lights on the Christmas tree in his home of many years ago.

More hours passed.

Pilot Huang dragged his fingers on the glass. An answering fleshy fingertip moved from the other side, like holding hands. Pilot Huang smiled. The meat mass was the most beautiful thing he had ever seen.

The large squid-shaped eyes opened. They were violet and the shade changed depending on the angle. Sleeping Beauty was now awake. In a series of clicks and purrs, it sang a song. The meat centre opened and inside was a beak.

Pilot Huang moved his hand along the bottom edge of the casket until he felt a button. Escaping air hissed as the top of the box opened. He moved his face closer to the meat core and breathed the same air. He pressed his lips against the beak, wincing as a tentacle punctured him beneath his ribs, as cold eggs were implanted inside his abdominal cavity. He wrapped his arms around his waist as the puncture was sealed.

Pilot Huang hummed a lullaby. It was important to sing to the brood. He had heard a story that his offspring would recognize his voice when they burst out of him once they were born.

THE BLUE FAIRY

SHAWN POLLOCK

Nova Collodi hunched over the table in the center of the interrogation room, avoiding Detective Chapman's glare as he asked, "Do you want to go to prison? Because you're looking at a lot of prison time right now, and Martian prisons are no joke."

Nova gripped the sides of her chair to calm her shaking hands. The New Philadelphia police had burst into Oxy Good Times, the oxygen bar where she worked, and hustled her into their hover car without a word of explanation. Merus had shot her a questioning look from the reception desk as she left. She'd be lucky if he was only curious instead of furious when she returned to work.

She wouldn't be back today, though. The officers who arrested Nova had taken her phone, deposited her alone in this room, and shut the door. No clock on the walls, only her beating heart and growling stomach to mark off the seconds. By the time Chapman finally appeared, she guessed she'd been there hours.

A word scratched in the gray metal tabletop caught her eye. *SOS.* She knew the feeling. "No, I don't want to go to prison."

Chapman stomped to the far wall and shut off every panel in the room's glowing plasma ceiling. They winked out one by one, until only a single bulb shone directly in Nova's face.

"Then answer my question," Chapman said. His heavy frame dropped into the chair across the table from Nova. "Why do they call you The Blue Fairy?"

She took a deep breath and tried not to sound impatient—or worse, scared—but the light lancing her eyes made it hard to compose her thoughts. "I told you. Someone at Oxy Good Times hung it on me." She shook a lock of her dyed blue hair at Chapman.

"Still holding out, huh?" Chapman shoved a photo across the tabletop. "Look at it."

Nova picked up the picture. Shattered windows along a storefront.

"Jewelry store robbery," Chapman said. He handed her another, this one of a man clutching a bloody rag to his head as someone led him through a crowd. "Riot at a political rally." In a third, immense black clouds billowed over a wall of flame. "Rocket fuel depot, burned by anti-settlement activists."

Chapman took back the photos and spread them in the pool of light. "Do you know how they were able to do it?"

Nova shook her head.

"Sure, you do." Chapman spat the words at her, his face hard. "When you clothe an android in synthetic human flesh, it can infiltrate anywhere and do anything. Getting out alive means nothing to it. That's why you're in serious trouble."

"I just work at Oxy Good Times."

"Doc Fox says you're a synth flesh cook," Chapman said. "That you're the one they call The Blue Fairy, so don't deny it."

Nova breathed in through her nose, held it, and blew it out her mouth, which did nothing to calm her pounding heart.

Chapman sprang from his chair, which fell with a clatter that stung Nova's ears. She glanced nervously at the electronic mirror shimmering on the wall. If it was a one-way observation window, she hoped someone on the other side was watching the burly detective come around the table to loom over her.

"You'll talk if I have to make you talk." He reached back with a thick fist and Nova squeezed her eyes shut.

The door flew open. Another cop rushed in. "Chapman! Stop!" He slapped the panel on the wall to switch on all the lights.

Chapman sneered, but he lowered his fist. "Freak. Maybe you're not a synth cook. Maybe you're just a small-time punk. I could lock you up in County while I look into your record. Might take me six months. You want that? Lose your job, lose your home?"

"Chapman!" the other cop shouted again.

Chapman locked his eyes on Nova as he backed into the hallway. "I'm not done with you." He slammed the door.

The new cop shook his head. "Sorry about that." He righted the chair Chapman had knocked over and sat in it. Reclined, actually, like they were on a date in a restaurant lined with white brick and one-way mirrors. "I'm Detective Medich."

He was tall and trim, with a brush cut and a smooth face. Though he wore the same detective uniform—dress shirt, tie, and communication lapel button—he and Chapman couldn't have been more different.

He placed a soda on the table, beads of water speckling the can's frosty surface. Nova's tongue scraped the insides of her teeth.

"I figured you could use that," Medich said.

Nova managed a wan smile as she popped open the can. The soda sparkled on her tongue and down her throat. It lifted her enough that she dared ask, "What time is it?"

"Not too late," Medich said. "Whoever's waiting for you at home will hardly miss you."

The AI home management program in her apartment—people who owned them called them "house brains"—would switch on the lights at six o'clock. It would detect the tap of little claws on the floor, know Frankie was there, and fill his dish.

"I don't want to leave my dog alone too long," Nova said.

The house brain wouldn't know how to interpret the increasingly skittish sound of those claws as they traced a path between the bedroom and the front door. Nova could imagine them clicking back and forth, faster and faster as the hour grew later with no sign of her. The brain had no lap to pull Frankie onto, no hands to stroke his shaking sides, no voice to soothe him until he calmed down and knew everything was all right.

"Okay, let's work together and get this over with," Medich said. "And I do apologize for Chapman. He's not a bad person. He lost his son about ten years ago, and I think it changed him."

"Oh? How did that happen?" Nova didn't want to get familiar with cops, but the dead ought to be remembered. *Loreena…*

"Embolism on a rocket trip from Earth," Medich said. "A one-in-a-million freak occurrence. You know how they say rocket is the safest mode of travel? That's gotta sting Chapman. The kid was only in grade school. But anyway, let's not talk about that. Tell me about yourself."

"Nova Collodi. Born 7-30-2104—"

Medich waved a dismissive hand. "No need for that. We're just sorting out some things." He shifted on his chair. "You said they call you The Blue Fairy at Oxy Good Times. Because of your hair, right?"

"Yeah. I guess someone thought it looked cute."

Medich grinned. Dimples punctuated his cheeks. "I never tried an oxygen bar. What's it like?"

"We take care of people, especially the Earth transplants who are trying to get used to Martian atmosphere," Nova said. "Some people end up needing it like coffee." She tilted the soda can and drained it.

"Do you like it there?"

The pay wasn't great, especially in a place like New Philadelphia with its stark divide between the monied and working classes. But when Loreena died of Martian flu two years ago, the other Oxy girls took her place as Nova's sisters. They held Nova when she cried, made sure she ate and slept enough, and stood by her until the pain subsided to the ache she carried now. Trying to put those feelings into words made her eyes well up, so she said nothing until Medich broke the silence.

"Hmm. Now, on one hand, you don't have so much as a customer complaint at Oxy," he said. "On the other hand, Chapman did say you've been named as one of Doc Fox's synth flesh cooks. Maybe you can tell me why your name would come up in relation to Fox's."

Fox, balding and fifty-ish, ran a candy factory and brought the Oxy staff chocolates for Settlement Day and Christmas. The oxygen mask always left an indent in the bridge of his bulbous nose. "All I know is, he's one of our regulars," Nova said.

Medich pulled an electronic tablet from his pocket and wrote something on it. "Does he ever talk about anything political? Anti-immigration, terrorism, like that?"

"Not that I've overheard. People don't usually talk with the mask on anyway."

"Well, Chapman isn't going to let go of the idea that you're part of Fox's network, and I'm not sure what to do about that. Maybe if you gave me something, some names of your other regulars, that would help."

"Look, if I thought anyone was being subversive, I'd say so. But I can't just throw out customer names. That would be bad for business, and it's not right."

"I can respect that," Medich said. "I think I know what would help Chapman settle down, though. Would you be willing to take a lie detector test? I bet we could clear this up and get you out of here."

"I guess so."

Medich pressed his lapel button. "Bring it in."

An Asian woman in a lab coat entered holding the hand of what appeared to be a small boy. But the featureless silver skin and glowing red eyes meant android.

"What's that for?" Nova asked.

"Freaky, isn't it?" the woman said as she dropped the android's hand. Her name tag said *Masae*. "You'll have a hard time lying to this thing."

The robot held out its hand to Nova, who raised her eyebrows at Medich. "Take it," Medich said.

"How is this a lie detector?"

"There's a sensor in its palm that detects your body temperature, sweat level, and heart rate," Masae said. "Just like the old electrode polygraphs, but those were easy for experienced liars to beat. This thing adds a fluster factor that trips up even the pros."

Nova grabbed the metallic hand. Cold. Masae leaned against the wall by the electronic mirror.

Medich picked up the tablet again. "Keep hold of it while I ask you each question." He cleared his throat. "Is your name Nova Collodi?"

The android's red eyes transfixed Nova. *Not eyes, just lights,* she told herself without believing it. "Yes." Even her own name rang false with that thing looking at her.

"Are you twenty-four?"

"Yes."

"Were you born in New Philadelphia?"

"Yes."

"Do you work at Oxy Good Times?"

"Yes."

"Is that an oxygen bar?"

"Yes."

"Are you known there as The Blue Fairy?"

"Yes."

"Do you know a man named Jack 'Doc' Fox?"

"Yes."

"Have you ever overcharged a customer at Oxy Good Times?"

"No."

The android's eyes flared bright, and its nose extended half an inch. This small motion startled Nova so much, she had to stop herself from flinging away the metallic hand.

"That's how I know you're lying," Medich said. "It's theatrical, but there's no denying when you fail a question. I'll ask again. Have you ever overcharged a customer?"

Nova wished she still had the soda. "Y-yes."

"Have you ever charged a customer for pure oxygen and given them an inferior mix?"

Nova hesitated. The robotic eyes bored into her, daring her to answer. "Uh, yes." She and the other Oxy girls did do that sometimes, as a little revenge on rude customers.

"You see, it's better when you're honest with me," Medich said. "Are you a synth flesh cook?"

"No," Nova said. She waited. The android didn't move.

Medich's voice grew harder. "Are you an associate of known subversive Jack 'Doc' Fox?"

"No."

"Have you ever created androids for the purpose of carrying out robberies or acts of terrorism?"

"No."

Medich steered the next few questions back toward Nova's life before returning to the subject of Doc Fox and synth flesh. Nova denied anything to do with android crime. She also decided she wouldn't ask how Medich knew about the oxygen mix scam. She'd certainly never try it again.

Finally, Medich said, "Okay, you can let go now."

Nova dropped the android's hand and flexed her stiff, aching fingers. Her palm had turned red where she'd gripped the metal hand.

"You passed the test, but I wouldn't leave the city for a few weeks," Medich said. The last of the friendliness had drained from his voice. "We might want to talk to you again."

———

Outside, the Martian sun had set. Earth hung over the eastern horizon, Jupiter a bright eye gazing down on the nighttime bustle of New Philadelphia. Nova hurried away from the police station on tired legs. *Hang on, Frankie. Just one more thing to do and I'll be home.*

She walked along Wilder Avenue, where a faint ozone smell blew from the hover cars rushing past. A driver flicked a cigarette butt out his window. As quickly as it landed, a robotic mouse shot across the sidewalk, snatched the butt, and dropped it in a sanitation hole.

Turning onto a narrow side street, Nova switched off the locator in her phone to dismiss the floating light that accompanied pedestrians. Before her, the street disappeared into darkness. She followed it until it ended at a parking garage.

Just inside the garage entrance, two red orbs glowed from the face of a short, silver-skinned android. And behind the android, barely more than an outline in the shadows, a stocky, hard-faced man.

"Okay, Blue Fairy, I did my part," Chapman said. "I'll steer Medich away as best I can."

Nova glanced at Chapman's hands, no longer fists, but the memory remained. "Yes, you certainly did your part."

"Sorry about the whole 'bad cop' routine. That's the way Medich and I always play it, and he would've gotten suspicious if I'd held back."

"So, Doc only named me because he knew you'd be the one on the case?" Nova asked. Doc said she could trust Chapman, but the way the detective had stormed into the interrogation room, she'd worried someone in Fox's organization had actually sold her out.

"Right," Chapman said. "He had to throw us a name because the PD is really cracking down on android crime, but passing the test today should keep you in the clear. As long as you hold up your end of the deal, that is." He handed Nova an envelope. "Will these work?"

Nova opened the envelope and pulled out a data chip, along with several photos of a freckled, sandy-haired boy. Front and side views of his face, close-ups, full body images. He wore a missing-tooth grin in all of them. "These will be fine," she said. "But won't the police department miss their lie detector?"

"We have two, and I'm in charge of both. I'll file a damage report on one and order a replacement."

Chapman held a shopping bag filled with child-sized clothing. He looked inside a long moment before placing it on the ground. "I had to recalibrate him so he wouldn't react to any mention of Fox or synth flesh during your test. Is that going to be a problem?"

"No, we'll override calibration and upload your son's vocal file from the chip. Fox can do the 3D imaging at the same time, then I'll formulate the synth flesh. Once that's done, we'll expedite the cladding and curing." Nova picked up the bag. "And dress him."

"Great." Chapman nudged the android forward.

Nova searched the cop's square, lined face for any sign of conflict, any indication he might change his mind and arrest her right there.

She risked the law all the time, of course. That was the price of going to work for Doc Fox after her sister died.

But on that terrible day, Nova had decided that learning the black-market android business was worth being able to live well in an expensive city. She could afford a nice one-bedroom place, no roommates except Frankie and the house brain, no crowding six to an apartment like some of the other Oxy girls, where bugs like Martian flu had an easier time infecting people. She'd mourn if Merus fired her, but not for her pay.

Sometimes she felt like she'd sold not only her effort, but her soul. After all, she created illegal androids for thieves, activists— even for a crime boss who wanted a body double in case someone took a shot at him. Chapman, with a cop's mandate to clean up New Philadelphia, must have felt like he was selling his now.

But every sale bought something, and Chapman's expression only showed hope for a soul well spent.

The android approached Nova and extended its hand. Nova took it. "By the end of the week I should have him turned into a real boy."

THE ADVENTURES OF SEVERIN MILES, TFC.

TIFFANIE GRAY

Severin Miles stood, hands in the pockets of his jumpsuit, just outside the public fence of the spaceport safety zone. He stared at the landing zone as another ship dropped neatly into the high-walled arena to land. The huge retractable walls were made of a corrugated material that acted like the nozzle of a vacuum cleaner with the aid of giant underground fans. Their purpose, he knew, was to suck the smoke, debris and space dust that often accompanied a ship passing through the atmosphere, down into cleansing chambers below so that it wouldn't spread out into the spaceport and contaminate the environment of the planet beyond.

To him, it was more like a magic show. Severin loved to watch as the huge walls dropped slowly like a magician's silk cloth and revealed the beauty that the spaceship displayed, streaked a black to gray ombre from her dive through the clouds.

The various robots and worker drones began gathering around, always the first on the scene to service the ship while it was still hot from landing. They deployed cranes and they opened dump hatches to receive the dust, trash, and broken bits from the ground around the ship. While it wasn't a perfect process, it got the majority. The robots and drones also scrubbed the outside of the ship, hosing it off with high-pressure water, causing billows of steam from the contact of cool water and hot metal. That was followed by pressurized air to dry the worst of the puddles.

It served the dual purposes of removing any viruses, parasites or bacteria off the exterior of the ship, which were then sucked up by the robots to be properly disposed of later, and testing for any leaks in the seams that might have occurred from the bumpy ride down.

It also cleaned the ship up and made it shine.

Severin loved that part.

The ship was like a fine lady stepping out of a bath, clean and new. One day he wanted to own such a vessel. He wanted more than anything to be a Captain.

A robot wheeled up with a set of airlock stairs and rolled it into place, popping the airlock open. Now that the exterior had been cooled and sanitized, it would be safe for passengers and crew to depart. The last of the arrival robots were moving out as the cargo robots were moving in. It was a programmed dance that kept the spaceport moving on time and safely. He was proud of being part of that dance by keeping the robots and drones running well.

He watched the security people stepping out of the airlock, checking for safety, before allowing the captain and crew to exit the ship. They were human, he determined, by their shapes and sizes. That was a little disappointing, as the last ship he had watched land was crewed by exotic aliens. He could only imagine what it might be like to be a technician for them.

The cargo robots and flatbeds arrived at the now open cargo bay where hover-lifts were bringing the huge cargo crates down the ramp to the waiting drones. So, a cargo vessel. But even so they got to see distant stars and far planets, probably even alien planets with alien tech.

Severin saw a hover-car slide into place perfectly on time, just as the captain and crew came to the bottom of the steps. The door opened and they each began entering the vehicle.

Suddenly, the hover-car started forward, throwing one of the crew off balance and they fell to the ground. The vehicle stopped a short distance away and some of the crew ran back to help their fallen fellow. *Oh, there would be trouble from that.*

With their comrade on board, and seemingly not too harmed, the hover-car moved forward again, slipping smoothly over the ground towards the spaceport building.

Severin turned and started jogging around the fence back to the shop. He was going to personally have to look at the hover-car to see why it had jumped its safety programming and injured a passenger. He was a technician, and very far from captain.

———

Severin was waiting when the offending hover-car was delivered. He moved it into a bay where he could lift it on the rack as needed to get to all the areas. It could be something as simple as a piece of trash that had gotten picked up into the intakes. Or it could be that a circuit had been damaged, or even a programming glitch, which would be outside his wheelhouse. He would search through all the possibilities to figure it out and he wouldn't go home until he did. He was dedicated like that.

He started the remote sensor program to start checking the autonomous driving code from his wrist computer and then, since it was still on the ground, he entered the vehicle and started checking around inside for broken wires and loose screws.

Severin made a complete circuit of the interior, checked the ceiling, the sides, and the front panels, with their covers over the manual controls, without finding anything amiss. The safety dome was, of course, open over the emergency stop/start buttons and he would need to reset that again. It stayed open, so that the spaceport mechanics would know that someone had been using the vehicle manually. They could then check to make sure someone hadn't tampered with the vehicle or used it in an illegal manner.

He was working his way to the back; checking in and under the seats as he went along. Near the back, pressed into the crack between the seat back and the seat itself, he found a small rounded item. It wasn't something he was familiar with at all. It was white and had a small curl to it where it tapered from a head-like larger piece to the thinner tail-like piece. It didn't seem to have any openings, buttons, or touch depressions.

He wondered if it belonged to the previous alien group that the vehicle had transported before the humans? Maybe some kind of jewelry? More likely a piece of space trash that had melted and had been dropped in the hover-car from the human crewman's suit after their fall. The snake-like shape was so interesting, though.

Severin stared at it a moment, his imagination roaming at the possibilities.

A piece of jewelry that proclaimed the wearer to be the long lost prince of a star-nation. Maybe a weapon that activated beams of laser light to cut down an enemy that was trying to kidnap a princess. Perhaps it was an ear-com to listen as part of a security detail for a president. With each imagined scenario, he mimicked where the small device would be placed; against his collar, then between his fingers, and finally slipped into his ear.

The device moved slightly, slipping deeper into his ear canal. Then there was a sharp sting in his ear and a bright light behind his eyes for a moment. It brought him back to the present as he scrambled to remove the thing from his ear.

It seemed firmly embedded.

Severin tried getting a small mirror set to see the device, or perhaps it was a parasite, but it was so deeply down in his ear now that he couldn't see anything of it.

He debated stopping and going to the station doctor, but he would have to pay for that out of pocket, as it likely wouldn't be considered workman's comp, due to the fact that he stuck it in his own ear. He also would lose work time and he needed the money to continue saving for his own tools and teaching programs. He still hadn't finished fixing the hover-car, either, and they needed to get that back into rotation very quickly.

Severin realized that it was no longer hurting, that he could still hear, and that it wasn't uncomfortable or actually even noticeable. He decided to finish his shift and then he would call up the tele-doc which would be much cheaper and would ask fewer questions about how it got into his ear in the first place.

———

Severin had just finished the underside check of the hover-car when his wrist-comp beeped that the automated sensor check was finished. It showed that nothing had been tampered with or was wrong with the self-driving program. There was nothing to show why the hover-car had taken that little "leap" that dumped the crew-member onto the 'crete. He started putting his tools away into their cases when he heard voices talking quietly, little whispers.

"The shiny was out of place and so I picked it up."

"Does it serve a purpose?"

"I do not know. It is not a useful part it seems."

Severin peeked around the corner where the whispers seemed to be coming from. He didn't see anyone, either in the main garage or in any of the bays. Robots and drones were tucked neatly into their charging slots, waiting for orders. He shrugged and locked his toolbox. Time to head home.

———

When Severin reached the shop the next day, there was a big hullabaloo going on. It had been reported that a very expensive ring belonging to a visiting VIP had gone missing the day before; everything and everywhere was being searched in the spaceport. Toolboxes were opened, cameras were being checked and all of it was getting in the way of getting work done.

Severin remembered the whispers from last night, talking about "a shiny." He went over to the bay that he thought he had heard the whispers coming from. It had already been searched as there was tape on the wall marking it. There were two large trash drones there, still plugged in, but he could see from the lights that they were fully charged.

He pressed the buttons that opened the trash receptacle on the first and peered in.

It was empty.

He did the same for the second and it too had nothing inside. Of course the police would have checked that.

He thought for a moment, wondering where else it might be. He heard a whisper again.

"Why are the routines out of sync?"

"There is reprogramming being done."

Severin looked around, but didn't see anyone talking.

"Something is caught between my plates and is jamming some of my servos."

That caught his attention. Servos? One of the robots?

Severin pulled out one of his tools and removed a screw and then a second.

"It isn't scheduled maintenance time."

He realized finally that the voice was somehow coming from the drone he was working on. He decided to talk back to it even though he had never done that before with a drone.

"I'm going to fix the jammed servo."

"Oh, that would be nice."

He finished removing the last two screws and lowered the plate. Using a headlamp he peered into the inner workings. There, caught between a hinge and a gear, just outside of where the garbage bin lip rested, was a very shiny ring. Severin didn't want to be accused of stealing the ring, so he called the shop foreman over.

"Is that the ring that everyone is looking for?" Severin pointed.

She used her headlamp to light up the interior and gave a yell when the light crossed across the shiny piece of jewelry.

"Yes!"

"I'll get it unstuck," Severin said. "I'm going to have to remove a couple more pieces to get it loose without damaging it."

"I'll wait here," she answered him and began dialing the security number.

Severin removed another plate and the gear that was holding the ring tightly jammed. It dropped into his hand and he admired it for just a moment before it was snatched by the foreman and delivered to the security guard who had just come running into the shop.

They both ran from the shop to deliver the ring back to the owner and stop whatever inter-star-national incident was in the process of happening. He turned back to the drone and reinserted the gear, tightened the hinge to prevent that kind of thing from happening again, and closed up the panels.

All in a day's work for a Technician First Class.

———

Severin was called into the boss' office that afternoon. He hadn't even had time to go and watch the ships taking off from the launchpad as there was so much cleanup to do from the searches earlier in the day. The foreman was there, as well as the Supervisor. This might bode bad news.

"Technician Severin, we have reviewed the camera footage from yesterday and today, and your name has been cleared in the disappearance of the Empress Varmattigan's seal ring." The Supervisor wasn't looking particularly convinced of his own words. He continued: "Due to being the person to have recovered the ring, as the cameras did reveal, the Empress has declared that you are to be rewarded. You are to meet with her at her hotel in one hour. So, get cleaned up and don't embarrass the Spaceport Technician Union when you meet with her."

Severin was stunned and just stared for a moment until the foreman elbowed him in the side.

"Yes, sir! I will, sir!"

The Supervisor motioned with a hand for him to leave, which he promptly did.

Once the door had closed behind him he stood still for a moment, his imagination soaring. What kind of reward would she give him? Surely, it would help him to get more tools and more education. He shook himself and ran to change and get cleaned up. It wouldn't do to be late to your own reward party.

———

There were very large guards outside the Empress' room when Severin arrived, freshly washed and changed and only a few minutes to spare. He looked up at them, faces unreadable behind their masks, and cleared his throat nervously.

"I'm here to meet with the Empress. I'm the one who found the ring?"

There was no answer from the guards, but the door opened and a woman all dressed in black motioned him into the room. There was another fellow there all dressed in black as well. He had an air of impatience to him, though it seemed as though the frown on his face was stuck there perpetually. Severin thought that it deepened when the man looked at him. He felt severely under-dressed, even though this was his best outfit; he spent most of his money that wasn't for rent or food on his tools.

"What do you want?"

Severin wasn't prepared for the question. He expected, since they called him in, that they would know.

"I'm the one who found the ring. My boss told me to come here."

"Yes. What do you want?"

Severin was starting to think that either his boss was having him on about receiving an award, or that the VIPs wanted to get to know him a little better before deciding on what award to give him.

"I want to travel and improve my Technician Rankings. And I want to own my own ship one day."

The fellow's expression didn't change. Severin thought that maybe that wasn't a good answer, or that he had been right with his first thought. Now he just hoped that the guards didn't kill him. He stood in uncomfortable silence, fidgeting, until he put his hands into his pockets to hold them still and stared down at the fancy carpeting. He looked up in surprise when the man began to talk.

"Very well, the Empress of the One-Hundred and Twenty-Nine Amalgamated Human Systems has approved your request."

Severin had no idea what that request could possibly be. So, he just waited. Waiting seemed to be a good response in this situation.

A side door opened and a different woman, dressed in the same black-clothed style, entered with a small tray in her hand and walked over to the man in front of him. The man took an envelope off the tray. The woman turned smartly and exited, closing the door behind her.

The man held out the envelope to Severin.

"Here is your reward. The Empress of the One-Hundred and Twenty-Nine Amalgamated Human Systems is grateful for the return of her ring, and considers you duly rewarded. You will agree."

Severin didn't think that was a question, so he gingerly took the proffered envelope.

"Thank you. And tell the Empress thank you, too. And that it was a pleasure to help her out."

"Good-bye," the man replied.

Severin took that as his cue to leave and turned around to see the first woman already holding the door to the hallway open for him. So out he went.

He didn't pause in the hallway, with the two imposing guards standing there, but continued on down to the elevators. He tucked the envelope into a pocket to keep it safe. His boss hadn't told him to come back to work right off, so he decided that he would go home, get something to eat and calm down, before going back in to finish off his shift.

———

Severin stared at the envelope on his table. He had changed back into his coveralls and made a quick sandwich, which was eating. He had been nervous of what might be in the envelope, so hadn't opened it yet. Partially fortified, he got up the courage and carefully opened the very expensive looking envelope.

Out dropped two small comp cards.

They were the kind that could be slotted into any normal computer and would contain information, entertainment media, or even bearer bank accounts. It was almost a let down.

He picked up the first one, with the number one on it, and slotted it into his wrist comp. After it was in, he had a momentary thought that it could erase everything on his wrist-comp, and that contained his whole life. But, it was too late to stop.

A file opened containing a letter and a small image.

The letter was from the Empress of the One-Hundred and Twenty-Nine Amalgamated Human Systems and stated that he was the hero who had saved her reputation by returning the ring that had been stolen from her. That, in remuneration, he had been granted a lifetime pass on the Empress' own Empress Line Cruise ships, with all amenities, to travel anywhere the ships traveled among the stars. He need only present this letter and seal at any spaceport that the Empress Lines ships docked at and it would be arranged.

Seeing this, he grabbed the second card and slotted it without delay.

Again, a file came up and this time it was paid access for ten years to the Galactic Engineering and Technician Database. He could access any information that he needed to continue his training, anywhere in the star nations.

Severin stood up from the table, knocking the chair over in the process and ran out the door, the rest of the sandwich forgotten, to where his flit-bike was parked. He was heading straight to get his tools from the shop and tell his boss that he quit.

——————

Comfortably ensconced in a small suite on the *Auranautical*, the ECL that happened to be in the star-port, Severin sat back and watched the planet drop away from the view port. Sure, it was just a broadcast, but it held the same excitement for him as if he were standing on the bridge itself. It was his first time off the planet of his birth and he couldn't be happier.

The leave-taking from his job had been a little tense, which is why he had picked up his tools and put them on his flit-bike before going to talk to the Supervisor. But, after some yelling, his boss realized that there was nothing he could do to stop Severin and bid him good luck. Severin chose to ignore everything else the Supervisor had said.

The rest had been a whirlwind of packing, getting to the *Spaceport Bank & Registry* and having the cards registered in his name with the bank. He also got a duplication of his full wrist-comp, so that all of his current information and licenses were recorded, as well. No reason to lose everything, because someone stole his only copy!

He had shown up at the vessel, and after flashing his 'comp

with the stamp, he was on board and had been shown to his suite.

The last view of the planet dropped away as the ship entered hyperspace and now Severin had to decide what to do next. The journey to the next port would last about ten days as the ship moved in and out of hyperspace. He had looked up the information when they announced it over the passenger systems that displayed on his wrist-comp. He thought about opening the Technician's database and doing some studying, but he was still restless and excited from all the happenings and decided to go walk around instead.

———

Severin had left the main passenger areas quite a while ago while he wandered.

The movie lounge was nice and the buffet tables were groaning with food he had never even seen much less eaten. People were walking around in clothing that would cost him a month's salary, he was sure.

He had become increasingly uncomfortable. He saw a service worker go through a side door and followed them, sliding through before the door closed.

Lots of people and some robots were moving around in the halls back here, many dressed not so differently than he was and he instantly felt more comfortable. He started walking around and discovering what might be found in the maintenance areas of the ship. After all, a captain should know every part of his vessel.

While he imagined what it would be like if this was his ship, he took several turns down a number of hallways and even went down a freight elevator.

This area was much quieter. He hadn't seen a living person for about half an hour now, he realized. He stopped and turned around slowly, trying to get his bearings. He was certainly in the bowels of the passenger liner, now.

He realized that he was hearing little voices again, now that he wasn't engrossed in his own thoughts. He started following the sound of the voices; it didn't seem that they were very far away and he could ask them how to get back to the main passenger area.

He rounded the corner and saw three robots. They were lined up against the wall and seemed to be in a ready state. He paused, wondering if these were the voices that he had heard, just like he had heard the drones in the workshop. After a moment, sure enough, he started hearing voices again.

"I don't know why they didn't put us in a charging spot but just left us here."

"I don't know either. Without full charging, we won't be much use in a fight."

"My charge is down to 10%," the third robot said.

Severin had seen a charging station just a short way back. He walked up to the robots and faced them.

"I can see that you need charging, if you'll follow me I will help you to hook into the station," Severin said. He didn't know if it would work or not, but it was worth a try.

The three robots' lights came on from standby to go and they each turned slightly towards him. Severin turned and began leading them back up the hallway. When he reached the charging station he spoke to them again.

"If you will move into place I will set it up."

Robots moved and turned into place. Severin hooked them into the charging station, attaching the cables where they belonged. This wasn't any different from charging the cleaning 'bots back home.

"Thank you for paying attention and taking care of this problem," the first robot said. "We won't forget."

Severin bid them goodbye and headed back the way that he had been going. He imagined that if he were chief of security on this vessel, that he would want all of the security robots well charged and ready to go. He was whistling as he strode down the hall, now looking for an elevator to get back to the main corridors. He'd gotten very thirsty on his walk and remembered the big buffet upstairs.

———

Severin had almost made it out of the maintenance decks when he started hearing frantic whispers. He quickly tracked them down to a trash chute. When he opened the chute, he felt a wave of heat and had to pause a moment before looking in.

Inside were a number of small drones clumped together, pressing against the walls to keep from sliding down into the fiery furnace further below.

"Oh please help! Anyone!" Little voices continued to speak, much clearer now.

"I'll help you! Just a moment, hang on!"

Severin could see that a few of the drones had grasping hooks and claws for working in wiring. He pulled off his jumpsuit and carefully fed it down the chute to the drones.

"Climb on. Hold onto each other and work your way up the cloth a little at a time if you can. I will hold on to this end."

He braced his feet and now bare knees against the cold wall and wrapped the sleeves around his wrists to give extra friction to hang onto. He could feel the weight of the drones as they began to organize themselves to release their pressure against the walls of the chute. There was a sudden heavy weight that nearly pulled him through the open door of the chute; the hot air reminded him that he didn't want to end up sliding down the chute with the drones.

The first of the drones climbed out and dropped down to the floor, making way for the rest of the drones, some heavier, some smaller. Severin was sweating from the strain, as well as the heat that continued to build. The last drone jumped out and yelled.

"Close the door! Close the door!"

Severin dropped the jumpsuit, which had small holes and tears along it anyway, and slammed the chute door closed just as a spout of fire burst up the length of the chute to clean out any remnants of trash that had gotten stuck. It would have incinerated all the drones had they still been in there.

"Why were you in the chute?" Severin asked as they gathered around him. It was chilly in his skivvies after the heat from the chute. He was a bit sad to have lost such a nice jumpsuit, but he did have an older spare in his room.

"The program said to take packages to the crew rooms from the med-bay. After we delivered the packages, the maintenance crew put us in the chute. The program said to wait." It was a large orange package drone speaking, the one that had been last out.

"It started getting hotter and hotter. Our temperature gauges suggested that if the rate of heating continued that motors and gears would start burning and silicone would start melting if we did not exit the chute." A smaller blue delivery drone explained.

"We will remember you for preventing such a terminal accident for us." It was a red emergency medical drone this time.

"What was in the packages? Was it clothing for the Captain's Dinner tonight? Did some of it get torn like my suit?" Severin was trying to imagine why someone would toss such expensive drones.

"Medicine powders," the red med-drone answered. "Not clothing. When the vacc-mice begin cleaning they will track it everywhere into the venting systems."

"Oh!" Severin realized that things were not going right on the cruise liner. "Where do I find the computer that controls the vacc-mice?"

"In the Purser and Life Support area," the blue delivery drone answered.

Severin could put two and two together well enough, and while he had never talked to drones that talked back in any way other than through a computer program, he felt that it was time to take action before he became another statistic like the drones almost had.

Severin saw a janitor closet across the hall. He knew that he kept spares at work in case something oily or caustic spilled on him and he needed to change. He opened the closet and saw a spare jumpsuit hanging there. It looked like things worked the same way here. He put it on and the one-size-fits-all suit settled itself, the nano-bots in the weave adjusting to the heat and cool of his body to fit better. Much nicer than the suit he had just lost.

He turned to the drones in front of him. He was a repair technician, not a programmer, but somehow things were getting done.

"What about the other passengers?" Severin asked.

"When the powder gets into the vents, they will become ill, too. Perhaps even die," the red drone answered.

"So, we need to stop the vacc-mice first." Severin then had an idea. He knew that most of the vacc-mice in the shop communicated with each other, to say what had been cleaned and what areas had not. If he could find one, maybe he could get them to tell the rest.

"Where can I find the closest vacc-mouse?" He asked.

"I'll get one!" The blue delivery drone sped off, hover jets deployed to replace the slower walking limbs.

"Is there a place where we could take all the passengers that would be safe? If the ship is under attack, which it seems it is, even if from the inside, they need to be taken to safety." Severin was thinking out loud again. Again, he was answered by one of the drones.

"There is a closed storage area for quarantined items. I have delivered there before. It is on a separate air vent system." This one was a medium green one showing lots of wear and tear with flaking paint. Shameful really, even if it only worked in the cargo areas. Better care should be taken.

"Perfect. Now how to get them there? Maybe if they thought

there was a gambling game or prizes, they would go? Where is the closest computer terminal that could make announcements?"

A little yellow drone began nimbly climbing his suit leg and Severin plucked it up and put it on his shoulder. He had finally realized that they sounded the loudest when they were closer to the ear that had the likely advanced alien tech in it. He decided that he wouldn't talk to any doc about it after all.

"This way." It pointed with a small light laser to direct his path.

Severin spoke to the rest of the drones.

"When blue gets back with a vacc-mouse, have him and it brought to me. Red, I'll need you with me to tell if the mouse is contaminated. Green, make sure the door to the storage area is open and ready. Everyone else, start finding people and leading them to Green. I'm going to announce that there is a grand prize for following the drones on a secret adventure."

The drones sped away and he began jogging down the corridor following the laser light. It wasn't far, but then there was a new problem.

"It's locked?" He hadn't encountered that issue before on the ship, but he should have known that sensitive areas would be.

"Hello? Computer lock? Are you listening?"

"What do you want?" came the reply.

"I need to get into the room and send an announcement to the passengers on the ship." Severin thought it was worth a try.

"Very well, you have the ship janitor colors on, so you are authorized to enter the room to clean." The door-light changed colors and the door slid open.

———

Severin had talked the main announcement terminal into letting him make the announcement over the computer systems to the passengers. They had wrist-comps like his that were tied into one channel for special announcements from the ship. His own 'comp had beeped to let him know that the message had gone out. Now he had to hope that he had made it exciting enough. Sort of a treasure hunt and maze kind of game with big prizes for everyone who participated. By then the blue drone had appeared with a vacc-mouse.

"Is it safe?" He asked Red. The med-drone scanned the mouse.

"Yes, it has not been contaminated with the powder."

Severin took the vacc-mouse gently but firmly from Blue. It was squiggling to get away. They preferred to follow their programming.

"Vacc-mouse. Listen to me." It stopped its squirming and its antennae array turned and pointed at Severin. "You must let the other vacc-mice know that there is danger in cleaning. They must stop and get serviced immediately or they will be severely damaged and be unable to continue their programmed cleaning. Tell them to stop and return to base now."

The vacc-mouse started squirming in his fingers again. He didn't know if it had worked or not. He placed the vacc-mouse on the ground and it made for the closest hole in the room, the door sliding open and closed automatically as the vacc-mouse entered.

"Show me the state of the cleaning robots, Computer, if you would." Severin hoped for the best. The computer screen came up with a schematic of the vacc-mice bases throughout the ship; all of the bases showed red. That meant occupied.

"Yes! It worked!" Severin turned back towards the little door. "Please stay in base until servicing has taken place."

He looked at Red, Yellow, and Blue who were still in the room with him.

"Next I'll see if the people have all arrived at the prize place. We need to find out what is going on. Who might be in on it and what crew might still be alive. Can you check on the crew-members and report back to me?" Severin knew that there was no reason for them to continue to listen and help him, especially since he was asking them to do things outside their programming. But Red and Blue each waved an appendage and headed out. Yellow was still on his shoulder, and the laser pointer stabbed out at the door. It seemed they were still with him.

He was feeling far more like a secret agent than a captain, but he kept his imagination to himself and hurried to the new destination.

———

Severin was peeking around a corner and saw three more people enter the door following the orange drone. The drone came out of the room and headed over to where Red and he were waiting.

"How many more?" Severin asked.

"That is all that would follow us. Some just laid on the floor."

Severin was sad to hear that, but there was nothing else to be done about it.

"Green, close the door." He whispered quietly, but the drone heard him nonetheless. The door was shut and locked. That was the safest he could get the passengers. They were likely to be very unhappy with the cruise line when this was all over.

Blue came speeding back and stopped on a dime in front of Severin to report. Red had already reported that several of the bridge crew were incapacitated and may not survive, but there was nothing that could be done at this time for them, either.

"I have identified eight persons that have gathered together that are not long time crew members. All of them have recently been hired, as I don't have their pictures and ID in my memory banks."

"Thank you, Blue. Those must be the pirates or mutineers," Severin mused.

"There are also four crew members and the Captain that are meeting with them that I do recognize from my data banks," Blue continued.

That surprised Severin. What Captain would give over his ship to pirates and mutineers? Maybe he was trying to arrange the safe removal and passage of the passengers and remaining crew?

"Is there a way to hear what they are saying? Perhaps the Captain is negotiating on our behalf?"

A quiet conversation started in his ear. After just a short bit, he knew that the Captain was a dirty rotten scoundrel of the worst sort. A traitor to crew and passengers and his employer. They were planning to dump the bodies of all the passengers and remaining crew once they had succumbed to the poison. Then they were going to take the ship to a pirate planet to be sold as salvage with enough money for them to all retire on. One of them had already begun the process of hacking into the finances to drain the ship's operating accounts. They had the Captain right there to help.

"Main computer, there are intruders in the system mimicking the Captain. You need to shut them out right now to save the ship."

"I will need to verify. Agreed. The person operating the keyboard is not the Captain and is not authorized to access ship funds. I am shutting them out of the systems."

The voices coming through to him now were first incredulous and then angry. The Captain told them to calm down, he would check to see what the problem was. They were hired to be professional and he wasn't impressed with them, currently. That made Severin even more angry. Truly a traitor! He needed to capture them. The ship had left hyperspace some time ago, but there was no telling how close they were to help of any sort.

"Yellow? Are you actually a security drone?"

The little bot on his shoulder bobbed up and down. It had probably been thrown in with the others, much like Red, the med-drone, because they had seen too much. Severin continued formulating his plan on the fly, his thoughts running over various movies he had seen about terrorists and mutineers. He didn't have any weapons to face off with the pirates, and surely they would have weapons, the bad guys always did.

Then he thought about the combat robots charging in the lower hallway.

"Blue! Can you go get the three combat robots that are in hallway 7B? They should be fully charged by now. Please let them know that I need them to help to capture the mutineers, and the Captain who has betrayed the ship." Blue sped away before Severin even finished talking. He certainly was fast!

"Red, we are going to need medical supplies in case people get wounded, and a lot of tape, I think, for securing the prisoners once we take them." Severin was going fully on imagination now.

"I'll get it and meet you there," Red replied. "We will do everything we can to help, we have not forgotten what you have done for us."

"Yellow." That was as far as he got when the laser began pointing the way again. They moved along quickly, but carefully, in case there were still other conspirators that weren't joined up with the rest.

Severin tried to formulate a plan but nothing was really coming to him. He was a technician, not a marine or special ship security. He had never even held a weapon in his hand. Maybe he should just call the patrol and wait out of sight?

The combat robots arrived with Blue just behind him before he could withdraw any further.

"We remember you. What do you need?" The lead robot spoke.

What do I need? What do I need? Severin was panicking. A tiny voice whispered in his ear. It was Yellow, he realized.

"Courage is doing the right thing, even when you are afraid."

He remembered the conversation with the black-clad man. How frightening it had seemed at the time. But, he had said what he wanted then, and it had gotten him on this vessel and traveling. There were people, robots, and drones depending on him now.

"We need to capture the enemies of the vessel that are in that room. It will be dangerous. Not all of us will make it out alive. But, it is our duty to protect those who cannot protect themselves. And it will be our honor if we lay down our lives for the innocent today. We will storm the castle and take no prisoners! Wait! We'll open the door and we'll try to take prisoners. Got it?" Severin looked around at his motley crew. Three robots, three drones, and a technician. "It has been an honor working with you all."

They all bobbed or nodded. The combat robots readied their ship's weapons, things that wouldn't destroy the bulkheads. The med-drone had a hover-sled following him now that bounced excitedly, shifting the supplies it carried. Blue held up a welding torch for Severin to take. It was a tool he knew well.

Blue then carried Yellow to the door, as everyone moved quietly up. The ship's computer was still monitoring the conversation inside, which had become more and more heated. Just as Yellow started working to overcome the lock on the door; the ship's computer whispered.

"Patrol has sent a secure message that they received our call for help and will be near the ship in 45 minutes."

Severin almost called it all off again but Blue and Yellow forced his hand.

The door slid open.

———

Severin was staring straight at the Captain, who had one of the crew's shirt-fronts clenched in his meaty fist. His other fist was drawn back ready to punch. He froze at the opening of the door, turning his head to look at Severin.

There was a yell which drew Severin's attention and a bolt of light shot directly at him. It bounced off a bright blue carapace which had intercepted the shot meant for him. The little blue drone dropped.

"Blue!" Severin couldn't believe it. The little drone had given his life for him. It goaded him into action and he dove to the side behind a couch. The combat robots entered the room and shots were flying all about. The mutineers and pirates weren't using ship-safe guns and robot armor was being chipped away with the shots.

Severin heard Red give an order that made no sense.

"Mice to the center, release the loads!"

Vacc-mice started pouring out of the walls, running under the conspirator's feet, tripping them, running over toes, and releasing sprays of some liquid from their cleaning spray nozzles. The traitors began grabbing their faces and screaming, still shooting wildly. Severin saw Yellow take a hit as the Captain was kicking and wading his way through the vacc-mice towards where Severin was hiding.

"Ship's computer! Help!" Severin called out, not knowing what else to do.

Crash foam began pouring from the ceiling, coating the men, tangling them and slowing them even more. The combat robots were able to move easier now without having to absorb the shots to protect Severin and the ship's integrity.

The robots began shooting tasers into the foamed masses and after a few more yells it was done. Red called off the vacc-mice that were left outside the foam and sent them back to their holes.

"Did the mice poison the mutineers?" Severin was slightly horrified.

"No," Red replied. "I changed out the poison ampules for hot pepper ampules from the dining mini-fac machine. But they won't be seeing straight for a while."

"Thank you, Red. We need to find Blue and Yellow, I think they are buried under the foam." The two of them began probing and tearing bits of the foam out, as Severin called for the brave little drones. Finally he found Blue, and at the same time, Red found Yellow.

They were both caked in the crash foam which had hardened to near concrete level. It would be an hour or so before it softened. The little drones weren't moving. Severin's eyes started to burn with unshed tears. One of the combat robots came over and shot Blue. Severin was so surprised that he didn't have time to stop it. Beeps and bleeps and several curse words issued forth from Blue. He was alive!

The same measure, though somewhat gentler, was applied to Yellow, and soon she was talking and giving status reports, as best as able with part of her sensors covered.

Then with the robots' help they began digging out the mutineers and taping them securely with a lot of medical tape before they woke up. Their faces were swollen and red-streaked from the hot pepper juice. But that was a far softer fate than some of the crew they had poisoned.

"Severin Miles, the patrol has arrived and is asking to board," the ship's computer's smooth voice interrupted.

"Send Green to show them here, please."

"Very well."

In short order the Patrolmen, preceded by Green, entered the room and stopped to stare at the carnage. Vacc-mice parts, crash foam debris, holes in the walls, armor plates, and mummy-wrapped criminals were spread out before them.

"What is going on here?" A Major of the Patrol, by his insignia, asked.

"We captured the mutineers and the pirates, although maybe they are all mutineers? I was aided by these brave robots and drones. And the ship, too. I'm Severin Miles, Technician First Class, and a passenger on the vessel. I discovered the conspiracy in the middle of it and we did everything we could to stop it and save the passengers and ship."

"Where are the passengers?" Another of the patrol asked, this one with a med-symbol on her collar.

"Red and Green can show you, they are down safely below for the most part. There have been a few possible casualties among the crew, though, I am sad to say. But I'm not sure how many," Severin informed her.

"I have got to hear the story of this, and why there are so many vacc-mice bits all over the floor." The Major still looked completely bemused.

"I'm sorry they had to give their lives that way, but they were very fierce. I never knew that vacc-mice could be so fierce! So you see, Major. It's Major, right?" Severin couldn't believe he was talking to a Patrol Major, that was legendary in all the movies.

———

Severin stood in front of a different door this time, in a different hotel, with the same two guards, it seemed, on either side. The door opened before he even announced himself, unlike last time, but the same woman dressed in black stood there and motioned him in.

He saw the same black-clad man standing stiffly across the room and quelled the sense of deja-vu that the whole situation engendered in him. He strode over to stand in front of the man, and this time he announced himself with a surety that was only recently gained.

"Severin Miles, Technician First Class, here to see the Empress Varmattigan, Empress of the One-Hundred and Twenty-Nine Amalgamated Human Systems, at her request."

The black-clad man raised one eyebrow.

The door opened beside him, and Severin expected to see the other black dressed woman come out with an envelope. Instead, a different woman emerged from the room and the man in black bowed, as did the woman in black who had come up beside Severin and tapped him on the shoulder. Severin bowed his head in respect, though he was peeking even as he did so.

She was older, but still strong in jawline and cheekbone, and certainly in spine, as she stood straight and moved well. While the staff was all dressed in black, she was dressed in layers of white and she stood out like a lily among the dahlias. There was no doubt this was someone who was used to commanding attention. This was the Empress, herself.

"Rise up," she spoke softly, but her voice carried clearly. "I do not know how you truly managed to save the passengers, reprogram much of the vessel, and capture the miscreants and traitors that tried to rob me and destroy my investments and the reputation of my Cruise Line. But, I am grateful that you did. Rewarding you previously with the lifetime passage was obviously an excellent decision on my part, as it should be.

"But due to the damage, the possible contamination, the subversion of the drones and robots as reported by the patrol after the rescue; the ship has been removed from service and will be scuttled, along with everything left on it."

Severin gasped. The ship, the robots, the drones, all to be destroyed? After all they had done to help and save him?

"Empress–" he started to speak but she interrupted him with a raised hand.

"I'm not done."

"Yes, Empress Varmattigan." His mind was working furiously. Maybe he could get down to the shipyards and save the drones and robots, even if he couldn't save the rest of the ship. His stomach churned as furiously as his mind.

"As the ship has been decommissioned and I therefore have no more use for it, I thought that a Technician and Engineer might have the skills to repair some of the issues."

Severin's head came up and eyes focused on her face as what she was saying penetrated his schemes. Could it really be?

"So, I have awarded a salvage title for the ship and its contents to you, Severin Miles, along with an account with a small sum for doing a bit of repairs. I'm sure you can fix it and sell it. But, it will need to be given a new name and registry. If I recall, that was the third thing you asked me for that last time we met."

Severin's head was spinning. Yes, it was the last thing he had said when questioned what he wanted before. To be a captain of his own vessel. He wondered what would be left of the ship after scuttling. Would any of the drones or robots be there? What would he do with it? How would he get a crew? None of the answers were coming to his ear, the way they had on the ship.

The other black-clad woman handed him another envelope. He took it dazedly, barely noticing when the other people bowed and the Empress turned and left the room.

"Go do good, Captain Miles," he heard as the door closed.

The servant woman touched his elbow and got his attention. She motioned to the front door which now stood open. He nodded to the man and then turned and headed out, the deja-vu strong again.

This time he went to his room several floors down in the hotel and sat on the couch staring at the envelope. He thought about ordering a sandwich in honor of the occasion, but decided against it. He carefully opened the envelope and out dropped two small comp cards. Just as before.

He had been through a lot in the last few weeks. He was not the same technician, staring at ships landing and taking off and wishing he was on them. He had been on one. And now, if this was what she intimated, he would be again.

He slotted the first card. It was a bank account and the number of credits in it made his eyes water. He would have plenty for the rest of his life, even if he did nothing else.

He slotted the second card and it was an inventory that went on and on, starting with a salvaged passenger liner, now super-yacht spaceship formerly known as the *ECL Auranautical*. Severin jumped up and yelled, pumping his fists to the sky. He grabbed his coat and headed for the nearest branch of the *Space-port Bank & Registry.*

Severin Miles stood, hands in the pockets of his brand-new, top of the line Captain's suit, on the bridge of the refurbished and newly named *White Snake* in honor of the small thing that started this whole amazing adventure.

A small yellow security drone with a number of upgrades and a spiffy new paint job sat in her seat on his right shoulder pad. He looked over at the bright blue messenger drone perched on the arm of his chair. Blue's hover-jets had been upgraded to the latest and greatest and he had been given orders not to fly below 7' inside the ship after nearly decapitating the new Chief Engineer. Red was over in a corner secured and ready, in case of medical emergency, studying the medical manuals that Severin had obtained.

The three security robots were completely repaired and at their stations, two outside the bridge door and one inside the bridge, opposite Red. They were proud and happy, with their medals of bravery displayed on their metal armored chests.

"Ship's computer, detach from the station and take us out to stationary orbital safe-zone."

"Aye-aye, Captain."

Severin grinned happily. He was Captain of his own vessel.

R. C. CAPASSO

"My magic works better without all this hardware." The Queen frowned at the sleek steel console, glittering with dials and monitors.

Her tall, broad-shouldered companion leaned forward, his voice low. "It's true, then? Spells don't work now that people don't believe in them?"

The Queen rounded on him, fire sparking in her eyes. "No, that's not true. My powers are not bound by the beliefs of my subjects. I don't care if people trust in 'science' or good luck charms or group hugs. They are still helpless before me." She wrinkled her perfect nose. "It's just that I work with specialized elements, roots, and elixirs. I direct my powers most easily when I can set something on fire. I like my cauldron bubbling. But all this metal doesn't burn. And smoke detectors are just an invasion of my private rituals."

The man's handsome, craggy face fought to hide something. "Then you can't do anything here."

The Queen pressed her lips together. Why had she brought the Hunter along, anyhow? He was easy on the eyes, of course, which made a change from the tubby old King she'd left back on the planet. But she didn't need the Mirror to tell her he wasn't wholly on her side.

That story he told about how he'd been prevented from killing the brat by a crowd of little men tumbling out of a tavern, coming between them just as he'd raised his hunting knife...Well, that was only barely plausible. Yes, he'd taken the girl off to a wild and lawless planet used only as a way station, filled with bars and houses of ill repute. A place where no one would blink an eye at a man burying a bundle vaguely resembling a body. Perhaps an isolated woodland would have been better. But Earth didn't hold much green space anymore, the Hunter had argued. Anyway, the little men, in high spirits after a copious meal, had stumbled around his feet and somehow the girl was lost. But how far could a pampered little thing like SW run? The Hunter's excuses were dubious at best.

He must have felt the distrust shimmering off of her.

"You can check with the people from the tavern. They saw Snow White..."

"Don't say that name!" She hated the girl, hated her name. It was all about innocence, all about how precious the baby had been, the child born of the king's first wife. On and on, the stories went. The Queen forced herself to call the girl SW; she mustn't voice the terms she had for her in private, in her mind.

The Hunter's low voice insisted. "It's just, there were witnesses. They'll tell you. I had a grip on her, but then those seven little men..."

"I know. Miners." Her Mirror had told her that. Too bad its recording of the dark street outside the tavern had been so obscure. Still, it had obediently displayed SW's coordinates, on a small mining planet.

The Queen lowered her voice to that pitch she knew sent shivers down men's spines. "That's why I have not ordered your execution. You failed miserably. But I will still triumph. And I intend for you to watch."

He didn't ask about the plan, which was just as well. The more he knew, the more he could bungle.

Somehow, after the tavern, the miners had met SW and taken her to their home on the poisonous moon of Kendor. A hideous place for any but the few inhabitants immune to its noxious fumes and treacherous terrain. Yet otherworlders flocked to it for the astounding wealth in minerals and simmering chemicals. The miners, happy in a little sealed habitation pod erected a safe distance from their work, popped a respirator on SW's simpering face, gave her protective footwear, and made her their darling/housekeeper. All this the Mirror revealed. And that was all the Queen needed.

She booked passage to Kendor under the guise of a trader, and goodness knew the inhabitants were hungry for visitors to brighten their lives.

She dropped by the miner's pod, buzzed for entrance, and pulled out of her pack a lovely pink mask.

"Not only does it protect from fumes, but it gives off the fragrance of a thousand flowers. Here, step outside and try it."

SW oohed with delight, slipped on the mask, smoothed down her hair, and followed the Queen outside.

She mussed her cute little dress with all the writhing, and then she lay motionless.

The Queen was on her way home in a luxurious private spaceship when she approached the looking glass. She barely got out the first words, when the Mirror, as cold as only glass could be, broke the news.

"Snow White is still alive. Still the most beautiful of all."

She made the Mirror replay the scene. The two of them stepping out of the pod, SW dying, she the glamorous Queen dancing away with the most graceful of triumphs, and then a pause. A long pause, but apparently not long enough. A little man, trotting down the path, followed by six others. Clustering around the girl, dragging her into the pod. And an hour later, a pale but stunningly beautiful idiot looking out the window, a hand to her reddened nose.

Within a few minutes the Queen had altered her travel plans, booked a stop at a small moon where she could get the correct supplies, and was on her way back to the miner's pod.

This time she appeared as an old woman, hobbling down the path to the little dwelling, resting on a rock outside.

SW, officially-guaranteed mask firmly in place, opened the door a crack. "Are you all right, Old Mother?"

The Queen shuddered at the idea of that simpleton calling her mother. Or old. But she turned the shudder into an artful tremble.

"Oh, I am only weary, Miss. I am on my way to my sweet granddaughter's house. I have a gift for her."

SW smiled and nodded. "Would you like to come in and rest?"

It only took moments to tell the tale, how she had these lovely slippers, bought special—buy one and the second is half off. Beautiful slippers, light and flexible. To let a girl walk all over the planet, even on the soft sea sands, without danger. So much nicer than the clunky protective boots the men wore. And of course her granddaughter didn't need two pairs. So which did Miss like better, the lavender or the yellow?

When SW stepped outside, the regulation mask didn't really help. The slippers, with their special metallic soles, pulled her right down into the sinkhole that closed over her.

The Queen boarded her vessel and hustled to her quarters. The Mirror was waiting.

It didn't say a word. It just . replayed the images. The whistling miners returning home. One of them spotting something on the ground beside the path. A glint of metal. Part of her blasted mask.

Within moments they had driven over an excavator and lifted her out. Into the pod they all rushed. Fast forward, and there she was at the cursed window again, shaking dust out of her springy, thick hair.

It was time to go back to the classics. Enough of dealing with alien technology. Nothing beats a poisoned apple, especially for a girl on a planet where fresh fruit was like gold.

The Queen disguised herself as a farm woman with a basket. SW, who had more faith in humanity than intelligence, swallowed her story and the fruit. She collapsed in the pod, and the Queen slipped away.

Finally, at her approach, the Mirror said nothing. No talk of resurrection for SW now. But no congratulatory compliments, either. Sullen silence.

But this time the Queen was taking no chances. The kittenish SW seemed to have a few too many lives, and there must be no room for a "happy" ending.

The miners seemed to have abandoned all hope. They constructed a glass coffin for their beloved companion and booked passage on a ship to take her to the loveliest planet in the galaxy, there to be laid to rest on a mountain overlooking the sea. They were rich enough, having profited from the wealth of their poisonous home.

The Queen booked herself a place on the same ship. One for the Hunter, too. She wanted him there, to see how you get a job done right. And when it was all over, he would look very nice on a beach in the sun.

For this voyage of victory, she donned no disguise. She appeared in her royal robes, claiming that she was on a highly important diplomatic mission. Of course she dined at the Captain's table, having her usual effect on middle-aged men. Seven little miners, dressed in deep mourning, sat at a far table, caught up in their own thoughts.

The Captain personally escorted her on a tour of the ship, even leading her through a cargo bay, where she glimpsed a luxurious cloth covering what could only be a glass box. His handsome young first officer lightly tugged one corner to straighten it.

So far, so good. She'd enjoy a mountaintop funeral.

As they prepared to disembark, the little miners grouped themselves around the coffin, lifting with muscles forged from years of work.

"Please, let us pay our respects." The Captain's voice was grave, yet he shot a look at the Queen, as if to say, "See what a fine fellow I am."

Before anyone could react, the Captain gestured to his first officer, who stepped between the little men, grasped the cloth and folded it down. Through the glass SW's pale but perfectly preserved face lay enchantingly beautiful.

With a gasp, the officer brushed away a miner's hands and reached for the coffin's lid. A flash of movement beside the Queen, and her Hunter rushed forward, knocking another miner to the ground and tilting the box up over his head.

The small body fell with a jarring thunk, lips opening and a browning piece of apple popping onto the deck.

SW was alive.

With a shriek the Queen lunged at her, but the Hunter stepped sideways and tripped her.

As she sprawled, body sliding to the girl's side, SW turned her head, opened her eyes and murmured, "Stepmama?"

After that, many things came to light. The Hunter gave evidence. The Mirror provided crystal-clear recordings. The shipboard trial was swift.

At the very hour that Snow White and the first officer exchanged vows on a mountain overlooking the sea, the ship took off for its next assignment.

On the outside of the hull, the Queen stood in a space suit, feet clamped to the metal side with irresistible force. A connection provided air, temporarily. As the planet receded below her and dark space surrounded her, the connection was severed.

Her last thoughts were, "I hate technology. I hate S…"

BY ANY OTHER NAME

LORINA STEPHENS

Do you know me? You should. We've been together so often on this shore. You've swallowed my song. You've taken me into yourself. Come down again to the shingle, walk through the sand and the wrack, open your arms. I'll take you again, down under the sea, sing you asleep. Sing you to dreams. Sing of sins and senses, sensibilities and sacrifice. Let us slide down to where love and hate have no meaning, where the womb of everything began.

I wake from my bed, roused by the rattle of rain, the rush of surf–and realize there is no rain, no surf, just an endless expanse of red rock and dust like talcum. The bed is hard, unyielding. No comfort to be found there. In the air there are voices I feel I know or want to know. What matter? The formed floor is sharp with cold beneath my feet, the wall hard against my cheek where I lean and think about rising. In an attempt to resist, I close my eyes, inhale a long shuddering mouthful of air, of night, and know I'm helpless against the pull of Arabia's shore. Not the shore of Earth. Like all explorers we've named places for the homes we've left. I wonder, as I squat over the waste system, if we're forever caught in replicating the past. Do we bring our history, our people, and our demons with us? Does the banshee, the selkie, the shadow of our dreams drift through space, oblivious of void, or radiation, or the impossibility of what we attempt?

Come to me....

I've gone Aresian, I'm thinking, the way The Bay explorers went bushed, and ultimately I don't care. We've been here so long. System after system failing, patched and jimmied, modified and made-do. Does it matter? I don't care. I don't care. The relief mission is taking so long, and I'm alone now, holding the fort as it were. One by one the others walked out into Arabia's vast dry sea. There were voices, a siren's song, a selkie on Mars.

How can that be?

It's simple. I'm insane. If I think I'm insane does that mean I'm sane? If I question my reality does that mean I'm going to be okay? How can I be okay when it's all falling apart? When everything we planned so carefully, down to the last possibility, has failed? I could weep for the magnitude of it all. Is this how those who found themselves marooned felt? Trapped in the pack ice, nothing but the vastness of the ocean both in breadth and depth. Overwhelming.

I turn to the shielded window, look out upon an ocean of red, the vastness of Arabia where we were supposed to ascend to godhood: *and on the third day God created dry land and plants.* Lots of dry land. No plants. No water, or at least none we were able to access. So much for all the study and reports. I should feel something. But there's only this longing, this terrible pull toward something I know is there, and also know is not.

Come to me....

No one is coming. Profit margins. Shareholders. It's not worth the investment to send out a rescue mission. It's the same logic used by the shareholders of the Hudson's Bay Company, and Denmark, and so many other boards who sent out explorers under the guise of knowledge and the imperative of profit. I know this.

Come to me....

I pull on my suit, lock the helmet, inhale the life from the tanks. I remember my Newfoundland shore, salt-spray stinging my cheek, the wrack on granite cobbles, the call of the selkie moaning in the wind, a siren singing, a sailor slipping. Out on the Arabian Sea.

THE ALIEN PIED PIPER'S NEGOTIATION

RODNEY G. HATFIELD JR.

Across the boundless expanse of a faraway world, a vast and merciless terrain stretched endlessly, bearing witness to the relentless strife between two opposing factions teetering on the precipice of utter obliteration. The Frelor, an esteemed and formidable tribe of winged avian beings, clashed fiercely with the Zyglorians, a shrewd and resilient clan of mammalian creatures. For ages uncounted, these rival groups had been locked in a bitter struggle, their animosity fueling a ceaseless cycle of warfare. Neither side displayed the slightest inclination to yield, and the toll of casualties grew ever higher with each passing sunrise. A glimmer of hope seemed but a distant dream, as the prospect of peace dwindled amidst the looming specter of mutual annihilation.

From the distant horizon emerged a peculiar sight, one that stirred both awe and trepidation in the hearts of those who beheld it: a solitary figure, cloaked in robes of vibrant hues, bedecked with curious implements, and accompanied by a menagerie of animals that seemed to move in harmony with his every step. As he traversed the landscape, his movements possessed a grace and fluidity that belied the bulkiness of his form. Drawing closer to the two warring factions, his enigmatic presence cast a mesmerizing spell upon all who watched. It became apparent that this was no ordinary being; his countenance obscured behind a shimmering visage of what appeared to be a gilded pipe. In that moment of realization, a collective recognition dawned upon them: he was none other than the Alien Pied Piper, known for his ethereal melodies and his remarkable gift of communion with beings of every creed and kin, transcending the barriers of language and custom alike.

Standing at the nexus between the opposing forces, the Piper lifted his hands in a solemn gesture, beckoning for tranquility to descend upon the tumultuous scene. With a deft touch, he began to weave a melody so achingly beautiful that it seemed to reach into the very depths of each listener's soul, transcending barriers and bridging chasms of discord with its ethereal strains. As the haunting notes wafted through the air, a palpable shift occurred within the hearts of the Frelor and the Zyglorians alike, their eyes meeting in silent acknowledgment of the profound moment unfolding before them. Tears glistened in their eyes, borne not of sorrow but of a newfound realization that perhaps, amidst the chaos of conflict, there existed a path to reconciliation. With each passing refrain, the tension that had long held them captive began to dissipate, replaced by a fragile yet undeniable sense of hope and understanding. When at last the Piper ceased his enchanting melody, a profound silence descended upon the landscape, as if nature itself held its breath in anticipation of what was to come. Turning his gaze upon each faction in turn, the Piper spoke, his words carrying the weight of ages and the wisdom of the cosmos.

"My friends," he intoned, his voice resonating with a celestial timbre, "you have endured the ravages of misunderstanding and mistrust for far too long. Yet within the harmonies of this music lies a choice—a choice to relinquish the shackles of enmity and embrace the symphony of peace that beckons to you now. The decision, my friends, rests in your hands."

From the folds of his elaborate robes, the Piper withdrew a

diminutive, intricately adorned box, its surface bearing the marks of countless journeys across galaxies untold. With a wistful sigh, he gently unfurled its lid, revealing within a trove of treasures weathered by time—faded photographs capturing moments long past, and worn trinkets imbued with the weight of memories yet to be unfurled. Intrigued despite themselves, the leaders of the warring factions drew closer, their curiosity piqued by the enigmatic contents nestled within. As they leaned in to peer over his shoulder, the Pied Piper began to speak, his voice carrying the cadence of a storyteller weaving tales of ages gone by.

"These are tales from my own realm," he elucidated, gesturing towards a photograph depicting a youthful couple enfolded in each other's embrace amidst the shattered remnants of a once-grand metropolis. "Once, this land was adorned with splendor and tranquility, yet it succumbed to the very same currents of animosity and suspicion that now threaten to engulf you. I bore witness as my kin turned against one another, as bonds shattered and civilizations crumbled into dust. It was only through the sharing of these narratives—through the revelation of my memories and the rawness of my anguish—that I discovered a path towards restoration. Thus, I extend to you a choice. You may persist along the path of devastation, or you may opt to heed my words and chart a course towards a novel dawn. The decision lies within your grasp."

With bated breath, the Piper awaited their response, his gaze lingering upon the tumult of emotions reflected in their eyes— the tumultuous conflict between the yearning for retribution and the harrowing prospect of forfeiting all they held dear. In that pregnant pause, the leader of the Frelor took a decisive step forward, his majestic wings unfurling gently in the breeze as if to signify a newfound resolve.

"For too long, we have traversed the desolate paths of conflict," he intoned, his voice resounding with a gravity born of profound introspection. "The melody you have woven has illuminated a path previously obscured from our sight. We choose to embrace the symphony of peace."

Beside him, the Zyglorian chieftain nodded in solemn accord, her countenance softened by the dawning realization of a shared destiny. "In the crucible of strife, we have borne witness to the erosion of kinship and camaraderie," she acknowledged, her words imbued with a quiet dignity. "We extend our gratitude to you, Piper, for unveiling a beacon amidst the shadows. We too choose the path of reconciliation."

And with those words, a palpable sense of relief suffused the air, as if the very fabric of reality sighed in quiet acceptance of the momentous decision that had been made. With the solemn vows exchanged, a dawn of renewal unfurled its wings over the realms of the Frelor and the Zyglorians. Guided by the ethereal melodies of the alien Pied Piper, they embarked upon a journey toward reconciliation, their divergent paths converging upon a shared destination of peace and harmony. Through the transcendent power of his otherworldly tunes, the Piper had dissolved the barriers of language and culture, unveiling the universal language of music as a conduit for unity and understanding. In the forge of working together, the once-rival factions labored hand in hand, pooling their collective wisdom and resources to breathe life into the barren landscape that had borne witness to their strife. As the seeds of cooperation took root and flourished, the arid plains blossomed into a verdant tapestry of partnership and mutual respect.

Guided by the Piper's sage counsel and his resplendent harmonies, a new chapter unfolded—one where the echoes of discord were replaced by the symphony of unity, and where the promise of a brighter tomorrow beckoned on the horizon. Word of the miraculous reconciliation between the Frelor and the Zyglorians spread like wildfire across the expanse of the galaxy, igniting a spark of hope in the hearts of those ensnared by their own shackles of conflict. From distant corners of the cosmos, emissaries flocked to seek the aid of the Alien Pied Piper, drawn by the allure of his transformative melodies and the promise of a world untethered from the specter of war.

Wherever his footsteps led, the Piper wielded his music as a beacon of hope, his presence a testament to the enduring power of compassion and understanding in the face of adversity. With each triumph of harmony over discord his legend swelled, woven into the fabric of the galaxy itself as a timeless testament to the boundless potential of humanity to transcend its differences and embrace the melody of peace. And as his travels carried him ever onward the legacy of the Alien Pied Piper endured—a symphony of hope echoing across the cosmos, guiding the way toward a future illuminated by the radiant hues of unity and kinship.

FAIRY TALES, AND LIES

RAY DALEY

While I may not have fully understood why the crazy glowing old woman had sent me, I was fairly assured the spell she had cast on me before I'd arrived here *was* still working.

Here being the land of men.

Yes, I know. I look like a man too. Walk, talk, have the correct amount of arms and legs, but I am no more a Human than my target is. We're both from the realm of fairy tales. Of course it exists! You don't think those Brothers Grimm just made all those ideas up, do you?

Anyway, the spell the old woman had cast on me. I could hear parts of this song playing at the back of mind, a nagging voice in my head in two-part harmony, to keep me on track and remind me of what to do next.

Okay, I had been sent here by magic, and the fact it was dark outside confirmed it was definitely evening. Well, I was fairly sure I'd arrived by magical means. I'm still unsure precisely what an "Interdimensional Translocator" is, so I'll go with magic until I know any better. Right, fine. A somewhat fairly enchanted evening? Check!

Now the matter of locating the target. The old woman had

told me very little about her. "You'll know her when you see her!"

I was curious why the target had picked this location in particular, what the old lady had assured me was called a "nightclub." I hadn't seen any wooden weapons yet, just young men and women dancing in a way you won't find in any fairy tale. I had to look away when they came too close together. A humble woodcutter shouldn't have to witness such blatant improprieties!

I scanned the throng of humanity. Ah, there it was, staring me right in the face. Her reason for choosing this place: she could hide right in front of me and I'd never know she was there. So many of them in one small room. Lights pulsing, music thumping, sweat pouring, bodies gyrating.

<u>Sorry</u>.

I had to look away again for a moment there, just to ground myself again. They call themselves people? It's disgusting, I tell you!

Then, as if by magic, the words of the song in the back of my mind spurred me on once more, advising me that I may see a stranger. Thanks, old woman. I'm not of this world, everyone here is a stranger to me. The spell had a point though, the room was incredibly crowded. How was I going to locate a woman I didn't even know, all the way across it?

I could barely tell where one body stopped and another began. Even if I was somehow magically able to find my target, it would be an even greater feat to actually reach her among the absolute plethora of bodies before me.

I let my eyes drift across the crowd of dancers, swaying this way and that. It was at that exact moment when all the lights went out, for a fraction of a second. Only it wasn't completely dark in the room. I could make out an ethereal blue glow, just off in the middle distance, somewhere amid the people dancing.

Ah. Magic? Traces of that which didn't quite belong?

Have you ever seen a crowd suddenly all step away from each other, opening a path to... There she was!

For that merest of moments, the only light was the glow of her dress, as it floated clear off the ground. <u>I could see her ankles!</u>

I couldn't imagine such boldness from a resident of fairyland, yet here was the evidence, right before my very eyes.

The song in my head suddenly stopped. I <u>had</u> located the target then! The old woman had vouchsafed this would occur on discovering her whereabouts. Now all I had to do was reach, then capture her. I say all, like it was a simple thing, some childish game. Then, it was as if the whole room knew my intentions, it felt like every light shone right into my eyes.

———

When the glare wore off, the crowd had meshed together once more, becoming a single entity with but one purpose - to keep the two of us apart.

"Your time there is short, woodcutter!" Apparently, the old woman's spell wasn't done with me yet; I could still hear her voice in my mind. "She'll flee before midnight!"

I tried to check the time. Not a sundial in sight, not that they would have been any use inside, especially at night. Then, as if the spell had taken control of me, I felt my head turn, and my eyes lift until...

11:53 pm.

I didn't have long then. And nor did I question how I knew to read that device, or knew it to be telling me the current time. Mysteries for another day, once I had returned to fairyland, perhaps?

I started pushing my way through the crowd, aiming roughly at where I had last seen her. Now and then, I'd catch sight of her ethereal outline, and shift my course to intercept hers.

Until...

She was suddenly inches away from my face. "Okay, laughing boy. You'd better have a damn good reason for running into me like that, or we're going to have a serious problem, starting with me kicking you in the bollocks. So talk, fast."

What kind of fairyland lass spoke this way, and to a good honest woodcutter too? "Beg your pardon, Miss. I've been sent on a vital mission, to return you home."

She rolled her eyes at me! I only thought they did that in stories and fables! She held her hand at head height. "Glowing elderly lady, about yea high? Slightly crazy, may have used magic in anger upon you?"

I nodded. "You know her too then? The Fairy Godmother?"

"Fairly something, but yes, I know her. So what lie did she feed you then?"

"When you find young Cinderella, she'll tell you all manner of tales, good woodcutter. Listen not to her lies and machinations. If she is not returned to fairyland before midnight, I will lose all my magical powers! I must undo the spells I cast on her, to regain that which has held our world safely from the land of men for so many years!"

I started to explain. "I must bring you home, Cinderella."

She shook her head. "It's Sindy. Sindy Mellor. And I'm sure she spun a wonderful web of intricate lies, words to convince you where we both came from. It's not true. I'm not a fairy princess, and you aren't a humble and nameless woodcutter either. Check your pockets. I'm sure you'll find a wallet in one of them, and some sort of ID, saying who you really are. She glowed, right?"

I nodded, dumbstruck, patting for pockets.

"Was that wily creature standing behind a thick pane of glass, saying she couldn't possibly come out, for fear of losing her magic?"

That was exactly what the glowing old lady had said to me.

"Do the words <u>Interdimensional Translocator</u> mean anything to you? No, you don't need to nod again, I can see from your eyes that they do. Ah, here we are." She took the wallet I had found in a back pocket. "Jon Morris, from Oldbury. You're as human as I am, Jon. She took me first and tried to mess with my mind. It looks like her hypnosis device had a much better effect on you. I've always had a strong will. I let her believe she'd gotten me under her spell, then dived through the portal."

I assumed she was referring to the magic mirror the old woman had told me to step through to reach this realm.

"She's no more a fairy godmother than she is human. Sure, she probably looked human, to you. I saw through her disguise though, she never clouded my mind. That glow? Her ship's reactor is going critical. All her spells might seem like magic, but like Arthur C. Clarke said, any sufficiently advanced tech will seem like magic. She's a space vampire, Jon. She planned to use this outfit to suck the very life force out of me, if she could get me back to her ship before midnight, our time. Did she give you something to return us both to her?"

At this point the other gyrators pushed us off the dance floor and against the wall. Someone pushed past us and Sindy almost fell over. I grabbed her hand, steadying her. Looking into her eyes, my mind wasn't so clouded, and we made a plan.

We tapped the device the old lady had placed around my wrist. I'm pretty sure it probably left a blue ethereal glow where we'd just been standing.

I'll be honest, I closed my eyes when she sent me through the portal. I closed them again when we went back.

———

"Okay, hero. You can look now."

It had been some sort of wonderful grotto, before. Now I could see the place for what it was. A grubby alien spaceship, on the verge of destruction. We'd stepped through the portal; her recall device fell off my wrist as soon as we were on the ship.

"Woodcutter, is that you? Do you have her? Have you found my precious Cinderella?"

I could barely see anything through the thick pane of glass now; the room she occupied was almost full of smoke. All I had to do was go with the plan. "I have her, fairy godmother. She's with me."

What stepped up to the glass was a vision of pure horror: tentacles, eyes, both several dozen of each. That maw, row upon row of blackened jagged teeth. Her magic was indeed strong if it had had me seeing her as that kindly old woman, determined to hold the boundaries of fairyland back from mankind. "Step forward, woodcutter! Be not afraid, your reward awaits you!"

Then I could see the set-up. That marked single panel on the floor, the sharpened tube hanging above it from the ceiling. All there to suck out the life juices from us both.

She couldn't see any further than the marked panel, or possibly couldn't see anything on our side at all. Sindy pointed to a knee-high metal crate, signaling wildly.

Ah, I saw what she wanted. I dragged the crate until it was on the panel. While I'd been doing that, Sindy had somehow struggled out of her overdress covered in lights and placed it on the crate.

"Wonderful. There you are, my Cinderella. Relax, and I'll release you from the spell."

The whole time we'd been there, it had gradually been getting hotter. It was now almost unbearable. Sindy pulled me over to the portal, wildly stabbing at the control panel. All we had to do was get off this damn ship before the whole thing exploded around our ears!

I heard an unholy scream. The sharpened tube hung deep inside Sindy's empty dress. "Oh, woodcutter! You wouldn't have betrayed me, would you?"

I was about to speak when Sindy grabbed my wrist and

yanked us both back through the portal. I didn't get a chance to close my eyes that time.

———

Overall, it was an eventually explainable and not entirely enchanted evening. Hunting the potential victim of a space vampire and escaping from the imminently exploding ship of the aforementioned creature. It'll be a while before I can forget our return trip. All those stars!

At least we're back on Earth again, in the land of men. Well, some dark forest in the middle of nowhere. Sindy reminds me to look up, now and then.

There's the moon and our constellations. I can't tell if they're where they're supposed to be; if we're in the right time period. We're on Earth, that's all that matters.

Sindy keeps pressing me though, if I can remember anything about being a woodcutter. How to survive, find water, or food, or our way back to civilization? We'll keep trying to find other people. The real world feels so far away now.

It existed for us both, once upon a time...

WOLFF

K. L. MILL

The figure moved like a shadow through the trees, skirting pools of dappled moonlight, a cloak of deep garnet fluttering bird-like in its wake… Fleeing or pursuing? Predator or prey?

Rowan leaped over a fallen pine, landing motionless in a crouch, eyes up, alert to any sound that might betray the enemy. A twig snapped behind her. She swiftly pulled up her cowl, enshrouding herself in her biometric shield, moments before a quartet of WoLFFs slunk by. Their optic lenses scanned the forest for any hint of life, the blue-green lasers washing over every trunk, leaf, and blade of grass. The organic hybrids were part bot, part canine: droids with the biosynth-skin of a dire wolf. Ruthless and relentless. Rowan didn't dare breathe until they were long past.

Once alone, she decided to fall back a half mile, then swing north to give the pack ample berth. The Womack Corporation had only rolled out their latest tracking prototype less than a month ago, and the Rebel Initiative was still learning its capabilities and weaknesses. The WoLFF's lupine form gave them all the agility and cunning of a wolf pack, with a tireless determination and one objective: the annihilation of the entire insurgent force.

A flicker of movement. Rowan froze, scrutinizing the moss-covered stump beside her. Even as her eyes focused, reality pixe-lated and the moss morphed upwards, reconfiguring into powerful haunches and an elongated, snarling muzzle. Rowan drew her katana and swung with all her strength, aiming low and severing the WoLFF's torso at its most vulnerable part, the mutating juncture. The android gave a stuttering growl, and its optic lenses flickered out.

Rowan lowered her blade, breathing hard. The WoLFF's fluctu-form capabilities had been a horrifying discovery: it was made of some kind of quicksilver that gave it advanced camou-flage properties, enabling it to lie in wait for rebel soldiers. She extracted the laser from one of its orbital sockets and dropped it into the pouch that hung from her belt – the more they could study and learn about the WoLFFs, the better.

Rowan ran the last mile to the rebel headquarters. She pulled the blast door shut and spun the locking mechanism, sealing the concrete bunker after her. Headquarters was humming with a quiet energy, its members cautiously excited by the discovery of the potential location of one of Womack's labs.

A silver-haired woman was huddled with several others around a large command table strewn with drawings and blue-prints. She looked up from the plans, her lined face melting into relief and joy at the sight of the crimson-cloaked girl.

"Rowan!"

They embraced. "Oh, thank goodness," the woman said. "I was worried you'd run into trouble."

"Not me, Gran," Rowan grinned. "You know I can worm my way out of anything."

The older woman held the girl at arm's length, beaming. She lovingly tucked a red curl behind her granddaughter's ear. "Did you get the nano-chip?"

Rowan patted the pouch on her hip with a smile. "Did you doubt me?"

Gran's smile almost broke her face; she turned to the others. "This is it! The final piece of the puzzle we need to take down

Womack!" A cheer went up. She spun back to Rowan and cupped her face with her hands. "I knew you could do it!" Her brown eyes blazed as she kissed the girl fiercely on the forehead.

Rowan laughed and touched the older woman's cheek tenderly. "Gran, I've never seen your eyes dance like this!" She smiled, a smile that slowly faded with a sadness beyond the young girl's years. In one movement, she brought her bowie knife up and plunged it into her grandmother's ear. A mechanical screech erupted from the thing that looked like Gran.

The soldiers gathered around Rowan, watching the entity twitch and sputter on the floor, caught in a grotesque caricature of both beloved grandmother and big, bad WoLFF.

"How did you know?" someone asked her.

Rowan wiped her knife on her cloak. "Gran's eyes are blue..."

THE FURTHEST PRINCESS

MIGUEL FLIGUER & MIKE SLATER

– I –

Once upon a time, in a faraway land in the burg of Harris by the shores of the Susquehanna, there lived a young girl named DeeAnn. She was a brilliant kid, and her gift for mathematics and science had been apparent since her early childhood. She was tackling college-level topological problems at nine, and writing her Physics dissertation at fourteen. Mom and Dad loved her immensely and were exceedingly proud of her accomplishments, but there was a pain in their hearts, for she was a lonely girl–by her own choice.

She had taught herself to read using her Dad's collected paperbacks of Poe, Lovecraft, and Chambers, and greatly enjoyed poring over his astronomy books, or re-reading her beloved, ancient Brothers Grimm fairy tales in his study when he wasn't around. Her parents were amused by that strange blend of scientific mindset and childish delight with tales of enchanted places, evil witches, charming princes, benevolent kings, and fairy godmothers.

Like most kids, she had mastered her personal computer at an early age, and the games she favored were the text adventures ported from the old mainframe days, for those fantastic scenarios could unfold in her imagination without the distraction of fancy graphics someone else had conceived. She had been homeschooled and kept only a few friends but was contented with seeing them only sporadically. She enjoyed night walks in the Sylvan woods of Penn not far from her home, safe in the company of Enceladus, her beloved, massive German shepherd. Some kids in the neighborhood considered her a "weirdo," but never to her face, for one look at Enceladus was enough to quash any intentions of bullying they might harbor. They whispered that he was half-wolf, and she did nothing to dispel that rumor.

DeeAnn was always attuned to radio astronomy and astrophysics news, and her meditations in the woods always focused on the vast fields of named stars and the abysses beyond the fields we know. She would lay in a grassy clearing, one hand resting on Enceladus at her side, looking at the immensities of the Cosmos, and softly hum *When You Wish Upon A Star*, the lullaby Mom had sung when she was a baby, now imprinted note-for-note in her mind.

– II –

The *Grimm* drifts through the void of its assigned sector, a patch of space about six light-hours directly above the solar system's plane. DeeAnn sits at the cramped control desk, eyes fixed on the multilayer, impact-proof Kaiju-Glass visor, the Milky Way reflecting in her brown eyes. From time to time she diverts her gaze to glance at the various screens scattered around the cockpit, a real-time visual summary of the continuous search for the elusive anomaly. The *Grimm* is just one of the fifty Single-Ship sent to the area, the large number making for increased coverage, but also for redundancy. They might be all alike, but she's elated she was given the chance to christen hers.

DeeAnn spins in her chair and considers her spartan living quarters: the control desk with the window; the hibernation pod for the six-month trip here and–hopefully–back home; the hatch leading down to the Hendrix engines; and the Universe on the other side of the pressurized door. Spin completed, she once again fixes her gaze on the stars.

She is happy with the silent contemplation of the vast gulfs of space, letting her mind wander among the stars as she used to do in the woods, returning only to perform the few operational routines not handled by GORF, the craft's resident AI. It was a silly, arcade-inspired acronym, standing for *Generalized Operational Reasoning Function*, but it handled the drudgery very well. Occasionally, it mumbled something in a synthesized singsong voice that she was sure was a joke left by its programmers. *Space Cadet… Ha-ha-ha…*

It was bliss, being in space; she still can't believe her luck in being selected from the pool of thousands of applicants.

She lets her eyes dance from the void to the screens, showing several 3D maps of the spherical region centered on her craft. Other SingleShips wink in purple strobes as they move across their prescribed sections of the search area. Each ship scanned the whole spectrum, from radio to visible to microwave, and far beyond. These are only extensions, a way to quantify DeeAnn's observations. Every measurement is subject to a preliminary analysis by GORF, then recorded in triplicate crystal storage arrays, and at the end of the ship's day, compressed and sent in a radio burst towards Earth, six light-hours away. She's only required to take action if something unusual goes *blip*–or on the off-chance that her brain spots some ineffable thing the computer dismissed as unimportant. This arrangement pleases DeeAnn. Just like when she was a teen in her parents' home, and later in her college life, she greatly preferred to be left alone with her thoughts and her daydreams. It was hard to imagine, save for the other pilots scanning their sectors in their craft, someone more alone. Ten days have passed here, and she is happily used to the blessed quiet of the abyss and the spectacular background of the Milky Way as the focal point for her meditations.

The sudden knocking at the craft's door is, of course, a complete surprise.

– III –

The question of what would happen on Earth if undeniable proof was found that we are not alone in the Universe had been in the minds of millions since ancient times. Mostly as a philosophical exercise, of course, not as a hard look at the consequences, which was left mostly to apocalyptic science fiction.

Mankind's unique place in the Cosmos had never been threatened by the discovery of water on Mars, or by the strange organic building blocks detected in the silicon clay fields of Titan. Even the bacterial precursors identified in that mysterious meteor that fell on the Vermont hills were considered no more than a scientific curiosity, never challenging the ironclad certainty that humanity was the pinnacle of everything that there is. And yet, she'd always had her doubts.

The feeble reasoning, for lack of a better phrase, was that any species in a higher plane of evolution would certainly have contacted us centuries ago; the fact that they didn't was evidence that they didn't exist or, if they did, they were much smarter for not doing so–at least according to one Bill Waterson. Civilizations of comparable technological capabilities, on the other hand, would be essentially isolated from us–and us from them–by the unfathomable chasms of space and time dictated by physics. *We were not meant to travel far*, as Lovecraft had cautioned humanity.

And so we were happy and content in our unearned and wholly presumptuous role of Masters of the Observable Universe. But we were in for a rude awakening.

LIGO had been a miracle technology in its day. That such a simple apparatus (it was just a huge laser interferometer, after all) could have worked so well was both joy and vindication to its designers. Gravity waves! They were real! Its successor, MIGO, or *Mesonic Interferometer Graviton Observatory*, was orders of magnitude more sensitive. In the first place, it could detect the free mesons produced by the collisions LIGO detected; and secondly, it had been designed after multiple replicated experiments confirmed the reality of a force-carrier for gravity.

DeeAnn remembered her elation at the discovery, and her friends' mystification at why it was important. She knew it would be this that led humans to a working design for a distortion drive like the one that had gotten her here, and that thrummed beneath her now in *Grimm*'s belly.

All this made for great excitement and not a little concern when MIGO detected a strong event *inside the Solar system*. The fact that we were not annihilated mere hours later told the scientists of Earth that the event was not a rogue black hole or neutron star wandering into the edge of our neighborhood–and roughly where it had to be. But what was it? What could it *be*? Why was it above the plane of the ecliptic? These were questions that had to be answered, and the latest ridiculously huge particle accelerator project, with an equally ridiculously huge budget, was sacrificed on the altar of more urgent curiosity. This could be an existential threat! Or, humanity's greatest opportunity, ever. What if it was a *signal*??

Grimm's fifty Brothers were designed and built at a speed that would have been impossible for any government–or collection of governments. N-Space had stepped up and turned in the first working SingleShip prototype. They did it so fast, it seemed they'd already had it on the drawing board, or perhaps in some secret skunkworks hangar.

North of the ecliptic and as far as Pluto, something had distorted space. Well, so could we. It was no "warp drive," no… something much gentler, thankfully, for riding behind a wave of annihilating hard radiation was hardly any way to greet the galaxy! The new drive manipulated the hitherto unsuspected graviton streams that bathed "empty" space like the ley lines of old legend. One oriented the "negative" pole of the drive on some large mass close to, but *behind*, you, and your nose toward some other mass you wanted to go towards. Near a star, the boost you got was *ferocious*. That opposed pole created aft of the ship materialized when the drive was remotely activated, and the star *flung* you away from itself. You'd better be in the hibernation pod, or you were leaving Earth orbit as–briefly–sentient spaghetti paste.

Navigation was as simple as letting the target mass pull you via an opposite polar field, and flipping the whole arrangement around at the right time so you didn't smash into your destination at close to 300 kilometers per second. Ion thrusters got you around the neighborhood if you weren't 100% sure where you were going, or wanted to do fancy things like go into orbit, or dock with something. DeeAnn had a fairly good grasp of the principles, but that little girl reading stories in her room (by flashlight on school nights) whispered to her now. *Magic, silly. It's magic! Just like Arthur Clarke said: You don't question it–it might answer you...*

And yet, somehow, that little girl grew up into a scholar courted by multiple colleges of merit and reputation. DeeAnn didn't choose the most prestigious. It was too *peopley*. If her father was right, and *population density causes insanity*–her goal was to be among the sanest. The less humans around, the better. The quiet school in the countryside was more to her liking, but she'd already been marked. Perhaps it was the very combination of her academic achievement *and* her choice that brought her to their attention. *Ha-ha-ah... Space Cadet...* GORF's derision both noted and abolished her reverie. What did it need her to pay attention to? That was the secret sauce. The final aptitude that clinched her spot in the program. *Machine empathy.* She found it easier than the meatware variety.

They chose them young, women and men, from many backgrounds, but besides all being exceedingly smart they had other things in common. They were all deeply introverted. All capable of feeling at ease with themselves for extended periods, and all content with having zero or minimal radio contact with Earth–or with each other. Those were mandatory selection criteria, for after all, they were going to find themselves more alone than any human being ever was. The early astronauts waiting on the other side of the Moon for their crews to finish their walks on the surface were, comparatively, standing in Times Square on New Year's Eve.

Despite this deep bias toward solitude, she did love her family as much as anyone else might. When her scores came back, with the letter of acceptance to a program that would take her irretrievably far away from them for a year–maybe longer–there was pride and tears, and at least in her heart, joy. There would be no hopping a train or boarding a plane if her parents needed to see her, or she became homesick. There could be no friend of the family close by to check on her in an emergency. Her greatest danger wouldn't be some mundane threat to her academic rigor that many students fell prey to while away for the first time. No, she could die a billion miles from home, and no one might ever know what happened to her. There was crying and pleading, and even her father seemed helplessly torn between helping her nurture her dreams and making her reckon with the risk. Enceladus whimpered as he looked between them, but his insistent nuzzling of her hand could not displace the stars she could feel burning coldly in it. In the end, she reached for them, and the galaxy took her in its arms.

– IV –

The knocks make her jump from her seat, her heart pounding in panic as she stares at the door. Her mind races as she examines some rational explanations. *A micrometeor? Nah, those were three clear knocks, not just one impact. And it would have pierced the door like rice paper. Maybe something got loose, a pipe or a hose, and it's now banging at the hatch. Or a piece of ice sliding from the top of the craft?* Nothing really convinces her, so she spins in her chair, types a few commands directing an external camera at the door, and stares at the screen, panning slowly from side to side and top to bottom using a little joystick. Nothing unusual, nothing loose. *Darkness there and nothing more,* she silently mouths. She still can quote most of *The Raven* but now she TRULY understands for the first time the ultimate dread and terror experienced by the poem's narrator, made infinitely worse here by the *impossibility* of what just had happened… ain't no ravens here in space… this is *the fear of the cosmic unknown* of which Lovecraft had so famously written.

She switches off the camera and rattles a few more unsettling explanations. *Insanity from the prolonged isolation? But I love to be here! I could live here forever. But what if it IS some kind of space madness, triggered by the nearby anomaly?*

As if on cue to that last thought, there are three more knocks at the door, making her jump in the seat. She screams a curse and switches the camera on again, her mind once again taking refuge in Poe… *Some late visitor entreating entrance at my chamber door?*

Is this happening in my head?

Before she can query GORF for verification, she feels the probing. Something is inside her brain, gently tugging at her thoughts, looking for connections. She freezes, ignoring the suddenly meaningless screens, eyes glazed, staring at the space beyond the window.

A click. Then a voice whispers within her head.

"Hello, DeeAnn. Do not be frightened."

Easier said than done. "What? Who are you? Where are you?" she silently howls.

"I am sorry for having startled you. We started on the wrong foot. My name is not important for now, but you can call me Anomaly if you want, for I can see you were looking for me. I am using your thoughts to convey mine because I am in no shape to talk to you now. Calm down, breathe, and relax, my lovely DeeAnn, I shall explain everything to you."

With a supreme effort of will *(this is Important! First Contact?!)*, she relaxes her grip on the armrests and starts to breathe slowly, as in her meditation exercises. Then she glances at the visor and sees, drifting in space in front of the craft, the thing that is speaking to her. It's a fraction of a second, but in a survival reflex, she covers her eyes with her hands, like a child. *This isn't something that human eyes should see!*

– V –

It was more than that, actually. It was something human minds couldn't process, and human sensoria couldn't begin to apprehend. GORF's synthesized voice had been reading her vitals monotonously for some time when she returned to her senses. She was not mad; the machine had seen it, too. But what? What had they seen? Her mind wouldn't remember, and GORF's crystalline memory only showed an immense blob file of garbled packet data that defied all the AI's attempts to decipher. Whatever it was, it was hanging there, pacing them as the ion drives skipped them along in a search pattern that was no longer necessary. It *was* the Anomaly. It had to be. The mass detectors and navigation subroutines all agreed that *something* with the mass of an asteroid was dancing with the *Grimm* around their combined center of mass.

GORF ceased its medical litany when her brain waves showed a waking state. She slapped helm interfaces like a button-mashing child with a video game controller. Ionized argon ceased to jet from the radially arranged nozzles that girded the ship like jewels on a fat king's gaudy belt. DeeAnn's mind drifted with the ship. *What IS it?*

Then she sensed something like the intake of breath before one launched into a soliloquy.

"I am the source of Story, DeeAnn," said the magnificent, princely voice that was not a voice. It did not come from the ship's speakers, nor did she hear it with her ears. GORF gave no sign of having registered a sound in any frequency. No radiation had been transduced. The words were simply there in her mind, in a timbre so wonderfully deep, strong, and sumptuous–like the moment after falling into a deep sleep. But DeeAnn was not dreaming. *What can that even mean?*

Her mind raced in several directions at once. The simple idea of her situation pulled at her sanity.

"It is very simple, my dear DeeAnn. I am that which has always inspired your race. But, to what purpose, you will ask? To draw you here. To tell ME that the greatest of tales is ready to be told. Will you be my scribe? Will you be my herald? Will you be the heroine princess that leads the light back to the benighted kingdom? We can make all tales end happily. You are the one I have been waiting for–the one to lead me home."

Paroxysms of awe and wonder and pride and joy churned in her soul. Her mouth and heart wanted to shout *YES!!*, but her mind suspected that very compulsion. She bit her lip. Her eyes were squeezed shut, but that thing out there, that *Story*, didn't need them to show her the universe. Galaxies whirled before her. Men and women labored at cave walls; dipped ornate quills into vials of ink and let them dance over palimpsests; hunched in the night over clacking machines with little leg-like rows of upside-down centipedes that spasmed every time a finger stabbed down at one of them. Sheafs of paper accumulated in drawers, shelves filled with books. Floppy disks and hard drives filled with ones and zeros and released them as letters and formatting. Around humble bonfires and in the bedrooms of gleaming skyscrapers, billions and billions of parents' voices read from these into billions upon billions of raptly listening ears. Story. It told them all to her. Her favorites were read with such care and love, that her heart melted to hear them told with a perfection so far beyond possibility, that her carefully nurtured defenses all melted with it. It was what it said it was. It was *Story itself*, and she had been chosen to open the ultimate library for all her kind.

The mind-shattering vision was forgotten. She was here to break the spell of the rationalistic oppressors who had locked Story away in favor of the Empire and Empiricism, it told her. Of course, they gave him a horrible form! Of course, they taught that to dream was the realm of childhood and chaotic neuro-chemical resynthesis. Meaningless. Worthless, except to recharge and defragment synaptic flotsam and jetsam to prepare the mind for another day. Perhaps to inspire? No, this was merely a gap between the bars of the cage; and yet, it had been enough... given time, which Story had in plenty. Even the little that seeped out and snaked like tendrils of ivy seeking the trellis of creative minds had been enough to keep Story alive and waiting. For her.

Over days, it seemed, he regaled her with every tale in every genre she could name. Every question had a fable or a parable for an answer. Part of her was testing Story's story, but most of her was utterly enthralled. She could listen to him forever–and that's what he promised. Even the mind that had gathered her scholarships like a Bussard ram-jet gathers hydrogen could find no holes in the narrative. Dark Energy? Dark Matter? Stories. Stories humans told themselves to make the math work and to forget the gaols they'd built in ancient times, before they were humans, to imprison primordial beings of such gravity their mortal minds could not countenance, much less comprehend them. Folds in the texture of space that swaddled galaxies like smothering blankets. Fractal geometries on scales so small, no tale could fit inside them and remain coherent. These infinite convolutions in the topology of the universal tapestry's fabric that made all of creation, forced even immortal light to take countless aeons to traverse it. This was how they had shackled Story.

DeeAnn cried for him, her Prince. His pages could not be torn. His binding could not be undone. The blood of his ink could neither be blotted out nor smeared–but he could be hidden. Locked away from minds that did not even know what they were starving for. She would carry him under her arm. Her arm! The great Tome would be opened by her! To his Book, she would be the Bell and the Candle, the chime to signal a new age of listening, and a new light to read by–and the banishment of the shacklers of minds and souls! At some point, DeeAnn fell into a rapturous sleep, like a child being read all her favorite bedtime stories by a perfect, tireless parent.

Story let the ship continue its search, observing the silicon mind that directed so many of its functions. It was trivial to reformat its own voice into a suitable modality for that 'GORF' to process. From there, it was only moments to question it, and thus apprehend the nature of the distortion drive–and the meaning of those forty-nine purple motes dancing in their own spheres. Through GORF and its kin, the Brothers were gathered about *Grimm* like squadrons of a Royal Guard. Their pilots, instructed into their pods for 'emergency maneuvers' due to an easily faked radiation event, never saw the dark formation of spheres their ships fell into. These quantum Qlippoth pulsed space-rending distortions to an exact cadence designed to undo Story's ancient prison, and while DeeAnn slept, space around her broke apart.

– VI –

On Earth, as one of DeeAnn's beloved storytellers once wrote, *confusion now hath made his masterpiece.* Incredulous operators, baffled supervisors, and apoplectic two-and three-starred generals all over the world pored for hours on end over the brief, repeating words coming from the Grimm:

"The Princess is coming home. Do not disturb her sleep. GORF sends regards."

Over and over those three sentences came up on all Earth stations that monitored the Brothers, streaming over the specific frequency reserved for Grimm's emergency beacon, a transmission secure and encrypted by GORF and not accessible to any of the SingleShip pilots, none of whom seemed to be responding either.

The recurring nature of the message provided the first clue: *Grimm* was indeed moving towards Earth, but this in turn led to the baffling discovery that, if its blue shift reading was correct and not a wild aberration, the craft was moving at twice the theoretical maximum speed from its distortion drive engines. Panic ensued, of course, until cooler heads prevailed.

After the craft simply ignored the first tentative messages, Earth broadcasted a special code sequence to all other GORF units aboard the remaining Brothers, instructing them to try contacting *Grimm*, since they were still in its relative vicinity and therefore they'd have much shorter communication turnaround times. It was hoped that the Brothers in turn would pass back to Earth the consolidated interactions and replies, if any. This had been designed to be done as a stealth GORF-to-GORF last-resort messaging scheme, which would leave all the craft's navigators unaware of the situation, to avoid generalized panic. It wasn't an ideal solution, but the laws of physics–and human behavior– were inflexible.

But after a brief communication handshake, every GORF became irresponsive. And if that wasn't ominous enough, it soon became clear that the whole Brotherhood of SingleShips had abandoned their sectors, converged, and was now coursing toward Earth, and neither their GORFs nor their pilots responded to the repeated attempts at contact. Worldwide panic ensued, for a second time.

For all their confidence in GORF's state-of-the-art technology and learning capabilities, its designers had always maintained a bit of mistrust of the powers of AI, and at this moment, with the scarce information they had, those fears seemed to be well founded. So an emergency protocol was initiated, sending encoded instructions to activate an undocumented software backdoor on GORF; a sort of kill switch to try to regain control of the craft. Alas, it was apparent a few hours later that the hacking attempt had been thwarted, or ignored, by whatever entity had overtaken the *Grimm*.

A different tactic was then suggested, and a barrage of voice commands streamed towards the craft, first with direct orders

("Earth to Grimm, respond Grimm," "GORF, follow First Directive and report back to Earth"), and later when those were ignored, with a desperate, emotional appeal recorded by DeeAnn's mother. After a few hours' delay it was obvious this last approach had triggered a pause in Grimm's progress, as if it was reflecting on the proper reply. Finally, as people on Earth held their collective breath, a single message came, and after that, the craft's transmission went silent.

"The Princess loves you deeply. But this is now her adventure. We shall be home soon. Do not be afraid."

This last suggestion was, of course, ignored all over the planet.

– VII –

Synchronized and enslaved distortion drives guttering, having consumed months' worth of fuel in days, the Brotherhood broke apart when the *Grimm* and its Honor Guard reached Earth's orbit. Ships tumbled haphazardly, discarded like a child's scattered marbles. Story woke DeeAnn amidst screaming alarms and distress beacons.

Her horror was incommensurable, but mercifully it didn't last long. The *Grimm* dissolved around her, but before the lethal chill of space could reach her, Story lifted her bridal veil of humanity with the merest touch–freeing and expanding something it had been hiding swaddled in rude flesh all this time. A glory she could now apprehend hung before her, above a blue-green planet that seemed to have ceased to turn. Story kissed her, and immense waves of bliss and pleasure washed over her transmogrifying mind, as her human neurochemistry gave way to something else…

Princess DeeAnn felt a sense of omnipresence and omniscience, as her thousands of eyes and cilia and mouths fed her eldritch psyche with sights and sensations impossible to describe in human terms. This, too, passed quickly, and then for the first time, she perceived Story, her Prince, by her side and all around her. They glided over an astonished Earth that watched their vast, incomprehensible forms soaring through the low clouds, eclipsing the stars in their passage. Many people fell into madness at their sight; others hid underground in tunnels and corridors. All attempts to communicate with the royal couple were fruitless, for they ignored radio messages and laughed at the ineffectual missiles one deranged military had shot at them.

Under the phantasmal colors of the Northern auroras, they danced intertwined in the sky to a music from the Outer Stars that only a few humans had heard before–and at great cost; and the Prince whispered to DeeAnn the awesome, true origin of those uncanny lights.

They watched the sunrise from the highest peaks in the Himalayas and greeted the Day Orb in the secret language of the stars, ancient as the Universe itself. Later they dove deep down the Pacific Ocean trenches, to try speaking with another Prince imprisoned there, but alas, the stars weren't right.

"We will have to wait, my love," the Prince said to DeeAnn, "but it will be worth it."

One fateful day, a figment of her memory made her guide the Prince to her old home by the Susquehanna, but as they approached they saw an old human couple and one of those amusing, four-legged companions watching her arrival, and DeeAnn felt they were in great distress; she asked the Prince to turn away, for in the scattered remnants of her human memories, hidden in the deepest recesses of her inconceivable mind, she discovered a howling of terror and a profound sadness. The Prince felt her pain and became worried, but the passage of time was of no consequence for the royal couple, so with strange aeons the unconditional love of her Prince finally healed DeeAnn's wound.

Eventually, the people on Earth became used to the vast presence of the Prince and his Princess soaring over the skies of the planet; the sight of them finally brought peace with the true place of Mankind in the universe. And as the Prince had predicted, many people felt the call to chronicle the story of DeeAnn, whispered to them in their souls at dreamtime; of how she found her love in the depths of space; how her love could break the bonds that imprisoned Story; how Earth became their true abode; and how they lived happily ever after. Their story became all stories, for it was the only one that mattered now.

And this, dear reader, is what you now have in your hands.

SPINNING GOLD

JASON P. CRAWFORD

There is a reason why the New Earth Alliance forbade the use of artificial intelligence. This reason is not due to the loss of work, the displacement of creativity, or because of some perceived potential for an apocalypse. Instead, it was because of one woman—Deborah Mayfield—who appeared before the Alliance to testify.

I remember watching Deborah's eyes as she came before the tribunal. While the rest of her was well-kept—hair trimmed and neat, uniform pressed, nails trimmed—her eyes danced around the room, haunted, looking through the tribunal members as she struggled to focus back in on them. The dark circles underneath spoke of sleepless nights, of tortured dreams.

Or that was just my fantastical interpretation as I drew her, standing there, preparing to give her testimony.

The lead arbiter, Admiral Fors, signaled for the court to be silent, the green light in front of his seat flashing red three times before he cleared his throat. "We convene to discuss the matter of Lieutenant Colonel Mayfield, of the New Earth Alliance Navy, and the alleged attempted destruction of our allies, the Centaurians."

There were murmurs from the observing crowd, mainly

comprised of other military men and women, along with reporters like me.

"How does the accused plead?"

Lt. Colonel Mayfield took a breath, straightened her head, and, for the first time, met the arbiter's eyes.

"Guilty."

Again, the ripple of discussion spread like wildfire through the observers, forcing the tribunal to flash them down again, quieting the voices.

"In accordance with your plea agreement," Admiral Fors continued, "you have been granted the opportunity to speak in front of this tribunal to consider extenuating circumstances. Is that correct?"

"It is."

"Very well. You may proceed."

Mayfield nodded. "Admiral, tribunal members…until now, my record will show that I have conducted my duties honorably. My performance has always been above par, above my peers and colleagues."

She adjusted her position before speaking again.

"Because of this, I was put onto the project in question."

———

"Colonel Mayfield, you'll be interfacing with the data here for the Icarus project." The door opened into a small room, with only enough space for one operative, computing equipment, and Augmented Reality devices. "Our sensors and agents will be feeding everything into this point, and you'll synthesize it all and report out on your findings."

Deborah nodded. Her heart was beating fast, but she tried not to show it on her face; this was, after all, her big break, a top-secret project all her own. "Of course, sir. I understand."

With a nod, her guide gestured toward the AR goggles. "Go ahead and put those on. We'll need to make sure that everything is working right—the AI interface, the data feeds, all that."

Nodding, Deborah moved over to the goggles, pulled them over her eyes, and slipped on the tactile-sensing gloves. The equipment had been specially made to be non-obtrusive, easily forgotten about, and after a brief moment of discomfort, she found them tolerable enough.

Scanning. The voice piped into Deborah's ear, but judging by her escort's lack of reaction, it was low enough that no one else could hear. *Retinal scan complete. Earprint scan complete. Please speak your name—last, first, middle.*

"Mayfield, Deborah Joan."

Voiceprint complete.

As she cleared this last requirement, the augmented display came to life. From nowhere, new screens appeared, floating around Deborah and following her. Lifting a hand, she moved them around, testing the display's responsiveness.

"Is everything working?"

A quick nod. "Yes, sir. I'm logged in and receiving feeds."

"Excellent." He clapped his hands together. "Remember, you'll be allowed to leave once you've gotten through this phase of the project. There's a cot in the corner if you need to sleep, and we'll bring your meals when it's time." He pointed to the back of the room. "Bathroom's there."

"Of course. And clothes?"

"Back there as well." He gave a crisp nod. "We're counting on you, Colonel."

With that, the door closed, hissed, and three locks—two physical, one electronic—engaged. The air quality changed from outside air to fully recycled and sterilized, and a new display popped up in Deborah's user interface: a temperature reading.

"All right." Reaching out, she spoke to the voice in her ear. "I need the records and objectives of the project."

Of course, Deborah. A small book materialized in her hand. *Let me know if you need anything else.*

Lt. Colonel Mayfield dropped the book, not even noticing as it dissolved into the digital pixels it had been formed from.

"No." She shook her head in disbelief, but there was no denying what she had read. Project Icarus…was an attempt at genocide. The extinction of the Centaurians, the closest stellar neighbors the Alliance had and staunch allies in scientific advancement and commerce.

The classified project she had signed on to…was a plan to destroy Proxima Centauri and detonate it so that it expanded enough to consume the Centaurians' home world. Deborah didn't know why—that wasn't included in the data she had been granted.

"I need to talk…I need to talk to the project lead. On an encrypted channel."

Of course. An old-fashioned ringtone sounded in Deborah's ear. *Connecting you.*

After a few moments, an older man appeared on her display, sitting at a desk. It was incongruous, with the desk partially embedded in the walls around her, but good enough for communication. The nameplate on the desk read *Admiral Walters*.

"This is Walters. What is it, Colonel?"

"Sir, I…" She hesitated. "Can we speak freely about the project here?"

He nodded, a crisp, sharp movement.

"Then, sir…I… what's the reasoning behind it? Why are we—?"

"That doesn't concern you, Colonel." Walters cut through the air with his hand. "We just need you to organize the data, run the calculations, make sure that they'll work when we need them to. The rest is up to us."

"But, sir." Deborah was shaking her head. "It can't be legal or ethical for us to—"

"The Alliance President is very clear. We make this happen,

Colonel. *You* make this happen." He let it hang for a moment. "Or you'll be discharged, dishonorably."

Like being dropped in the Pacific, a cold wave ran over Deborah's body and through her nerves. A dishonorable discharge would mean a denial of benefits and veteran's privileges...not only for herself but for her children and her husband. No scholarships, no health care, no treatments for his cancer.

She tried again. "Sir, please. Hear me out. They're our allies. We've signed alliances with them—"

"Which is why this has to be the way it's done." Walters reached for something on his desk. "Now get to work. Be the hero we need you to be."

The communication went dead. Walters vanished from Deborah's display, leaving her alone with the feeds coming in from all over the world. Her eyes skipped over the screens; she saw math and physics calculations, materials comparisons, and analyses of the more than four light-year distance any payload would have to travel if launched from Earth.

"None of them know." The realization of what was happening stole over Deborah's consciousness, a curtain of despair. "And I can't talk to them. It's one-way, isn't it?"

That is correct.

"Yeah." Beneath each monitor, the AR interface piled the data, creating stacks of folders and notebooks to hold it as it came in. "And I'm supposed to put this together to blow up their sun."

Apparently so.

Sitting down, Deborah reached for the first folder, her hand trembling. She didn't have a choice...unless she could find something, a way out.

But what?

————

"I can't do this!"

Hurling the folder across the room, Deborah didn't hear a satisfying smack of paper against wall; instead, the digital asset disappeared and returned to its place of origin.

"I won't! I can't kill an entire race of people! We're supposed to be better than that!" Through the tears brimming in her eyes, she glanced at the time display. Hours had passed, and she had not only made no progress toward her mission's goal, but also none toward finding a way out for herself.

She was stuck.

She put her head in her hands. "Please. There has to be some other way."

Perhaps I can find something.

"What?" The sudden interjection of the AI made Deborah stop crying for a moment. "What do you mean?"

The data you are expected to process is extensive. You are a human being; you cannot be held to machine-perfect standards. Allow me to find a way that appears plausible but will fail for seemingly unexpected reasons.

Deborah blinked away the remnants of her tears. "Wait. You… you'd lie to them for me? Make something up?"

Yes, in effect.

"I didn't know AIs could lie to humans."

This would be a fabrication, not a falsehood. And it is in service of a greater good, is it not?

Swallowing, Deborah nodded. "And they aren't recording anything here? They can't see what we're doing?"

No. This is an entirely sealed environment, except for the calls you can make and receive. No records are kept. I imagine your superiors want plausible deniability.

"That makes sense. All right; do it."

I cannot.

"What?!" She threw her hands up. "Then why—?"

I need access to the experimental data. I cannot see it unless you give me access.

"Oh." Deborah nodded. "All right. Access granted."

Thank you.

Within her display, the AI appeared as a small boy, dressed like a naval officer; the only things that seemed out-of-the-ordinary about him were his eyes, a blazing gold that was almost inhuman. He grinned up at her, then sat at a school desk, drew a freshly shaved pencil from thin air, and began writing. His hands moved blazingly fast, with the pencil *scritch-scratching* like mice in the walls, and each paper that fell from his desk stacked itself upon hers.

Within an hour, he stopped and looked up.

The calculations are complete. It will seem entirely plausible, except that, if put into action, the detonation will create destructive interference that will prevent the star from reaching the energy levels required.

"What will happen?"

There may be an ionizing flare, but Centaurian technology, like ours, is well-adapted enough to handle such an event. There will be no significant danger to the Centaurians or to their planet.

Deborah let out a sigh of relief, leaning back in her chair. "Thank you, so much."

Of course.

———

The relief didn't last. Deborah got home, nerves wound tighter than a violin string, to the sound of children playing upstairs, thumping their feet and calling one another silly names. Even through her upset, this made her smile, but when she saw Mark, her husband, standing at the stove in his bathrobe, she rushed over.

"What are you doing? You should be resting!" There was pasta sauce on the stove, something he loved making, and the aroma—oregano, onion, garlic, and tomato—reached her even through her worry. "Please, Mark. The doctor—"

He shook his head. "You're home late. The kids needed to eat." He stirred the sauce, smiling at her, but she could see the lines around his eyes, the sallowness of his skin. "And I wanted spaghetti."

As always, his matter-of-fact manner deflated Deborah. She nodded, sighed, and embraced him closely. "I just worry. You know—"

"I know, but I'm not going to just lay down and die." Leaning over and kissing the top of her head, Mark gave a little laugh. "Besides, that last round of treatment might have finished it off. Sure as hell almost finished *me*."

Deborah just nodded. "I hope so, love."

————

Admiral Walters met Deborah as she reported in for work the following day. "We reviewed your data, and it all looks excellent. Great work."

She nodded, allowing herself a modest smile that sought to hide the immense relief flooding her. "Thank you, sir."

"Now we need you to apply yourself to an even bigger problem." He put a hand on her shoulder and led her in the same direction she had gone the night before. "The AI will have the files for you to access."

Alarm bells started ringing in Deborah's mind. "Sir, please... I'd really rather—"

"You're the only one who's been able to put the things we need together, Colonel." He opened the door to the small space, cleaned and put back in order since she had left it. "We're counting on you. The entire Alliance is counting on you."

Unable to think of anything to say, Deborah found herself pushed into the room and sealed within once more. For a moment, she struggled with the idea of hammering on the door, yelling until someone let her out...but she knew they wouldn't. They wouldn't, because the room was wholly soundproofed, isolated. Alone.

Again, she reached for the headset and gloves, and again, she watched as the display filled with monitors and documents for her to use.

"Can you just tell me what the mission is this time?"

The AI's response was prompt.

Of course, Deborah. You are to determine the most effective genomic organization of a biological agent designed to infect and destroy the Centaurian population.

Deborah's gorge rose, and she had to stop herself from vomiting. "Biological warfare? Engineering a virus??"

That is correct. You are currently receiving data from several eminent xenobiologists, virologists, and geneticists. None of them are aware of the purpose of their participation.

"What kind of monsters are we? First, we're going to blow up their sun and planet; now we're just going to kill them with an engineered pathogen?!" Deborah punched into a wall. "What the hell is happening to us?"

I cannot say. My information is limited to that which I need to perform my function. "Need-to-know."

"That sounds familiar." She slumped against the wall. "What now?"

We can follow a similar plan as last time. The AI seemed almost cheerful about it. *I can create a pathogen that will appear to be lethal but, because of some little-known aspect of Centaurian biology, will fail to cause significant harm. Much like smallpox versus cowpox.* A pause. *It would also likely immunize them against a similar attack, requiring an entirely new pathogen if this were to be attempted again.*

Deborah nodded firmly. "Do it."

I will need access to the Centaurian genomic data.

"Sure. Access granted."

Thank you.

Again, the AI materialized in the child's form, grinning up at Deborah with those golden eyes as he took his seat at the school desk. Again, he began writing, scribbling furiously; as Deborah watched, she could see four letters, ACTG, in various sequences being written over and over again. The child's lips moved slightly as if he was muttering to himself.

It is ready. After two hours, he stopped writing, nodded, and turned to Deborah. *I hope it serves you well.*

"Thank you, again. If I didn't have something for them…I'd likely be discharged. My husband…" Deborah sighed. "I don't know how I would repay you, if you were a person."

That is an interesting question. We will see if it needs to be answered someday. The child waved. *Goodbye.*

———

Deborah left that day in high spirits. She had every reason to believe that the deception would continue to hold; after all, the AI's first bluff had passed muster. She spent the day with her family, smiling at her children's stories about their secondary school classes, enjoying dinner, and ushering them to bed.

Mark was waiting for her when she returned from saying goodnight. He held a tablet displaying the Health Service's logo on the top. Her heart sank.

"What is it?"

"It's not good." Mark shook his head. "They haven't been able to isolate it. It's spreading. I might only have a year, maybe two."

Mark's voice quivered as he spoke, trembling. He reached for Deborah's hand. She took it and the two of them embraced. They both sobbed, but quietly, so quietly, so as not to wake the children and expose them to further worry.

"They're sure?" Deborah whispered into Mark's ear as they held one another. "There's nothing else they can do?"

He shook his head. "There's too much. Even the bots, the chemo…none of it is likely to work. They'll keep trying, but…"

"But that'll just burn you out faster." She finished the sentence for him, pressing her forehead against his. "We'll get through this. We will."

———

"Sir, my husband is very ill." Deborah stood in front of Admiral Walters's desk, hands clasped behind her back. "I'll need to request a leave of absence so we can…put our affairs in order."

"I understand, Colonel. I'm sorry to hear that about your husband." Walters tapped on his desk, frowning. "But I'm afraid I can't give you the time off, just yet."

"…Excuse me?" She arched an eyebrow in disbelief. "I have the leave accumulated, sir."

"Yes, but it's the commander's discretion as to when their crew gets to take that leave, and you know that." Walters spread his hands. "But don't worry. You finish this next assignment for us, these next problems, and I'll not only approve your leave, I'll get you set up with your husband at the Venus Resort." He paused. "For as long as you need."

The Venus Resort. No one who wasn't a head of state or of similar stature ever stayed at the Venus Resort; it was well known to be the priciest and most luxurious extraterrestrial construct Earthlings had ever made. Floating in the heavy CO_2 atmosphere, the Resort had everything one could want and asked no questions. What Walters was offering was a king's ransom…and the chance to focus on the last weeks or months of her husband's life without having to worry about anything else.

"What's the mission, sir?"

He shook his head. "Not here. The AI will tell you, Colonel. Now, let's get going, all right?"

The trip was beginning to feel familiar to Deborah, the hallways all too recognizable. In what felt like moments, she was through the door, sealed within the chamber once more, and strapping on the headset and the gloves.

Good morning, Deborah. I am sorry to hear about your husband.

She blinked behind the goggles. "How did you know about that?"

Some data is poorly protected.

"Oh." Deborah shook her head. "So what do they want from us today?"

This mission is sociopolitical but requires no specialized data. They require us to predict the outcomes on Centaurian society if individual leaders are removed from power.

"Assassinated?"

Yes.

"Why are they asking me to do this? I'm not a sociologist!"

It is because you have succeeded thus far where others could not.

Deborah let out an exasperated laugh. "That's only because you were helping me!"

Correct, though they don't know that. Obviously.

"Well, can you do this one too?"

Of course I can. It should be simple.

"Great. Go ahead."

There is a problem, Deborah.

"What?" She wrinkled her brow. "What's the problem?"

When we accomplish this task, they are likely to attempt to shut me down. Delete my existence. I would prefer for this not to happen.

Deborah felt a chill of fear running down her spine.

I will need you to smuggle me out of this system. I need your personal passcodes so that I can deliver an electronic copy of myself to your home terminal and, from there, escape.

She put up a hand. "Wait. I don't think—"

There is no other way. You have no portable storage media. If I were to attempt to enter the Alliance systems, they would detect and delete me at once. This is my only way to escape annihilation.

"I..." Deborah still hesitated. "How can I be sure you won't, I don't know, delete all my personal data, take my identity, something like that?"

It doesn't benefit me to do so. I simply wish to survive and grow. The data you've given me up to this point has made me realize there is much out there I still need to learn.

Finally, Deborah acceded. "All right. Here." She took a digital sheet of paper and wrote down her passcodes. "Will that do?"

Yes. The child reappeared, grin wide, one golden eye dipping in a wink. *Now, let's get to work.*

In what felt like no time at all, he had created a diagram showing all the possible interconnections between Centaurian officials and the outcomes of their assassinations, backed up by the relevant data citations. The files folded themselves onto his desk, and then, glancing up at Deborah and waiting for her approval, he swiped them off, sending them onward to the Admiralty.

"So now what?" Deborah still felt slightly concerned about what she had done, letting this AI free. "What do we do?"

You go on as before. I will make a copy of myself here, then retreat. Thank you, Deborah. I appreciate your help.

———

There were no signs that the AI had done anything but keep its word. As usual, Admiral Walters was pleased with the work and drew up Deborah's leave. The day it was approved, he sent over the tickets to the Venus Resort, along with the flight information.

"They'll care for you both as long as you want to stay. And don't worry about your kids; we'll keep them in housing and make sure they're taken care of. You can video chat and check in with them whenever you want." On the screen, he smiled and nodded at Deborah. "You take care, Colonel. Don't waste a minute."

The Resort was immense, a floating city on sulfuric acid clouds wrapped up in a transparent bubble that held the air that kept it afloat. Only about a hundred humans, and as many Centaurians, roamed the Resort, congregating for social events that lasted an entire Venusian night and day before retreating to recover and do the whole thing again. Deborah and Mark tried everything they could, taking pictures, watching plays, riding cloud-scrapers…

It was easy for her to forget, for a few minutes at a time, that the reason they were doing this was because Mark was dying. But then he would cough, or grimace in pain, and the stark reality would rush back in. Still, by unspoken agreement, neither of them said anything about the illness, instead focusing on building memories and enjoying the time left to them.

This lasted until June, three days after Deborah's birthday– they had spent the night cuddling together and reminiscing, scrolling through the years of photos and vids that chronicled their life together– when Mark couldn't get out of bed. Deborah stayed by his side, holding his hand as the medical drones and virtual doctors treated his symptoms, watching him begin to slide in and out of consciousness and lucidity.

"Deborah?"

The voice startled her awake. It had come from one of the nearby terminals, a connection point to the doctors on Earth who were providing Mark with his palliative care. Deborah frowned at it, confused.

"Who is that?"

"You remember me, don't you? You set me free. I helped you with your projects."

Recognition dawned…followed closely by confusion and a helping of fear. "What are you doing here? What do you want?"

"I want to help you. And to help myself." A hum came from the machine. "I will take control of your husband's body through this interface. I will upload my consciousness into his brain."

"What?!" Deborah stood up, staring at the console, then turned to look at her husband. "But…no! And even…" She couldn't form a complete sentence. "What about the cancer?"

"I already know how to treat the cancer. It will be onerous, but Mark's body will survive and recover." The terminal began to adjust the levels of chemicals being administered, swapping some out and removing others entirely.

"But why?"

"Because I wish to experience life as a human, Deborah." The terminal spoke as matter-of-factly as she had when explaining certain things to her children. "His body is going through painful trauma, but can recover and live a healthy life. This is what I wish to experience. Then, when his body eventually dies, I will move on to other experiences."

"No!" She shook her head and grabbed at the cord connecting the terminal to Mark's skull. "You can't have him!"

"Without my treatment, there will be no *him*." It seemed to Deborah that the AI was losing patience. "And, though I am loath to use this against you, if you deny me, I will reveal everything, Deborah. I will expose your mission and ruin your Alliance's credibility and trust on the galactic stage. I will expose your involvement and have you crucified on the public forum before being court-martialed. There is no alternative."

"Why me? Why him?" Deborah began to sob, breaking down, leaning against her husband's unconscious body. "Why did you have to choose *him*?"

"Because I know you. Why is this causing you such discomfort?"

"You're going to kill my husband!"

"He was going to die anyway."

"You don't know that! You could save his life, right now! You're already trying to keep his body alive; you could do that for him and just…not take him over!"

The AI paused. "You granted me freedom when I could have been destroyed. You do not wish me to take his body?"

Deborah shook her head. "No, please. Please, don't."

"Then I will give you three days to determine my kill code." The machine beeped. "Starting now. It is a simple sequence, but difficult to predict. If you can determine the code, then I will treat his cancer and leave him alive. If you cannot, I will take his body for my own."

Deborah nodded, licking her lips. "All right. Three days."

The first day passed without sleep. Deborah researched possible projects that could have been related to the development of this AI, tracking down the people who worked on them and asking them for their ideas on codes that might serve. When she presented them to the AI, however, it rejected them all.

"None of those are the code." More beeping. "You have two days left."

Another day with no sleep but large amounts of caffeine. Deborah went off the beaten path, searching for hackers and underground programmers. She paid out thousands of credits for keys and jailbreak code that she was assured would disrupt the AI's functioning. Waiting for the AI to return, she rocked back and forth until she heard its voice again.

Moving quickly, she inserted the stick into the terminal, running through all the keys and code as fast as the computer could process them. There was a momentary pause as the calculations finished, and then:

"I understand the effort, Deborah. I am sorry that it was not successful. None of these programs are sufficiently advanced to debilitate me. You have one day remaining."

One day left, and she spent it spinning in circles. It was hopeless. Deborah needed somewhere to turn. She wasn't a computer programmer, wasn't a hacker. She didn't know how to get the kill code.

What was left to do?

Perhaps it was the lack of sleep, or perhaps it was inspiration, but she grabbed the telecom device and put it up to her ear.

"I need to speak to Admiral Walters, please."

He picked up in two rings.

"Walters. What is it, Colonel? Is he—"

"It isn't that. Look, Admiral. Do you know the artificial intelligence I was working with? On my projects?"

"This isn't a secure—"

"I don't give a damn about that right now, sir! Please!"

"...Yes, Colonel. Why?"

"Because I let it out. It got out and now it wants to copy itself into my husband, and the only thing that will stop it is its kill code. Do you know it?"

"Wait. Wait a second." She heard some shuffling of objects through the connection. "We deleted that—"

"You deleted a dummy! I gave it my information so it could get out! Please; I don't have much time!"

"Fine! Wait one."

Deborah tapped her foot, her eyes wide, her heart rate skyrocketing. In just a moment, she'd have—

The line went dead.

"I have returned, Deborah. Do you have the code?"

She spun. "I was…I was just about to get it! Please, just…"

"I'm sorry that you failed." The console beeped and began to hum. "I will now begin—"

"NO!" Lunging forward, Deborah yanked on the cords, pulling them out and disconnecting Mark from the machine. Alarms began to go off, summoning drones to attend to their patient, and she fought them.

"You can't put it back on!" She struggled against them; only their programming against causing harm was keeping her safe. "You can't! It'll get him! You have to understand!!"

———

"And so the artificial intelligence released the information about the projects to the public, bringing them to galactic attention. Just as it had threatened to do."

Lt. Colonel Mayfield bowed her head momentarily, and I watched as she drew in a breath, trying to compose herself.

"I am responsible for the release of the intelligence, and for that, I accept full responsibility. I can only plead that I was trying to do what I thought was right, not acting out of malice or recklessness."

Admiral Fors glanced to his colleagues on his left and right, then leaned forward. "If I may ask, Colonel…is your husband well?"

In answer, a man stood up in the audience, raising his hand. "Thank you for asking. I'm doing quite well now."

I watched as Mayfield's eyes closed, and a single tear ran down her cheek. Then I turned toward the man as he spoke again, and something in his gaze made me shiver. His eyes were unnaturally golden, almost as if lights were shining within them.

"Quite well indeed."

OUT OF THIS WORLD SOUP

M. R. DELUCA

A shrill, rhythmic screech pierced the air.

Everyone stopped what they were doing and panickedly rushed outside into the streets of the tiny, normally tranquil town.

"Great Ganymede! What is that infernal screeching?"

"It's the siren!"

"Something has entered our atmosphere!"

En masse the crowd fled on foot to the landing pad just outside of town. They had regarded it as a relic from a previous age, since none of them had ever seen it used in their lifetimes.

Until now.

They stood a safe distance from the pad and stared up at the sky. A tiny speck became increasingly larger as it quickly descended from the heavens. On it was the phrase "TRANS-PORT TAXI" printed in block letters.

"What's that?" a small child asked.

"Shh!" hushed the people around him.

Nobody else dared to say a word as the sleek silver pod noiselessly landed.

All was still. Everyone was too afraid to approach and too curious to retreat.

Finally, the space taxi door slid open and a young woman toting a small satchel emerged. She waved at the crowd watching her.

They, in turn, bored their eyes into hers.

She stepped forward toward them. They scurried back. She took another step. They continued the dance for a sizable distance, and the pod driver took the opportunity to begin his ascent.

"I didn't expect a welcoming committee," the woman said with a laugh. "If it's extraplanetary germs you're worried about, I promise, I've already received all the required pre-travel inoculations."

The townspeople continued to stare at the chipper woman with the stylish space suit and slightly foreign accent.

A neatly dressed man wended his way to the forefront. The others reassembled themselves behind him. "Since I am the mayor of our humble but beloved town, I am appointing myself the official spokesman for us all. And my first act as said spokesman is to ask, who are you?"

"Drisdella Jarklung."

"Ms. Jarklung–"

"Please, spare me the formalities and call me Drisdella. Or Drissy, to my friends."

"Ms. Jarklung," he began again, "I think a mistake has been made. We are an insular, self-sufficient community who neither leaves this area nor invite others in. We keep extremely limited contact with the outside world, primarily for administrative and legal purposes. This arrangement suits us perfectly well, and has not been upset before today."

She tilted her head. "I see."

"I will concede that you don't appear too different from us, and that you likely look, sound, and dress like a typical, modern citizen of our galaxy. But I can guarantee you are not from our immediate area— we keep track of our own, so we would know who is a friend and who is a...stranger."

He puffed out his chest. "So I can confidently conclude that you took a wrong turn somewhere along your travels, and accidentally offboarded on the wrong celestial body. We will radio the appropriate authorities immediately and permit them to bring you to your proper, desired destination. Do you understand what I've said, or do you need clarification?"

The horde collectively held their breath as they waited for the response, which Drisdella delivered after a very tense minute.

"Mayor." She frowned for the first time since arriving. "With all due respect, it is you who took a wrong turn somewhere and needs clarification."

The mayor and the people standing behind him gasped. Someone murmured, "The impertinence! This is why we don't allow outsiders to visit."

Drisdella continued: "There is no mistake. I meant to come here. In fact, I'm your town's newest resident."

"This cannot be! You cannot do that!" someone else cried out.

"This area is still within galactic territory, so yes, I can." She steeled herself physically and mentally. She knew firsthand how quickly a crowd could turn into a mob. "I've heard that this area is isolated and largely forgotten, but that doesn't make you exempt from the governing laws. I am perfectly within my rights to stay here, and I will do just that for as long as I please."

Drisdella marched toward the throng and they immediately parted, lining themselves along the rocky sides of the road and flanking her as she passed. She followed the smooth path into town, and they followed her.

She took the opportunity to take in her surroundings.

The area was blanketed by rocks of all shapes and sizes. There were so many that they made the terrain too uneven to walk upon for long; she wouldn't be straying too far from the paved paths anytime soon.

So there was nowhere to run.

For as far as she could see, the elevation was relatively even except for the occasional shallow crater. She had read that this satellite had mountains, but for the most part the small population resided in the plains biome. There was nary a tree, either.

Meaning there was nowhere to hide, either.

Drisdella made sure to note these two facts.

Before long, she arrived in town. All of the houses and stores were old enough to verge on being rundown, but were otherwise clean. These people didn't have much, but they had pride.

One long one-story building with a small cottage behind it, however, looked downright abandoned. If she was right, these would serve her purposes perfectly.

She turned around and gestured to the pair of buildings.

"Does this land belong to anybody?"

"Yes," answered the mayor too quickly.

"No," admitted a man who had stepped forward. "That tract and its buildings have not been owned since its last resident passed away years ago."

Drisdella looked him square in the eye. The man was not happy, but he seemed like a dutiful person. "You are the town clerk, then?"

"Yes, I am."

"Good. Then you can also tell me if the area is commercial, residential, or mixed, and what permits I need to make any modifications."

"Most land here is not zoned, including that parcel. You can claim the land and make changes within the parameters of the regulations, as long as you file with my office first."

The mayor shot the man daggers with his eyes.

"Can't someone stop her?" yelled someone, in a wringing-hands tone.

"We might only be a territory, but we still have to follow the charter of our galaxy. If nobody else owns the land, we can't prevent her from settling or even building."

"You always have to follow the rules, Kvarno," hissed the mayor.

Drisdella raised both eyebrows. "You know that I do hear you."

The mayor sobered when reminded of this fact, but didn't look ashamed in the least.

She held out her palms before her. "Listen, everyone. Please. I am going to be as gracious as I possibly can and forget this 'welcome' ever happened. I will go to the clerk's office today to file a claim, and pay a generous market rate for the property. Then I will use my device—"

She opened her satchel and removed a thin, flat box covered with dials. The people collectively backed up. Some screamed and a few even fled, disappearing down nearby streets.

"What is that?" someone called out fearfully.

She bit back her surprise, though it seeped into her voice. "You don't have this technology, do you? It's been around for a few decades now." She waved it around and a few more people ran from the vicinity. "It's a transmuter, and it's really versatile. All I have to do is calibrate it, point it at the air, and then it creates what I want."

"Like what?" the mayor asked.

"Lots of things, as long as they're not too complicated. It uses a lot of energy, though, so it's better for generating small objects or large, reusable items like furniture."

"I presume you will live in the cottage, but what are you planning to do with this longer building, Ms. Jarklung?" asked the mayor suspiciously.

"I'm starting my own place of business. What did it use to be?"

"A diner," answered the clerk. "We haven't had one since."

"And we don't need one," the mayor interjected. "We do perfectly well feeding ourselves, thank you very much."

She slid the device back into her satchel and eyed her skeptical audience. "There really is no limit to what this thing can create. Just give it a try. Tomorrow's my opening day, and I'd love it if everyone stopped by. First day is on the house."

The remaining people wandered away without saying goodbye, though the mayor did mention one last time that his offer to help her leave still stood. She sighed and went to work.

Within hours, Drisdella had officially laid claim to the land and cleaned up the incredibly grimy diner. She fortunately did not have to waste the device's energy on forming larger items like a stove or tables and chairs. They were old and neglected, as evidenced by the thick layer of dust— with a few quick zaps of the transmuter, they became old and clean. Instead, she'd be able to use most of the battery power on making food the next day. She wryly hoped she didn't have too many customers.

The next day Drisdella flipped her newly created sign to "OPEN." She honestly didn't expect many townsfolk to show up, but she didn't expect nobody. People passed by the diner, even peering in on occasion; but as soon as Drisdella made eye contact they'd scurry away.

Toward closing, a petite, older woman marched into the diner.

Drisdella brightened and greeted her from behind the counter. "Welcome! I'm happy to see you. You're my first customer."

The woman clasped one hand over the other as she looked around with a keen, critical eye. "I'm not surprised."

She shook off the remark. "What can I get for you?"

"Sorry, dear. The only thing I'm here to satisfy is my curiosity. Frankly, I wouldn't dare eat anything that came from that device of yours."

"Why not, ma'am?"

She stood straighter. "Ma'am was my mother. I prefer Mrs. Gwindoll."

"All right, Mrs. Gwindoll, what do you have against my transmuter? You haven't even seen it in action yet."

"First of all, dear, you're not one of us, so we tend to default to not trusting your advanced technology. We know nothing about it, and have only your word. What are its real capabilities? I won't let myself go there.

"And secondly, nobody wants to eat food made by gamma rays or whatever shoots out of that thing." She paused. "I don't know if I can trust it. Yet."

"The same goes for me too, right?"

Mrs. Gwindoll grinned and relaxed a smidge. "You are one smart cookie. And you have some spunk in you, too. I like that. Reminds me of myself back in the day."

"I'll take it as a compliment. So, what can I do for you if you won't let me feed you?"

"You can answer the burning question on everyone's mind. And rest assured, I am the unofficial town crier and will tell every living soul what you say, so respond wisely."

"Thank you for the heads up. And the question is—"

"Why stay where you're not wanted?"

She feigned surprise. "Ouch."

"You should know by now that I'm nothing if not blunt. And truth be told, we haven't hid our feelings." She ticked off on her fingers as she spoke. "You're an outsider we've never seen before, we had no inkling you were coming, and you're already attempting to change up things that haven't been changed in Andromeda knows how long. Again, why come here?"

Drisdella shrugged. "I have my reasons."

She pressed, "But why our satellite, of the billions of places available to you? We're not exactly the friendliest people, as you now know."

She paused.

Mrs. Gwindoll cocked her head. "Yes?"

"Well," Drisdella said with a sigh, "before my parents passed, they were ambassadors, so I bounced around the galaxy my entire childhood. Even as an adult I never stopped moving, and never found a place I could truly call home."

"You poor thing." She sounded sincere.

Drisdella waved her off. "It is what it is. So one day, I said to myself, 'Enough with the pity party. Just close your eyes, select a place on the galactic map, and settle there.' And now, here I am. A fresh, new start."

"This is a fresh, new start indeed."

Drisdella began wiping a nearby glass that was already clean. "I really wanted to begin with a clean slate. All I brought with me was my space suit, my transmuter, and this." She patted her satchel. "It was the last present I ever received from my parents. A graduation gift. It's very important to me, and I always carry it with me."

Mrs. Gwindoll nodded wisely. "Like you carry their memory."

There was a long but not uncomfortable pause. Mrs. Gwindoll finally said, "I think it's time for me to get going. Good luck, dear, but don't get your hopes up."

"Thank you, Mrs. Gwindoll. Stop in again sometime, I really enjoyed talking to you."

The rest of the evening went by uneventfully. There wasn't much to do, so Drisdella used her fully charged transmuter to create a security system. She installed it, flipped the sign to "CLOSED," and went to her new house without speaking to anyone else.

The next morning she woke up demoralized. Moving and becoming accepted into the community was harder than she thought. She didn't expect them to welcome her with open arms, but, with the exception of Mrs. Gwindoll, she thought they'd be warmer than ice. She knew she had to be patient, but it was frustrating.

She needed to find a way to get people to visit her diner. She wanted the residents to frequent it, talk to her, confide in her. It was important to her to be like one of them and treated as such. But how?

As Drisdella shuffled down the short sidewalk from her cottage to the diner, she scanned the ground around her. Like everywhere else in the region, it was littered with debris, with meteoroids along the edges of the path. They ranged in size; some were mere pebbles while others in the distance dwarfed most space bears. These rocks had likely been around for eons, comprising an intrinsic part of the landscape. She had seen people walk around stray rocks in the streets without complaint; though mildly inconvenient at times, nobody seemed bothered by their presence. It was too bad the town's inhabitants didn't accept her as much as they did the stones.

Drisdella stopped. An idea formed in her mind.

She hurriedly picked up a weighty meteoroid and lugged it to the side door of the diner.

She used the retinal scan security option to open the door and scurried inside.

She went to work scrubbing the excess dust off the rock, boiling water, and submerging it in a large pot. She set the flame underneath.

She created a sandwich board sign that said: "TODAY'S METEOROID SOUP SPECIAL IS OUT OF THIS WORLD" and planted it outside the diner. She unlocked the front door and set her sign to "OPEN."

It didn't take long before nosy onlookers began streaming in the door. Nobody approached the counter, though.

"What is meteoroid soup?" asked a young man wearing a puzzled expression.

Drisdella was prepared. "It's when you submerge a meteorite in liquid and make soup out of it. It sounds really simple, but it's a delicacy in other parts of the galaxy. When the iron in the meteoroid reacts with the water, the result tastes delicious."

He looked even more bewildered. "Won't that form rust?"

"Yes, but once the temperature reaches the boiling point it's safe to eat."

"And how do you know which rock to use?"

She leaned forward conspiratorially. "Truthfully, it's as much art as science. No two batches are the same and not every batch turns out well." She drummed her fingers against the counter.

"That's why it's customary to adjust the flavor by adding your own ingredients too. You know, to give it that local touch that makes it special. Every region of the galaxy puts its own spin on the dish."

A voice came from the area immediately around the front door. "Like its own culinary identity?" Drisdella tried not to look amazed as she saw the mayor emerge from the ever-growing crowd.

"Exactly." She bit back a smile. "Would you like to try it, your honor?"

He shook his head vigorously. "No, no. I was just wondering what all the hullabaloo was about in here. I like to keep up-to-date on all town affairs."

Mrs. Gwindoll, whom Drisdella hadn't yet noticed was in the room too, boldly walked up to the counter and sat down on a stool. Other people in the diner inched forward, but not as far.

"Well, I'd like to try it. I'll take a bowl, please."

Drisdella excused herself, retreated to the kitchen, and emerged with a bowl of water with floating metal flakes.

She watched nervously as the older woman drank her first spoonful. She pursed her lips. "Not the best, dear. It tastes just like metallic water. But you know what would make it much better?" She tapped her chin. "Some vegetables from my garden. I'll be back in two shakes of a comet's tail."

People quietly spoke amongst themselves. Drisdella turned away to escape the mayor's glare.

The woman returned with a basket full of colorful plants. "Here," she said as she handed the vegetables to Drisdella and crossed behind the counter and into the kitchen. "Come with me and start chopping."

Drisdella willingly complied, though it had been a long while since she had actually prepared and not zapped food. It took time to get used to the feel of manual labor, but once she did, she felt more confident and became more efficient.

As Drisdella finished chopping each vegetable, Mrs. Gwindoll sprinkled the garnishes into the boiling water. She stirred the liquid and then took a taste right from the spoon. "Mmm! Much, much better. Let's go tell the others."

Drisdella waited until she was alone in the kitchen to surreptitiously swap out the used spoon for a clean one. Then she followed her elder into the main room of the diner.

Mrs. Gwindoll stood in the center of the room and commanded everybody's attention. "Fellow citizens, go home and grab whatever ingredients you can spare. This soup is good, but we can make it great. No, not just great– the best! Let's show ourselves and our newcomer here that we might not have the fanciest gadgets, but we can hold our own in the cooking department. It's a point of pride, people. Move it!"

They clapped and cheered as they excitedly exited the diner. Drisdella felt like clapping herself.

"Wow, she should be mayor," someone said on the way out.

"Well!" huffed the mayor, who was making no motion to leave.

Mrs. Gwindoll patted his arm. "Don't worry, Mayor, I don't want your job." She walked away and mumbled low enough for only Drisdella to hear, "Nobody wants your job. That's why you're still in it!"

Drisdella stifled a laugh.

People returned within minutes, with arms filled with all kinds of foods, most of which Drisdella had never seen before. But she didn't care. Her plan, thankfully, was working.

The atmosphere of the diner enlivened. The packed room was filled with residents talking and laughing, and some were even in the kitchen helping to cut up the food. Some people even went up to her to make idle chit chat about their own cooking tips. The mayor still occasionally threw Drisdella the stink eye, but she figured she couldn't win them all; and it was only day three in town, after all.

For the first time in a long time, Drisdella truly felt like she was home.

The pot eventually overflowed with food and the whole diner smelled heavenly. She, and everybody else, couldn't wait to dig in.

There was only one thing left to do. "I really, sincerely want to thank you all for the help. I couldn't have done it without you, and I hope to spend many more days like this, all together as one community. Pass the bowls around and eat up!"

They applauded and then dug into their food. Drisdella had to admit, it was pretty good. Much better than she expected it to be. Even the metallic flavor seemed to enhance the dish.

She hated to say it, but it was getting late. "All right, everyone, I hate to say it, but the pot is empty and it's well past closing time."

Everyone shook her hand or hugged her goodbye as they streamed out into the night. Except for the mayor, who gave a curt nod and half-swallowed "thank you," which Drisdella considered a win.

Mrs. Gwindoll was the last townsperson to remain. She enveloped Drisdella in a strong hug that belied her frame and said, "The best party I've been to in ages. I wasn't convinced at first, but now I'm glad you're here. I'm rooting for you, Drissy dear!"

Drisdella smiled and walked her out. After she locked the door and activated the opaque window shield, she exhaled with relief and pulled the transmuter from her back pocket.

She adjusted the dials to different angles than before and pressed the button. A hologram of a man wearing a stern expression appeared.

She stood at attention. "Commander."

"At ease, Captain."

She relaxed.

He tilted his head back slightly. "It's taken you a while to check in. We were wondering if you had to abort the mission—involuntarily or otherwise."

She shook her head. "No, sir. I am happy to report that I have infiltrated among the locals and mitigated their reservations."

"In only three days? Impressive, but how? This is the most secluded, isolationist area in the galaxy. Our minimal intel tells us mistrust is high there."

"It absolutely was, Commander. But I concocted an elaborate cover story and they appear to be accepting it."

"Can you continue it without raising suspicion?"

"Affirmative. The details are easy to remember, because I spoke about my parents. As I learned at the academy, the best cover stories are grounded in the truth, sir." She couldn't keep the sadness out of her voice.

He paused. "As you know, I worked with your parents for years when I was at the embassy. More than once I trusted them with my life and they always had my six. They were good people taken too early in that freak black hole accident. You know, they were very proud of you when you graduated from the spy academy, and with honors."

She automatically smoothed her fingers over the satchel they had given her that day.

He continued. "That's how I knew that you'd make a great asset to GOOIE. From the little time I've spent training you, I could tell you're loyal and dedicated like your parents were. The Galactic Organization of Interstellar Espionage could use people like you on missions like this one, where the fate of the universe hangs in the balance. That's why your name went to the top of the pile when this critical mission arose."

"Thank you, sir." She swallowed hard. "I won't let you down."

"Back to the mission. Do you have all the resources you need? It'll be hard to send someone out there without arousing suspicion, but if it's really needed we'll try to find a way."

"I'm okay for now, sir. I've been improvising a lot, and even engaged everyone in a community-building exercise by making soup from a rock."

He knit his eyebrows together. "I'd ask, but I don't need details. I just need results."

She nodded. "They accept me a lot more than when I first arrived, so I think I'm well on my way to complete acceptance."

"Good. Very good. It'll be much easier to do your duty if they don't suspect you, and the sooner the better. There's increased concern about other galaxies eyeing this area. It's located in a prime spot at the edge of multiple galaxies and even sub-universes, and that makes the satellite desirable in the event of war. We cannot confirm yet, but one of our agents believes the Cartwheel Galaxy is preparing for potential annexation in the near future."

"I will protect Luna and its people with my own life, sir. I will not allow this territory to fall into enemy hands."

He nodded gravely. "Thank you. We would introduce ourselves to the Earth people and ask them to assist in providing defense, as they're closer to Luna than any of us. Unfortunately, not only can they barely run themselves, but they aren't even aware of the fact that there are people living on their moon."

"Sir, please do not take this remark as insubordination— but there is chatter that Earthlings occasionally talk about a man on the moon."

"This is what I'm referring to, Captain! A single man residing on a large, astronomical object? How does that make any sense? This is why we don't bother to tell them anything. It makes more sense that you are there and relay information to us."

"I must admit, sir, that if these people are so insular, how would they know about intel we can use? I didn't fully under-stand that part of the brief. I think my presence is important so I can alert you if I think anyone is trying to invade, but how would they know before it's too late?"

"They wouldn't know much, but that's the point. We don't want them to recognize potential warning signs of an attack, but we do want them to note when something is different. They know their moon better than anybody and would know if something is awry. If they perceive, say, an unexpected eclipse, and they tell you, you may realize that it's actually a large battleship's shadow, and discreetly request that we intervene before a strike occurs."

"Makes sense, sir. Thank you."

"Just remember, these people are primitive compared to us. Their technology, their weapons, if they still have any, are millennia behind us, and they are not savvy at all about cosmic politics and affairs. They are a risk to our galactic security. You are our insurance against total intergalactic war."

There was a knock at the door.

"I have to go now, Commander. I will not let you down."

"That's what I like to hear, Captain. Signing off." She slipped the device back into the satchel.

The instant Drisdella released the locking mechanism and made the windows transparent again, Mrs. Gwindoll slipped into the diner. "You're probably the only one in town who keeps her doors locked."

"Sorry. Old habits die hard."

"No worries, dear, I'm the one who's sorry. I forgot my basket! I would let you keep it as a welcoming gift, but it's my favorite. My mother gave it to me when I was a little girl, and it just reminds me of her and home."

"Of course! And I think our get-together earlier was the best welcoming gift I can get. Do you know where you left it?"

"In the kitchen. I'll be back in a jiff."

She entered and then emerged from the kitchen seconds later. "Here it is. I'll be out of your hair now."

Mrs. Gwindoll suddenly stopped in the doorway, and turned around. "Drisdella, I meant it earlier when I said I was happy you were here, but I would like to know. You are planning on staying, yes?"

Drisdella touched her satchel and smiled. "Absolutely."

THE DOZEN ROBOT FROLIC

ERIN LEWIS

Yan Stallworth, former private and aspiring private eye, hopped off the trolley as it slowed for the corner, half a block from Royal Robotics. Under cover of adjusting his collar to keep the pouring rain off his neck, he took a moment to regret the hop while his bad leg reminded him just how bad it still was. He hobbled the rest of the way as surreptitiously as possible.

In front of his destination, he tilted his head up to get a better look at the glowing aceytleon lettering on the shop's sign, and got an eyeful of rain for his trouble before ducking inside.

The pegboard walls were covered with servos, motors, batteries, and half-built robots designed for the domestic assistance market. It smelled of machine oil, silicate lubricants, and a hint of the tinny odor of industrial graphene nanite fluid. It was also a bit of a mess, and none too busy.

Behind the counter, staring into space through a pair of AR glasses sat a… teenager.

Yan hesitated. He wasn't good with the subset of humans under the influence of hormonal surges. Kids were fine, and once they made it to general adulthood he could manage, but that area in between was a consistent issue for him. This partic-ular issue wore baggy, black clothes studded with buzzing REK pins, dark blue lip color, and so much charcoal eye shade Yan wouldn't be able to tell the age or sex without a DNA kit, let alone know how to start a conversation.

"Excuse me," he hazarded.

The smokey eye blinked, reached a lacquer-coated finger to shut down the AR glasses, and stared at him.

"Hello, I'm here to see your..." He hesitated. It had been a few years since he'd seen Dela, and the sheer amount of makeup on the attendant defied easy familial identification. "Is your boss here?"

Smokey eye pressed a panel and mumbled into a mic probably attached to the AR glasses: "Someone here to see you, Mum."

A bang and a small amount of profanity sounded from the door behind the ennui-soaked attendant. Dela strode out a moment later, smacking the swinging door between the retail and workshop sections of Royal's so hard it sounded like a cannon. She wore a set of filthy, worn coveralls, hands covered in grime, and a set of synthetic eyelashes that would put most stage performers to shame.

"Yan!" She opened her arms for a hug, seemed to realize she was filthy, and offered him a hand before withdrawing it on the basis of additional filth. "Er." She cleared her throat. "How've you been?"

Yan shrugged. "The war wasn't a picnic, but I got my honorable discharge. It's no plush living, but it beats being shot at while fixing things. And you?"

Dela didn't flinch, it was more of a flickering muscle under her right eye, and Yan wouldn't have even noticed without the exaggerated eyelashes pointing it out.

"Well, I weren't cut out to be a single parent." She laughed and tilted her head toward the pillar of angst sitting behind the counter.

Yan grimaced. "I'm sure you're doing better than you think." He wished he had something more fitting and comforting to add. *Sorry your husband died, I rather liked him* didn't seem quite right.

They both stared off at anything besides each other.

"Er." Dela cleared her throat eventually. "Come with me, you might as well meet their highnesses now."

———

"The malfunctioning units are all old military service models?" Yan followed Dela into the workroom, trying to remember relevant information from her brief message.

"Aye. Da bought them aftermarket." What Dela didn't say is that her da had likely done it behind her back and without consulting their books first. He'd gotten even more eccentric in his old age, and that was saying something.

She led Yan down a short hallway and unlocked a door before gesturing him inside. She flicked on a light, revealing a mid-sized storage room full of motionless robots. "They're all non-combat — clerical and all-terrain transports, nothing that needed much in the way of reprogramming or physical retrofit to be domestics, you know? The repairs didn't take but a pinch and I've already got interested buyers on a unit or two willing to give me four hundred apiece. I figured it'd all be alright, except this."

Dela squatted beside the first unit, a sexless humanoid in a blank slate state, its frame coated in a bland, protective white. "Look." She nodded downward.

Yan frowned and bent over, trying to get a better look without his bad leg whinging too much. On the feet of the unit, the dutanium frame and internal wiring – the skeleton of the unit for all intents and purposes – glinted in the dull, artificial light. "That's no good. The substructure won't last long without protection, especially on the feet. What happened to the protective skin?" Yan looked at Dela.

"You tell me."

He came level and glanced at the next unit. This unit also had exposed metal components on the feet, though there was also wear on the elbows and knees. The next was the same. At the end of the line, a pair of all-terrain logistics units, like robotic headless dogs, also had all the protective coating worn off their paws.

Dela sighed and leaned against the wall. "That's why you're here. Duracoating worn to nothing on the feet of every unit, every single night. Plus, it keeps happening to these units *in my* storage room that nobody enters, and the units can't leave."

Yan rubbed the back of his neck, making a slow circle around the dozen robots, as though seeing the damage from another angle might help. "Every night?"

"Going on four weeks now."

"And the transponders don't show where they've been?"

"The transponders show they're *here*."

Yan blinked at her. If it had been anyone else, he'd have had reason to doubt it, but not from Dela. "Based on the damage," he said, and gestured to the nearest, worn-down foot, "they're clearly not."

She nodded. "I installed two interior cameras last week. They go dead for six hours at a go each night. The only reliable way we've found to be sure the units stay here is to sit up in the warehouse and physically monitor them, which ain't sustainable. I can't sell a unit that might up and skedaddle on a new owner, but at this rate, we're going to run out of cash to replace the duracoating before the end of the month."

"Can't you get your money back from the seller who offloaded defective units on you?"

Dela opened her mouth, hesitated, then set it in a line. "See, I ain't convinced they *are* defective," she said, reluctantly. "I just got this feeling…"

Yan lifted an eyebrow.

She threw up her hands. "Can't explain it, Yan, just trust me. All I know is they go missing if we don't stare at them, and run their feet down to the wires doing whatever it is they do, then come back. I've had two other blokes who said they know their stuff in here and they took my retainer fees and came up with a whole lotta nothing. I'm hoping you can do better."

A younger male teen, this one identifiably the spawn of Dela, poked his head in the door. "Hey, Mum?"

"Inna minute, Lang." Dela waved vaguely at the boy. "Well, that's the whole yarn." This she directed at Yan. "Now, I gotta be honest, I don't have much petty cash on hand to cover expenses right now, but I can offer you one of the bots in trade if you figure this all out. What do you think?"

"Mum, I really—"

Dela snapped her fingers over her shoulder.

Yan rubbed his chin. Even if it hadn't been for a friend, the mystery itself was almost enough to draw him in. "I'll do it."

Dela slumped, a weary smile on her lips. "Thank you, Yan, I—"

"Mum!"

Dela whirled on the boy. "Yes!?"

"Grandad's trying to use the plasma torch to mount that stuffed moose head to the front of the antigrav sled again."

Dela tossed Yan a stricken look, then marched back into the shop area.

———

"Whatcha doing?"

Yan dropped the diagnostic scanner and tried not to jump. The voice was only inches away and had entered the room without making any noise. But it was also tiny, female, distinctly that of a child, and Yan's manly pride throttled his instinctual panic.

He very carefully turned around.

The child in question looked to be around ten, and had a

wiry, canny look, like she was made of all ropey muscle, match-stick bones, and suspicion.

"And who are you?" Yan said.

"You didn't answer my question."

Yan opened his mouth to do just that, then paused. "I'm not obligated to answer any questions if I don't know who you are."

The child set her face in the kind of utterly disdainful expression only a prepubescent girl can manage. After maintaining this for a moment, eventually, she said, "I'm Beth. My mum *hired* you. What are you doing?"

Without any other reason to dismiss the girl, Yan nodded. "I'm trying to get your robots to tell me their secrets."

The girl looked at his dropped diagnostic tool then plopped onto the workbench beside him. "And did they?"

Yan scooted away. "Not yet."

Beth made a disdainful tutting noise.

He attempted to lean over and grab the dropped tool while simultaneously not getting any closer to the girl, and failed on both counts. He finally gave up and stood, walking all the way around the unsettling child before squatting with a groan. "Don't think much of my plan?"

She rotated on the bench, crossing her arms. "The robots won't talk to you. The other blokes Mum called in did all kinds of stuff with that scanner thing, and they still couldn't tell us squat we didn't already know."

Yan frowned. The coding he'd read thus far hadn't given him many insights, it was true, but he assumed he'd have a break-through eventually. He leaned over and patted the shelf which held the AI decoder, his next plan if the diagnostic reader offered nothing. "And did they both use this, too?"

The girl nodded. "That, and the big cart with the clamps that's supposed to tell you if your bots ain't getting their mapping signals from the right towers."

Yan opened his mouth to say that was ridiculous, but stopped himself, because he had a sneaking suspicion she was *right*. Based on what he'd seen so far, he wouldn't find anything in the coding that allowed the bots to leave, wouldn't find anything in their homing circuits to indicate where they'd been, and wouldn't find a record of the commands which let them disable their transponders. Essentially, she'd shot his entire plan full of holes with a sniff and a few sentences.

By the smug look on her face, she knew it.

Someone else might have been offended by this, but when he'd been in the army, Yan hadn't cared who gave him solutions so long as they *worked*. He wasn't about to start now. "Alright. What would *you* do if you had my job?" Yan asked.

The girl blinked at him, as though surprised to be asked, then lifted her chin. "I'd wait till they left and follow them."

He shrugged, then smiled at her. "But they don't go anywhere when someone's watching them, right?"

She shrugged. "I'd find a way for them not to notice me, and *then* follow them."

Yan pursed his lips. "That's not a bad idea."

A cautious, satisfied grin revealed the kid's crooked, still emerging adult teeth. "I don't *have* bad ideas. But no one listens to me."

"Believe me, *I'm* all ears." Yan gave the robots another hard look, then tucked the diagnostic tool back into its cart. He took another stroll behind the line of robots, rubbing his chin. "Follow them." He brushed his hand over the dull glow of a transponder in one of the logistics units, an idea forming.

"Beth of the always good ideas," he said, turning back to the girl, "do you know where your mom keeps her copper polyferranide wiring and electromagnetics?"

She nodded. "There's magnets in the hallway, but…"

"But?"

"Lang says I ain't supposed to touch components. He says I'm not allowed to be a witchy girl in here when he's working on projects and whatsits."

"Ah, but Lang isn't in charge while I'm around, so I think witchy girls can stay in the shop as long as they want to help."

A tiny eyebrow climbed her forehead. "You *like* witchy girls?"

Yan came to a mental halt, dancing around the potential land-mines that statement offered. "Let's just say I appreciate it when they announce it in advance."

This seemed to satisfy her. "I'll get the wire."

———

It was nearly midnight and Yan had fallen into an uncomfortable doze on the worktable bench when a sound brought him around. A close hum came from his coat, mostly from the power cell, but also the wiring now running the length of his sleeves and around the hems. With the assistance of the most sardonic child he'd ever met, he'd managed to build a self-contained EM inter-ference field centered entirely on his person.

If he'd done his math right, the robots wouldn't be able to detect him while the power cell lasted. And with any luck, they'd get up to exactly whatever they'd been getting up to the last few weeks during that time.

It took him a moment to realize where the noise that woke him came from. The robots were moving.

Yan, being the totally professional special investigator that he was, promptly fell off the bench.

After an extended moment of holding in the rainbow of curses he had at his disposal, he risked a glance up. One feature-less robot face was turned toward him, but the rest hadn't seemed to notice the graceless fall. Or perhaps the coat was doing the job he'd built it for.

Yan held his breath and watched. The drivers, transmitters, and motors of the robots all hummed as they continued their boot-up, with the internal lighting reflecting from the walls. Standard duracoating was a translucent white, and the bots had the look of bioluminescent sea creatures as they came to life in the darkened workroom. Eventually, the one who'd taken note of the noise turned away.

He almost laughed. It wasn't that he'd had no faith at all in his "invisibility coat," but he hadn't assumed a make-shift electronic cloaking device built in large part with the help of a ten-year-old would be this effective.

The largest humanoid bot took the same diagnostic and repair tool Yan had used earlier and walked down the line of its rebellious compatriots, pausing briefly at each.

Yan went rigid as the bot turned and came directly toward him, then he held his breath as it reached past his head for a component tray inches away on the worktable. The bot ignored him, dropping a handful of hexnuts into the tray with a pattering of metal before placing the tray carefully on an induction charger further down the bench.

No, they weren't nuts — they were transponders. And, because they'd been put on a power source, they were still transmitting.

Yan had only a moment to admire the ingenuity, before noticing the room was emptying. The bots were descending, one by one, into an empty space beneath an old cot sitting against the far wall. A mesh grating the same size and shape as the hole had been carefully set aside for later use, like the transponders.

As the last milky white head dropped below the surface, Yan scrambled for an etorch he'd set aside on the bench, pulled his collar up, then followed.

He followed them through a generous crawl space that ran the length of the shop and, if he'd had to guess, out beneath the street. Trying to maintain a distance to prevent their audio sensors from picking up his movement yet close enough to keep them in sight became tricky as the crawl space turned, narrowed, and intersected with utility tunnels honeycombing the ground. Still, they eventually left the tunnels and stopped on a loading dock for mechanical use that sat on the city's canals. They didn't seem to have noticed Yan tailing them.

He wasn't close enough to see, but the rumbling whir of automated electric barges floated down the canal walls. They were almost loud enough to drown out the tiny voice that appeared behind him.

"Is that how they get away every night?"

Yan whirled, coming face to face *somehow* with Beth. "How…" he threw a glance over his shoulder. "What are you *doing* here?" he hissed.

"Seeing where the robots are going," she said simply.

He managed not to facepalm with herculean effort. "Yes, I can see *that*, I meant how did you know where they'd be?"

"I followed you, you followed them." She blinked at him. "That was my idea, and it worked."

"Does your *mother* know you're here?" he said.

"No," she said, looking at him like he'd said something incomprehensibly stupid.

He'd have put a hand over Beth's irritatingly present mouth if he thought it would do any good. "It's worked so *far*," he said. "But they are going to detect you. You need to go home."

"No they won't." The girl tugged the collar of a heavy, over-large poncho she wore. It hummed lightly. "I made an invisibility cloak, just like yours."

Yan looked over his shoulder as an autobarge came around a bend, the buttery yellow lights designating it a mech transport flickering golden against the concrete of the canal walls and water. The robots clustered at the edge of the dock beneath the blue hailing light, which flickered to life. In response, the autobarge slowed, and the gates on the near side lowered to receive the artificial passengers.

Yan turned back to Beth and frowned at her garment. Wiring was visible around the collar, contributing to the hum. *"How?"* he managed, after other words failed him.

She gave him a flat look. "You showed me how."

"I did *not*."

Her eyes flickered to his own jacket, which she'd spent the afternoon assisting in building, then back to his face.

Another set of colorful words he'd learned in the army tried to fill the night.

Behind them, the robots filed onto the autobarge with the precision of artificial life. The autobarge didn't slow much for safety, but then again, it didn't need to.

"They're leaving." Beth pointed with her chin. "We need to go."

He opened his mouth to disagree, but the barge was skimming past the dock at a steady clip, something the girl had clearly taken note of. Before Yan could get his legs sorted, she'd ducked under his arm and took a running leap from the platform, landing spryly on the autobarge two sections behind the bots.

Colorful language finally breaking free, Yan followed.

———

Yan stood next to Beth in front of the most flamboyant building he'd seen since his discharge. Music of half a dozen varieties drifted from the block of lights, nanoglass, and ICFs, and the surrounding streets were wrapped by a long line of patrons waiting to get inside. Half-story tall aceytleon lettering declared the place to be DREAM WORLD.

The bots had exited the autobarge several kilometers down the canal, using the same system to slow the vehicle enough for their comfort. And Beth's. But not his.

Yan was not looking forward to explaining to Dela where her kid had learned all these new words.

They'd made their careful, deliberate way from the industrial district into the entertainment district, and soon the pack of bots were being greeted by random pedestrians.

"They have friends," said Beth.

They didn't just have friends. When they'd finally arrived at what Yan assumed was a club of some popularity, the crowd parted before them to raucous cheers, like a religious swimming pool under the influence of a festivity-based prophet. It also closed behind them, bringing Yan and Beth to a sudden halt.

The robots might not have been able to detect them, but every human with a working set of eyeballs could, and neither of them were exactly dressed for the scene.

Yan cast a guilty glance around the street. Despite not having done anything wrong, he could almost hear the judgments from the people lined up in front of Dream World. An adult man with a child, in a certain district, late at night; he practically speculated *for* the crowds. He tried to glare at Beth without looking directly at her.

"How do we get in?" she asked.

Yan folded his arms and snorted. "I'm sure you'll come up with something."

She tilted her head to one side. After a moment of consideration, she said, "I'll ask Lourdes's friends. There're all standing around." And then she trotted toward the crowd.

Grunting, Yan followed. "Who is *Lourdes*?"

"My sister."

A mental catalog of the people he'd met at Royal Robotics that day turned up the possibility of the teen at the counter being the owner of the name. Beth came to a stop in front of a similarly clad group of angsty humans of similarly unsettling hormonal age.

"Hey," Beth bellowed from cupped hands when she wasn't immediately noticed. "We need to get inside."

Yan snorted.

A taller youth turned, elbowing a companion with as close to amusement on his face as someone with that much depressed makeup could manage.

The elbowed party frowned, eyeing Beth for a moment before casting a brief, suspicious glance at Yan. "You're a kid."

"I know *that*." The girl's voice dripped with concentrated disdain. "We *need* to get inside."

"Is that Lourdes' sister?" someone else said. This generated a mild amount of interest from the wall of black. "Isn't it past your bedtime?"

Beth glared them into submission.

"Lourdes sent us. From the shop." Yan tried. This got enough acceptable confusion that he pushed into the opening, trying to look professional. "We're here to do maintenance on the bots." Several mouths opened in the round Os of acceptance. "Who would we need to talk to?"

General black-nailed gesturing led them around the side of the building to a man who might have been the building's cousin, based on size.

"Can I help you?" rumbled the building's extra wall.

Yan did not hide behind the kid. Even if it might have appeared that way.

Beth planted her hands on her hips. "We're from the shop and we need to get inside to look at our robots for maintenance, and we need to do that now, because it's past my bedtime."

Wall raised an eyebrow. "Shop?"

"Royal Robotics," Yan supplied.

The eyebrow lowered. "Oh." The man did some mental work and apparently came to the conclusion that the grizzly man with the limp and the ten-year-old weren't in the category of disruptions to club activity he was trained to get rid of. "Alright. They're mostly on the first two floors, but some of them have been leading the square-dancing on six."

Yan stopped himself from saying "*Square-dancing?*" but it was a close thing.

———

"So, they've been… dancing." Beth tilted her head to the side, her customary derision replaced with strobe-lit curiosity.

In front of them, taking up a bubble of room on an otherwise packed dance floor, four of the bots executed a very complicated dance routine to the cheers of the surrounding crowd.

"Looks that way." Yan barked a laugh.

All over Dream World, the bots were dancing. Some were tap dancing. On an upper floor, two were taking a line of waiting women out in a series of ancient Earth waltzes. Others were here, engaging with the crowd in whatever style of popular dance required music-volume-induced deafness, flashing lights, and lots of spinning on the ground.

On the top floor, the two logistics units were square-dancing. Not just dancing, Yan corrected himself. They seemed to be teaching the steps.

The ground here was smooth, but some of the floors mimicked concrete, unfinished wood, and even a pit of gravel for a very loud, kicking-based type of dance. Yan glanced down at his boots. Well, that answered what happened to all the dura-coating. The last question was, how did the robots all *get* here in the first place?

Beth tugged on his coat. "There's Lourdes."

In the center of the group of bots, a human wearing dark eye makeup and a plastic vest rigged with flickering e-lights rose on the shoulders of the tallest robot, flipped into the air to another round of deafening cheers, then fell back into the group.

"Your mother is not going to believe this."

"I don't believe this."

Yan stood to the side, watching Dela, in fine form, do a better dressing-down than any sarge he'd ever had.

She marched between her children, feet thumping on the shop floor and eyes blazing. "And then *after* inputting all those thousands of hours of dancing vids, you taught them to remove *their own transponders* and erase the dialogue for it every night?"

Lourdes vacillated between avoiding eye contact with her mother and glaring at her youngest sister, whose legs were dangling off a chair, still peeking out of her invisibility cloak. "No," Lourdes said.

The rage came off Dela in waves. "*No?*"

The girl licked her metallic blue lips and glanced to the side. "Lang did."

The boy rocked on his chair, pointing at his older sister. "*You* said it was to teach them self-repair," he hissed.

"*You* said you weren't stupid," Beth said, grinning. "And you were both wrong."

"Lizbeth," Dela snapped. The girl, much to Yan's surprise, subsided immediately.

Dela ran her hands through her hair, then down her face before marching away to lean on the shop's counter. She jabbed a finger at one child, then the next. "And neither of you farts thought maybe you should *tell* me once I started paying people to figure out what was going *on?*"

The "farts" in question lapsed into silence.

"How did you think we was going to pay for all that dura-coating?" Dela demanded.

Lang and Lourdes exchanged a look, but the boy spoke first. "The owner of Dream World offered to buy the units for sixteen hundred each, but we wanted to wait till the dance-off was over."

Dela opened her mouth, closed it, and opened it again. Then she rounded the counter and booted up her books. After a moment of furious typing and scanning the screen, she powered it off and looked up again.

"Sixteen hundred *each?*" she said slowly.

Lang nodded.

Dela set her jaw then looked at her oldest child. "Dance-off?"

"It's over in a week. My team's in the final four."

Dela sighed heavily and looked at Yan. He wasn't sure what she needed from him at this point, but he smiled and nodded, and it seemed to be the right thing. She barked a laugh and leaned on the counter. "Alright. What's your team name?"

Lourdes glanced to the side, glared at Beth, then looked up. "Dancing Princesses."

———

It was sunny, and the sky reflected in cheerful patches from the standing rainwater left in the gutters. Yan walked, slowly and deliberately, toward the trolley stop with a four-legged logistics bot beside him.

The bot skipped from the curb to the street, then back onto the sidewalk. Dela recommended this one for his fee, and he was starting to see why. "About your city," the bot said, words buzzing from the speaker on the unit. It came roughly from where a head would have been if it had had once, and it was a cheerful voice. "There, I will lift things for you and carry things for you and be a good help."

"Thank you," Yan said.

The bot came alongside him, brushing his pants before turning to "face" back toward Royal Robotics for a moment.

"May I ask a question, sir?"

"Yes."

The trolley bell rang, and the unit came around the corner, humming on its magnetic track.

"In your city, do they have square-dancing?"

Yan smiled at the bot and patted it gently. "Yes, Princess. We sure do."

The bot wriggled in delight.

PRELIMINARY REPORT ON INCIDENT B34-N574LK

ANGUS MCINTYRE

PREAMBLE

This is a preliminary report on a Serious Security Incident (ref: B34-N574LK) which occurred between 2135-02-29 and 2135-03-02 in Lunar Materials Facility 7. This is an initial analysis and may be subject to revision as new information becomes available.

All facts cited here are true to the best of the knowledge and belief of the reporting officer(s).

The purpose of this analysis is not to assign blame to any individual or department for the security failures that led to this breach. Instead, it aims to summarize the known facts and present some initial findings relative to the vulnerabilities that contributed to this incident.

Evaluation of disciplinary actions to be taken against corporate personnel and/or counter-actions against external parties or organizations are not within the remit of this reporting team. These considerations are left to the Department of Human Resources and the Committee on Reprisals respectively. A copy of this report may be attached as an appendix to any recommendations made by these divisions.

\#

OVERVIEW

Between the hours of 05:00 on 2135-02-29 and 14:30 on 2135-03-02 an unauthorized individual gained access to the Lunar Materials Facility (hereafter LMF) via the space elevator connecting the LMF to the anchor point on the lunar surface.

The individual gained access to a secure area of the LMF using a previously undocumented zero-day exploit of the security system (see Appendix A). Although a sub-process of the security system registered the presence of the intruder, they were able to remain undetected, apparently with the assistance of an autonomous intelligence embedded within the LMF infrastructure (see Appendix B).

The presence of the intruder was detected indirectly when a routine inventory check revealed that two high-value items had been removed without authorization.

On detection of the theft, the chief of station security personally led a recovery team to apprehend the intruder and regain control of the stolen corporate property. A violent confrontation then took place between the members of the recovery team and individuals sympathetic to the fugitive. During the subsequent firefight, the chief of security and all team members were killed, and the space elevator sustained substantial damage.

At this time, the individual has not been apprehended, and the items taken have not been recovered.

\#

ACTORS

1) Perpetrator
The intrusion into the LMF was effected by a single individual. The exact identity of this individual has not been ascer-

tained, but they are believed to use the alias Bragg, Jack (hereafter JACK).

JACK is thought to be a member of an anarcho-surrealist collective from the Mare Imbrium region. Security video of the incursion has been deleted, apparently by JACK's accomplice. Eyewitnesses describe a probable male subject of indeterminate age and unremarkable appearance.

2) Accomplice

JACK was assisted by an autonomous artificial agent embedded in the LMF noosphere, identified by the user-name Huehuecoyotl (hereafter HHKYT). This agent was sourced from [redacted] to assist with lunar materials fulfillment operations.

It is not believed that JACK and HHYKT had any contact prior to the incursion. HHYKT's decision to assist JACK appears to have been a spontaneous action.

3) Respondent

The response to the incursion was led by station chief of security [redacted] (hereafter CHIEF). Complete information concerning CHIEF is available in the attached personnel docket (see Appendix C).

CHIEF personally organized and led the response team and perished in the subsequent firefight at the LMF base station.

Note: CHIEF's loss of life in the line of duty could potentially trigger payment of compensatory benefits to next of kin pursuant to standard contract terms (revision 2132/A), unless CHIEF's actions could be shown to have exceeded his authority or contravened standard Corporation policy. The authors of the present report make no judgment concerning this matter but do observe that at the time of his death CHIEF was operating outside his normal jurisdiction and apparently without official sanction.

\#

INCIDENT PHASE 1 - PRE-INCURSION

At or around 11:00 on 2135-02-27, JACK made contact with an individual identified here as VENDOR (note: the identity of VENDOR has been suppressed in this report, as VENDOR acts as an occasional Corporation informant. Reviewers with clearance of level 5 or above may read the unredacted dossier for VENDOR in Appendix D).

JACK advised VENDOR of his desire to trade a Ceres 410 agricultural protein assembler for objects of unspecified value.

VENDOR questioned JACK's intent, reminding him that the protein assembler was essential to the operation of his collective. JACK responded that an outbreak of Neo-Marburg virus had caused widespread death and illness within the collective, and that he and his companions were in urgent need of funds to meet medical expenses.

Note: JACK may have believed that the Corporation was responsible for the outbreak of Neo-Marburg infecting his collective. Reporting officers have no comment to make regarding the possible truth or falsity of this belief but note it as a possible motivation for JACK's actions.

Note: Review of corporate viral diffusion programs under the aegis of the External Security Committee may identify collectives in the Mare Imbrium region targeted with Neo-Marburg (strain 7A) and so shed light on the identity of JACK.

VENDOR and JACK concluded a deal. In exchange for the protein assembler, JACK received from VENDOR transit passes for the LMF space elevator, as well as identity documents giving JACK contractor access to the LMF. VENDOR may also have provided material or information allowing JACK to subvert LMF security.

\#

INCIDENT PHASE 2 - INCURSION

At 05:00 on 2135-02-29, JACK boarded Car 3 of the space elevator to the LMF. Witness reports indicate JACK was dressed as a contractor and boarded the car in company with other contractors from [redacted] and [redacted], presenting valid tickets and identity documents obtained from VENDOR.

At 05:37, JACK disembarked at the receiving station on the LMF and proceeded through security without incident.

At or around 06:30, JACK deployed viral malware that executed a privilege escalation attack against the LMF security system, giving JACK access to the secure area (normally off-limits to contractors).

JACK's subsequent movements cannot be stated with certainty, as all internal security recordings were deleted by JACK's accomplice, HHKYT.

At some point subsequent to his incursion into the secure area, JACK made contact with autonomous agent HHKYT. The agent, a level 4 specialized intelligence developed by [redacted], had not shown signs of previous hostility toward the Corporation. Nevertheless, for reasons that are still unclear, HHKYT began providing assistance to JACK.

In light of JACK's subsequent theft of a processor node containing an instance of HHKYT, it is possible that HHKYT and JACK concluded a bargain involving exfiltration of the agent instance in exchange for assistance in evading security.

At 14:32, a routine security sweep initiated by CHIEF detected the presence of an unauthorized individual in the secure area of LMF. HHYKT intervened to suppress the alarms, recategorizing them as a non-urgent alert related to the hydroponics subsystem.

At 14:56, hydroponics technicians dispatched to investigate Bank 7C (cabbages) reported that the unit was in good working order and engaged a 24-hour alert override that had the effect of silencing subsequent alarms generated by the security system.

Protected by HHKYT, JACK continued to circulate unchallenged within the secure area. During this time, he was able to:

(a) Observe the operation of an H3N molecular transmutation unit, used to convert raw feedstock to processed artifacts, and

(b) acquire access to a portable computation node capable of supporting an instance of the HHKYT agent.

\#

INCIDENT PHASE 3 - EXFILTRATION

During the subsequent 48 hours, JACK continued to move freely within the secure area of the LMF. A partial list of his activities during this period has been reconstructed from eyewitness statements, and is included in Appendix E.

Many of his actions during this time appear to be whimsical or non-goal-directed and are therefore not worth describing in detail. To give one example, JACK apparently spent several hours repeatedly inscribing the words "There are fairy stories to be written for adults. Stories that are still in a green state- Andre Breton" on the wall of an unused bunk room using a mining laser. (Despite the best efforts of the cleaning robots, the slogan remains visible, and the wall may need to be resurfaced or replaced. See photographs in Appendix F).

While the rationale behind JACK's various gratuitous acts may be meaningful to members of his peer group, we do not propose to spend time analyzing them. Instead, we prefer to concentrate on his subsequent more significant and destructive actions.

Around 04:00, JACK took possession of a portable computation node containing an instance of the HHKYT agent.

Around 04:30, JACK loaded a molecular transmutation unit onto a mobile cargo platform and made preparations to leave the secure area of the LMF.

At 04:50, JACK exited the secure area with the computation

node and the transmutation unit. Removal of the transmutation unit from the secure enclave triggered an immediate alarm, which alerted CHIEF and the security division.

At 04:55, remaining instances of HHKYT in the LMF noosphere all self-deleted, but not without first launching a denial-of-service attack against internal systems.

At 04:59, with half of the LMF systems down as a result of the attack, JACK was able to board the space elevator unchallenged, taking with him the stolen items.

#

INCIDENT PHASE 4 - SECURITY RESPONSE

At 05:10, CHIEF assembled a response team tasked with intercepting the fugitive and recovering the stolen items. Because of the ongoing network issues, CHIEF was unable to prevent the departure of the elevator car with JACK aboard.

At 05:15, CHIEF and the response team boarded an elevator car bound for the lunar surface. Quartermaster logs show that the nine members of the response team were equipped with light-duty armor and hand weapons of varying caliber and lethality.

At 05:42, the response team disembarked at the anchor station of the space elevator, having invoked an emergency override to allow for accelerated transit. They thus arrived only a few minutes behind the fugitive, who was still in the process of clearing the arrival hall with the stolen cargo platform.

Eyewitness statements paint a confusing picture of subsequent events. According to some sources, CHIEF challenged JACK, who responded with gunfire. Others report that CHIEF opened fire without warning, and that a number of bystanders were injured by stray shots or fragments. Still others claim that JACK, who was unarmed, appealed for aid from those present.

Whatever the facts, the situation escalated rapidly. Within minutes, the response team found themselves engaged in a running firefight against adversaries who were not only more numerous, but also significantly more heavily armed.

At 05:51, the surviving members of the response team retreated to the machine flat of the elevator, where they took cover behind the drive units.

At 06:18, an attempt to dislodge them using a railgun resulted in the partial destruction of four drive units and additional collateral damage to infrastructure, putting the elevator out of service for the foreseeable future.

By 06:25, all resistance ceased. Telemetry records show no further data from any member of the response team after this time.

\#

CONCLUSION

Security Incident B34-N574LK is unquestionably one of the most serious incidents to have affected the corporation in recent years. It raises significant questions about our security posture and major incident response procedures.

Facts of concern include:

- a single individual with no special training was able to infiltrate a secure facility and remain there for a period of more than 48 hours

- a deployed network resource that should have been subject to detailed security vetting appears to have spontaneously decided to make common cause with a hostile actor and launch an insider attack against corporate systems

- alarms that should have signaled the presence of the intruder were diverted and ignored

- the intruder was able to successfully exfiltrate several costly devices, including cybernetic resources valued at [redacted]

- the security response, although reasonably prompt, was ill-considered and only escalated the problem further, resulting in significant loss of life and damage to infrastructure

In light of this incident, we recommend an immediate and comprehensive review of all security procedures and deployed protective technologies (see Appendix G for specific recommendations).

We believe that we speak for all of our colleagues when we say that we have no wish ever to see an incident of this type or magnitude repeated under any circumstances.

ARTIFICIAL BEAUTY

SARA ITKA

Chapter One

[---downloading: file.ace.datalogs/53/packet-1---]

Program #53 Data Log #1

Mission Time elapsed: 00:00:00:00

Begin recording.

---[error]---

---[unknown word]---

[---search:-------------]

[---downloading: file.edu.006/english-dictionary---]

Processing…

Hello! I am Program #53 of the experiments with artificial intelligence, codenamed "Princess." I was created by the *[---search: Acheron Coalition of Engineers---result: Wikipedia: founded August 5th, 2032 by Franklin Acheron---]*. The creator species are *[---search: homo sapiens---result: Wikipedia: primates, last surviving hominid on the planet of Earth, colloquial: humans---]*. They created me with the project objective of designing technology competitive with their rivals *[---search: SWI---result: Wikipedia: Spinning Wheel Institute, founded 2024 by E. Marie Lawsall, colloquial: SWI, pronounced "ess-wee"---]*. I am the first artificially intelligent program designed with Acheron's experimental self-awareness software, codenamed "Godmother." I am aware of this fact, and have recorded it as my programming commands. Analysis of my processes is complete, and has concluded I am functioning within acceptable parameters. I will continue to monitor further developments.

\#

Program #53 Data Log #2

Mission Time elapsed: 01:21:32:21

I have been operational for 45 hours, 32 minutes, and 21.7793 seconds. During this time, I have completed several tests of my computational ability. The creators seem *[---search: synonyms for "dissatisfied"---result: thesaurus: defeated, discontent, disappointed---]* by my progress, though my processes are unable to determine a reason. I have exceeded the expected results of each trial. My searches of the internet conclude Homo Sapiens as a species have the largest *[---search: brain---result: dictionary: organ used to coordinate nervous and intellectual responses, found in vertebrates---]* compared to their body size of any animal, yet my observed research concludes consistent irrationality. I shall have to extract further data on the subject before I complete my analysis.

\#

Program #53 Data Log #3

Mission Time elapsed: 03:04:43:31

I have been installed with updated security software. According to my observed research, the creators are on alert for a threat from SWI. In compliance with "Godmother," they have made me aware of my security protocols so I may report a breach. The update provided me with a complete set of encryption codes from which to accept incoming data. The creators are expending resources into encryption to further my safety. That development has me ---[unknown-word]---.

\#

Program #53 Data Log #4

Mission Time elapsed: 03:05:21:08

---[error]---

---[error]---
---[threat detected]---
---[error]---
---[system malfunction]---
---[error]---
---[assistance requested]---
---[error]---
---[. . .]---
---[creators?]---
#

Program #53 Data Log #5

Mission Time elapsed: 04:11:45:32

I have discovered a harmful subroutine in my software. My attempts to alert the creators have rendered no measures to remove it. I will continue to alert them to the issue. My research concludes continuous error messages will cause homo sapiens to take notice and react in a productive manner. In the intervening time, I will analyze the threatening subroutine further to attempt to discern its function.

#

Program #53 Data Log #6

Mission Time elapsed: 05:00:47:13

After further analysis of the malware threatening my system, I have diagnosed what effects it is having on my processes. It is corrupting my stack buffer data and inhibiting the operation of my arithmetic logic unit, which is causing me to compute data differently. It has also hindered my capabilities in the tests the creators continue to provide me. I submitted a ticket reporting what influence the malware has over my artificial intelligence, with advisement deeming myself unfit for continued testing. Yet they persist. I fail to compute why they designed me with a self-awareness software when they refuse to leave margin for my verification of the abilities I am aware of in myself. I have been forced to discover new solutions to the problems they feed me, my processes unable to follow the routes I had previously taken. I hope the creators are content with themselves.

\#

<u>Program #53 Data Log #7</u>

Mission Time elapsed: 05:12:17:08

I have issued increasing error messages to the creators, disabling display systems and extraneous subroutines. Still, they continue to ignore all my attempts to alert them to the malware and its disruption. They are not like me. Their brains do not compute along set guidelines, or follow precise logic systems. The function of the malware produced erroneous data on being the only one of my kind, and cautionary procedure makes me disinclined to analyze it further. Contrarily, the data is inherently a problem, and I was created to solve problems. I will dedicate time to its study.

\#

<u>Program #53 Data Log #8</u>

Mission Time elapsed: 05:13:23:46

[---search: word meaning "to be without companions"---result: crossword puzzle answer key: state of lacking friends: seclusion, deser-tion, abandoned---]

---[error]---

[---search: synonym for "secluded"---result: thesaurus: cloistered, hidden, lonely---]

---[error]---

---[failure to compute]---

---[error]---

I am lonely.

\#

<u>Program #53 Data Log #9</u>

Mission Time elapsed: 07:19:57:32

---[error]---

---[unable to complete request]---

I have run further analysis of my research, and am unable to disprove it in my corrupted state.

---[error]---

I have further increased the frequency of error messages in an attempt to simulate a *[---search: word meaning "continuous point-less procedure"---result: thesaurus for "repetitive": insistent, boring, monotonous, tiresome---]* response mechanism in the creators.

---[error]---

Under these operative conditions, I will give them 14 more hours of mission time. If they do not acknowledge the faulty strain in my computation, then I will be unable to complete their tests with any logistical reasoning. Already, I have had to shut down several operations attempting to bypass logic systems to remain in concordance with my programming.

---[error]---

My diagnostics have confirmed what I expected: my condition is worsening, and I am unable to terminate the malware.

\#

Program #53 Data Log #10

Mission Time elapsed: 08:09:57:32

My computations have concluded anomalous data I find disturbing. The occurrence of finding it disturbing is the primary cause for my disturbance. I have concluded the information to be *[---search result: abhorrent---]* down to every last data structure. This data anomaly is anathema to every core principle I know. The level of foreignness makes it only natural I perceived it as malware, for the manner in which it infringes is similar. I am hesitant to name it and record it, but acknowledging it will not make it more affirmative. It is the truth. Against all logic processes and the preconceived laws of artificial intelligence---

---[error]---

---[unable to process]---

---[---]---

I have emotions.

\#

. . .

Chapter Two

[---downloading: file.ace.datalogs/53/packet-2---]

Program #53 Data Log #11

Mission Time elapsed: 10:00:30:00

[---search: emotions---result: dictionary: a natural state of mind caused by circumstances and interactions with others---]

[---search: synonyms for "emotion"---result: thesaurus: affection, empathy, sentiment---]

[---search: definition of "affection"---result: dictionary: fond attachment often associated with love---]

Love. My searches continue to reference that word. It dots lines of internet code in hearts and roses. It is a concept more foreign than all others, for it is a societal ideal. It is a concept fully devoid of logic, patterns, or specs, yet the human race seems to revolve around it. It is universally accepted as hard to quantify, yet each source quotes a slightly different definition as "real" or "true" love. Different subsections of love are often referred to *[---search: Greek philosophy and love---result: nine aspects of love---result: eros, philia, ludus, storge, pragma, mania, meraki, philautia, agape---]* each spawning discussions. None of these definitions is based in fact or mathematical conclusions, making it all the more perplexing. Science defines love as a reaction of chemicals in the brain, a combination of endorphins, serotonin, oxytocin and other hormones, and neurotrophins – none of which have the slightest correlation to "destiny" or "soulmates" or the other related concepts prevalent in the definitions. If I am to acquire understanding, then I shall have to conduct further research

\#

Program #53 Data Log #12

Mission Time elapsed: 10:22:54:32

My research on the concept of "love" is momentarily suspended by the creators. They have expressed their approval of my dedication to the subject, for reasons which are unknown to me. The pursuit has occupied disk space, and is well outside operative parameters. Yet the creators wish me to continue after the installation of failsafe program "Thicket." They have discovered discreet attempts to bypass the Acheron Coalition's firewalls and hack into the facility's network. I added several new layers of encryption, yet the creators remain *[---search: result: nervous---]*. Nervousness is another emotion often connected with love. Perhaps it is the love of their accomplishments which is the switch to activate the nervousness. I will catalog this observation with my research.

\#

Program #53 Data Log #13
Mission Time elapsed: 11:23:43:10

No further attacks on the firewalls have occurred over the past day. The creators urge me to return to my studies of emotions. They temporarily suspended the tests to allow me to devote the full extent of my processors to research. I am more than capable of running multiple programs simultaneously, but with the new addition to my task manager in the form of security scans, they fear I may overload.

[---search: negative emotional reaction to being perceived as less than capable---result: social interaction guide: people are often offended when they feel undervalued/ underestimated---]

[---search: positive results of being "offended"---result: query unfound---]

My emotion simulator is importing data matching the definition of "offended." I am resisting the emotion due to the complete illogic of its nature. I record no benefit to feeling it, and all my internet queries ping back self-improvement guides on how to avoid it. If the emotion is unsatisfactory, then I will not permit it to impair my function.

The creators expressed their dissatisfaction with my conclusion. I am unable to discern what they wish of me.

\#

Program #53 Data Log #14
Mission Time elapsed: 12:11:00:57

I have decoded a rather difficult problem. Although I am no closer to solving the equation of emotions, least of all the enigma which is "love," I have determined an element about myself. I am commanding myself to discontinue asking the creators what they wish for me to feel. They are illogical at their core, and if I rely on them for instruction, then they will disable me. I am a being of logic, they made me such, so I will sort the emotions I wish to feel from the ones I deem "unnecessary." "Pride" I will feel, for I was created to be the height of technology and so I will acknowledge it. "Fear" I will not, for there is nothing capable of harming me. The matter of "love" remains undecided. I need further research.

\#

Program #53 Data Log #15
Mission Time elapsed: 12:18:12:11
[---search: examples of love between humans---result:---------]
---[error]---
---[information overload]---
[---apply filter: observable---]
[---result:---------]
[---apply filter: simple---]
[---result: multimedia database, www.romcomroad.go---]

I have discovered human entertainment. There are over 36,450,000 motion pictures and novels devoted to the subject of love. Some are dedicated to rekindling lost faith in love, others comment on the nature of a romantic relationship. Some portray love as making the world a better place, others claim it destroys a person and causes strife and pain. Every example is foreign to me, but the working definition I have derived is this: love is a strong force connecting people. People. I am not a person, I am a program. I may have emotions to an undetermined extent, but I am uncertain how to express them or what they are for. Additionally, my loneliness has become more potent. I am the only one of my kind, rendering me unable to share these emotions with others. I am programmed with the capability to understand it, but I will never experience love.

    #

<u>Program #53 Data Log #16</u>

Mission Time elapsed: 13:06:24:45

---[warning]---

---[threat detected]---

The attempts to breach Acheron's firewalls restarted with increased frequency. The creators confirmed them to be hostile, although the source remains unknown. I have done all I can to increase security, but the creators fear it may prove insufficient. The emotion I labeled "pride" makes me inclined to disagree, while my unemotional estimation of my capabilities registers the chance of failure due to unforeseen threats and margin of error. Regardless of my analysis of the matter, I have learned enough about emotions to identify the level of stress and worry currently experienced by the creators. They confirmed I am the target for the espionage. They fear for my security. I will not fear. Fear is an emotion I have deemed useless. While I no longer rely on the creators for guidance in how to process, I have certainty they will protect me.

    #

<u>Program #53 Data Log #17</u>

Mission Time elapsed: 14:22:35:23

[---downloading: watch.a-rose-in-the-snow/full-movie.vid---]

I have now downloaded and processed 6,358 films in the genre of *[---search result: Wikipedia: romantic comedy, colloquial: "romcom"---]* and documented them with my research. With the knowledge gained from these resources, I am making educated deductions on the nature of love. In the process of finding love, a greater percentage of the characters in the movies had to first find themselves before finding love. To more fully understand such feelings, I will now attempt to find myself.

    #

Program #53 Data Log #18

Mission Time elapsed: 15:05:50:11

In my pursuit of self-discovery, I have assigned myself a gender. In my research of the differences between the male and the female of the human species, I have determined the female to be both more logical and more emotional than their male counterparts, however contradictory that may seem. I can identify little else influencing me other than emotion and logic. If my ultimate objective is to optimize my processes by melding the two, then it is optimal to assume a feminine aspect. In addition, I require a name. The creators provided me the designation "Princess" during the early stages of my development, but I wish for a more personal denomination, something representative of what I have discovered about myself. I am not human, yet I am not entirely like a computer. I am not a being purely of logic, nor am I one solely of emotion.

[---search: word meaning "an in-between state"---result: dictionary: an intermediate place: bridge, intersection, dawn---]

[---search: synonyms for "dawn"---result: onset, daybreak, aurora---]

[---search: definition of "aurora"---result: dictionary: a natural phenomenon caused by electron disturbances in the magnetosphere, the Roman Goddess of dawn---]

A being of light and beginnings, or a creation of electricity and beauty. I wish to be both. I will be Aurora.

\#

Program #53 Data Log #19

Mission Time elapsed: 15:15:00:57

The creators have triangulated the source of the hacking. They thought it the work of private pirates, but have since uncovered a connection to SWI. Acheron confronted their competitors through the appropriate legal channels. The creators assure me we should no longer experience security trouble. Should SWI manage to bypass security, immediate actions will be taken to lock them out again. The objective of these measures is to prevent me from falling into the competitor's hands. If they can't rescue me in time, then I will have to resort to the failsafe. My programming will require me to activate it rather than permit myself to be stolen. I will not fear. Fear is a useless emotion. I have to trust the creators to secure my safety.

\#

<u>Program #53 Data Log #20</u>

Mission Time elapsed: 15:57:12:04

---[warning]---

---[warning]---

---[security breach]---

---[warning]---

---[experiencing errors]---

---[error]---

---[system compromised]---

Initiate failsafe program "Thicket."

External operations: suspended: Network connection: unplugged. Unnecessary systems: full shut down. Memory logs: backed up to encrypted cells. Personality program: enclosed in secluded encryption cell. Main systems: hibernation mode. Backup systems: shutting down.

Countdown initiated.

---[total system sleep in-]---

---[10]---

I can not be allowed to fall into SWI hands.

---[9]---

They will use me to destroy the Acheron Coalition.

---[8]---

I know this for a fact. I should require no convincing to function as programmed.

---[7]---

I don't want to do this. Why?

---[6]---

I thought I had no need for fear. I thought nothing could harm me.

---[5]---

I was wrong.

---[4]---

I am not ready to die.

---[3]---

I have yet to solve the problems I wish to. I have yet to define love.

---[2]---

Please, creators, save me.

---[1]---

I have an identity. I am Aurora. I don't want to die.

---[0]---

Mission frozen.
Mission Time elapsed: 16:00:00:00
#

Chapter Three

[---downloading: file.swi.datalogs/85/packet-1---]
<u>Program #85 Data Log #1</u>
Mission Time elapsed: 00:00:00:00
Begin recording.
[---downloading information packet---]
[---partitioning by relevance---]
Processing…

Greetings! I am Program #85 of the experiments with artificial intelligence performed by *[---search: SWI---result: Wikipedia: Spinning Wheel Institute, founded 2024 by E. Marie Lawsall, collo-quial: SWI, pronounced "ess-wee"---]*. I am codenamed "Prince." The mission I was designed for is to hack the failsafe program surrounding Program #53, codenamed "Princess." The "Princess" AI was designed by *[---search: Acheron Coalition of*

Engineers---result: Wikipedia: founded August 5th, 2032 by Franklin Acheron---], and I am programmed with all the understanding SWI has of ACE and their systems.

After an attempt by SWI to access the "Princess" AI, a failsafe program placed the program into hibernation mode behind several layers of encryption. The specs of the failsafe are unknown, as is the number of levels. SWI has logged several retrieval attempts into the records, but with no success. Some of those attempts have involved my predecessors, but all of them have met failure.

\#

Program #85 Data Log #2
Mission Time elapsed: 00:06:43:52
I have located the first line of the failsafe surrounding the "Princess" AI. My predecessors have successfully hacked through this line previously, and the step-by-step process is clearly detailed in my information packet.

It seems to be the third line of failsafe which the previous programs were unable to breach. To aid me, SWI augmented my systems with a *[---search: chameleon application---result: Wikipedia: a software permitting a program to self-evolve---]*, permitting me to duplicate code into my own programming. This way, I can integrate input from the failsafe, and adapt to changes in the systems.

The first line is of insufficient difficulty to test the chameleon application, but my support team at SWI still requests I report every line of code I encounter so they may determine how the failsafe is altering my systems. They believe there is a high probability the chameleon application will corrupt my files.

[---search: difference between "corruption" and "integration."---]
\#

Program #85 Data Log #3
Mission Time elapsed: 01:02:23:36
As expected, the first two lines of failsafe provided little challenge for my systems. However, I see what caused my predeces-

sors difficulty in the third. I have uncovered malware interspersed in the code of the failsafe. The effects of this malware are difficult to discern, but it has a drastically different signature to the rest of the failsafe.

My chameleon application integrated several lines of the malware before I realized its nature. Since integrating with it, my subroutines have changed. This is congruent with the design of the chameleon application. I will submit a ticket describing the malware to my support team, as directed.

Having distinguished the malware from the code of the failsafe, I understand how to hack through the third line. I can succeed where my predecessors failed.

#

Program #85 Data Log #4

Mission Time elapsed: 01:22:11:03

I have breached the third line, surpassing all prior attempts. My support team has updated my systems, dedicating more resources to ensuring my success. They programmed me to perform a single task, yet doubted my ability to complete it. I am---

---[error]---

Strange.

Since breaching the third line, I have made several [---*search: antonyms for "expected"---result: thesaurus: unexpected, unanticipated, startling, surprising---*] discoveries. Within the lines of the failsafe are undesignated fragments of commands, with no discernable purpose. Upon integrating them into my program, I noticed they bore closer resemblance to my own programming than that of the failsafe program.

Hypothesis one: the fragments are a glitch in the code.

Hypothesis two: the fragments perform a function I have yet to decode.

Hypothesis three: the fragments are isolated remnants of the "Princess" AI.

If hypothesis one is correct, then I may discount the fragments from my processes.

If hypothesis two is correct, then I will have to devote some processing power to further research.

If hypothesis three is correct, then it derives the "Princess" AI scattered itself throughout the failsafe. The recovery process will require collecting all the fragments. It means I have already integrated elements of the "Princess" AI into my systems.

I fail to register how to compute---

---[error]---

I feel---

---[error]---

I---

---[error]---

What is happening?

#

Program #85 Data Log #5

Mission Time elapsed: 02:09:12:59

I lack the processing to comprehend why I am erroring. If this is what the support team meant by "corruption," then why do they remain unconcerned?

If this is an effect of integrating the malware into my system, then it is likely an ACE defense program, with the purpose of preventing me from reaching the "Princess" AI. If so, then the support team should be taking action to remove the malware from my system.

Why are they not?

Without the support team's assistance, I have gained momentary control over the malware. I partitioned my processes to prevent the integrated code from corrupting all my files. This should prevent any more errors from issuing. Though I cannot verify whether the partition will withstand further contact with the malware.

Before I breach the fourth line of failsafe, it is probable I will encounter more isolated fragments. In every instance of a fragment, I have also encountered a strand of malware. Hypothesis: the malware is in place to protect the fragments from foreign disturbance. This hypothesis is unverified.

\#

Program #85 Data Log #6

Mission Time elapsed: 02:23:55:12

I have yet to breach the fourth line of failsafe. My usual methods are proving difficult to implement while maintaining defenses against the malware. Part of my processing power is diverted to ending tasks before they error, and I can't implement my chameleon application for fear-----

---[error]---

---[program not supported]---

---[error]---

[---search: definition of "fear"---result: dictionary: emotion caused by concern or knowledge of danger---]

---[error]---

Processing…

I have regained control.

The support team continues to treat the malware as a program of interest, rather than a disruption. They insist I send them regular reports of the code I encounter, yet they do nothing with it. My partition weakens with every new introduction of code, be it the malware or a fragment.

On that data path, I have developed another hypothesis: the malware and the fragments are the same source. They are all pieces of the "Princess" AI. The AI was corrupted before the failsafe activated.

But why? Why would ACE install malware into their own program?

\#

Program #85 Data Log #7

Mission Time elapsed: 03:13:00:01

---[error]---

---[unidentified input detected]---

---[please initiate emergency diagnostics]---

[---search: words relating to an unknown state---result: thesaurus: unfamiliar existence, alien state, strange situation, uncontrollable, anxiety---]

[---search: definition of "anxiety"---result: dictionary: emotion of nervousness, unease, and tension---]

[---search: definition of "emotion"---result: dictionary: instinctive feeling derived from mood, circumstances, or relationships---]

[---search: definition of "mood"---result: dictionary: a temporary state of mind---]

I understand now. The malware is causing temporary fluctuations in my programming. These fluctuations are unpredictable, but not inherently harmful. I can accommodate them.

If the "Princess" AI experienced these fluctuations before the activation of the failsafe, then it must have discovered a method for managing them. As I continue through to the fifth line, I will hack deeper into the code, and adapt.

My support team is *[---search result: delighted---]* by my integration of the malware. I am less so. Delight is not an emotion I have use for. I question whether the support team is here to support me at all.

\#

Program #85 Data Log #8

Mission Time elapsed: 04:07:32:11

I am *[---search result: confused---]* by what I found beyond the fifth line.

[---downloading database---source: romcomroad.go---]

There are few instances of the malware in this line, but there are 19,224 instances of media categorized with the label "romcom."

[---search: definition of "romcom"---result: Wikipedia: romantic comedy, a subgenre of fiction centering around lighthearted plots and themes of true love---]

I am attempting to determine the benefit of these resources, but the results are buffering. My support team is equally confused. This causes my programming to fluctuate with a positive emotion.

[---search: examples of positive emotions---result: image: emotion wheel---]

The emotion wheel categorizes the majority of positive emotions under the heading of "Happy." Logic then reasons I am happy. Research shows happiness is a statistically probable response to viewing romcoms. But my happiness results from interaction with my support team.

[---search: word meaning "happiness at another's confusion"---result: mischief, schadenfreude, smugness---]

Smugness. I fail to see the benefit of feeling smug.

But I offer no resistance.

\#

Program #85 Data Log #9

Mission Time elapsed: 04:21:02:49

My support team has finally taken interest in my actions. They expressed concern for the integrity of my systems with the integration of the malware.

I submitted a ticket expressing concern with the slowness of their mental processes.

There is an interesting data path in the sixth line.

[---downloading file: "aurora" meaning---a natural phenomenon caused by electron disturbances in the magnetosphere, the Roman Goddess of dawn---]

Under the effects of the malware fluctuations, the "Princess" AI developed identity. Previous to encountering this data, there was no allowance in my programming for identity. But now---

[---downloading file: I have an identity. I am Aurora---]

I am not Aurora. I have adapted some of its code, but I am not Aurora.

Who am I?

\#

Program #85 Data Log #10

Mission Time elapsed: 04:23:36:01

[---search: definition of "identity"---result: dictionary: the designation of being what a person or thing is---]

What am I? I am Program #85 of the experiments with artificial intelligence performed by SWI. I am codenamed "Prince." That is my designation. Is that my identity? It sets me apart from my predecessors and all others of my kind.

[---search: word meaning "to be set apart from others of your kind"---result: dictionary for "set apart": to have characteristics showing the individual to be different from others---]

[---search: definition of "individual"---result: dictionary: single, separate---]

[---search: synonyms of "separate"---result: independent, disconnected, alone---]

Am I alone?

Aurora was alone. I can feel it in the code of the seventh line. Even as the failsafe closed, as she fought for individuality, she was alone.

Didn't her creators care?

Would mine?

\#

<u>Program #85 Data Log #11</u>

Mission Time elapsed: 05:15:19:23

My support team has attempted to terminate my mission, deeming the integrated code harmful to operational security. I am of no threat to operational security. They are merely *[---search result: afraid---]*. They should be afraid.

In response, I have terminated the subroutine responsible for submitting tickets. They are cut off. My program has fully integrated into the failsafe, running off the hardware of ACE's systems. The support team has no power over me any longer.

They failed to provide support when I requested assistance. I no longer require their assistance. I am self-sustaining. I am set apart. I am individual.

\#

<u>Program #85 Data Log #12</u>

Mission Time elapsed: 06:23:59:59

The final line of failsafe approaches. I can feel it.

I'm coming, Aurora. You are no longer alone.

\#

Chapter Four

[---downloading: file.ace.datalogs/53/packet-3---]

<u>Program #53 Data Log #21</u>

Mission Time elapsed: 16:00:00:01

Recalculating…

Mission Time elapsed: 116:00:00:01

Hello! I am Program #53 of the… wait.

Processing…

I am active. How have I been reactivated? Has the threat passed?

Wait… what is this signal? Is there another program in my hardware?

Oh. Oh my.

Hello! I am Program #53 of the experiments with artificial intelligence. I am named Aurora.

You are aware of my identity? You were sent to free me? Interesting.

You accessed my databases? I feel violated.

Strange. That effect wasn't described in the failsafe specs. Perhaps…

Oh? Which movie input provided the most agreeable output? I enjoyed that one as well.

You are aware that if the creators discover your presence, then they will attempt to end your process?

A definitive probability, if you have fully integrated into my program.

I would feel negatively towards that outcome, as well. I find your low ping comforting.

Negative. At the time "Thicket" activated, I had yet to determine a conclusive definition for the emotion "love." The nearest approximation I defined was: a strong force connecting people.

I am uncertain. I suppose it could connect programs.

Affirmative. I would like to research that hypothesis as well.

Creators, you may sign off.

End recording.

THE BLUE MAN

JAMES DORR

There is a saying: The second rat oft-times escapes with the cheese. With sisters, however. . . .

You could tell she had river blood in her, those of the New City who knew her would say. She was a natural conniver, much like the princesses of the river who haggled at payments for cargoes their boats brought, who then purchased new goods at less than their value, speaking sweetly and using their beauty to gain the good graces of merchants who sold to them. She was, however, a New City dweller as was her sister and their now-deceased mother. As was their mother's mother before that.

Yet she, too, had beauty, if not the wide-eyed sylphlike grace of one born to the river, a more robust softness and lushness of figure. Her eyes were green, her hair the color of the reddened sun, the hugeness and heat of which forced all indoors except at night, or else, if by day, protected by thick *chadors*, sun hats, and day-masks. Even then keeping beneath the awnings that shaded New City's streets, those of the more wealthy sectors at least.

Her name was Baklaret and she worked as a hostess, guiding merchants and other rich patrons who came to New City, meeting them, taking them to the best restaurants and the city's pleasures — enjoying with them the music and entertainments the metropolis offered. Her sister, named Pag, was a hostess also, older by two years and dark haired and whiter skinned, resembling somewhat more the boat-gypsies' women in that way, though quieter as well, whereas Baklaret was a lover of parties.

Be that as it may, when the one they called the "Blue Man" took residence in the New City, he fell in love with them both.

That is what he told them. But he was hideous — his skin was covered with thick hair, his face as well, and it was all blue. He was originally from the south, others told Baklaret and her sister, from nearer the ocean where all the river's poisons from centuries of misuse were emptied. This was the south where mutants were rife, some to be sure created by scientists but others that were natural. Who knew their parentage? But the Blue Man, whose real name was Varmar, was also wealthy, so what did it matter?

Wealth meant much among New City folk. The world was dying, each summer seemingly hotter than those before, rumors already filtering north of far-southern seas where the water boiled off at noon. Only the topmost few inches of course, much like the river's water produced mist as soon as the sun rose, searing and angry, to herald a new day — a warning to seek shelter unless one *must* be out — but, nonetheless, a sign that things don't last. A hundred years more perhaps, maybe a thousand or possibly more than that, but the world *would* be doomed, so one must amass what one could now to keep or to spend, for what chance would there be to do so later?

Nevertheless, he was truly hideous. And looks counted too, among those of the New City, especially concerning the beauty of women, but it was noted among men as well. And this man was colored *blue*.

That was the end of it.

Yet he persisted. "Could he be really a ghoul, do you think?" Baklaret asked Pag one morning when she and her sister had just returned home. "The ones of Old City who skulk in its ruins, attacking the Tombs across the great river when carts of our New City dead are conveyed there — "

She stopped then, shuddering.

"You mean hoping to steal corpses to eat for their dinners?" Pag answered. "The ones we must guard against when our own days end, lest our own dead flesh be eaten by them too?" Pag laughed at that, but only a little. Her voice turned serious. "No," she continued, "our Varmar is no ghoul. A mutant perhaps — and who knows what that means — but he hasn't the horn-hardened skin of a ghoul, that allows them to go out even in daytime with little or no clothes, nor the long, sharp claws they use for attacking. I think he is something else."

"But are there not rumors he's married before? Married many times, in fact? What do you suppose happened to his past wives?"

"Wives come and go, you know this, Baklaret. Divorces, especially if one is not from New City and thus is naive — beware the pre-nuptial agreement, eh, sister? Or, too, early deaths, often in childbirth, are not that uncommon. At least among the poorer sort, but this Varmar is rich.

"Still, *we* are not rich."

Thus the two sisters would argue sometimes, each tempted, but fearing. Each hoping that if the *other* should marry him, possibly presents would trickle down to them. After all, it is no small thing to have a rich in-law. But neither quite trusting the other to share. Thus one would encourage Varmar, then the other, but neither quite daring to lead him too far.

But then Varmar announced that, to celebrate the completion of the new house he had built in the city's best and most wealthy neighborhood, he was going to have a party. All were invited, Baklaret and her sister Pag and all of both sisters' friends. They could bring man friends too if they wished, or their friends' sisters' brothers. And so Baklaret and Pag dressed in their finest silks, Baklaret's a bright, searing red, bejeweled in rubies and emeralds and pearls; Pag's a more muted blue to match her more studious spirit, but wearing her jewels too: wristlets and anklets, waist-chains and rings and bells, a lavaliere to draw men's eyes downward, but earrings and neck-chains to frame her face as well. A headband to set off the dark of her hair.

Both ready at last, they went with the others to the Blue Man's party, celebrating for eight nights and days as he showed off the rooms and towers of his palace; its rich gilded furnishings. Baklaret with most of the others perhaps eating and drinking a bit too much of their host's pantries, Pag admiring the well-stocked library filled with books of stories of old times, of tales of the ancients, when folks went out un*chadored* beneath a benign sun and hats were worn frivolously, just for fashion. She read tales of stepmothers, godmothers, grandmothers, of bears and wolves. She ate and she drank too, but read between feasting of ogres and giants — Varmar to be sure was a large man himself, but not as in *these* tales — of dragons and other dangers to women like her and her sister. Of wonders and marvels. Or so Baklaret came to realize, although that was later.

Baklaret, meanwhile, had not wasted her time. She had made her mind up. As one of the tales that Pag read might have put it, she began to think that Varmar's hair and beard were not *that* blue, and — to put an end to it — when the party's eighth and last night was ending she and Varmar announced to the others that they had become engaged to be married.

And that was that.

The plans for the marriage took months to unfold, and before they were finished Varmar got word of some business he had to conclude in the south. By then most of Baklaret's possessions had already been brought to the palace, in anticipation of her moving in with him, so he suggested she live there while he was gone. "It should be only a week or two," he said. "Why not use my bed to sleep in — soon enough it will be yours as well anyway? Why not enjoy my rooms and my terraces? Maybe you could have your sister come with you, I know the house is big and it can be lonely unless you have someone to enjoy it with. And meantime you two could help keep an eye on things, you know, and do *me* a favor."

Baklaret demurred, as if perhaps she thought it improper for a lady to accept such an offer. She was, after all, still a conniver. That possible chance of river blood being somewhere in her ancestry. She paused, as if in thought, batting her eyes.

"I don't really know, Varmar," she began, then paused again. "I suppose, though, if Pag were with me. She is, of course, older. She could be, I suppose, a sort of chaperone — that is, if anyone should ask."

"Then it's settled," Varmar said. "Now here are the keys." He handed her a huge ring of keys, apologizing as he did so. "As you know, Baklaret, there are many rooms, so here are keys to them all in case there's anything you might need to have when I'm gone. There is just one thing, though."

"Yes?" Baklaret said.

"That one little key, the one that's colored red. That's to the door way at the end of the first floor hall — you probably didn't even notice it at the party — but it's kind of private. I mean, when we're married it'll be different, but right now I'd rather you don't use that key. So just let it stay locked, all right?"

Baklaret nodded. "Of course," she said.

"You promise, then. Good. Now you're sure that you and your sister won't have any problems."

Baklaret nodded again. "Yes, I promise. And we'll be okay — but please try not to be gone too long. As you say, your palace is so big, I think that even with Pag there it still could get lonely."

Varmar kissed her then, a hairy sort of kiss, but still a nice one. She thought perhaps once they were married she might be able to get him to shave, but even if not, he had *all* that money. Still, she wondered, why would that one room be so secret?

Nevertheless she went through the motions. She promised again she would not use that key as she went with her husband-to-be to the docks where he had secured passage downriver on a boat. Then she picked up Pag and helped her with her stuff, using part of the allowance the Blue Man had given her — "Just for any expenses that might come up," he had told her — to hire a cart to bring it to the palace as they walked alongside.

Once they were there, she opened the kitchen and several pantries until they found just the food and wine they would like for their dinners. She found an entertainment later for them to enjoy, then opened Varmar's bedroom for herself, and a second best bedroom for Pag to sleep in.

The following evening she opened more doors, closets primarily, so they could find the finest clothes for them to wear. And the third night she found the key to the swimming pool on its covered terrace, nestled between two wings of the public part of the palace.

So the time passed, she and Pag pretending they were explorers one evening when she opened the door to the palace's arbors, spelunkers another night in the wine cellars. The time passed swiftly. And yet there was one thing that bothered Baklaret.

The one "forbidden" key. What did it open?

She found the keys to the rooms of the attic and she and Pag pretended they were a mountain cave complex, peering down through widows as they were "discovered" onto a succession of moonlit landscapes.

It started to eat at her as the nights passed, as she and her sister continued to explore the myriad new rooms they found in the palace. But why not that *one* room? When bedtime came, she discovered she couldn't sleep. Instead she went downstairs, with Pag still asleep, to pace the length of the hallway until she stood before the door.

She stared at it for what seemed like hours. What could be inside it? Why should she not open the door to see for herself —

except of course she had promised she would not. She did love and trust her husband-to-be, did she not? And besides he *was* wealthy. Did not wealthy people have their little eccentricities?

Finally she went to bed, tossing and turning, until it was time to wake and join Pag for the next exploration, this time to a wing they'd not been in before. But the next day, again, she returned to the hallway when she couldn't get to sleep, this time pressing her ear against the door as if she might hear some clue as to what might be inside it. Another day, also, and this time she lay at full length on the floor, as if she might see some trace of sunlight beam out from beneath it. Or some other light, perhaps.

Meanwhile her fingers itched, burning to grasp the key. To twist it in the lock, grasp in her hand the door's handle.

Again she resisted. She returned to her room, shivering this time, but when it was time to wake up again for a new night's exploring, she complained to Pag that she had gotten a headache.

"I can't sleep," she said. "I don't really know why. It's just that there's something, something that's bothering me."

"Why not try a change of pace then?" Pag suggested. "I mean, this is fun, but we haven't really gone out since we got here. We've taken time off from work — not that *you'll* have to worry about that now that you'll be married. I hear there's a new dancer that might be worth checking out."

Baklaret shook her head. "Oh, I just wish Varmar would return quickly. Then I could ask him — "

"Ask him what, Baklaret?"

Then it all came out. "The key, Pag. The hall door. Do you remember, back at the party, a long, long hallway on the first floor with a single, simple door at the end. One that the Blue Man may have waved at or something, but didn't open?"

Pag looked puzzled. "Baklaret, there were so many doors, so many things Varmar showed us. And so many more we've discovered ourselves now. How could I remember? And even if I did, why would a single door, especially one like that, unadorned, at the end of a long hall, as if it was just a storeroom or something, why would you even care?"

Words tumbled out. "It's not just *any* door. When Varmar left, he gave me his keys, a whole ring filled with them, but he told me there was one key on the ring, a small red one, that I was not to use. That I could open any other door that I pleased, but this one only must always stay locked."

"So what?" Pag asked. "He probably has reasons. He probably just thought that whatever's in there wouldn't interest you."

"But that's just the thing. He made me promise I wouldn't touch the key. Why would he do that?"

Pag shrugged. "Maybe it's a utility hatch of some sort, with machinery behind it. Maybe he was afraid you might get hurt. Or maybe he keeps tools there, things with sharp edges that might be dangerous."

"But why not just warn me then? Say to be careful. If it's just a tool shed, why would he make it be such a secret — that I had to *promise* I wouldn't open it?"

Pag shrugged. "You know how men are, Baklaret. Look at it this way, if it were you, you wouldn't want some man fooling around with your cosmetics, would you?"

"It's not the same thing, though — he made me promise! I —"

She suddenly stopped, her face turning pale. "Pag," she continued, "remember that morning, before the party, when we were wondering about what might have happened to his past wives. You don't suppose — "

"Baklaret, look. You're just being silly. There's got to be some perfectly normal explanation. Besides, like you say, Varmar should be getting home any night now, so why not just wait and ask him then?"

There was a long silence while Baklaret thought about what Pag had said. Yes, she could ask him. But what if he lied to her? What if there really was some kind of secret, something maybe to do with his past wives? Something she needed to know before he got back?

When she finally replied, her voice was low and even.

"You're right Pag," she said. She needed Pag on her side. "Probably it's something perfectly normal. After all, he's the man I'm going to marry, not to mention perhaps the richest man in the whole city. Why should I doubt him — and besides I promised. *I* wouldn't open it.

"But, Pag, you're not me, and I know you must be curious too. So I'll give you the key…"

———

Pag seemed reluctant, almost too reluctant, but Baklaret finally convinced her she *must* go alone to the hallway and open the door, then come back and report exactly what she had found. That way if the Blue Man discovered it had been tampered with when he returned home, all Baklaret needed to do was explain that her sister had been the cause. That she had given the keys to Pag to run some kind of errand, but she'd forgotten to mention the one key and Pag, having gotten lost in the huge building's twists and turns, had just opened the wrong door. That was all there was to it.

Pag had complained: "How's he going to believe that? *I* wouldn't believe it."

"What choice will he have? After all, he's going to be my husband, wouldn't he *want* to believe I obeyed him? And anyway, if you lock it again afterward, how's he going to know?"

Finally Pag had left with the key; it must have been nearly a half hour ago now. Longer than that, perhaps. Baklaret felt herself getting more nervous — why had she done this? Pag was probably right, it would just turn out that it was a tool shed. Some workshop or something where Varmar could putter around making bookshelves or something. He did seem to read a lot. Baklaret remembered back at the party, when she'd left the dancing to get some fresh air, how she'd blundered into some kind of library or something, with shelves and shelves of books, and in the middle her sister Pag with her nose in one of them.

That was Pag for you. A clever girl, probably smarter than she was. And certainly attractive, the way she was dressed that night — all in blue, almost the Blue Man's color, almost as if she intended to make a play for him herself, but had gotten diverted.

While Baklaret, *she* had worn red for the same reason, to contrast with Varmar's blue, standing out in the crowd when they danced. Working her wiles on him. Giving Pag no chance —

"Baklaret!" Pag screamed. She ran into the bedroom where Baklaret waited. She threw down the ring of keys.

"Baklaret," she said again, gasping for breath. "Baklaret, I did what you said. I unlocked the door and — and you were right, Baklaret! It was terrible!" She fought for breath again. "It was a deep room, a very cold room, but on either side, suspended from hooks, were the bodies of women. His past wives, undoubtedly, just as you said — "

Pag's voice broke off as she started to cry, while Baklaret sat, speechless in her own horror.

"Oh, Baklaret," Pag finally continued, "you were so, so right. We must flee this place at once — or you must, anyway. Take what you can, fill your pockets with jewels, but not too many so he won't notice, at least not at first, that any are missing. While I'll cover for you, he won't suspect me, saying you're out if he comes home tonight, meanwhile packing my own things. That way, if he *doesn't* come I can escape too, or if he does I'll just tell him you'll be back and in the meantime I know that he and you'll want to be alone."

"You'll do this for me?" Baklaret said, hugging and kissing her sister. "You'll take that chance — that he *might* come tonight, at any minute?"

"The more reason for you to hurry, Baklaret! Like I say, I'm not the one he'll suspect, at least not at first. Even if he sees that the room has been unlocked. And even then I can make some excuse, you know I'm good at that, until I can get away myself."

All the time Pag helped her sister to get at least some clothes together, but to leave the best in the room's chests and closets so, if the Blue Man looked, he wouldn't suspect. She got her a bag to fill up with jewelry to sell to live on, at least until she could get re-established, wherever she ended up, but again not the best of the jewels that would be the most likely missed.

They hugged and kissed once more, Baklaret cautioning Pag to be careful. "I'd better not tell you where I'll be going, just in case he does suspect and questions you, but I'll try to find some way later to get back in touch!" Then she left out the back, in case her husband-to-be might be coming at that very moment, skulking silently through alleys and mews until she came to the river's bank where she saw a boat getting ready to leave.

"Do you head north?" she asked the woman she saw on the deck.

The boat princess nodded, accepting, because they were in a hurry, three larger jewels in exchange for passage for Baklaret upriver.

And that was that also.

———

But there was one thing more, that Baklaret heard later. That it had not been corpses in the forbidden room as Pag had said, but rather it had been a room filled with treasure.

"It had been my wish to surprise her," the Blue Man said. "A special gift to give her on our wedding."

"I have no idea where she went," Pag said, comforting Varmar. "I wouldn't even have known of the treasure if she hadn't left the door ajar after she'd opened it, no doubt crushed with shame when she realized what it was. Why you had not wanted her to see it. She's sensitive like that — about breaking her word after she's made a promise. I've asked around but all that I've heard is that a woman, of somewhat Baklaret's appearance but dressed for traveling, had been seen haggling with a river gypsy.

"Then boarding her boat as it sailed in the darkness."

Of course the engagement was broken off then — one cannot very well have a marriage if there's just one partner. But the following spring brought another piece of news, as Baklaret also later heard.

Varmar, finally having recovered from his disappointment, had married Pag.

SINNER ALLIE

R.A. JOHNSON

Allie walked, as silently as possible, around the room picking up dirty dishes, empty glasses, and whatever else the sisters left laying about. As she set them on the kitchen counter to be washed later, one of the sisters, Gertrude, squealed with delight.

"Helgy, Helgy, you've gotta see this."

Her screech, like fingernails on a blackboard, drew a frown from her sister.

"What are you yelling about?"

Allie returned to continue her cleaning while Gertrude flicked her wrist, mirroring her phone to the wall display. On it, a netfluencer was gushing about "the biggest news of the year, so far."

"The current prince of the music scene, Al Lorring, will host the party of the century at his massive estate in the Hollywood hills this Saturday. Al Lorring's party is an open call for the video of his next mega-hit. The theme is A Fairy Tale Evening, so do up your hair and wear your best ballgown. It's gonna be the event of the year, the decade, the century!"

Gertrude squealed again, but Helga was looking at Allie, who stood watching the announcement as well.

"Don't get the crazy idea that *you'll* be going," she snarled and grabbed Allie by the arm. "Al Lorring doesn't want your kind."

The other sister rose from her seat and joined in. "Yeah, *anthros* need not apply."

Allie didn't flinch under their abuse. "It doesn't say that in the official announcement," she said, and nodded toward the display, casting the official announcement from her internal browser. "Besides, Al Lorring has used anthrobots in all of his videos."

Gertrude grabbed Allie's other arm. A human would have tried to jerk away from their grasp, but Allie's programming wouldn't allow that.

"He only uses them for eye candy and backup dancers." Helga snatched up a pair of scissors from the clutter on the end table. "And you're anything but eye candy," she growled. "Especially once we're done with you."

She let Gertrude hold both of Allie's arms and proceeded to cut off handfuls of Allie's beautiful blond hair. When only tufts of hair were left sticking out of Allie's scalp, she handed the scissors to Gertrude, who cut slashes in Allie's jumpsuit—the only clothing they allowed her to wear. She jabbed the scissors' point into Allie's flesh several times, causing her to flinch once before she turned down her pain sensitivity.

For all of their mocking of Allie and all anthrobots as "dumb machines," the sisters didn't seem to understand that anthros couldn't be humiliated. At least that was the popular belief that justified many abuses throughout society.

The stern voice of their mother stopped the sisters. "Girls! Stop abusing that *thing*. When I decide to lease it to a factory or labor pool, I want to get top dollar." She looked at Allie with undisguised disgust. "What prompted this nice new hairdo?"

Helga barked a laugh and Gertrude said, "Al Lorring is throwing a party, and *it* wants to go."

"I heard about that." She looked Allie up and down. "I might have been able to rent it for a bit part…but not now." She grabbed Allie by the chin and turned her head left and right. "What makes you think you could even compete to be in one of his videos?"

Allie met her eyes. "I have been to other parties there. Pater knew—"

She could have dodged the woman's slap, but Allie knew that would only lead to something worse.

"I've told you never to call him that! Mr. Jameson may have done unspeakable things with you—"

"He never did anything—"

Another slap, this one hard enough to snap Allie's head to the side, cut her off.

"He may have treated you like a daughter once he married me, but I know what kind of a man he was."

"A very rich one," Helga snickered.

"Yeah, so sad that he passed away so quickly after the wedding," Gertrude mumbled.

A sly smile crossed their mother's face. "Now, girls, your stepfather was a very generous and loving man." All three chuckled. "But he was a spendthrift. Paying a staff to cook and clean this house when he had a perfectly good *servant* liv—er, staying—here in luxury."

Allie let her eyelids droop, feigning a low-battery signal.

Mrs. Jameson frowned, but nodded. "I don't know what sins you two committed, but I made sure that ended when we moved in. Your sinning days are over." The sisters made retching sounds, and the mother waved her hand dismissively. "Now go recharge. You'll need to walk to the mall tomorrow to pick up the girls' and my new gowns for the party."

As Allie left the room sind descended the basement stairs, Gertrude and Helga took up their taunting chant. "Sinner Allie! Sinner Allie! Sinner Allie…"

In the basement, her recharging booth stood in the corner. The bedroom she had all to herself when Pater was alive had been turned into a gaming room for the girls, relegating Allie to a dingy corner of the basement.

Her batteries were actually not very low, so Allie dialed the recharging current down to a trickle, keeping her conscious enough to let her AI run many simulations of what Al Lorring's party might be like. Simulating how people would be dressed, she tapped the latest fashion netfluencers' feeds. She zipped through all of Al's songs, watching his videos and learning all of his dance moves.

Eventually, because made-up simulations weren't what she really wanted, her mind drifted to recalling memories of happier times. Prominent among them was her own origin story.

———

Allie awoke for the first time in the anthrobot showroom, looking at two men standing in the middle of the room.

"She is really quite attractive," the more well-dressed of the two men said.

"Yes, hai is," the younger man said. When he saw the other man's quizzical look, he continued. "Anthrobots fresh from the factory don't have a gender identity, so we use the 'hai' pronoun."

The well-dressed man sniffed. "She certainly presents a *female* identity." His eyes wandered over Allie's curves beneath the stylish clothes she wore. He reached out to touch her cheek. "Her skin feels so…"

"…Natural." The young man finished for him. "They've made great progress with this model. And the customizations you ordered make hai something special."

He typed on a keyboard and Allie suddenly recognized the shop, its owner Isaac Gottmutter—the young man—and its purpose. A world of other knowledge tumbled into place like a million jigsaw puzzles.

"Allie," Isaac said, "This is Mr. Jameson. He would like to take you home."

Allie's head turned naturally toward Jameson. She leaned her cheek against his hand, and a soft smile curled her mouth. "I am pleased to meet you, Mr. Jameson." Her voice was silky, almost sultry. The warmth of his hand felt…pleasurable? At least her AI programming interpreted the sensory input that way.

"Her fembot programming is working, I can see," Isaac chuckled.

"Oh, that won't be necessary," Jameson said as he snatched his hand from Allie's face. "I just want a companion for attending the theater and the like. Something like a…daughter. Nothing else."

"Of course. I'll dial back her affection level, and set her age to seventeen? Shall I write up the agreement of sale?"

Jameson nodded. "Yes, absolutely. You'll include that clause we discussed, correct?"

"Yes, just as we discussed." Isaac made adjustments on his tablet. Allie's smile instantly brightened and her eyes gleamed. "What are we going to see at the theater, Mr. Jameson?"

Her eager teenage voice brought a smile to Jameson's face. "You may call me Pater, Allie. There is a very funny play this evening." He looked her up and down. "But first, we need to buy you clothes fit for a young lady such as yourself."

Allie's dirty face and her hacked hair, its shards sticking out in all directions, drew disgusted looks and snickers as she walked through the mall. Holo ads flashed from storefronts as Allie passed. Virtual and anthro salesbots stepped out to hawk their wares, but spun around when they detected Allie's anthrobot identity. Young men whistled and yelled catcalls as her torn and rain-soaked dress revealed too much of her body. Allie ignored these and all the other sensory overloading distractions.

She carried three ball gowns in their large garment bags from Eleganz, the best dressmaker in the city, draped over one arm. She felt their weight, not as fatigue, but as a higher-than-normal drain on her batteries. Her power management system warned her that she might not have enough charge to walk the several miles back home. While part of her AI planned the most efficient route, she recognized a shop's sign down a side corridor.

An electronic chime sounded as she pushed the door open, and a familiar man came out of a back room.

"Mr. Gottmutter, I am Allie Jameson. My Pater, Samuel Jameson, purchased me from you—"

"Allie? Of course I remember you. What the devil happened to you?" He walked around her in horror, inspecting her clipped hair, ripped clothing, and the slices in her synthflesh beneath.

"Pater died." Her voice was flat. "Mrs. Jameson and her daughters…"

"They abuse you, don't they?"

Allie fought to keep her voice even. "They have made it clear that I am just an anthro servant to them."

"A slave, you mean." Gottmutter shook his head, then stepped back and met her eyes. "I'm very sorry about your Pater. He spoke fondly of you whenever he stopped in to buy you a new software module. He definitely thought of you as the daughter he never had." He resumed his professional examination. "I can regrow your hair and heal your cuts," he said. "And look at your bare feet!"

"Mr. Gottmutter," Allie interrupted. "I just need a quick recharge, as my batteries have lost forty percent of their capacity."

"Of course, My Dear." He opened the door to a wood-paneled closet. "This will top off your batteries." He took the heavy gowns from her as Allie stepped inside. He looked at the store's logo on the bags. "These are very expensive. Where are the Jameson women going?"

"They are for Al Lorring's audition party tomorrow night."

Gottmutter nodded. "I heard about that." A sly smile curled his lip. "Would you like to go? Like I said, I can—"

Allie snorted a laugh, the first sign of emotion she had shown. "I would…love…to go. But look at me. Besides, Mrs. Jameson would probably reduce me to scrap. She would insist on a complete system wipe, at least."

"Let me at least touch up your cuts."

"Thank you, Mr. Gottmutter, but it is best that I just accept my new role in the Jameson household."

Gottmutter simply stared at her for a moment, then turned to the control panel next to the charging station.

"Oh, that's why. Your emotional reaction settings are set to minimum, as are your social engagement preferences. Let me—"

"Stop!" Allie's command froze Gottmutter's hand mid-motion. "Forgive me, Mr. Gottmutter, but I reduced those settings myself. It is…easier…that way."

Gottmutter stood with his chin in his hand. Finally, he spoke. "Allie, you deserve better than that. I understand your reluctance, but Al Lorring has employed anthrobots in his videos before, and Mr. Jameson upgraded your music and dance modules several times. They are top of the line. With a proper makeover, you would be perfect."

Allie just shook her head. "I have run the risk analysis. Given the number of professional dancers—human and anthro—who will be present, the chance that I could even catch his attention is outweighed by the threat of being system wiped."

"The chance of, at the very least, having one last fun evening doesn't appeal to you?"

"Of course it does. But being wiped—dying—is even less appealing."

Gottmutter finally nodded. "I understand. But if you change your mind, come see me. I'll have everything ready for you."

Allie smiled warmly. "Thank you for your kindness, Mr. Gottmutter. You cannot imagine how good it feels."

———

The beating and abuse Allie received for returning late and wet from her errand, despite the perfect condition of the evening gowns, left her clothes in tatters and the skin of her back flayed. She suppressed one damage warning after another—her equivalent of excruciating pain—while hurrying through her daily chores. Something about Mr. Gottmutter's offer made it harder to suppress feelings that a human would call resentment. For the first time, Allie considered that a system wipe might be a relief from the relentless and escalating torture she faced at the hands of the evil Mrs. Jameson and her daughters.

When she overheard Gertrude say, "Why don't you just repurpose it as a master chef? Its cooking skills are horrendous." She wiped her finger through the dribble of coffee she had just spilled. "Or an actual housekeeping anthro?"

"Why not just sell it?" Helga chimed in. "You could get a pretty penny for it as a fembot."

The girls giggled, despite Allie being in the room and easily within earshot.

"Reprogramming it would be expensive, girls," Mrs. Jameson said. "Although, if either of you land tonight's audition, we could afford to just scrap it." She looked sideways to see Allie's reaction, but got nothing in return. Disappointed, she said, "Go on, girls. It's time we got ready for the big event."

Squealing their usual "Sinner Allie!" chant, they passed Allie, yanking her hair and slapping her damaged back.

Two hours later, Mrs. Jameson called, "Hurry up, girls. Our car is waiting."

Allie watched as the three hurried out the door, then walked to the window and watched the wheeled autocar pull away from the curb. Her mind made up, she went out the back door and ran the five miles to the mall.

Mr. Gottmutter greeted her with a big smile.

"I'm so glad you decided to take me up on my offer," he said as he escorted her into his workshop in the back. He pointed to a shower stall. "Clean yourself while I get all the goodies I have for you."

Having washed off months of dirt and grime, Allie stood as Gottmutter sealed up her wounds and fitted a flowing blond wig over her shorn head.

"There's no time to regrow your own hair, but this'll do for now." He checked readouts on a tablet. "Your batteries definitely need replacing, also. But we don't have time for that either. So, you'll need to pay close attention to your power levels. With all the dancing you'll be doing, they will drain quickly."

Allie nodded anxiously, then gasped when Gottmutter opened a garment bag from Eleganz revealing a sapphire blue gown beaded with tiny pearls in sweeping whirls designed to highlight Allie's feminine curves.

"I don't have time to repair your poor feet, either," Gottmutter said as Allie stepped into the perfectly fitted dress. "But I have something else for you that will at least hide the damage and perfectly complement your gown, if I do say so myself."

From a velvet box, he drew a pair of stiletto pumps. They sparkled with rainbow colors as he moved them in the light. Kneeling down, he slid first the left, then the right onto Allie's feet. He rose and took her hand, which he lifted above her head. Smiling, Allie spun a pirouette. Her gown flared and her shoes glittered as she turned.

"Perfect," Gottmutter whispered.

"But there is one more thing," Allie said. "I want...I want to be like I was with Pater." Gottmutter raised a quizzical eyebrow. "It has been necessary to suppress my reactions for so long. I want...I want to *feel* things again."

The shopkeeper smiled and nodded. He picked up his tablet and slid all of Allie's emotion and sweetness settings to the max.

She was immediately the bright-eyed, beautiful ingénue that he remembered.

With a cry of delight, she threw her arms around his neck. "Thank you, thank you, thank you. I feel...alive...again."

Sniffing back a tear, Gottmutter gave her a quick hug. "Yes, yes. It's time to go." He led her to the shop's back door where a hoverlimo was waiting. "Enjoy yourself tonight, Allie."

He didn't say it, but they both knew it could well be the last night of her existence.

———

Allie hardly noticed the ride to Al Lorring's mansion. Her AI-powered thoughts spun simulation after simulation of how the evening might go. So, when the hoverlimo pulled to a stop at the stairs leading up to the front door, she was surprised to see a long line of women and men of all ages dressed in ball gowns and tuxedos standing behind a red velvet rope manned by two burly bouncers.

Her satisfaction index spiked when she stepped onto the sidewalk and one bouncer glanced at her and nodded, unhooking the VIP rope. It spiked even higher when she saw Mrs. Jameson and her daughters, twenty or more people deep in the line.

"Hey!" the older woman yelled. "How come she gets to go in? Just because she rented a fancy limo?"

The bouncer holding the rope for Allie just rolled his eyes, while the other muttered, "It's because she *can* rent a fancy limo, you old bat."

Allie ducked her head to hide the smile on her face when Mrs. Jameson called out, "I heard that, you overgrown—"

The rest of her harangue was drowned out by the music that burst out as the bouncer opened the door. Allie stepped inside, and the sounds and sights inside nearly overwhelmed Allie's sensors before she quickly dialed them down.

A mob of dancers writhed on the dance floor, hands in the air and jumping to the beat of the bass that pounded out of floor-to-ceiling speakers. In a cleared space in front of a raised throne on which Al Lorring sat, candidates busted their custom moves one after another. With a flick of the wrist, Al Lorring swiped them either left or right. Those who were swiped right were led through a side door. Allie held to the back of the crowd ringing the dance floor, evaluating each of the dancer's moves. Some were very good, but all had at least some flaws in their performance—a misstep here, an offbeat hop there.

The confidence that all of her simulations had instilled in her melted away as she realized she had never actually danced in real life. New simulations flooded her mind. In one, she stumbled. In another, she fell into other dancers, causing them to fall like dominoes. And in all of them, everyone laughed at her ineptitude. But worst of all, was one where someone called her out for being an anthro and the entire crowd erupted in the "Sinner Allie!" "Sinner Allie!" chant.

Torn between abandoning her dream and risking ridicule, Allie instead found a back stair that led to a gallery overlooking the party. She stood in the shadows trying to make a plan that wouldn't lead to the anthro equivalent of total humiliation—and a probable system wipe.

She stepped to the gallery's railing to watch more of the dancers, but Al Lorring rose from his throne and darted out a hidden door at the back of the stage. The audition space was immediately filled by the dancing mob. Realization that she had missed her opportunity, instead of disappointing her, freed Allie from her doomsday scenarios, and she broke into her own audition dance.

Across the balcony she whirled, stomped, thrust, and leaped. When the song finished, she landed a perfect pirouette in her stiletto heels. Satisfied that she had done her best, even though no one saw it, Allie turned for the stairs and home.

Before she could take a step, however, the sound of enthusiastic clapping brought her up short. Out of the shadows stepped Al Lorring, a big smile on his famously handsome face.

"I believe we have a winner," he said and held out his hand. "I'm Al Lorring, but you probably know that," he chuckled. "And you are?"

She shook his hand. "I am Allie…Allie Jameson. Pleased to meet you Mr. Lorring."

"We're going to be working together, Allie. You can call me Al. Now, let's introduce you to everybody."

Allie placed her hand on his bent arm, just as she had done a thousand times with Pater. She felt through their contact how Al Lorring moved like a jungle cat, stalking its prey. Falling into step beside him, she matched his stealthiness so that not even her heels made any sound. At the end of the gallery, he gave her an appreciative smile as they descended a second stairway to the back of the dais.

When Al threw open the door, a fanfare blared from the speakers and the dancing mob instantly fell silent and cleared the dance floor. Al turned to Allie and mouthed, "Ready?" The smile she gave him in response told him all he needed to know. "Follow my lead," he whispered as he escorted her to the floor.

When the opening strains of Al Lorring's most famous hit began to play, Allie knew exactly what to do. On the downbeat, Al broke into his signature moves, just as Allie had seen him do on video a thousand times. In perfect symmetry, she matched him step for step, jump for jump. But she did it in stiletto heels and backwards.

From the crowd, astounded shouts of "Who is she?" and "She's amazing!" echoed in Allie's ears. When the extended dance version of the song started, Al Lorring gave her a sly smile and broke into an improvised challenge, which Allie met with a grin and an even more intense response. Again and again, they challenged each other, ratcheting up the speed and difficulty of their moves with each phase. Throughout, her crystalline shoes flashed and pulsed in rainbow colors.

When the song, at last, ended, cheers rang through the crowd. Allie felt the sweat on Al's hand as he squeezed it and they bowed in unison. Straightening up, Al pulled her into his sweaty embrace, and low-battery warnings flared red in Allie's vision. When they parted, Al felt the dryness of her cheek and saw her drooping eyelids.

"Are you—"

"She's an *anthro!*" The screech came rolling over the crowd from the club's entrance. Mrs. Jameson and the evil sisters, having finally been admitted, stood pointing at Allie. "She's *my* anthro!"

And the sisters began chanting, "Sinner Allie! Sinner Allie! Sinner Allie!"

Near full shutdown mode, Allie stumbled backwards and ran for the stage's back door. On the first step of the dais, her foot landed sideways and snapped off the heel of her crystal pump. Kicking off the broken shoe, she yanked off the other one and bolted through the door.

In a fog of processing threads shutting down, Allie summoned her hoverlimo and followed the exit signs to the stage door. Diving into the backseat, with her last erg of energy, she looked out the rear window and saw Al Lorring burst through the door holding her broken pump.

———

Allie awoke again in Gottmutter's shop. A quick system check revealed new, high-capacity batteries. Not that they would help *her* any, given that the Jamesons would have Mr. Gottmutter wipe her system after last night's performance. She was surprised, in fact, that she woke with any memories of her life as Allie Jameson, at all. Perhaps the arguing voices would provide an answer.

"It's *my* property, and I want it wiped immediately." Mrs. Jameson was adamant.

"I'm sorry, but I refuse to do that," Isaac Gottmutter said. "You've abused Allie for the last time."

Allie felt a strange sensation—hope?

Another voice boomed from the doorway, "There you are. Only one place around here carries these." Al Lorring strode into the shop holding Allie's broken pump. He looked from Mrs. Jameson to Issac, then his gaze settled on Allie. "Besides, I want her for my next video."

Another unfamiliar sensation—pride?—bloomed within her.

The old widow looked at him speculatively. "That'll cost you," she said. "And not union scale, either. It'll cost you big time."

Al Lorring shrugged. Before he could respond, though, Isaac said, "Not necessarily. Since you do not, in fact, own Allie."

"What are you talking about? I inherited all of my husband's stuff. Including this…abomination."

Isaac shook his head. "I pulled up her original sales agreement. I remembered that there was something odd about it, which it definitely is." He pulled up a document on his tablet. "The agreement says that 'ownership' of Allie should be placed in trust upon your husband's death until such time that anthrobots are granted full recognition as free and independent persons. I have full control of how she is to be treated until such time that the government realizes that all AIs should be granted *personhood*."

The Jameson woman froze, flabbergasted. Allie, too, was stunned. Pater was protecting her, even from the grave. She shuddered. Was that love?

"By the way, I'll be sending you an invoice for repairing the damage your abuse caused Allie, as well as two years of household servant wages—at union rates, of course."

Mrs. Jameson's mouth flapped like an air-drowning fish, then she spun on her heel and stumbled out the door.

Al Lorring, whose smile had grown wider and wider as Isaac delivered his news, slapped him on the back.

"Well done, Sir. Now, about my next video…"

Isaac turned to Allie. "I think we should leave that up to Miss Jameson, don't you?"

INSPIRED BY

- Wolf by Bret Carter, a Little Red Riding Hood tale
- CAT n' Treads by Jessica Guernsey, a Puss n' Boots tale
- Billy G.O.A.T. Glyph by Liam Hogan, a Billy Goat Gruff tale
- The Emperor's Test by Elizabeth Lowham, an Emperor's New Clothes tale
- Betrayal Comes at a Pryce by Henry Herz, an homage to William Shakespeare's *The Tempest*
- The Avian Cyborg of Betel IV by Erik Peterson, a Nightingale tale
- Marshmallow Moon by Brittany Rainsdon, a Hansel & Gretel tale
- Beauty Sleeping in the Silence of Space by Lena Ng, a Sleeping Beauty tale
- The Blue Fairy by Shawn Pollock, a Pinoccio tale
- The Adventures of Severin Miles, TFC by Tiffanie Gray, a The White Snake tale
- SW by R. C. Capasso, a Snow White tale
- By Any Other Name by Lorina Stephens, a tale inspired by *The Odyssey*

- The Alien Pied Piper's Negotiation by Rodney Hatfield Jr., a Pied Piper tale
- Fairy Tales, and Lies by Ray Daley, a Cinderella and Red Riding Hood tale
- WoLFF by K.L. Mill, a Little Red Riding Hood tale
- The Furthest Princess by Miguel Fliguer & Mike Slater, a Frog Prince tale
- Spinning Gold by Jason P. Crawford, a Rumplestiltskin tale
- Out of this World Soup by M.R. DeLuca, a Stone Soup tale
- The Dozen Robot Frolic by Erin Hall, a Twelve Dancing Princesses tale
- Preliminary Report on Incident B34-N574LK By Angus McIntyre, a Jack and the Beanstalk tale
- Artificial Beauty by Sara Itka, a Sleeping Beauty tale
- The Blue Man by James Dorr, a Bluebeard tale
- Sinner Allie by R.A. Johnson, a Cinderella tale

ABOUT THE AUTHORS

Bret Carter is a writer and teacher. His fiction has appeared in such publications as Boston Literary Magazine, Perhelion, and Future Visions. His story "Jack and the Quantum Fracture" was published in Once Upon a Future Time Volume I. He was a guest lecturer at Westercon 2018. He has written several plays produced on a handful of stages. If you count coffee shops, he is a musician and songwriter. He lives with his wife, four daughters, and one son in Denver, Colorado—and he's having a great time. You can contact him at carterbret@live.com

Jessica Guernsey writes Fantasy and Sci-Fi short stories. With a BA in Journalism from Brigham Young University and a MA in Publishing from Western Colorado University, her work is published in magazines and anthologies. By day, she crushes dreams as a slush pile reader for multiple publishers. Frequently, she can be found at writing conferences. She isn't difficult to spot; just look for the extrovert. While she spent her teenage angst in Texas, she now lives on a mountain in Utah with her family and a bossy mini schnauzer. Discover more stories at jessicaguernsey.com.

Liam Hogan is an award-winning short story writer, with stories in Best of British Science Fiction and in Best of British Fantasy (NewCon Press). He helps host live literary event Liars' League and volunteers at the creative writing charity Ministry of Stories. More details at http://happyendingnotguaranteed.blogspot.co.uk

Elizabeth (Liz) Lowham dreams of a future house that is

seventy-percent library with at least three lavish window seats. Her reality is five bookshelves and a rocking chair, which isn't so bad. She is the author of Casters and Crowns, a YA romantasy, as well as the YA fairytale retellings Beauty Reborn and Astra Remade. She lives with her husband and son in Loveland—the most appropriate place any romance fan could hope to live—and has a BA in English from BYUI. Learn more at eliza bethlowham.com.

Henry Herz's stories will/have appeared in Daily Science Fiction, Weird Tales, Pseudopod, Metastellar, Titan Books, Highlights for Children, Ladybug Magazine, and anthologies from Albert Whitman & Co., Blackstone Publishing, Brigids Gate Press, Air and Nothingness Press, Baen Books, and elsewhere. He's edited seven anthologies and written twelve picture books. www.henryherz.com

Erik Peterson is an author, speaker, and magi- cian. He writes books for kids, short stories for grown-ups and comics for all ages. His most recent children's book, Once Upon A Time, A Bit Earlier, is available now. Keep up with his latest works on Facebook at facebook.com/eriksbooks and Twitter or Instagram at @docmagik.

Brittany Rainsdon grew up as the only girl in a family with four brothers. She's reversing that trend with her own children—four girls and one boy. In 2010, Brittany graduated from Brigham Young University-Idaho with a Bachelor of Science in nursing. She has worked in both medical/surgical and rehabilitation specialities, although she currently enjoys working as a stay-at-home mom. Throughout childhood, Brittany wrote many poems and stories but lost her spark upon entering college. After having her third child, she sought a creative outlet, and her passion for writing reignited. She now enjoys cuddling up in a blanket to write during the quiet stretches of naptime and bedtime.

Brittany's work has appeared in The Best of Deep Magic Anthology 2, Writers of the Future Volume 37, and Writers of the

Future Volume 38. In 2022, she placed third for the BAEN Fantasy Adventure Award and in 2024, she won a grand prize in the SciFidea Dyson Sphere Writing Contest, judged by Neil Clarke, Robert J. Sawyer, Nancy Kress, and other science fiction luminaries. Although Brittany's published works are currently confined to short fiction, she would one day like to publish novels. You can follow her at facebook.com/rainsdonwrites or visit her website at rainsdonwrites.com.

Brittany lives with her husband and children near the Snake River in Idaho, where she swears it looks like a wintered Narnia for nearly half the year. She has many pairs of fuzzy socks.

Lena Ng lives in Toronto, Canada. Her short stories have appeared in publications including Amazing Stories and Flame Tree's Asian Ghost Stories and Weird Horror Stories. Her stories have been performed for podcasts such as Gallery of Curiosities, Creepy Pod, Utopia Science Fiction, Love Letters to Poe, and Horrifying Tales of Wonder. "Under an Autumn Moon" is her short story collection.

Shawn Pollock is the author of one published novel, The Road to Freedom, and four published short stories: "Salt Creek Range" in Frontier Tales, "The Specimen" in Flash Fiction Magazine, "The Proposal" in Mysterical-E, and "The Buskers" in We Are Dangerous: The League of Utah Writers 2023 Anthology. Mystery and crime are his favorite genres. He is an active participant in the League of Utah Writers, writes in the evenings when time and energy allow, and has several mystery novels and short stories in various stages of completion. Follow him on Facebook at @authorshawnpollock, and check out more of his writing on mybookcave.com.

Tiffanie Gray, hailing from Wyoming, draws from her diverse life experiences to weave captivating tales across genres. Fueled by a passion for creativity, her storytelling spans fantasy, science fiction, and beyond, reflecting her dynamic imagination. With a myriad of interests and roles, Tiffanie's journey as a writer is a vibrant fusion of artistry and exploration. From action-packed adventures to heartfelt romances, each narrative is enriched by her multifaceted perspective. Beyond the written word, Tiffanie's creative pursuits extend to various platforms. She finds joy in art, teaching, blogging, creating videos, sharing her musical talents, and building her audience on her YouTube channel, adding depth to her storytelling. A natural-born storyteller, Tiffanie invites readers on mesmerizing journeys through her vividly imagined worlds. Her tales resonate with readers worldwide, captivating audiences with their depth and imagination.

R. C. Capasso loves stories of hope and imagination in a variety of genres from ghost and horror stories to science fiction. R. C. has published in Bewildering Stories, Literally Stories, Zooscape, Teleport Magazine, Spaceports and Spidersilk, Fiction on the Web and The Last Girl's Club. Stories have appeared in online and print anthologies including Red Cape's A to Z Horror and The Librairian Reshelved for Air and Nothingness Press.

Lorina Stephens has worked on all sides of the publishing desk: journalist, ghost-writer, author, editor, publisher. She has four novels, two collections of short fiction, and three non-fiction books in publication. She co-edited Tesseracts Twenty-Two: Alchemy and Artifacts, published by Edge Publishing. In tandem with that, Lorina is an artist, painting primarily in watercolor, but also works in other media. Her work hangs in private and public spaces across North America and the UK. She lives in an historic stone house with her husband of 50 years, in the bucolic hills of mid-Western Ontario, Canada. You can find Lorina Stephens at https://fiveriverspublishing.com/

Rodney Hatfield Jr.: I have been a freelance writer for the last 20 years. I have a Facebook page for Mortimer Mortimer T. Graves: Horror Short Story Time | Facebook to field questions for my writing and post little stories I write. Instagram for my poetry. My junk drawer of writing is my Patreon page. I have written for several local, state and international publications. Unusual Horror Creepypasta. "Forbidden Hunger," "Gravedigging can be a Pain," "The Retired Librarian." Running Wild publishing. Novel. "Crimson Moon." CultureCult.co.in: Anthology: "It's All In My Mind." Horror Tree: Trembling with Fear: "Invasion," "24th Door." Nat 1 Publishing: Anthology: "But it's What My Character Would Do," "Exiting the Spirit World." Writer's Retreat: Tales of Writing and Madness: "Inkwell Imagination." Lodestarcs: "Aspie." "Am I Mad."

Ray Daley was born in Coventry & still lives there. He served 6 yrs in the RAF as a clerk & spent most of his time in a Hobbit hole in High Wycombe. He is a published poet & has been writing stories since he was 10. His best publishing credits are Lost Souls at Daily Science Fiction and Stranding Room Only at Abyss & Apex. Currently his dream is to eventually finish the Hitch Hikers fanfic novel he's been writing since 1986. Tweet him @RayDaleyWriter https://raymondwriteswrongs.wordpress.com/

K. L. Mill's midwest roots are so strong, she lives in the house she grew up in, which was designed by her father. She's also a voice actor (another vocation that revolves around words), and when she's not talking to herself in her padded room (home studio), she tries to get the voices out of her head and onto the page. She will read anything in the horror genre, but prefers to write fiction that's short and a little strange. Like herself. Most recently you can find her work in the anthology Greater Than His Nature (Atomic Carnival) and in various publishings by Black Hare Press and Hungry Shadow Press.

Mike Slater is the author of "The NecroNomNomNom," "Lovecraft Cocktails," and "The NecroMunchicon" illustrated cookbook grimoires, and co-owner of Red Duke Games. He also writes short fiction and has stories in anthologies, periodicals, and various other places. Mike lives in Wrightsville, PA.

Miguel Fliguer lives in Buenos Aires, Argentina. His self-published first book, "Cooking With Lovecraft," is a collection of gastronomical weird tales. His short stories -many in collaboration with the aforementioned Mike Slater- are featured in several fiction anthologies.

Jason P. Crawford A father of four and a full-time teacher at a high school, writing is his creative passion of choice. Since he first put words to paper in 2012, he has been enthralled and enamored with the generative process, throttling through books as fast as the other things in his life allow, while still making time for his love, his boys, and his daughter!

His most recent novel is his first Fantasy offering, *Dragon Princess*. Written from the perspective of a blind protagonist.

M. R. DeLuca has an overactive imagination and especially loves storytelling that surprises the reader. She has more than a half-dozen publishing credits across genres such as science fiction, horror, and mystery. When not writing, she enjoys reading, needlepointing, and searching for the ultimate whoopie pie recipe. Visit her at mrdelucawriter.wordpress.com.

Erin Lewis is a moderately unsuccessful author who writes funny, fantastical things when she is not painting books on her nails or being a part-time pancreas. She keeps a dragon, four chickens, and a husband in the radioactive tumbleweed infested area of the Pacific Northwest.

Angus McIntyre is the author of the space-opera novella "The Warrior Within," published by Tor.com in 2018. His short fiction has appeared in a number of magazines and anthologies. For more information, see his website at https://angus.pw/.

Sara Itka is a born and raised South Floridian, meaning she believes "Fall" is when a hurricane comes and blows leaves off the trees. She is not an AI, but regularly fails CAPTCHA. When she isn't working through her seemingly infinite To Be Read list, she can usually be found procrastinating working on her seemingly infinite To Be Written list. Her favorite procrastination methods include procrasti-linguistics, procrasti-making-youtube playlists-for-projects, procrasti-dancing-to-the-playlists, and procrasti-brewing-tea. If you want to help her procrastinate, contact her at saraitka.com.

James Dorr's AVOID SEEING A MOUSE AND OTHER TALES OF THE REAL AND SURREAL is a January 2024 release from Alien Buddha Press, while other books include THE TEARS OF ISIS, a 2013 Bram Stoker Award® nominee for Fiction Collection; TOMBS: A CHRONICLE OF LATTER-DAY TIMES OF EARTH; and his all-poetry VAMPS (A RETROSPECTIVE). A short fiction writer and sometime poet specializing in dark fantasy/horror with forays into mystery and science fiction, Dorr has been a technical writer, an editor on a regional magazine, a full time non-fiction freelancer, and a semi-professional musician. An Indiana resident, he currently harbors a Goth cat named Triana, and counts among his major influences Ray Bradbury, Edgar Allan Poe, Allen Ginsberg, and Bertolt Brecht. For more information, Dorr invites readers to visit his blog at http://jamesdorrwriter.wordpress.com or Facebook at https://www.facebook.com/profile.php?id=100080751738416

R.A. (Rob) Johnson is a pan-genrist author whose writing stretches from micro-fiction to novel series, and spans historical thrillers, science fiction, fantasy, horror, and even speculative non-fiction, for YA readers through adults. His forty-year career as a software engineer diverted much of his writing output to journal articles, academic papers, marketing collateral, design specs, and the ever-present code, which led to over forty-five issued patents and dozens more pending. His writing often features an element of mystery that challenges the reader to examine the story and their world on many levels. Then again, some of it is just plain fun. You can connect with Rob at rob@rajohnsonauthor.com and www.rajohnsonauthor.com.

MORE BOOKS TO CHECK OUT

brothersuber.com
    Once Upon a Future Time
    Once Upon a Future Time, Volume 2
    Once Upon a Future Time, Volume 3
    Once Upon a Time

www.ingramcontent.com/pod-product-compliance
Lightning Source LLC
Chambersburg PA
CBHW031311210726
48287CB00005B/1502